Come With Me

To Erica,
   my TLC PYT !♡
I have loved getting
to know you ever since
you told me to fuck off.
I'm so happy for you and
your new job. You made having
this job so much more bearable
and I will miss you!!! Keep in touch ♡
   ~ Michell

Come With Me

Annie Swank

LANGDON STREET PRESS

MINNEAPOLIS

Langdon Street Press
212 3rd Avenue North, Suite 290
Minneapolis, MN 55401
612.455.2293
www.langdonstreetpress.com

ISBN - 978-1-936183-54-8
ISBN - 1-936183-54-4
LCCN - 2010935548

Cover Design by Alan Pranke
Typeset by James Arneson

Printed in the United States of America

Introduction

Thanks to Ash, Cons and Spades for your input and support...

...and to Mr Taylor, please forgive me

Introduction

I took his virginity. Maybe I should feel guilty, but I don't. I've never been prouder of anything I've ever done. He was seventeen, I was sixteen, and I knew the first time I saw him that I would be in love with him forever.

He consumes my mind, even to this day. It's been a twisted road full of extreme ups and crushing downs, but it's a hell of a story.

It all started in 1977, what a pivotal year. The world was changing, at least from my perspective. The art, the fashion, the music . . . it was an incredible time to be young.

I was fifteen years old when my father's job transferred us to Cambridge, England. I didn't mind terribly, we moved a lot. Originally we were from the suburbs of Detroit, where my parents worked for a major automotive company. But, from the time I was very young we had to move around the country every so often. That meant we didn't get to see our family much and I rarely had the opportunity to make lasting friends. It was just the three of us, me and my parents, Rick and Paula Casey.

I had developed kind of a thick skin by this point in my life. My parents were never around much, they were very involved in their careers. I was used to being a bit of a loner, used to starting new schools in new cities, but I hadn't ever lived in a foreign country. I had no idea what I was in for.

Also, I wasn't very confident and, as a result, not very outgoing. I usually tried to fly under the radar. It worked well. On the outside, I was nothing spectacular to see- brown hair, blue eyes, pale, ordinary. I wasn't a flashy dresser, I suppose I didn't want to call attention to myself.

Besides that, there is nothing else worth mentioning about my life before I met him. As far as I'm concerned, there was no life before I met him.

Chapter 1

"I was never so thankful in all my life for anything"

So, there I was, totally uprooted, right before my junior year of high school. I wasn't excited to be living in England. I didn't know how long I'd be there, all I did know was that in two years, I would be starting college- wherever *I* wanted, for a change.

More than any other time, I dreaded starting this new school. On my first day, my mother dropped me off at the door. Usually I didn't feel the urge, but that morning I wanted to cling to her and have her protection. Looking out the car window at the looming gray building on that cloudy morning conjured up images of haunted castles. I knew this old building was not likely full of ghosts and wicked creatures, but it was so unfamiliar and seemed unfriendly. This place was not my home, I was an alien here. I was scared. I hesitated to get out of the safety of the car, but I took a deep breath and did it.

"Good luck. Have fun," my mother encouraged.

I didn't reply, I just shut the door, feeling abandoned and nervous. I slowly walked toward the school's main door, sensing that I was in for a major upheaval.

England had a different type of curriculum than I was used to in America. I appeared to be the youngest person in my class and although at first I felt intimidated by the towering eighteen-year-old students surrounding me, I was never so thankful in all my life for anything.

Alphabetical order put me behind a boy I didn't notice at first, my surname being Casey, his being Blake (I would later find out). My desk was the last in the row and in the back of that classroom. It was getting a little noisy while the teacher was scrambling to get his materials organized. Everyone else was socializing, but I just shyly kept to myself, doodling on my notebook. The boy in front of me was turned sideways in his chair to talk to a friend across the aisle. I was concentrating on my drawing when I was distracted by a cherubic laugh. It was so bright, so enchanting and sweet that it startled me. I looked up. I'll never forget seeing him for the first time.

He was insanely beautiful, and yet, it seemed like he was as plain as could be to the rest of the world. I stared, unnoticed for what must have been a long time as I studied every detail of his face, totally transfixed. Shaggy, longish brown hair, unbelievable brown eyes (though hidden behind glasses), incredible high cheekbones, and a sharp-angled jawline. I marveled at his smiling lips, his wide grin, and his perfect mouth with adorable teeth just out of alignment.

Luckily, he was too engaged in his conversation with his friend to notice me. All the staring was making my eyes hurt- either from the lack of blinking or the dazzling sight. I quickly looked down, closing my eyes to rest them. The teacher began talking, but I didn't listen. Before I knew it, papers were being passed down the aisle.

"Take one, pass it back," the teacher said, though I barely heard him.

The handsome boy in front of me attempted to casually pass me a sheet over his shoulder. I wasn't looking and didn't take it, so he turned around to hand it to me. That got my attention. I looked up, startled. He smiled politely and gently laid the paper on my desk. As he turned back around I felt my face redden, thinking I must already look like an idiot. I soon calmed down when I realized the once meaningless sheet of paper in front of me was now a collector's item because he had touched it. I quietly sighed and tenderly touched the paper.

The teacher's voice was loud and intrusive, breaking my girlish thought processes. "Has anyone read Jane Eyre?" he asked.

A few people raised their hands, including my gorgeous neighbor.

"Good!" he exclaimed. "What is it about?" He looked for someone to call on. "Nigel?"

To my shock, the handsome boy spoke. "Um . . . love and pain. Like a sad love story."

"Mm hmm, and did you like it?"

"Well, yeah. It was good. I liked it."

"Great." The teacher began to lecture, but I didn't hear any of it. I tried to replay Nigel's voice in my head. What a brilliant name, what a brilliant voice. It was a bit gritty, a little deep, and with a sweet, subtle British accent. I picked it apart in my memory and hoped the teacher would call on him again soon so I could hear him say something new.

When class let out, I tried to get close enough to Nigel to touch him, or smell him, or read his thoughts, or something . . . I'm not sure. I noticed he was pretty tall and had a lanky build with broad shoulders, and I really liked that. I didn't even know why. There was just something about him that was completely alluring. Every cell in my body was tingling with lust.

I had maneuvered right behind him when I dropped my purse. He kept walking away as I bent down to retrieve it and when I looked up, he was gone. I was disappointed. I searched for my next class with a heavy heart.

I was wondering if I would be lucky enough to see him again that day when I saw him standing outside the door of the room I was heading for, talking to the same boy. My heart jumped and I tried to conceal my smile. They briefly looked my way, still continuing their conversation as I slipped inside the open door.

This class was art. I sat at a table and wondered if he would sit by me. We did not have to sit in alphabetic order. The students began filling the room. By the time he came in, the only vacant seat was across from me. He apparently knew the other two at the table and sat with us. He seemed very comfortable. I was far from it.

The teacher was some kind of New Age hippie. As she walked around, handing out paper and pencils, she told us all to sketch something that would inspire her. Art had always been a passion of mine, but I only liked to create it on my terms. I started drawing something abstract. The teacher roamed between the tables of quietly buzzing students, surveying and commenting on their work. I was concentrating on my piece when she came up behind me.

"Very interesting. What's this about?" she asked.

"Um . . . this is a man who is like, searching for, like, something unattainable. And this circle represents eternal hope." I blurted out and immediately felt embarrassed, hoping I didn't sound foolish.

"Wow, that's very creative!" She picked it up to show the class. "Not a run of the mill still portrait, real art! Very good. What's your name, dear? And where are you from?"

"My name is Michelle and I'm from America, outside of Detroit . . . Michigan." I clarified, assuming none of them were very familiar with American geography. I had all of their attention, most notably, Nigel's attention.

"Ooh, I love fresh blood!" The teacher clasped her hands with delight. "Your table-mates can tell you about me and how I run things. I think we're going to have a smashing year. I can feel it!" she exclaimed and walked off.

I didn't know whether to be scared or optimistic, but I was grateful she gave me the excuse to talk to Nigel.

The girl next to me started first. "Well, love, Ms. Trudy isn't very strict," she began.

Nigel snorted in agreement. I looked up. Nigel's neighbor chimed in. "Oh, yeah. It's easy to ace her classes."

"She kinda lets us lead and decide the lesson plan," Nigel added.

"Really?" I breathed, responding only to him.

"Oh yeah, love," said the girl on my right. "I'm Angie, by the way. That's Tom, and that's Nigel," she explained, pointing to the boys across the way.

"Oh, hi. I'm Michelle, like I said."

"So, what's Detroit like?" Angie asked.

"Well . . . " I started, noticing Nigel was looking, waiting for a response. This was my chance to appear interesting. I tried to think of something to say, but before I could begin, Ms. Trudy broke in.

"Oh, I forgot to give you your drawing back! Here. Now if you don't mind, I'd like to pull up a chair and watch while you work on this." The others at my table stifled a laugh, but I didn't mind. I wasn't sure what to say and I had no idea how to make a good first impression with Nigel. I wanted him to think I was worldly and sophisticated.

Really, I wanted to be whatever would appeal to him. But I wasn't much of an actress. I was as readable as a book and had no talent for lying. I just hoped he would like me for who I was.

"Nigel, what have you got there?" Ms. Trudy asked.

"It's my name in block letters," he admitted, embarrassed.

"Let's have a look. . . . Oh it's quite nice. Nigel John Blake." She read it slowly and it echoed in my head. Nigel John Blake- what a beautiful ring that had. I was swooning. I looked at his artwork, it *was* nice. He had shaded it and carefully drew it out. I liked it. I was staring at it and he caught me.

"It's not very imaginative," he confessed to no one in particular.

"It's interesting, though," I remarked, my eyes on his paper.

"It is?" His eyes widened.

I nodded. "I really like it. I never would've thought to do that."

"And that's what this is all about!" Ms. Trudy exclaimed excitedly. "Taking all these ideas and bringing them forth. Thirty students make thirty different pictures and they're all wonderful," she proudly gushed.

I smiled a bit, looking at her. I caught Nigel smiling too, but he was looking my way. I smiled back at him. Our eyes locked for a second, just a second before the bell rang. Angie tapped my arm, breaking the trance. "What class have you got now, love?"

"Umm . . . " I started, looking for my schedule. I looked up just in time to see Nigel and Tom making their way out the door. I watched them go as Angie studied my reaction. "You fancy Tom, eh?" she poked.

"Huh? Oh, he seems alright," I answered.

"Yeah, he is. A lot of girls like Tom. You'd probably have a chance with him, too. See, we've mostly all been in school together for ten years. We're a bit bored of each other, but you, you're exotic."

"Exotic?" I was shocked. I had always thought of myself as pretty plain.

"Oh yeah! Guys like American girls. . . . These guys would like any new girl."

"Really?" I softly replied, deep in thought. I had a chance with that wonderful, beautiful boy? Angie looked down at the schedule in my hands.

"Arithmetic, that's where I'm headed as well. Come on." She dragged me down the hall and when we got there, Nigel wasn't in the class. I was disappointed.

I had a hard time paying attention. I didn't like math much and Nigel was on the brain. Luckily I had lunch after that, and I knew I wouldn't have to focus there. When the bell rang, Angie walked with me to the cafeteria. We sat at a table full of Angie's girlfriends. She introduced me. "Everyone, this is Michelle. Michelle, this is everyone."

"Hi everyone." I tried to sound friendly.

"You're American!" one of the girls called out.

"Yes, I am," I replied, sitting down. A barrage of questions ensued. Angie was right, being new meant being popular. I was not too wrapped up in the conversation when Tom walked closely by, carrying a tray of food.

"Gettin' the scoop, girls?" he coyly asked, walking away. The girls giggled and gossiped in hushed tones.

"Oh, Tom is so cute!" one girl said while staring toward a few tables over, where he sat with his friends, including Nigel.

"Well, you're not the only one who thinks so," Angie teased in a mocking tone, winking at me. Some of the girls laughed or commented, but one said "Really? Cuz she's been starin' at Nigel Blake since we sat down."

I blushed and looked away.

"What? Nigel?" Angie asked, confused.

I didn't answer, not knowing what to say. I was always a very honest person, but I didn't know if telling them about my crush would be wise. Although, maybe they could fix us up; or tell me if he was really bad news. I was thinking it over quickly, but before I could decide, one girl interrupted my thoughts.

"Well if you like Nigel, that's a different story," she informed me.

"What do you mean?" I asked quickly and eagerly.

"Oh, well, Tom has a list a mile long of girls waiting to date him. He's a bit of a challenge. Nigel, well, I don't know if Nigel has ever really had a girlfriend here."

"Really?" I questioned quietly.

"Actually, Nigel would get a kick out of you, I think."

I was all ears.

"He is sort of quiet, but smart."

"And funny," another girl added.

"Oh yeah, funny, too. And artistic and creative."

"He's got art with us!" Angie beamed.

"Oh, that's good!"

"Michelle is good at art," Angie explained.

I was full of hope, and I liked everything I was learning about this guy. Another girl chimed in.

"I think Nigel is bored with the ordinary. No wonder he doesn't want to date any of us girls. You're fresh. You're probably perfect for him."

I smiled, looking across the cafeteria at him, my heart full and beating fast.

"What's so attractive about him?" another girl asked.

I was shocked. Couldn't everyone see his stunning, unique beauty?

"Oh, he's alright! Not bad looking, just . . . kind of plain," Angie commented.

Plain? They were delusional!

The girl responded, "Maybe if he didn't wear the spectacles. I don't know . . . brown eyes and brown hair. Tall and skinny. Pale. Boring. I'd like a tan blonde with green eyes and big muscles. You got those in America, I'm sure. Gorgeous cowboys!" The rest of the girls were all laughing and agreeing. I had to defend my boy.

"American men have a lot of different looks, it's such a mix. There's something for everyone, for sure . . . but I don't know. I've never seen anyone like *him*. I think it's love at first sight," I said softly.

All the girls at the table looked teary and emotional. I instantly felt stupid, opening up to all these people I barely knew. After that, the rest of the lunch hour was spent talking about boys, boyfriends, love, and Nigel.

My next two classes didn't have Nigel or Angie in them. I did my best to be friendly to the strangers around me. Luckily everyone was eager to make nice with the American.

My last class of the day was writing, and Nigel was in it. There were no empty seats by him, but I sat as close as I could. I was curious to see if those gossiping girls were right about Nigel's creativity. I wanted to check out his writing abilities and share mine with him. In this class, we'd have a reason to talk, first about the assignments and then our inspiration for writing. Pretty soon we'd be sharing our work, then dating and kissing and getting married and having babies. . . . My mind was racing with possibilities.

The whole period, the teacher was explaining the projects we'd be doing and what he expected of us. No sharing of our creations today, like we did in art. I was disappointed. Before I knew it, class was over. I was gathering my things as the room emptied, so was Nigel. As we made our way out at the same time, he gestured for me to exit first.

I appreciated that. "Thank you, that's very gentlemanly of you."

"Um, no. I just like to let the girls go first- for the view," he said with a wink. I laughed, perhaps a bit too hard, titillated over his perverted joke. He looked proud and smiled widely. "Do you take the coach home?"

"The what? Oh yeah, the bus. Yeah, I'll be doing that from now on, I guess."

"Me, too. I can walk you there- that is, unless you know what you're doing and don't need an escort." He was shy, quickly retreating to not seem presumptuous. It was endearing.

"No, that would be really nice, thank you." I accepted. He smiled and looked a bit more self-assured. We walked down the halls together. I guess the girls were right, I thought. Maybe I was just up his alley. God knows he was right up mine.

"So, I'm Nigel. We didn't get properly introduced."

"Yeah, Nigel John Blake, I remember. It's nice to meet you. I'm Michelle Lynn Casey."

"That's a nice name."

"Thanks, but I can't take credit for it," I joked. He smiled.

"I hate my name," he admitted, disgustedly. "It's so nerdy and boring. Nigel. I'd just like to go by my middle name, John."

"I think Nigel is a lovely name. It's unique. I've never met a Nigel before."

"It's not a unique name in England," he pointed out.

"Well, I think it suits you- I mean, not nerdy or boring. Lovely. You look like a Nigel," I told him. He gave me an unconvinced look.

When we reached our bus, he went first through the door. I followed closely.

"Do you want to sit by me?" I asked, trying not to seem too desperate. "I don't really know anyone," I explained.

He looked at the back of the bus at his friends and waved to them, then turned to me to answer. "If you want me to."

I nodded. It was uncharacteristic of me to be so forward with a stranger, let alone such an attractive stranger who made me feel quite nervous. I guess I just felt like now was not the time to be shy. I saw what I wanted and didn't want to waste time, or an opportunity to get close to him. Besides, the girls at lunch gave me quite an ego boost. I had confidence this boy may get to like me as much as I was getting to like him.

He chose a seat and sat by the window. I sat also, not too close, but not too far either. "How was your first day?" he asked, getting the ball rolling.

We talked the whole way home, which took at least forty-five minutes. He gave me the low-down on teachers, classmates, rules, everything. I loved listening to his beautiful, sort of deep voice, every word accented with his perfect tone. He made me laugh. I made him laugh a bit, too; it felt great.

Something about him was so comforting and familiar even though he was totally new and exhilarating to me. I couldn't put my finger on what was so attractive about him. It wasn't just his looks. He had a charm about him that was unique. A total lack of arrogance, but a confidence that radiated from within. It was as if he didn't know how special he was, but I did. I could already feel the spell he was casting over me.

All too quickly, the bus approached his stop. My heart did a back flip when I realized how close he lived to me. It looked like he lived in a neighborhood just like mine: cute, small, two story cookie cutter houses crammed together on a tree lined street. He got up and turned to me. "Well, goodbye. I will see you tomorrow, then?"

"Tomorrow, yeah. Goodbye Nigel." He smiled and exited the bus. I watched him out the window as long as I could before the bus rounded a corner. I was falling in love.

When I got home, I raced to my room. I jumped onto my unmade bed, sighed, and closed my eyes. I wanted to rerun all of Nigel's scenes today; everything he'd said, how he looked, all the information the girls had given me about him. I faded into a deep thought process for I don't know how long. I drifted off to sleep and dreamed about him and I on a beach. He was sitting in the shade on a big rock, looking sad and lonely. I was walking along and spotted him staring off in the opposite direction towards the water. I wondered what he was doing here, and why he was alone. It was cold, he didn't belong here. I approached him from behind and put my hands on his shoulders. He turned around and smiled. "Come with me, my sweet love. Come with me," I sang. He took my hand and I led him to the shore, away from the gloom of the shade. Beams of sunlight cloaked us with warmth and we felt instantly better. It wasn't just the warmth, it was the fact that we had found each other, and that seemed to be the key to our happiness. His smile was radiant, he was like a new person and so was I. We were like angels, we seemed to be floating, I couldn't feel the ground beneath my feet. All I could feel was him and his presence, and that made me complete. I wondered if this was what heaven was like- two people united, becoming unearthly happy together.

I vaguely became aware of a sore face from smiling too long in my slumber. I opened my eyes, it was getting dark.

"Dinner!" my mother called. I hadn't even heard her get home. I reluctantly picked myself up and went downstairs. I sat down and tried to clear my head. I hoped my raging emotions were not obvious to them. My parents asked me about my day and I briefly filled them in. They didn't ask too many questions and I didn't really want to talk much. We had a strained relationship, but we never spoke of it. I was an only child but I always felt like I was on the back burner to them. Careers and status first, kid second. I had always been left alone far too much while they advanced the corporate ladder. Maybe that's why I escaped into art so much. Writing and drawing took me out of the now and into a fantasy world of my creation.

I picked at my dinner while my parents kept their focus on the nightly news on the television. I got up and put my plate in the sink, barely noticed.

Back in my room, I picked up a notebook from my backpack. I wrote a journal entry. I wrote some poem verses. I made a sketch. All of which inspired by Nigel John Blake.

෮

The next morning I got up early, after barely being able to sleep the night before. I meticulously picked out an outfit, did my hair and makeup, and rushed out the door. I got on the bus and he was there, looking out the window, seated alone. I didn't want to appear forward, so I sat across from him and casually said "hi."

"Are you not going to sit by me today?" he feigned affliction.

"Oh, can I? Yes, I will," I stammered and rushed to his side.

"So, did your parents give you the third degree yesterday?" he asked.

"No, not really."

"Really? Are you an only child?"

"Yeah."

"Me, too. My parents are on top of me with everything."

"Huh. Mine aren't like that. They're very busy."

"Oh, that's rough."

"I guess," I replied. He looked down, the mood suddenly heavy. I tried to lighten it. "Well, it's okay, I'm used to it. . . . And I like my privacy."

He looked at me. "Optimistic attitude, I like it."

I smiled, he smiled back at me. We had such an easiness between us. We talked all the way to school, and all the time while we walked to our literature class, continuing until the teacher quieted us all down.

In art, we were allowed to be more open and speak while we worked. We talked about art and what we liked, what we created, what we wanted to create. He was planning on going to art college, I was fascinated. I wanted to know everything I could about him and all that I found out, I liked. Tom stared at us as we bantered away, astonished by our sudden connection. He was about to voice a comment, but Angie kicked him under the table to stop him. We both noticed and looked, Angie quickly smiled innocently and Tom just gave us a quiet nod. Nigel and I locked eyes briefly, but long enough to convey the mutual feeling that something serious was beginning between us.

Nigel walked me to my next class and Angie followed close behind, watching and listening. "Maybe we can sit together at lunch," he suggested.

"Cool, yeah. I'll find you."

"Cool." He smiled and walked away, waving goodbye.

"Whoa, what happened between you two?" Angie asked, wide-eyed.

"Um, we just clicked." Then I began gushing excitedly. "He's so wonderful! And, oh my gosh, he's so gorgeous. I feel like I'm going to melt when he looks at me!" I knew I was babbling on, but I needed to tell someone and Angie was so interested in the drama, she wanted to know every detail.

We chatted about Nigel as much as we could in class. Again, I was unable to focus on math. It was so unimportant compared to everything else going on. After class, Angie and I were walking to the cafeteria. "So, you're going to eat together?" she asked.

"I guess so, but I'd still like to sit with you and your friends. Everyone was so nice." Not to mention they gave me the confidence I needed to talk to Nigel.

"Maybe we can all sit together," Angie suggested. "The girls would die to have Tom sit with us."

"Great."

At lunch, I found Nigel and we agreed to sit at a long table with enough room for all of us. The girls all stared at the interaction between Nigel and I, smiling and whispering. I felt so special, envied by them and accepted by him. I loved England already.

On the bus, headed home, we continued to chat, just as we had been doing all day whenever we had the chance. By the end of the ride, we had exchanged phone numbers and addresses.

The next afternoon, he decided to walk me home; he said it was because it was such a nice day and he wanted to be outside. I saw through his ruse. I thought it was sweet that he felt he needed an excuse to stay with me longer.

We talked as we walked, all the way to my house. When we arrived, I invited him in. My parents weren't home and wouldn't be for a few hours. I was nervous. I tried to act casual and busy myself, suddenly uncomfortable for the first time with him. Unsure what to do, I retrieved the mail and tossed it on a nearby table. Nigel looked at it, interested in something. "You got a card?"

"Did I?" I picked it up. "It's a birthday card from my grandparents."

"Your birthday is coming?"

"Well, this card is early. They probably wanted to give it enough time with the distance and all."

"When is it?"

"October first ."

"Oh, a Libra! And you're turning seventeen?"

"Um, no, sixteen."

"Sixteen! Wow. I turned seventeen over the summer."

"And when is your birthday?"

"June nineteenth."

"Ah, a Gemini. The twins. Duel personalities. . . . Well it's been nice knowing you, but-"

"Now, hang on, Libras and Geminis are compatible with each other," he blurted.

I looked away, blushing at what he was implying. He thought we were compatible! Did he want to date me? I looked back up at him. He looked a bit embarrassed at the forwardness of his words.

" . . . But I don't know. Fifteen? . . . " he joked. I smiled at him. "I don't know if I want to be the old man with the young girlfriend, so maybe you're right, I should go." He started for the door.

"No, wait. I like older men." I reached for him, lightly brushing his hand. It was the first time we had touched. It felt electric. He turned around and looked at me. Our eyes locked. I could tell he was starting to have feelings for me, too. His beautiful brown eyes were warm and intense, they were powerful. It nearly took my breath away.

"No, I think I *should* go," he said seriously and I understood why. If he had stayed, things probably would've progressed too fast and neither one of us was actually ready for that, even though it was obvious we had a real connection. I guess our little relationship was moving fast, but there couldn't have been any other way. We clicked so deeply, it felt like we'd known each other for our whole lives and yet I didn't know that much about him or vice versa.

"Okay. Let me walk you out." I led him out the door and onto the porch. We faced each other. "Thanks for walking me home, and hanging out and stuff. It's been fun," I admitted apprehensively.

"Yeah, it has been fun. I like talking to you," he confided, looking down with his hands in his pockets.

My heart swelled. I tried to act casual. "I'll see you tomorrow morning."

"See ya." He walked away. I watched him go until he was out of sight, suddenly feeling depressed. I didn't understand what was happening to me. I never felt like this before. My heart was aching when he left but at the same time I was also brimming with excitement for the next time I'd see him.

I closed the door, wishing he was still in the house with me. I couldn't believe it, but I felt like I was on the verge of tears, overcome with sadness at his departure. At the same time, I thought I was going to bust, smiling and laughing- so happy to have him in my life. And he wanted me too? Incredible!

In four days, my whole life had changed. It wasn't because I moved away from everything and everyone I knew- none of that mattered anymore. The only thing that mattered was what was materializing for me and Nigel, the love of my life.

Chapter 2

"Maybe we would start sharing more."

Nigel had gotten into the habit of walking me home after school. I loved it. In school, we were inseparable, talking and passing notes as much as we could. Our lunch hour was spent side by side, laughing and flirting. On the bus we would sit together, a bit closer than friends should. His friends were becoming my friends and we all sat by each other in the back of the bus, gossiping, laughing, sometimes singing, or having one massive group conversation. Of course, Nigel and I had a private thing going on amidst the uproar. We were in our own little world most of the time. It was clear to everyone around us that we were an item, though we never defined it. I don't think we had to. After the long ride home, he would follow me back to my house.

My parents did not get home until after six o'clock during the week. I don't know if Nigel didn't want me to be alone or if he just didn't want to go home to his own parents or if he wanted to be alone with me in a private place. Whatever the reason, I definitely didn't mind. Most days, we'd have a snack and watch TV or listen to music. Nigel was really into music- maybe even more than me. He would introduce me to bands I'd never heard of and make me see why they were geniuses. I turned him on to a few bands that were popular in America, though I really liked British music more than anything. Somehow I connected to it more. It seemed fitting when one day while sitting on the floor in my room, listening to records, Nigel told me he was learning to play guitar.

"Really?" I said incredulously.

"Yeah, I'm just learning. Well, I'm teaching myself," he explained.

"That's awesome! I can't wait to hear you play."

"Well, it will be a while. I'm not good."

"Yet. You're not good yet. You will be. You have musician's hands." I picked up his right hand with mine and traced it with my left. "You have big hands. With long, slender fingers," I admitted, continuing to stroke his hand, eyes cast down on it. At first, I didn't mean anything by it, I wasn't trying to arouse him. His hand was getting warm and moist. So was mine. My heart was racing, touching him and his perfect, sexy fingers. Dirty thoughts quickly came to mind before I realized it was no longer appropriate for me to be holding his hand. I gently released. He was looking down, not at me, and I was relieved. My face flushed. He was good at not blushing, but I was learning that he was a quietly passionate and emotional boy. Smoldering. He put his hand on my knee. I was nervous and excited. Part of me was scared, but the majority of me wanted to begin a physical relationship. Right now. He lightened the mood.

"I'll play you a song soon," he told me, looking me in the eyes. He then slid his hand off my knee and got up to change the record.

With his back to me, I let out a long exhale, realizing I had been holding my breath for the whole exchange.

"T-Rex," he stated, placing the needle on the record.

"Cool," I answered halfheartedly, still distracted by my sexual frustration.

"Mark Bolan was the best," Nigel said, smiling and reading the back cover. He sat down beside me, teaching me interesting music tidbits. I listened intently, watching him ardently discuss the who, what, and why.

"You're going to be a great musician one day, Nigel."

"You think?"

"Oh yeah. You're made for this. One day, some kids are going to be sitting around talking about you. And I'll be able to say I knew you when . . ."

He beamed at me proudly. I meant every word. I believed in him. He was proving to be talented and devoted; full of integrity. Sometimes that's not the recipe for success in the music industry, but he also had drive. That would get him far.

"Would you ever want to learn an instrument? Maybe we could both learn guitar and start a band!"

"Like Sonny and Cher?" I blushed again at my precocious comment. I hadn't meant to imply marriage. It didn't faze him.

"No, way cooler than Sonny and Cher," he said, rolling his eyes.

"Right. . . . Well, we'd have to be," I joked, trying to regain composure.

"Yeah." He looked at me, and then looked at the clock. "I should go."

"Oh, okay. I'll walk you out." I followed him to the front door. "Wait, your records! I'll go get them."

"No, just keep them for now. If you want to. I'll get them later." He smiled. I smiled back, knowing that what he meant was he planned on making this a regular date. And he wanted me to be a part of his life! Or at least, to share his music. Maybe we would start sharing more.

"So, what are you doing this weekend?" he shyly asked.

"No plans yet."

"None at all?"

"No, you?"

"Well . . . I was thinking we could go somewhere. Together."

"Really? Yes, let's."

"Cool. We'll talk more tomorrow."

"Okay." I wanted to kiss him goodbye, at least on the cheek, but we hadn't gotten there yet. No formal titles in our relationship. I stood there awkwardly. We were both silent for a moment.

"Okay, goodbye, then," he eventually said.

I tried to hide my disappointment. "Goodbye Nigel," I returned with a smile. I watched him trot down the porch steps and away from the house until he was out of sight. I went back to my room and played the records he'd left with me. I pored over the liner notes and jackets. I was truly interested in what interested him. He inspired me. He was my muse. Because of him, I was writing the most amazing poems and songs every time my pen touched paper. Maybe one day, I would share them with him.

I couldn't believe how fast I was falling for this boy. No one had ever captured my attention the way he did. When he did any little thing, raise an eyebrow, stumble over a phrase, laugh, my heart stretched to breaking point. I thought about him constantly, I felt like I was going crazy. I couldn't eat much, couldn't think straight, and couldn't sleep at night, always twisted up in the sheets, anxious for his body beside mine, imagining his touch, his kiss, his smooth whispers in the dark . . .

Luckily for me, not everyone noticed how incredible he was. If he had any idea, I was sure he would realize that he was too good for me. I wasn't sure what I offered to him. I thanked my lucky stars for his naiveté.

慘

My sixteenth birthday was approaching. I didn't really want anything this year, I'd already gotten the most amazing gift. Even if Nigel and I weren't a real couple, just having him in my life meant so much.

This year, my birthday was on a Saturday- and this just happened to be the weekend that Nigel wanted to spend time with me. I wasn't sure if it was a date, and I certainly didn't have my hopes up for any birthday surprises from him. I doubted he remembered, and that was fine. I was just excited to see him on a non-school-day for the first time.

When Saturday came, I went downstairs for breakfast in my pajamas, lured by the smell of cinnamon in the air. My parents were waiting for me.

"I know you're going out later today, so I thought we'd surprise you first thing!" my mom proudly stated.

"Oh, thanks," I said sleepily. I had forgotten but I must have mentioned my plans to her earlier. I was surprised because normally my parents didn't make a big fuss over me.

"Well, I made a huge breakfast and we're having *coffee* cake, but I still put candles in it."

They seemed to be trying hard to make this birthday special. I went along with it. "Oh, that's sweet. It smells good in here."

"Before we eat, let's open your presents," my dad insisted.

"Okay," I agreed and they went off into another room, returning with two large boxes.

"This one first," my dad said quickly, looking nervous. I lifted the top off the box and found a small calico kitten inside.

"Oh! What a sweet baby!" I cried, picking her up. "I love her already." I cradled her furry little body to my flannel-clad bosom.

My dad beamed. "We wanted to make this birthday as special for you as we could. I know this has been the toughest move ever. I hope this little cat will keep you from feeling so lonely."

"She's not lonely. She has that boy," my mom corrected. I looked up, shocked. She knew about Nigel?

"What boy?" my dad demanded, though not angrily. I was silent and stunned. Would they be mad? Was I not allowed to have boys over? It had never come up before. I was worried this would ruin my birthday before it really began.

My mom explained. "Oh, it's fine. A few weeks ago, I asked the next-door neighbor, Gertrude, to kind of look out for you before we got home from work. When I was talking to her recently, she said I shouldn't worry because every day you were being escorted home by a young man and you two seem quite chummy."

I had no idea I was being watched. So, did she know Nigel and I were alone together in the house for hours most days? She didn't seem suspicious or displeased. She sounded like she trusted me.

"I think it's nice that you have a friend." My mom smiled at me.

My dad relaxed. "Okay . . . Well, now you have two friends," he said, pointing at the kitten. I relaxed too, and finally quietly exhaled the breath I'd been holding for too long. "Open the other box."

It was full of cat supplies: toys, food, everything we'd need.

"Thank you both so much!"

"Well it's not a car, but I don't really think you need one here. And anyway, I think I'd rather you learn to drive the American way in an American car," my dad informed me.

"Oh, we don't know when we'll be back in the states!" my mom reminded him. My heart skipped a beat. I hadn't thought of moving back home since school started. I had missed America, but now . . . things were complicated. I didn't even want to think about moving now.

"That's true," my dad admitted. It relieved me to hear there were no plans of us moving anytime soon, maybe ever.

"Let's eat!" I cheerfully exclaimed.

ༀ

After breakfast, I took the cat to my room, put on Nigel's records, and prepared and over-prepared for my upcoming afternoon. I changed my clothes five times, I changed my hair three times. I didn't quite know how to dress because I didn't know if this was meant to be a date or a casual outing with a friend. I didn't want to overdress nor look too casual; and, above all, I wanted to look enticing.

I played out every possible scenario in my head and then resigned to the fact that I had no idea what was going to happen today. I settled on a short sleeved white eyelet lace blouse and a knee length denim skirt. I pulled my some of my hair back with a barrette and added some bracelets, a necklace and earrings. I also decided to wear shoes with a bit of a heel to increase my height for Nigel's sake. Very carefully, I applied some makeup, trying to look as naturally perfect as possible. When I was satisfied with my appearance, I sat down and began responding to the few birthday cards I'd gotten from friends and family in America. I was interrupted when I heard a knock on the front door. I dropped my pen and darted downstairs, the kitten slowly following.

Nigel was here. I wanted to let him in but my mom beat me to it. She opened the door. I peeked over her shoulder as she studied the tall boy on the porch.

"Hi Nigel," I spoke from behind her.

"Nigel," my mom repeated. "Please, come in."

He looked slightly uncomfortable, but entered demurely with a typical polite English attitude. He was dressed up a little bit, wearing a nice deep red sweater and slacks. He had styled his hair. He looked more handsome than I had ever seen him before. I could smell a hint of cologne on him. He was prepared for a date! My heart leapt.

"Pleasure to meet you, ma'am." He offered his hand to my mother.

My mom cooed at his good manners. She looked pleased. "Hi, I'm Paula."

My dad came in the room with the kitten in his arms. "Look who I found." Then he noticed Nigel. "Oh, company."

"Dad, this is Nigel. Nigel, this is my father, Rick Casey," I introduced.

"Nice to meet you, sir." Nigel extended his hand. My dad handed me the cat and firmly shook Nigel's hand.

"Nice to meet you, too, young man. I'm glad Michelle has made a good friend."

Nigel looked a bit surprised when my dad said 'good friend'. I groaned, embarrassed. He changed the subject and focused on the cat. "And who is this?"

"This is my birthday present. I haven't named her yet."

"Well, it's nice to meet you anyway, dear," he said to her, shaking her tiny paw. My heart melted. I think my mother's did, too.

"I don't think we need to hang around, do we?" she asked my father. "Let's go get more cat food." She took his hand and led him away. Apparently it was okay to have a boy in the house.

I sat down on the floor; Nigel sat beside me, fixed on the kitten.

"What should I name this sweetie?" I asked.

"Maybe something along the lines of September or something. She has all those autumn colors in her."

"I should call her Autumn!" The cat looked up at me. "Is that your name, baby? Autumn?" Her ear twitched. "That's her name!"

Nigel stroked her little head, I watched him. He was so tender, and so handsome. I was one hundred percent in love with him. He felt my stare and looked up at me. I looked away, but grinned. "So, what's on tap for today?"

"I have the whole day planned," he answered.

"You do?" I was shocked. Why would he go to such lengths? It seemed like too much for a friend to do.

"Don't get all excited. It's no big deal."

I didn't believe him. "I'm ready. Let's go." I put the cat down on the floor and grabbed my purse and jacket.

"Okay, let's." He stood up, looking a little nervous.

ভ

We started off walking; he led the way. We ended up on a country lane I had never seen before. It was lovely. We talked the whole way and the time flew.

"Your parents seem nice," Nigel observed.

"They can be. I mean, they aren't that bad, they're just kind of controlling. Like, they're good when I'm doing exactly what they expect me to, but if I'm not perfect, if I ever do something they disapprove of, they can be . . . difficult to deal with."

He nodded, listening. It was nice to have someone to confide in.

Eventually we came to a dead-end, a small house on a huge property at the end of the lane. We paused, and then he continued walking, right up the dirt driveway. I stayed behind, not wanting to trespass.

"Where are we?" I loudly asked. He turned around, not realizing I wasn't following him. He returned to me, put one arm around my waist and led me up the drive. My whole body quivered at his touch. My heart sped up. Even though I felt scared and sick, I was comfortable and happy next to his warm body. He smiled at me as we walked. I wondered if he felt the same.

"This is my grandmother's house," he explained. "She's away on a visit." We approached a gate and he went in first. The yard was beautiful. Lush green grass stretched out on low hills. Wildflowers sprung up all around. The air smelled clean, yet fragrant with the scent of early autumn and the changing of the leaves.

There was a large pond in the center of the huge, sprawling property. Close to the edge of the pond was a big yellow blanket. He must have set it out before he picked me up. He brought me to the blanket and knelt on it, so I did the same. It was gently heated by the sun, it felt so good. I felt like I was right where I belonged. It reminded me of the dream I had when I first met him. Upon remembering how that dream ended, I scooted closer to him as he stared out at the peaceful scene.

"This is really nice," I softly said.

"Yeah, I love it here. I've spent so many summers here. . . . I've never brought anyone here before. . . . "

"Really?" I gushed. We were both silent, nervous and thinking of our next move. "Nigel, have you ever had a girlfriend before?"

"Well . . . not really. You?"

"Oh, many girlfriends!" I joked and we laughed for a moment. "No boyfriends, though," I said quietly.

"Why not?" He seemed surprised.

"Well, we move around a lot. It's hard to make friends, let alone start a relationship. Anyway, in America, I'm a dime a dozen, nothing special. The guys never look at me twice. But here, I guess I'm different and exciting. . . ."

He had a perplexed, almost angry look on his face. "Different and exciting, yes. Nothing special? Never. Not in any country could you be a 'dime a dozen.'"

It was very forward of him to say that. In the past month, we had become fairly close but we hadn't spoken our true feelings to each other. I didn't know he felt like that about me. "Thank you," I almost whispered the words. Suddenly I felt like reciprocating his generosity. "Thank you for everything, Nigel. You have made this experience so warm and fun. I was really not looking forward to moving to England, but I am so glad we did. I already like it more than home."

"Why?"

" . . . Because you're here." I confessed.

He took off his glasses and looked me in the eyes. The intensity was thick between us. For some reason, I had the nerve to be totally open with him.

"God, Nigel, you have such beautiful eyes. Everything about you is beautiful. I loved you since the first time I looked at you and I haven't been able to think about anything else since." I was talking so quickly, I would've been shocked by my unabashedness if I had time to think. My heart was doing all the talking. "You have taken my dull, gray world and filled it with color and life. You've inspired me to make beautiful art. You've opened my eyes and ears to new ideas and music. You woke my heart up . . . "

I was slowing down now, realizing the impact of what I was saying. We couldn't go back to being friends now. What if he was just being polite and friendly? What if that's how all the English were? I was in too deep now, it didn't matter; so I took a chance and spilled it all. "I never understood the movies or books or songs about a love that was so strong, you'd do anything, but I'm beginning to. I feel so passionate about you. I admire everything about you. I believe in you. You are amazing." I looked down, a bit worried about his reaction. "You must think I'm some obsessed freak now, but even if you don't want to hang out with me anymore, you should know," I looked back into his eyes, "you're the best."

He was stone, his lips parted a bit, his eyes wide and emotional. I looked away, my face burning, but I wasn't sorry I said all that. I really cared for him, and he needed to know that.

The silence was unbearable, but I knew he was processing my admission. The seconds passed like hours as I waited for his response.

He didn't say anything. He took my hand and squeezed it. The blood drained from my face. I looked at him, our eyes locking again. He pulled me close. I stopped breathing. He gently touched my face. I couldn't stop staring into his deep brown eyes, they were mesmerizing. I was helpless, his for the taking.

Without thinking, I said the only thing in my mind. "I love you, Nigel."

Then he kissed me. I felt out of body, like a dream. Yet I could feel his lips so vividly, soft and moist, meeting mine. I felt whole, physically reunited with my counterpart.

It seemed like time ceased to pass, but all too quickly the kiss was over.

"I love *you*," he told me, though it was obvious from the kiss. I fervently embraced him and squeezed him as though he and this moment could slip away. He hugged back, almost harder. My eyes stung with tears that I tried to hold in. He just kept holding me. "Thank you for saying those nice things," he mumbled into my shoulder.

"I meant every word." I tried to make my voice sound uncluttered of the tears.

He loosened his embrace. "I didn't quite know how you felt about me. . . . I mean, we've been getting close but, you never said anything before. And I've been trying to work up the nerve to tell you . . . I'm glad *you* had the guts. And now we can stop trying to hide our feelings. It's a relief. My plans for today would've been embarrassing if you only liked me as a friend."

As a friend? Impossible. He was far too special.

"Now I can give you your surprise."

"A surprise?" I thought that bringing me here was my gift.

"It's nothing much, just close your eyes. I'll be right back."

I laughed and did what I was told. He ran off. I sat there with my eyes closed, trying to listen to what he was doing. I could hear him sneaking up behind me moments later. I heard him set something down, then sit down in front of me. "I had to make sure things were right before acting on my instincts. I mean, I thought you felt the same way about me as I do about you. And I was right." I could hear the smile in his voice as he spoke those words. My heart swelled. He felt the same way about me? He cared about me that much? It was too good to be true. Did he really mean it?

"Okay, open your eyes."

I did. The only thing in front of me was him, but that was alright, he was all I wanted anyway. I was content. I grinned a big grin at him.

He pulled out a card from behind his back. It was handmade. The front was covered in huge letters reading 'HAPPY BIRTHDAY'. It had the appearance of the sketch he'd done in art class that I admired so much. I sighed happily and opened it. The whole inside was filled with his sort of messy handwriting.

> Michelle,
>
> Getting to know you this last month has been great. You are a wonderful girl and I am lucky to know you.
>
> I was quite lonely before I met you, but lately I find myself smiling and happy all the time. I just feel good when we are together. You are unique and brilliant and beautiful. You are everything I could want. I fancy you quite a bit and I flatter myself to think you feel the same way as well.

I was so overcome, I could hardly see straight. I had no idea he was going to come out with all his feelings today. I wasn't even sure he had those feelings!

The last words of the card were:

> I want to give you the best birthday of your life because I've fallen in love with you.

Blinking away tears, I looked up at him. He was studying my reaction.

"You were going to tell me you loved me today?"

"Yeah," he said shyly. "I had to wait until you were sixteen because I didn't want to look like some cradle robber, dating a fifteen-year-old," he said laughing.

"God, I'm glad I'm sixteen! So, wait, does this mean we're dating?"

"No, not yet."

"Oh." I was disappointed. He took my hand.

"Michelle, will you be my girlfriend?"

"Yes, Nigel, I will." He smiled widely and took me in his arms for another kiss. This time it lasted much longer and was far more serious. He held me close to him and parted his lips. My hands slid down his neck and back, trying to touch him anywhere I could. I wanted to touch him everywhere. The intimacy was addictive. His kiss was glorious. I wanted to undress him so badly, right there, in broad daylight, at his grandmother's house no less!

His body felt eager, we were both ready to take things further. He shifted to lay us down together and when he did, he stretched out his leg and knocked it against something. The sound of clinking glass startled me. I sat up and looked, he had hidden a picnic basket.

"So that's what you were getting? You made a picnic?"

"Yeah," he said sheepishly. "But we can go back to what we were doing!"

I laughed, pleased that he wanted me as much (or possibly more) as I wanted him. "What's in the basket?"

"Well, picnics in the movies always have the same things, so that's what I tried to go for. Wine, cheese, fruit, biscuits, jams, that sort of thing."

I was so touched. I couldn't believe a teenage boy could be so thoughtful and do something so romantic. This boy was different than the rest. I began to realize how lucky I was that he chose me as his object of affection.

He didn't seem to notice while I stared at him with appreciation as he pulled two wine glasses out and expertly uncorked a bottle. I'd barely ever drank before, the laws in America being tighter than European ones. He'd brought a very sweet wine, a dessert wine. It was very easy to drink. I was pleasantly surprised. All the little goodies in the basket were unfamiliar to me, and that made it more special. English food was so different from what I was used to.

We bantered about that and our customs and such so effortlessly. I nibbled the snacks; he gobbled them down. I had to remember Nigel had the appetite of a seventeen-year-old boy . . . and not just for food.

After the picnic, he gave me the tour of the house, sharing stories and memories with me. I was honored to be the only girl he'd ever done this with.

We walked the grounds, slowly meandering around the huge property. We managed to be touching the whole time, either holding hands or draping our arms around each other's shoulders or waist. It really felt like we belonged to one another. The previous month of getting to know each other now culminated into an explosion of truth as we poured out our hearts and realized all our budding feelings were mutual. *Budding* was not the word, they were budding when we met. By now, they were full blown, deep and intense.

It was starting to get dark. "Time to move on," Nigel said.

"Oh, what's next?"

"Let's get ready to go."

He picked up the blanket and basket, refusing to let me help. I followed him in the house to freshen up while he tucked away our supplies. When I was done, he flashed me a set of keys. "Let's go."

He was borrowing a car from the garage. I waited on the front porch. He pulled around in a little black English car. Quickly he got out and ran to the porch. He led me to the car and opened the door for me. I was confused for a second as I thought he wanted me to get in the driver's seat, but I had forgotten it was backwards from what I was used to. I slid into the passenger's seat and he closed my door for me. He bounced into the driver's seat and informed me "I'm taking you on a tour."

I clapped my hands. "Oh, fun! I haven't been anywhere yet!"

He seemed very pleased at this. "Tonight, we're going everywhere!"

Once we were out of the countryside, the drive was more exciting. The city was booming, it was Saturday night and everything was lit up. The kids were out, sporting funky punk clothes. So different from American kids. Nigel pointed out the coolest hangouts, what bands played where, all the best places to find whatever you needed. He knew a lot about the art, music, and fashion scenes. I listened with awe and absorbed every word.

We ended up at a place called 'American Joe's'.

"Here we are," he said.

"A taste of home, eh?" I joked.

"You can tell me if it's authentic."

Once inside, I started laughing at the décor. Stereotypical American memorabilia was everywhere. The waiters and waitresses all wore white T-shirts tucked into blue jeans, cowboy boots, and cowboy hats.

A waitress came by and led us to a table. "Yous guys want some Cokes?" she asked in what was supposed to be an "American" accent but sounded like Brooklyn slang barely covering her thick British accent. Nigel looked at me with questioning eyes.

"Yeah, sure. Two Cokes, please," I answered the waitress.

She smiled. "Good accent," she complimented, no longer disguising her own. We laughed.

The menu was hilarious. Fried chicken, fried potatoes, steak, burgers, hot dogs, and apple pie á la mode—just fatty, unhealthy foods. *What must they think of us?* I wondered. Southern-style rock music played in the background. Pictures of presidents on money were blown up on the walls. A big Elvis statue stood by the restrooms. This place was unique.

"What do you think?" Nigel asked, looking around.

"I think . . . " I started, slowly choosing my words, "that it's very sweet of you to take me here."

We talked about the real America over dinner. I answered his questions about home and I asked questions about England. We seemed to find each other fascinating. I was unnaturally glad to be a foreigner.

After dinner was over, we got back in the car. "Where to next?" I asked.

"You'll see."

We drove out of the city and toward home. I wasn't quite sure where we were headed, though. He pulled down a vaguely familiar street and into a driveway.

"We're here," he stated.

"Where?"

"My house."

"Oh!"

"Is that okay?"

"Yes, absolutely. I'd love to see it."

Again, he hurried around to open my car door for me, and then he led me to the front porch. He opened the front door and entered; I followed close behind. His parents were sitting in the front room.

"Hello," he greeted them.

"Hello," I repeated. His parents stood up.

"This is Michelle," Nigel explained.

"Come in, dear," his mother offered. She came up to me and offered her hand. I shook it. "Oh, what a pretty thing she is, Nigel."

I blushed and looked at him. He obviously told them about me.

"I'm Jan, and this is Joe," she informed me, pointing to her husband. I shook his hand also.

"It's nice to meet you Mr. and Mrs. Blake."

"She's formal," Joe noted, apparently not knowing what to expect from an American.

"Did you have a nice day today, dear?" Jan asked. My first thought was the kissing and confessing of our love, which I had quite enjoyed, but I think what she meant was *how did your birthday go?*

"Oh, yes, very nice," I answered momentarily.

"That's wonderful. Well, Nigel, I'm glad to see you picked up your room. It looks very good," she said, winking at him.

"Thanks, mum. Excuse us." He took my hand and led me upstairs to his room. *Lenient parents*, I thought. *They don't mind that their only son is taking a strange girl up to his room on a Saturday night?*

When he opened the door for me to enter his room, I understood. He had balloons tied to a vase full of flowers sitting on his desk. Beside the vase was a small but elaborately decorated birthday cake with sixteen candles on it.

"Nigel," I choked out, a lump in my throat.

"My mom helped," he explained, avoiding taking all the credit. He closed the door behind him, giving us privacy.

I walked over to the desk to examine the cake, balloons, and flowers.

"Aww," was all I could say. The picnic was an incredibly thoughtful gesture, but by this time, I was floored. I wasn't used to being treated special and I couldn't fathom why anyone, particularly someone so divine, would go to such lengths for me. "Nigel, this is too much."

"It's been my pleasure. I've never had a girlfriend to spoil before. I like it."

"I like it too," I confessed with a little laugh. "Thank you for all this."

"Well . . . there's one more thing."

"No."

"Yes. I wrote you a song." He picked up a guitar from the corner of his room. "Sit down and I'll play it for you."

I sat on his bed, across from him, as he stood and strummed, carefully positioning his fingers on the frets. He was just learning, but it was clear he'd practiced this many times. He played a beautiful melody—more beautiful to my ears than anyone else's, I'm sure. Just the thought that he had written music for me amazed me, but I really enjoyed it, it touched my heart.

When he was done with the last note, he slowly put down the guitar and cautiously looked up, fearing I had hated it. I stood up.

"Oh, Nigel. I loved it. It was perfect. Will you play it again?"

"Yeah. Soon. Maybe I'll write something new for you."

I threw my arms around him. "Thank you so much. You're the best."

He put his arms around me and hugged back. "I'm glad you liked it."

"More than anything! Today has been wonderful."

"Well, it's not over yet. You still have to make your birthday wish!" He released me and I did the same. He lit the birthday candles and turned out the light. Only the flame from the cake and the moonlight outside illuminated the room.

"Sit on the bed," he gently commanded. I did as I was told. He sang me the birthday song. "Make a wish." I did silently. "Blow out your candles."

I did- all sixteen on the first try. I really wanted my wish to come true. He set the cake down on his night table and turned to me. It was fairly dark, but I could see him well enough.

"What did you wish for?" he asked.

I grabbed his shirt and pulled him onto me. We fell into a passionate kiss, our hands wild and exploring. I could feel his hardness rubbing against my leg. It was so thrilling; I wanted to go further. He was kissing my neck, his eager hands moving up from my waist, inch by inch. I knew what he was going for. I wanted to let him. I wanted to let him take me, take whatever he wanted. We were deeply involved in our lust, forgetting where we were and our restrictions.

A loud creak outside the door made us both jump. Footsteps paced away and back outside his door. We were frozen. The footsteps stopped and so did we. He sat up and ran a hand through his thick, brown hair, taking a deep breath. "I'm sorry."

"No, no. I started this."

He stood up and turned on the light. "Did I go too far?"

"No, actually, I was really enjoying it."

He smiled. "I'm glad. But that wasn't meant to be part of the gift."

I laughed.

"Hey, my mom will be offended if you don't eat this cake."

"What? You didn't make it?" I teased. "Well, if we can't fool around, we may as well eat cake!"

After we finished the little cake, he helped me gather my gifts and say goodnight to his parents. They didn't look suspicious or judgmental. I was relieved.

Nigel drove me home and walked me to the door.

"I can't tell you what an incredible day this was," I said.

"It was my pleasure." He kissed me on the lips and lingered a moment. "Happy birthday."

"The happiest," I whispered, smiling. He walked away, getting into his car.

"Nigel," I called out. He looked up. "I love you."

He smiled a smile so incredible I will never forget. "I love you, too." Then he got in and drove away.

That night, laying in my bed, my head spun with ways to make it up to him. He had been so wonderful to me and so thoughtful. I wanted to give him something very special. *A gift?* I thought to myself. Maybe something meaningful. Something he'd always wanted. I could guess what he wanted most right now, remembering how we had been interrupted while getting physical earlier that night. *Something sexual.*

If he'd never had a girlfriend, he should never have had his first sexual experience. The one you'd always remember. I could give him that. I played with the idea in my head and fell asleep with a big smile across my face.

୪

The next day, I was floating on a cloud. Nigel occupied my mind. I wrote about him in my songbook. I daydreamed about him. I called Angie and told her every detail, minus the inappropriate ones.

As I was hanging up the phone, it rang again before I could walk away. "Hello?" I answered.

"Hi." It was Nigel. He had never called before. "I just wanted to see how you were doing."

"Oh, um, really good. You?"

"Good . . . I've been thinking about you all day," he admitted.

"Me, too," I gushed.

"I didn't want to wait until tomorrow to talk to you."

"Really? I'm glad you called. I missed you."

"Oh yeah? I miss *you.*"

Though we'd spent nearly twelve hours together the day before, we seemed to need to talk for another hour on the phone, conversation endlessly flowing about this and that until I heard his mother call him for dinner.

"Sorry, I have to go now."

"Okay. I'll see you in the morning."

"Okay . . . Goodnight . . . I love you." He spoke the last part quietly so as not to be overheard by his parents.

"I love you, too. Bye." I hung up, not hearing my mother sneaking in behind me.

"I *love* you?" she repeated wide-eyed.

"Yes, mom," I sighed. "We're in love."

"*In love,*" she again repeated cynically, as though it wasn't possible.

"You should have seen him yesterday. He brought me to the country and made a sweet little picnic for us and drove me to the city and took me to dinner to the only American restaurant in England and he introduced me to his parents and surprised me with flowers and balloons and a cake." The words rushed out of my mouth at a mile a minute, as they so often do when I'm passionate about something. "He gave me the best birthday. He cares so much about me and I adore him, since the moment I met him. And he's so beautiful mom, he's the most gorgeous thing I've ever seen!"

My mother listened with wide eyes at my confession. Normally I kept quiet about personal issues and didn't confide in her. This was a rare mother–daughter moment. "Did he kiss you?"

" . . . Yes. Four times," I swooned.

"All you did was kiss though, right?"

"Yes!" I said with a tone implying *of course that was all!* Though in my head I thought, *we were rudely interrupted or else I couldn't say that with a straight face!*

"Well, I'm happy for you. He *is* cute. And he seems very nice."

Nice? "It's more than that. I'm gonna marry that boy. You'll see."

Her smile vanished, she stared at me. "You just turned sixteen. This is your first boyfriend. I'm sure you do love him, but you'll meet so many other guys. Who even knows how long we'll be living here? Just promise me, you'll take things slow. Don't be in a rush to grow up . . . or do grownup things," she finished with a tone that I understood to mean, *stay a virgin!*

I nodded. "Okay." But I knew in my heart, I was right. I was going to marry him.

The next morning on the bus, waiting for Nigel was like a heroin addict waiting for a fix. When I saw him board, the jitters quit and I was complete. He sat next to me, closer than usual. He put his arm around me immediately and kissed me.

"I missed you," he said sincerely.

"Well, what have we here?" Nigel's friends mocked, spying on us.

"Making it official, eh?"

"I guess you're not a homo after all, Blake!"

The boys were bad, the girls were worse, in their own way.

"Oh my God, you guys are so cute!"

"This is so sweet!"

"You look so happy! You look like you belong together!"

I was blushing and embarrassed, shrinking away from the taunters. He just held me closer and smiled at me.

"Oh my God," he mimicked. "We're so cute!"

I looked at him, and all the staring faces. Suddenly feeling brave, I took his face in my hands and gave him a long kiss on the lips. The crowd roared and hooted. I didn't care. I sat back, satisfied. Let the world know, I was proud and I was in love.

⅓

From there on out, Nigel and I were a couple publicly. We were always together. We became one unit, and no one could break that. I was so happy. When he wasn't with me, I was thinking about him. We were getting closer, sharing our dreams, our past, some plans for the future. Then there were the times when we didn't talk at all, if you catch my meaning. Those were very good times.

We still had so much alone time. On weekends, we would go out or to his grandmother's house when she was away. During the week, we'd be in my room. It was getting harder to restrain our physical relationship. I ached for him, eagerly awaiting him to become one with me. I wanted to stay pure because I was so young, but my urges were too loud to ignore when we were in the throes. He was a masterful kisser. His lips were gentle, yet always pushing forward. His eyes were hypnotic, I never wanted to close mine when we were kissing; he was so gorgeous, I felt like I was dreaming. But I always did end up closing my eyes, too dazed to keep them open when he'd get me all worked up. I would completely succumb to the sweet feeling of his lips on my neck and his big, masculine hands wandering over my body. He would hold me by the hips, pressing his into mine, or dare to try to get under my shirt. Patience wasn't his strong suit. Being seventeen, being a virgin, being so close to someone he loved (who loved him and would do anything for him)-it was tough.

One night, alone in his grandmother's house, we were upstairs on a guest bed. I was lying under him as we made out, innocent kissing turning quickly into something more serious and demanding. I was so desperate for satisfaction, I took his hand and put it under my blouse. In the darkness, I could barely see his face but I'll never forget the sound he made. A sigh, sort of shocked, very grateful. I was titillated. He became ravenous with desire. In seconds he had stripped my shirt off and got on his knees to tear off his own. I didn't feel violated; I was totally comfortable having him undress me. I had been wanting to see more of his body. I traced my fingertips along his perfect, young, smooth chest. Touching his manly body for the first time put me in a frenzied lust that I could barely control. I wanted him *now*. I pulled him down on the bed and perched on top of him. I kissed him, starting at the neck and slowly moving down to his waistline. He was writhing excitedly. I could feel his erection strapped down by his snug jeans. As I contemplated unzipping him and relieving him, he grabbed my hand and pulled me down to lay on top of him. He put his hands behind my back and though I could barely see his expression, lit only by the light of the moon through a bare window, his eyes were asking if it would be alright for him to remove my bra.

"Take it off," I whispered. With a slight struggle, he triumphed. He groaned and squeezed me tightly to his body, rolling us over so he could be on top. So carefully and gently, yet so naturally skillful and seductive, he kissed and sucked my breasts, exciting me on a new level. I was no longer a girl. I felt like a goddess with a virile young man worshiping me on his knees for a taste of heaven.

Nigel's strong, lean body dominated me as he grinded his hardness into my attentive erogenous zone. We kissed madly, both feeling ready to take the next step. I groped around for his waistband so I could take off his pants. His eyes met mine and I could read his mind. *Are you ready? Are you sure?*

I bit my lower lip, thinking it over once more and was about to proceed when the phone rang. A look of panic and disappointment crossed his perfect face.

"Oh shit," he grunted and carefully rose from the bed. I could hear him quickly thud down the stairs, rushing to the phone. He loudly cleared his throat before answering. "'Ello?"

I sat up and put my clothes back on, not knowing who was calling or what was coming. I turned on the light and tried to straighten myself up. Moments later, Nigel was back with me, cheeks flushed. "That was my mum. She wants me to pick up some milk on my way home. She said I ought to be on my way soon. I guess it's late."

I looked down, ashamed. His parents knew we were here. They probably figured out what we were doing. He tried to make me feel better, taking my hands and kissing them. "I had such a good time tonight."

"Yeah, I thought so," I coyly remarked.

"That was . . . more than I expected. I wish we hadn't been interrupted. I would love to take you away, where we could have all the alone time we want with no one to answer to."

I smiled, imagining him and me in a fancy hotel room with a DO NOT DISTURB sign on the door. "That sounds nice."

"It would be. It's so hard to say goodnight to you and leave. I want to say goodnight and watch you fall asleep next to me. I wish we could be together all the time. And I can't wait until I can make love to you. It's going to be so special and so wonderful. I'm going to make you so happy." He stared into my eyes. I was instantly at ease. A second ago, I felt like a filthy slut, then he made me feel like some amazing person who wasn't guilty but who was fulfilling her destiny with her prince charming.

I kissed him. "I love you Nigel."

Chapter 3

"...to be able to give him something no one else would ever be able to give him..."

Christmas was coming and we were going to fly back to America for a week. It would be good to see my friends and family, but to go a whole week without seeing the one who made my world go round? What kind of Christmas gift was that?

I also had the dilemma of deciding what to get for Nigel. I wanted it to be as special as his birthday gift to me. After some thought, I figured it out.

I wanted to see him before we left, and that worked well because the day before our flight, there was no school and my parents had to work, so we would have privacy. I invited Nigel over.

He arrived early, right after my parents left. I barely had time to prepare. I pretended to be sleepy when I answered the door, still wearing my robe.

He looked stunned. "What? You're not even dressed yet? Do you want me to come back later?"

"No, no. I'm sorry. I guess I slept in. Please come in." I gestured for him to enter.

"I told my mom and dad that I was going to Tom's today. I said you were already gone so they won't suspect a thing. They aren't expecting me home until dinnertime." He handed me a wrapped box from behind his back. "Happy Christmas," he said cutely, handing me the gift.

"Oh, honey, thank you."

"Oh, wait, wait, wait!" He pulled a sprig of mistletoe from his pocket and held it over his head with a gleefully expectant expression. I laughed at his darling charm and kissed him firmly.

"Should I open the present?"

"Well, we could wait. Let me see what you got me first and then I'll see if you deserve this gift," he said playfully.

Laughing again, I agreed. "Your gift is upstairs, come on."

There was a big red bow on my bedroom door. He looked at me questioningly.

"Open it," I commanded gently. He suspiciously opened the door. Inside he found lit candles and soft romantic music playing. There was also a box of condoms on the nightstand. As he looked around with his back to me, I put another big red bow on my robe.

He turned around. "What's this?"

"I wanted to do something special for you, like you did for me for my birthday. It's no picnic, but I thought maybe we'd try something new."

"You're wearing a bow."

"Yeah. Your gift is . . . me." I said feeling a bit unsure. "I'm giving myself to you for Christmas. I hope you like it because you can't return it."

"No, I won't want to return it." He looked at me hungrily.

"Well, unwrap me Nigel."

He took off the bow, and then slowly untied the sash of my robe. I was naked underneath. A garbled moan escaped his mouth. He hadn't seen me totally nude before.

He held my body, kissing my neck and shoulders. I was breathless with anticipation. My heart was beating a thousand times per minute, yet he seemed so calm, so focused and so sure. He let go of me, walking behind me, kissing the back of my neck. Slowly his fingers slid down my limp arms, then up my sides, caressing my stomach and hips, around my outer thighs, carefully avoiding the sweet spots.

I was trembling, my skin was flushed and hot, my body willing and ready. From behind me, he undressed. Shoes and socks first, shirt, pants down. I tried to watch him out of the corner of my eye, still facing forward. I was nervous, but the excitement was heightened, not knowing what he was doing or what was coming next. He took a step closer to me. I felt him press his naked body into mine, holding me close by the waist. I felt his body hair lightly touch my skin. I felt his erection on my backside. I wanted it in me so badly. "Take me," I whimpered.

We got in the bed and under the covers. It began with kissing, very heated, passionate kissing. The last tortured kisses of virgins dying to go further. His fingers ventured between my legs. "Oh God, you're so wet," he moaned. "Are you ready?"

I nodded, eyes wide with fear and desire. Moments later, he had slipped on a condom and was ready for entry. His eyes were fixed on mine. "I love you, Michelle."

"I love you, Nigel." He kissed me hard and entered my body. I gasped. My eager insides filled with his manhood. He sighed deeply with a sort of shocked pleasure. At first, we were both stunned and nervous; it took us an awkward moment before nature took over. He rhythmically rocked us, first slowly and shallowly, then more forcefully and with more speed. I could tell he was torn between trying to be gentle and easy and ravaging me to quell his own needs. I was surprised at how little it hurt. I was intoxicated by the intimacy. I had wanted to be closer to him, to be one, and with him inside me, I finally achieved that. It felt so right.

Our bodies knocked together in a beautiful dance. He was gripping me tighter and tighter. Unable to control himself anymore, he was grinding into me, deeper and quicker. He tried to suppress his moans and grunts by kissing my face and neck. He didn't have to, I wanted him to scream right in my ears. I loved that I was giving him this pleasure. I could feel a throbbing inside me, he was panting and suddenly with a low howl, he released into me. "Oh my God. Oh my God," he kept repeating, crashing down next to me, then gratefully kissing me everywhere.

With closed eyes, he laid on the bed, trying to catch his breath, his hand pushing his hair from his sweaty forehead. After a moment to compose himself, he turned his face to me and stared into my eyes as if telepathically thanking and worshiping me. I stared back, returning the message. He put his arms around me and pulled me close, face over my shoulder. "I'm so in love with you," he said, his voice rich with emotion.

It felt so good to hear that, but I wondered if it was coming from his heart or his groin. I pushed the thought away. "I'm so in love with *you*," I returned. He smiled and kissed me. Then again. Then again with more passion. The kissing led to fondling, groping, and grinding. Before long, we were making love again, this time longer and less awkward.

I was really glad to be his first, to give him something no one else would ever be able to give him again. I was also glad we were learning together. I didn't know what to expect from sex, but I liked it.

We stayed in bed for hours, talking, cuddling, kissing. Eventually I looked at the clock, we had less than two hours before my parents would be home.

"Look at the time. I think we should get dressed," I said.

"I like this better," he joked, his fingers dancing on my bare skin under the blankets.

I laughed. "Me, too . . . We could take a shower together."

He perked up. "I won't say no to that."

The shower took too long. It was hard to stop touching each other now that there were no boundaries. We washed each other, desperate to keep our hands on the other, but also wanting to take care of the other. We weren't just horny teens, we really were in love, in a true and meaningful relationship.

Fully dressed, all evidence of our lovemaking hidden, we sat on the couch in the living room trying to look composed and innocent in case my parents got home early. Still, we couldn't help constantly touching each other.

"It's going to be so hard to be away from you for a whole week," I complained.

"Especially now. I feel so close to you. I don't want to be apart."

"Me either. I wish you could spend the night tonight, at least."

"Me, too. One day, we won't have to worry about parents, and then we can spend every night together."

I don't know if he realized what he had said. *Every night?* Was he insinuating that he wanted to marry me one day? I sat there, replaying the words in my head, picking them apart, totally lost in thought.

"Did you hear me?" he asked. "Do you want your present now?"

"Huh? Oh, oh yeah." I nodded. I already felt like he had just given me the best present of all. It was hardly a proposal, but I knew his intentions.

He got up to get the gift and handed it to me.

"So, I guess I'm deserving of it," I teased.

"Do you know how long it's going to take me to pay you back for the present you just gave me? A lifetime!"

There it was again. *A lifetime?* He was planning on spending his lifetime with me? My heart bulged in my chest. With shaky hands, I opened the box. The first thing I saw was a stuffed animal, a lion.

"I know you love cats," he explained, "and that you'll be lonely without Autumn. I wish I could be there with you on your trip, but since I can't, I'm sending the toughest cat of them all to protect you, but also to love you. You can call him Nigel, if you want- though he's not as cuddly as me," he smiled.

"I love him!" I exclaimed, squeezing the lion.

"There's more." He sat beside me, inspecting my reaction to the gifts, nervous as to whether I would like them or not.

In the box, below several sheets of tissue paper was a stack of envelopes, fat with letters inside of them. They were labeled December 23, December 24, and so on, one for every day I'd be gone. I looked up for an explanation. "A letter for each day we're apart. That way, it will feel like I'm there with you. Just promise to open them on the correct day. Don't read them all on the plane. . . . Actually, you should read them in private."

"Okay. Wow, I can't believe you did all this. This is so thoughtful."

"There's one more thing in there."

A thin, flat box was beneath another layer of tissue paper. It was a stationary set. It had been opened. I looked inside the box. Nigel had self addressed and stamped seven envelopes.

"I figured out the postage from Detroit to Cambridge." Also in the box was lovely stationary, nice matching pens, and a matching journal. It looked expensive. "I thought, if you wanted, you could write to me everyday, too. Or if you wanted, you could just put down your thoughts or whatever in that journal. I know you like to write. And you're good at it, so maybe while you're gone, you'll be inspired to write something brilliant, but maybe you wouldn't have had anything to write on or with. Now you will."

He had really put a lot of thought into my gift, and it was perfect. Carefully, I put the set back in the box. "I love it Nigel, and I love you." I put my arms around him and kissed him. And kissed him again, and again. Then, we were making out, unable to pull away from each other. We shifted positions on the couch, him now lying below me. Immediately our bodies went back into humping mode. I wanted to do it again and by the hard bulge in his pants, I knew he felt the same.

The grandfather clock in the next room rang out for the six o'clock hour. I bolted up. "Six already?" I was in disbelief. My perfect day over so soon.

"Damn," he muttered, sitting up slowly. "I should go."

"Wait! I'm not ready to not see you for a week!" I felt robbed. I knew my parents would be home any minute. I thought quickly. "Okay, we are going out for dinner tonight, no one wants to cook or clean up a dinner mess," I spat out in a hurry. "I'll get out of it. I'll say I was doing homework all day and didn't pack and I'm so busy and stressed that I don't have the time or desire to eat. I'll say that you're coming over later, at a time when they should be home so they won't be suspicious that we're alone at night, so that we can exchange gifts and say goodbye."

He nodded, intently following along my crazy train of thought. "So I should go and come back later?"

"No! Don't go! You can call home and say you're staying at Tom's for dinner and you'll be home late. Just hide out here until my parents leave. Then, when they get home, we'll say that you got here early, just a few minutes before they did, and that we already opened our presents. Then, you can still stay for a while because I'll be all packed, homework done, and we'll be chaperoned."

He nodded, comprehending. "Okay, yeah, sounds good. Just one thing. What if they ask you what you gave me? Can I tell them?" he asked with a sly smile.

The plan worked perfectly. Nigel called his mother while I hid his present to me. I scattered some homework on the kitchen table to back up my claims. When the car pulled up to the house, Nigel ran upstairs to my room. A couple of minutes later, my parents walked in. I tried to seem frustrated and exhausted. I gave them my story and told them to go to dinner without me. They agreed without blinking. My father claimed to be starving, so they hurried back out the door in a matter of minutes. I felt bad about lying but the thought soon flew out of my head as I remembered my prince was waiting in my bedroom for me. I ran to the front window in time to see them pull out into the street and zoom away. I sped upstairs.

"The coast is clear," I stated.

Nigel stepped out of the closet. "That was kind of thrilling."

"I'll show you 'kind of thrilling!'" I pushed him onto the bed and began undressing him. Moments later, we were making love again.

Each time was getting better and better. This third time, he was able to hold out a lot longer, his hips moving in a steady, rhythmic, deliberate motion. We were getting the hang of it. He was a natural already. It felt different this time. The blood rushed to my face, and then drained away, all going between my legs. I was panting hard. Then, moments later, I couldn't feel my legs, or anything but the sensation from where we were connected. I felt myself tighten around him. He looked at me with an unexpected enjoyment. I had to look away, squeezing my eyes shut. The pleasure was intense. My hands gripped his back, my legs bucked. I felt tears welling in my closed eyes, then all I could feel was the throbbing, heightening, heightening to extreme satisfaction. I cried out loudly. He put his lips on mine to stifle my sounds. I held him tight as I climaxed. It was my first orgasm. After a wave of endorphins rolled over me, I relaxed a little, but was no less excited. My vaginal muscles still clenched around him, still crying for more. He reacted to my stimulation. He was swelling inside me and thrusting deeper. He was panting and gasping; then, seconds later, huffing and groaning with his last thrusts. He collapsed onto me.

"Oh, honey . . . " He was barely able to speak. He kissed my lips and all over my sweaty, tear-stained face. I was still, unable to move. He pulled out of me, the shock of his exit brought me back to earth.

He lied beside me and swept the hair from my face. "Are you alright?"

I turned my face to his and looked into his eyes, but I couldn't speak. His beautiful eyes were deep and full of concern. I kissed him. He relaxed and held me tight. I felt even closer to him now. We were lovers; we were in love. A moment ago, we were children. Then, we found our soul mates. Now, it felt like we were in heaven, surrounded by sweetness and happiness and love. We settled in the bed, snuggling and holding each other, trying to prolong the moment.

Eventually we had to get up. Nigel excused himself to get cleaned up in the bathroom. I got up and noticed the mess I'd left in the bed. This time, my hymen broke, leaving a bloody stain along with the wet spots on my bottom sheet. I quickly removed it and pulled the clean blankets up, so no one would notice. I put on my robe and hurried to the laundry room to wash away the stain. I left the wet sheet to dry and rushed back.

Nigel was in my room when I returned, his back to me, almost fully dressed. I stopped in the doorway, watching him pull his shirt on, desperately wishing he didn't have to. I approached him, hugging him from behind. He turned around and embraced me. He was so tall. I loved having my face pressed against his firm chest when we hugged. I felt so safe.

"You should get dressed," he suggested. I groaned, but I knew he was right. I also needed to clean up in the bathroom. I brought my clothes with me. After washing up, I glanced in the mirror- I looked like someone who just had sex. I combed my hair and tried to look normal and presentable, but I still had that look.

I was a woman now. I was different. I wondered if everyone would be able to see it, too. I hoped not.

Back to my room, I checked and rechecked to make sure nothing looked suspicious. There was no visible proof of any wrongdoing. Even our used condoms were buried well in my trash, soon to be taken out. We were golden.

I began packing up, since that was what I was supposed to be doing while my folks were gone. Nigel sat on my bed, keeping me company and playing with my new stuffed lion, making me giggle.

My parents came home not long after I finished packing. Nigel and

I raced downstairs, trying to appear guiltless, sitting apart from each other in the living room.

"Hi. Nigel got here just a minute ago," I explained. They seemed preoccupied and barely heard me. It made me nervous. I got up and joined them in the kitchen. There was a box of pizza on the table.

"Eat all that up, I don't want any leftovers spoiling in the refrigerator while we're away. We gotta go pack. I have a million things to do before tomorrow," my mother said as she and my father removed their coats and shook off the cold. They trudged upstairs. I was relieved to have more privacy with Nigel. I was also glad to have food. We hadn't eaten all day and we definitely worked up an appetite.

For the next few hours, my parents rushed around, packing and preparing, pretty much ignoring us. I was happy with that. Nigel and I sat in the living room alone with the TV on, though we weren't watching it. We were trying to soak each other up before we had to part.

"Michelle, you should be getting to bed!" my father yelled loudly from another room. I groaned. Then I remembered I would have to retrieve my sheet and make my bed before I could go to sleep.

We got up and I walked Nigel out to the porch. It was cold and windy outside, but I didn't care. I would have slept outside that night if I could stay by his side.

"Travel safe," he instructed.

"I will. Thank you for everything today, Nigel."

"No, no, thank *you* for *everything*," he drew the last word out.

I smiled proudly. "My pleasure," I insisted, truly meaning it.

"I love you."

"I love you, too." We kissed one last time, a long warm kiss in the chilly darkness. We pulled away from each other, smiling contently. He started walking away.

"Write me!" he called out.

"I will! Merry Christmas!"

"Merry Christmas!" he returned, and then he disappeared into the night. I missed him immediately.

Chapter 4

"Nigel wasn't perfect, but he was perfect for me."

The next day was tougher than I thought it would be. On the flight, I could feel the plane ripping me away from him as the miles stretched. I kept that stuffed lion with me, hugging it tightly and trying to lapse into my dream world. I focused hard on the day before, trying to remember the things we had said, the feel of Nigel's body, the smell and taste of his breath, the surges of pleasure . . .

I nodded off with sweet dreams of Nigel, shirtless and smiling in the sun in his grandmother's yard. I was in a white sundress, lying on that warm yellow blanket of his. He asked me, "Can I make love to you?"

"Oh, yes, Nigel, make love to me," I answered. Instantly he was inside me, swaying us together in a gorgeous, rhythmic dance. "Oh, Nigel," I kept repeating in ecstasy. "Oh, Nigel."

"Oh, no!" he said.

"What?"

"You're bleeding. Oh, no!"

"Oh, no!" I cried, looking down at my ruined white dress. I had bled all over it, a big red circle between my legs.

"I hurt you, I broke you!" he screamed in horror.

"No you didn't! I'm fine!"

"Your dress! Everyone will see! Everyone will know!" He was shaking.

I held him. "Let them see. I don't care who knows. I would do it again. I would do anything for you."

"Michelle, I never meant to hurt you. Do you believe me?"

"Yes, darling, I know you would never hurt me on purpose. Please don't worry. I love you and I will always be by your side. You're my everything."

His worried face softened. "We're almost there," he said.

"Huh?" I asked.

"We're almost there," he repeated. My eyes popped open, dream interrupted.

"We're almost there," my mom said again.

"Oh . . . okay," I drowsily muttered, hoping I didn't talk in my sleep.

The week in America dragged on. Luckily there was constantly some function to occupy my attention, but every little thing reminded me of Nigel. I thought about what it would be like to bring him here one day, to have him as part of the family and how happy that would make me to be his wife. I thought about the children we would have, running around on Christmas morning.

I didn't care about gifts this year, I already had all I ever wanted.

Every day I would excuse myself and get away to read Nigel's letters in private. They all began the same way, *"Hello, my love,"* and went on to say what he would likely be doing that day and wondering what I'd be up to. He would say how much he missed me and loved me and counted the days until I'd be back. The letters were all so charming and each one made me laugh without fail. I never opened one prematurely, though I wanted to. But I read and reread all those letters until I had them memorized.

I wrote back to him every day, too. I would comment on his letters and tell him what I was doing. I wrote about America and what was going on there- news, family news, music news, all that. And, of course, the better part of the letter was babbling on about how much I loved and missed him and although the lion was good at keeping me company, it was a poor substitute. Two days before we left, I stopped writing to him, knowing I would reach him before the letters would. I saved the envelopes and instead wrote in my journal.

When we arrived back in England, it was very late, later than expected due to bad weather. Too late to call Nigel. It really bothered me because I promised I would call him as soon as I got home safely.

I called early the next morning. He answered the phone, "Hello?"

"Hi, honey. I'm back!"

"Why didn't you phone me yesterday?" he demanded. It was not the response I'd been expecting.

" . . . It was late. I didn't want to wake your parents," I replied quietly, hurt.

"Well, it kept me up all night! Jesus, I thought your plane crashed!"

"I'm sorry, Nigel. I wanted to call, but I didn't think it was the right thing to do." I had a lump in my throat that made it hard to talk. I had never seen this side of him before and it scared me.

"But the right thing to do was to keep me worried sick about you for the past twelve hours?"

I was speechless. We were silent for a moment. "I'm sorry," was all I could manage.

"Fine. I'm glad you're alright. I'll see you at school, then."

"But, what about New Year's- ?"

He hung up. With shaking hands, I hung up the phone and moped back to my room. As soon as I shut the door behind me, I began crying uncontrollably. I flopped onto my bed, face first into my pillow, soaking it immediately. Whenever I managed to open my eyes, I saw him there, smiling, contented, and naked; memories of the incredible day we had shared right before I left. I felt so close to him, even the thousands of miles between us didn't change that. But our recent conversation had. All I wanted was to come home to him, to hold him and be held by him, taking in his smell, staring into his eyes, hearing his perfect, sweet voice . . .

Sweet? Right. Maybe I didn't know him as well as I thought I did. Maybe he was just so charming until he got what he wanted. Possibilities flooded my mind.

Was he right? Was it so wrong for me to wait to call that I deserved that reaction? Did I just catch him at a really bad time? Maybe something terrible had happened and my late call was the final straw. I bolted up. "I need to see him," I said out loud to myself.

I hurried to the bathroom to splash some water on my face and pull myself together. I brushed my teeth and straightened up. I flew downstairs, grabbed my coat and purse, and announced, "I'm going out! I'll be back later!"

I practically ran the whole way to Nigel's house. When I got there, I rang the buzzer impatiently. His mother peeked through the window, and then I heard her yell "Nigel, it's for you." Momentarily, he answered the door, appearing uninterested.

"Hello," he said coldly.

"Hi," I returned, still out of breath from the jog. I couldn't think of anything to say anyway. I had no plan.

"What are you doing here?"

"I wanted to see you."

He snorted in disbelief, but he let me in.

"Can we talk in private?" I begged.

Without words, he led the way up to his room. Upon entering, I saw the letters I'd sent him in a pile on his night table. They looked well read. "You got my letters," I commented.

"I got some. I didn't get any the last couple of days," he said flatly. I could tell he was hurt. My heart sank. I felt so low for wounding him. The lump returned to my throat. "You want to talk? Talk," he coldly insisted.

I tried to compose myself. "I'm so sorry I upset you so much. Our plane came in late and I didn't want to bother you or your parents and . . . " I started choking up. "I missed you so much when I was gone. All I thought about was you and coming home to you and kissing you again-" I was sobbing and sniffling now.

His icy demeanor melted, his intense brown eyes softened. He uncrossed his arms and held me. I sobbed harder as he squeezed me to him and lightly stroked my head. I buried my face against his chest.

"I should've written you more letters. I just thought that it didn't make sense to keep sending them, but now I see that you really looked forward to them and you must have thought I didn't care enough to respond," I mumbled into his chest. I would have felt that way if the situation had been reversed. His letters meant everything to me, I'm sure it was the same for him. We were so much alike. Kindred souls.

How could I let him down? I felt the pain he surely felt. I understood the animosity he exhibited.

He put his hands on my shoulders and gave me a light shake to stop my babbling. "Hey," he said softly, "you wanted to kiss me? Kiss me."

I managed to hold back the sobs and brought my face to his. He very tenderly kissed my lips. My crying was done with instantly. I looked into his eyes. They were compassionate; mine were wide and completely entranced. A moment ago, he had me feeling so low; and now, I was eating out of his hand. I just wanted him to love me. I wanted him to kiss me again and take us back to that happy place.

And he did. He kissed me, longer and deeper this time. He parted his lips and peeked his tongue between mine. His arms squeezed me tighter as his hands brushed my back and backside. His kiss became more forceful, his hands groping me. He had a hungry look about him. I wanted him to take what he needed from me. He stopped kissing and pushed me onto his nearby bed.

I was breathless, waiting for his next move. He went to the door, locked it, and then turned to me, like a predator moving in on his prey. He hovered over me, ripping off my clothes. He had me naked on his bed while he was fully clothed. He was on top of me, kissing and grinding; then he put his hand down- never stopping the kiss- to unzip himself. I was ready and willing, but still caught off guard when he plunged into me. I gasped. He put his hand over my mouth to quiet me. He thrust into me, deep and hard. I was surprised and beyond excited; also, I was grateful that his bed didn't squeak. He was fucking me, there were no other words for it. He continued, harder and deeper for what was not long enough when he suddenly pulled out.

"Oh my God, I almost came in you."

I was disappointed. I wasn't ready to get pregnant, but I wasn't ready to stop either. He sat on the edge of the bed, breathing deeply to try to calm down. I sat up and thought for a moment. Then, I sprang up and knelt in front of him, putting my lips around his penis. He gasped, shocked but pleased. I sucked him. He relaxed and his head flopped back, his face to the ceiling, though he never opened his eyes. Slowly, he grew unable to control himself and let nature take over. He held my head by my hair, instinctively guiding me in time to his rocking hips. He was trying so hard to be quiet. I clamped my lips together tighter around him. With his mouth wide open, but no sound escaping other than his exhaling, he ejaculated into my mouth. It surprised me. I swallowed.

He fell back on the bed, depleted. "Wow," was all he said. I got up and then lied beside him, proud of my work. "I can't believe you did that," he said quietly, looking at the ceiling.

"Well, I couldn't leave you the way you were."

"Oh," he breathlessly responded.

"We're going to have to keep some condoms here, too," I suggested.

"Yeah." A thought came to him, his mood changed. He turned to me. "I was mean to you. I made you cry. Then, this is how you repay me? Should I be mean to you all the time?"

I laughed. "I hurt your feelings first. I feel like we know each other so well, but I guess we still need to figure each other out. I think you're a bit more sensitive than I thought, and I can be a little calloused sometimes. I should've known better, but now I do. I never want to hurt you again."

He stared at me, and then he smiled. "I think I was out of line. I don't know why I yelled like that, I wasn't that mad. I was relieved you were safe. I'm glad you came over, that's what I was hoping you would do."

"I guess I know you better than I give myself credit for," I teased. "But, I know you would never hurt me on purpose, and no matter what you do, I'll always forgive you. You're my everything." I smiled at him, remembering my dream.

He hugged me. "I love you. I'm glad you're here. This is where you belong."

I felt the same way. I wanted to stay beside him forever, but I knew I couldn't. "I should get dressed- "

"Later. Let's get under the blankets. I want to hold you for a while."

I couldn't say no to that. He situated me comfortably next to his warm body. Under the blankets, he caressed me soothingly, and then he began venturing with his fingers. "What are you doing?" I asked smiling.

"You can stop me if you want to," he almost threatened, confident that I wouldn't. He was right. He began exploring me with his hands under the blankets. He kept his eyes on my face as he blindly felt around between my legs, reading my reaction, very attentive to what I liked. He was so focused, I was totally distracted, pleasure getting the best of me. My bucking and panting didn't faze him. He was tuned in to my body. I bit my lower lip and breathed heavily through my nose, trying to be quiet as his masterful fingers brought me to orgasm.

It turned out to be a good day, a very good day after all.

We spent the rest of the day talking about our time apart over the previous week. The tension was gone; we were laughing and easy going as usual. I enjoyed having the Nigel I knew back, but I wondered about the drastic shift in his behavior. I never knew him to have a temper at all, then boom, he was like Mr. Hyde. I tried to keep it out of my mind, but I would wonder what could turn him like that again. I didn't want to walk on eggshells around him, but I figured I probably would if I had to for the rest of my life. If that was the price I paid to be with him, so be it. I really would do anything for him.

New Year's came and went, and then it was life as usual again. I was almost glad to get back to the old routine. Everything was like it was before the break, and it was refreshing. I was looking forward to 1978, a new year with Nigel.

The first day back in school, my history class went to the library to do some research. As I was hunting for books, a brightly colored book jacket caught my attention. *The Zodiac Complete.* I picked it up. It was a thick book and it contained everything there was to know about astrology, the zodiac, rising signs—you name it. I wondered if it would give me more insight into Nigel's characteristics. I flipped through it quickly, careful not to be seen by my teacher, and decided to borrow it. I hid it under my pile of history books and made my way to the librarian's desk.

The rest of the afternoon, I tried to read parts of it whenever I had a chance, but in my last class I kept it hidden. I didn't want Nigel to see me reading it for some reason. He bounced into class, looking happy to see me, and took his seat beside me. "Hi," he said with a grin.

I returned the smile and greeting, feeling guilty on the inside. Perhaps it was because of the book. I only rented that book to investigate Geminis. He didn't know I was on a mission to spy on him without his knowledge or permission. Actually, I was just trying to understand him better.

On the bus, riding home, I was pretty silent, my mind wandering. I was desperate to read that zodiac book, to figure out Nigel's psyche. He was talking to the boys behind us. I stared out the window, preoccupied but unnoticed. Every once in a while, he would turn to me and ask if I was alright. I would smile and convince him I was, then he would go back to his friends and I would go back to my thoughts.

Nigel walked me home as usual. "What do you want to do today?" he prodded.

I got the feeling he wanted to get physical. "Oh, I don't know. What about you?" I asked playfully.

"Well, we could . . . braid each other's hair."

I laughed at him. "Do our toenails?" I gave him a playful push.

"Go crazy on each other?" He looked at me hopefully. How could I resist? He was too adorable, too charming. I tilted my head to the side and acted like I was considering it. "I'll make it worth your while," he promised as we approached my house.

"Oh, in that case . . . " I teased. He smiled and kissed me in a playfully carnivorous way.

I opened the door and let us in. I dropped my bag and before I knew it, he had my hand and was leading me upstairs.

We spent many wonderful, unforgettable afternoons in my room. Exploring each other, teaching, learning. Beyond physical, the sex was almost just a way to get closer to each other than we could without it. Our bodies received total pleasure, but our souls received sustenance. We needed each other so much that it was physically painful to be apart.

He was also becoming quite a musician. He spent hours practicing his guitar, teaching himself. He often played me the short songs he created. I loved listening to his subtle genius. He was never as proud of his work as I was. He was easily embarrassed by a bad note or chord, but I didn't care. I could listen to him all day.

Many times, after we'd make love in his room, he'd sit on the floor and pick up his guitar and play for me, shirtless and barefoot while I lied naked in his bed, watching and listening, blissfully fulfilled.

Other times, we'd just hang out, playing records and talking. Occasionally, I'd let him browse through my own poems and songs. He'd ask what inspired me to write them, to explain certain references. He was quite interested in my creations also.

Sometimes we would dance, not very well, but we would dance when our favorite songs came on the radio. We'd sing along. I could always sing a bit; he wasn't terribly good, but I didn't care. I loved the sound of his voice, in tune or not.

It amazed me that the more time we spent together, the better I got to know him, the more I enjoyed him. I loved every moment of being with him. From what I read in the zodiac book, it was like he was specifically designed for me. Before we met, I had been lonely and felt so unloved. It was in his nature to be the caring, nurturing partner who almost obsessively throws himself into his relationships. I needed that. I was used to being ignored, but his world revolved around me. I had so much love to give and I felt the need to provide a loving environment for him, which is what he craved. As a Libra, I always strived for balance. I could be the first to give, but if I wasn't getting anything in return, I would stop. That wasn't an issue with Nigel. He reciprocated with precision- we almost seemed to try to out-do the other, as if we competed to see who could be the more generous lover.

When springtime had arrived, Nigel had to make college plans. He wanted to go to art school and was excited about that. I was excited for him, too, but I was also thrilled that he was going to stay local. I couldn't bear to think about distance between us.

Sometimes, though, when we were in the same room, there was more distance between us than an ocean could provide. Nigel was such a warm, friendly, witty guy most of the time, but he had dark tendencies that would sometimes get the best of him. I learned that from the zodiac book, too. Geminis are torn between two personalities, the outgoing Taurus and the brooding Cancer.

Sometimes, I would say something and think nothing of it, only to face cold silence as he mulled over my words and asked, irritated and offended, "What do you mean by that?"

That was a huge source of tension between us for me, and I guess also for him. I never meant to sound critical or judgmental when I joked around with him, but I was blunt and honest and he was self-doubting and easily hurt.

I learned I would just have to be patient with him. Sometimes he would act up or make mistakes or get very emotional, but that was just who he was. I had to accept it and forgive him and let him know that I still loved him and would always be there for him. I wanted him to feel like he was always safe and taken care of. I loved providing that security for him and he rewarded me with an incredible amount of love and devotion.

Mostly, though, we didn't clash. Nigel wasn't perfect, but he was perfect for me. His minor imperfections made him unique and although sometimes they were hard to deal with, they only endeared me to him. It amazed me how much I loved him.

I often wondered what he saw in me. To me, he was everything, but I didn't feel anywhere near up to par for him. He always looked at me as though he was the lucky one. I felt honored to be the one who got the chance to love him. And I did. With every fiber of my being. It was a gift to have my soul mate at only sixteen years old.

We were so young, probably too young to be in such a serious relationship.

Chapter 5

"...fate had other plans for me."

When June came, Nigel was graduating high school and was just about to turn eighteen. I wanted to celebrate these landmarks with something very meaningful. I decided to give him a gift, but it would have to be a very special gift. I scraped together all the money I could get and bought him an amp. I really wanted to support his dream of being a musician, and he was too broke to afford one himself.

Unfortunately, after I bought it, I too was broke. Yet, I wanted to do more for him, so I settled for homemade presents. Of course, I would bake him a cake. I was pretty good at cooking and I knew how much he loved chocolate, so that was an easy decision. But I needed something else, something he would really cherish, something he would have forever.

As I was sitting around, trying to figure it out by jotting down ideas in my notebook, it came to me. I can write him a song! It seemed perfect. The song he wrote me for my birthday was the most amazing gift I had ever gotten. I couldn't play an instrument, but I thought I could sing it for him.

The song had to be perfect. I wanted it to embody all my love for him. I wanted it to really grab his heart and convince him how deeply I cared for him. I chewed on my pen, trying to summon up all of Nigel's wonderful qualities. He was always at the forefront of my mind, his face haunted me, and his words echoed in my head- he was my constant muse. It didn't take long before I was inspired, and then I was able to put my feelings into verse.

I carefully and neatly transferred the lyrics of my song to a piece of the stationery he had given me. I was proud of my work and hoped he would enjoy it. Now I would just have to figure out a creative way to give him this gift.

After school let out for the summer, Nigel and I had even more alone time. He had a summer job and he worked odd hours, but on his days off, he was all mine. I asked him to choose a day during the week where I could have him to myself at my house while my parents were at work. I wanted to keep everything a surprise and he was getting excited about my plans.

It was reminiscent of Christmas, but I couldn't let things get stagnant. I had to keep him guessing. I planned every detail of his private birthday celebration with care.

When the day came, Nigel arrived in the early afternoon.

"Okay, I'm ready. What do you have planned?" He rubbed his hands together, anxious to start the show.

"Hasty, aren't we? Patience is a virtue, Nigel," I casually mocked.

He chuckled. "Come on, I've waited a long time," he complained.

"Alright, come with me, I'll give you your present." I started walking toward the hallway. He followed.

"Oh, is this going to be like Christmas when you had the red bow and-" he cut himself off, remembering our first time. I could almost hear his mouth watering.

"No, not like Christmas." He looked disappointed. "But," I continued and his eyes lit back up, "there may be some similarities." He was curious. There was a thick, red ribbon on the floor. I picked it up and handed it to him. "Happy Birthday."

"What is this?" he asked.

"Follow it," I encouraged.

He did as he was told, letting the string guide him through the house. Before long, he was led around the corner and had made it to the first stop. I had the ribbon tied to the amp, with my trademark big red bow. He gasped.

"You bought me an amp?" He was astonished. He knelt down on the floor to get a closer look.

I didn't answer, I just smiled, watching him play with the knobs and stroke the black box, unbelieving. I was proud and so thrilled that I could give him something that made him so pleased.

"Baby, thank you," he said gratefully. He was so engrossed in his new toy that he didn't notice the ribbon didn't end at the amp. There were more gifts for him to find. I let him check out his first present for a while, and then he realized there was more coming.

"What's at the other end of this ribbon?" he asked me innocently.

"Why don't you go find out?" I wanted to keep him in suspense for as long as I could.

He followed the ribbon again as it twisted around and led him to the kitchen. It was wound around a pedestal cake platter. On it, he found the creation of my laborious search for the best cake recipe I could find. His eyes were big.

"Triple chocolate cake with an inner layer of chocolate ganache and frosted with fudge mousse," I explained. "Made entirely from scratch, with love."

"Ooh, I can already feel my teeth rotting," he joked. "When can we eat this beauty?"

"Now, if you want to, or we can finish with your presents."

"Um . . . I don't know. I'm torn."

I laughed.

"Okay, I'll do the presents, then dive mouth first into that cake."

"Okay. Whatever you want. This is your day."

"Oh, in that case," he came up to me and put his arms around my waist, pulling me close to his body, "let's take that cake to your room and turn it into an appetizer."

I giggled. He was serious and he was making me excited. "If you say so."

I picked up the platter and followed him as he followed the ribbon out of the kitchen and up the stairs. The ribbon disappeared under my closed bedroom door.

He looked at me. "Ah, so it is like Christmas."

"No, not the same," I corrected. He seemed curious and he opened the door.

"No sexy music playing?" he questioned.

"I told you it's not the same. But there will be music."

He was perplexed. He looked around my room and noticed the ribbon was loosely wound around my bed frame. He began figuring things out.

"We're gonna have sex, though, right? That will be the same."

"We're gonna have sex, but it won't be the same." I continued my mysterious act. I set the cake on the nightstand, next to the envelope that held his birthday card and the lyrics to his song. He noticed the envelope had his name on it and reached for it. I gently grabbed his hand to lead him to the foot of my bed.

"You can have that later," I promised. He didn't oppose, I think the tone of my voice assured him that something better was coming. I pulled his shirt off over his head. He smiled a sexy little smile and reached for mine.

"No." I pushed his hands away. "I'm in charge."

He was surprised, but intrigued. I picked up a blindfold and put it over his eyes. He softly laughed with a shocked and nervous excitement.

I was only sixteen years old, but I was not innocent, and by this time, I was no longer a novice when it came to sex. Nigel brought out a very primal urge in me, animalistic, almost. He evoked lust and desire and wild sexual cravings. In the last six months, we steadily progressed to more creative approaches to love making, and today, I wanted to take the next step. He had no idea what he was in for.

I wanted to keep him in suspense, I wanted to keep him wondering. I knew exactly what I wanted to do to him. I put aside my insecurities and tapped into my inner confident sex goddess. I sank onto my knees and unfastened his belt.

"I wrote you a song," I casually told him.

"Oh yeah?" he asked, a bit distracted as I unzipped his pants. "When can I read it?"

I slowly and carefully pulled his pants down. "Do you want it now? I'll give it to you," I said in a sultry voice, indiscernible as to whether I meant the song or his joyride.

He was quiet for a moment. "But, I can't read- "

"Nigel, honey, I'll take care of you. Don't you worry."

I saw a little smile cross his lips before I pushed him down on the bed. I started singing my song as I removed the remainder of his clothes.

"Take it slow. Make me wanna make you make me, make me.
Here I go, Heading for the sky, kiss the angel most sweet
Let it flow. Take me, wanna you to take me, take me.
And you know, no one else can make me feel so…
Only you. Only you can make me spin and fly, laugh and cry,
My, my, my."

It was a sensuous love song and as I softly sang it, he was almost frozen. His lips parted a bit, he smiled as I sang his gift to him. He was still, trying to pay attention to the words, leaving him vulnerable to conquer. And I wanted to dominate him.

I crawled on the bed beside him. I paused my singing. "Scoot up," I whispered.

He tried, but he was unsteady since he was blindfolded. I guided him, with one hand behind his head, leading him to gently land on a pillow.

I straddled him and began singing again as I took one of his hands and stretched it over his head. I tied it to the headboard with the ribbon. I repeated with the other arm. He opened his mouth to comment, but didn't object- like he thought better of it. He must have been a little leery, but he seemed quite excited by it all.

"Only you. Only you can make me come and then, wonder when
Again, again, again."

I dismounted him and stood up. I inspected his incredible naked body strapped down to my bed, and felt absolutely full of lust. He was breathing deeply, anticipating my next move. I stopped singing. I let him dangle for a moment. I wanted to keep him in suspense, to only be able to hear what I was doing. The unzipping of my pants. The sound of my clothes coming off and falling into a heap on the floor. Giving these little clues was the only way he knew what was happening. I saw he was ready to continue the game. His cock was half hard on his thigh. With the softest touch, I traced my fingertips from his toes, up his leg, very slowly along the inside until I almost touched his manhood. He turned his body in anticipation to enable me to stroke him.

I pushed his hip down. "No, no. I'm in charge," I reminded him.

He relaxed back. I again traced my fingertips on the other leg from his toes up the inside of his leg, against the grain of his hair with a feathery touch. As I approached where he wanted me to fondle the most, I veered away at the last moment and let my fingers dance on his lower abdomen. I started singing again. It was a bit of a distraction, but I wanted him to associate the song with this moment forever.

"Only you, only you, only you…"

As I was finishing the song, I again straddled him, just far away enough so our genitals weren't touching.

"Now, Nigel, I am going to take advantage of you. I have you tied up. I can do with you whatever I want. And there's nothing you can do about it," I told him.

He inhaled deeply, preparing himself. "Okay."

"I didn't ask your permission," I sternly replied.

He closed his mouth. With open palms, I ran my hands up his sides, leaning forward to reach all the way up to his face. With his beautiful face in my hands, I kissed him. At first he was afraid to kiss back. I kissed him like I had never kissed him before- like he wasn't the wonderful boy I loved so dearly but like he was my sex toy that was only there for my gratification. I was a little rough, but the desire was so strong, he fell right into my trap. When he was kissing back with more hunger than I was, I lifted away. He strained to continue, I pushed him back down to the bed. I didn't want to give him too much satisfaction right yet. I wanted to draw it out, so I changed tactics. Again, I dismounted and instead, sat on my knees beside him on the bed.

"I really like your body, Nigel," I said, stroking him again. "I love these long legs." I grabbed his inner thigh and dug my nails in, little by little until his face showed the slightest bit of discomfort. I kissed the area I had just wounded and he relaxed again. Then, I began sucking the region and letting my tongue lap over his supple skin. I made my way over a bit, gradually moving toward his penis. I could feel his body rising and falling quicker as his breathing increased. I put my lips around his erection and sucked him until it seemed he was enjoying it too much; then I stopped to concentrate on a less sensitive area. Then,

I would go back, and in less time, he was getting too worked up. I had to stop.

"Now, Nigel, I'm not ready for you to come yet. And you have to do as I say." I took my hands off of him. "Nigel, part your lips."

He did as he was told. I scooted closer to his face and leaned toward him until my breast barely grazed his lips. He opened his mouth farther and sucked it greedily.

"Good boy," I groaned. "Now, I want you to kiss me. And when you kiss me, I want you to show me how badly you want to be inside me."

I shifted so my mouth was over his mouth. He did what he was told. His tongue was wild, desperately searching for mine. His lips were forceful, it was clear that he wanted to be in me that instant. I decided to end his longing. I reached over to get a condom off the nightstand.

"Okay, Nigel, I'm ready to use you. Hold still." I slid the condom down over his shaft and mounted him. He moaned when he penetrated. I got into missionary position and continued like a man fucking a woman.

I continued with my dirty talk. "Yeah, I really like your body. I like your chest, and your neck. I started kissing him on the chest and neck, sucking and licking his sweet spots. He was trying to keep his moans low, but whenever he seemed too excited, I would stop.

"Don't come yet," I would tell him. Then I would go back to fucking him, slow and deep, trying to prolong the ecstasy. When he had settled down enough, I would try to excite him more until he was reaching his peak.

"Don't come yet." It was getting harder and harder for him to hold off. I was also getting closer and closer. "Don't come yet. Wait for me."

As I slowly humped him, painfully drawing out our ecstasy, I carefully reached over to the cake on the table beside the bed. I decided to surprise him with a taste. I dug my index finger into the frothy layer of icing, covering it well. Carefully, I danced my clean fingers over his lower lip: first my pinky, then my ring finger, applying more pressure with each finger to gently open his mouth. Then I used my middle finger to pull down his lip even more and to slip my sweet index finger into his parted mouth.

He didn't see it coming. At first, he was startled, but quickly content-ed. "Mmm." He licked the frosting off of my finger.

When he had gotten the majority off, I said, "Suck it."

He did what he was told. It was an incredible turn on to see him perform this phallic gesture. "That's it, suck me."

He hesitated, understanding the homoerotic conveyance. It was not his style. But I was in charge. "Do as I say," I commanded and he continued. The delight of being subservient outweighed the shame of swapping roles.

It was becoming too much for me to take. I was grinding harder and quicker into him. I knew I wouldn't be able to prolong my orgasm from approaching and I was pleased that he was able to hold out as long as he had. It was time.

"Nigel, come with me. Are you ready? Come with me." I prepared to take us to the breaking point. I kept repeating. "Come with me. Come with me," as I rode him harder and faster.

And like a good boy, he did what he was told.

❣

We had a very nice summer, enjoying our youth and freedom. Nigel continued to work his summer job at a nearby store and I earned some cash babysitting for a neighbor. We spent most of our money on each other or on going out together and that was fine. We lived for each other and that's all we wanted.

That fall, Nigel started college at the local art school. I envied him quite a bit. I hated that I was left behind in high school, learning useless information while he was moving on without me to collect the skills and knowledge he'd need to become a successful artist.

Although he was living the dream, we were on the same page. Both of us lived for creativity, music, art, and literature. And neither of us had narrowed down the career we wanted, we only knew where to start.

But, there I was, stuck at high school (which I disliked immensely now that he wasn't there), and he had moved on to college. We still saw each other every day after school and stayed as close as ever. In the afternoon, he would tell me about the exciting things he'd learned that day or about a new project he was working on. I was jealous. My school life was boring, but he wanted to hear about it anyway. I felt young and naive compared to him, and I didn't like that.

He never made me feel as if I were beneath him or that I was the stupid kid I felt like. He made it clear that he viewed us as equals and that we were on a journey together.

We would sit around and talk about our future. Our grand plans. He was confident in our success, and it was contagious. All I really cared about was having him in my life, but he wanted it all. His eyes would blaze with passion; he was so intense about everything, so ready to make it big.

By the end of his first semester in college, he had met some other guys who shared his interests in music. This only fueled his aspirations of starting a band. I was very excited for him, and I was happy that I only had one more semester of high school left before I could join him and his journey to fame and fortune.

But fate had other plans for me.

In mid January of 1979, I came home from school and when I opened the door, I saw boxes filling the living room. I was instantly horrified- I knew this scene all too well. And still, I asked, "What's going on?"

"We're finally moving back home," my dad announced cheerfully.

"Home?" I stopped considering a country that didn't have Nigel in it *home*. "Why?" I was irritated and upset.

"What do you mean, *why*? We've been stuck here for the past fifteen months. Now my work is done here, so why would we stay?"

"I *want* to stay!" I tried to fight the tears.

"Well, we can't. My work is in the states now. Our friends and family are there. I want to go back home. Don't you?"

"No! I don't want to leave!"

"Why? Wait- because of your boyfriend? I'm sorry, but we have to move. We'll be back in Detroit in five days. You're going to have to say goodbye to him." He turned his back and continued packing.

There was no stopping the tears now. I had a hard time breathing. I ran out the front door and all the way to Nigel's house. I knew he wasn't home yet, but I wanted to be there when he arrived. I didn't know what else to do anyway. I couldn't just go to my room and start packing. I needed to be with Nigel.

I was pacing in front of his house, looking down at the ground, distracted by my own worries, when he approached me.

"What are you doing?" He noticed my tears and haggard expression. "What's going on?"

"I- . . . I- . . . I- . . . " I couldn't speak, I just choked on the words.

His face was panicked. He put his hands on my shoulders. "What?"

"I'm moving!" I spat before I broke down.

His arms fell. He took a step away. I tried to watch him though the tears blurred my vision. He looked as if he was going to fall down. I just stood there, heaving, hiccuping, and bawling. I looked down at the ground, unable to watch him hurting. Instead, I concentrated on the tears rapidly falling from my face and splattering on the sidewalk.

He put his arms around me and held me close to him. He cradled my head to his chest and rested his chin on my shoulder. He stroked my hair, trying to soothe me. It helped. After a minute or so of weeping on his jacket, I calmed down enough to pull back a bit so I could look into his face. His eyes were red and teary, his face was streaked; he sniffled.

I had never seen him cry before. He wasn't ashamed. When he looked into my eyes, he broke down and wept as violently as I had been. He squeezed me again and we just held each other, sobbing on the sidewalk.

I knew he didn't care if anyone saw us. I didn't care about anything at the time either. After a short while, he tried to compose himself.

"Let's go in the house," he said with a low, cracking voice.

I followed. Luckily, his parents weren't home yet. He took my hand and led me to his room. He shut the door behind us. I sank down onto his bed; he did the same.

"I have been dreading this day," I muttered.

"Yeah, I kind of thought you'd have to move back. I was just hoping I was wrong; or that if your parents had to go, you could stay."

"Me, too. I hate that they can just pull me in whatever direction work takes them! I get no say in the matter. *I* didn't choose to have a career that places me all over the damn world! Why do *I* have to deal with the consequences?"

He nodded, looking into his lap. I continued, "I thought the next time they moved, I'd be eighteen and able to make my own decisions. I thought I would be in college by then, probably the same school as you. They wouldn't take me out of school, so I'd just have to stay, you know?"

"Maybe they *will* let you stay, because you *are* in school. Maybe you can live here with us! Do you think your parents would go for that?"

"Do you think *your* parents would go for that?"

"I don't know." He sounded defeated so he must have thought our parents wouldn't agree to that. I looked down, my last shred of optimism vanquished.

He looked at me and noticed my melancholy expression. He grabbed me and pulled us both down to lie on the bed. I cuddled snugly into him, trying to appreciate our last tender moments together.

We just lied there, holding each other for hours; Mostly silent, not wanting to talk about the bitter reality. It was getting dark, and I should have gone home. I should have at least called my parents to check in, but I was angry and wanted to punish them. Nigel's mother knocked on the door. It wasn't locked, so she let herself in after a brief pause. She saw us lying there in his bed, but I guess the scene had an air of sadness that didn't cause her to panic.

"Hi, Mrs. Blake," I croaked, sitting up.

"Is something the matter, dear?"

I lost it again. "I'm moving!" I wailed as the tears ran.

"Oh no, I'm so sorry to hear that!" she embraced me.

I cried onto her shoulder. I really liked his family, I didn't want to say goodbye to them. As she held me, I noticed her look at Nigel to check up on his feelings. He sniffled and quickly wiped away some tears with his sleeve.

"I don't know what we'll do without you, dear," she said with soft eyes. I knew what she really meant was that she didn't know what Nigel would do without me there. I knew that, but I appreciated her confirming the fact that I was special and had changed his life. I nodded silently, trying to control myself and stop the tears.

"Um, just take as long as you want up here. We won't bother you," she added and let herself back out. It was really nice that she understood, and trusted us. She obviously cared about her son more than anything and wanted to spare him whatever pain she could. However, I knew she wouldn't agree to me moving in with them while my parents lived across the ocean.

Eventually, it became too late for me to stay with Nigel, so he walked me home. When we got to the porch and were about to say goodbye, my mother opened the door.

"You're home! Your father said you ran out earlier without a word. You didn't call us to say where you were or when you'd be back. Luckily, Nigel's mother called a while ago to say you were over there."

"I should go," Nigel quietly interjected.

"No, wait a minute. I want to say something to both of you. I truly am glad that you both found each other and it's obvious you are in love. But I think this may be the best thing, to separate you, because you're too young for this. Michelle, you're only seventeen. You don't need to get pregnant and throw your life away on the first boy you meet. And don't take that the wrong way, Nigel, you're a great guy; but we belong in America. You shouldn't be tied down here. And you shouldn't marry the first boy you date. I know this is going to hurt and you're going to hate me and your father, but this really is for the best. It's time we go home, and say goodbye."

I looked at Nigel, he appeared wounded and shocked and uncomfortable. It felt like a dagger in my already bruised heart. I had no words, for my mother or for him. He looked down, unable to face either one of us.

"Say goodnight and get in the house," my mother said quietly but sternly. She retreated into the living room to give us privacy.

"Nigel . . . I'm sorry. . . . Are you alright?"

"I need to go. I just need to go. It's been a long, difficult day. I just need to go." He backed down off the porch. "I'll call you tomorrow."

The dagger in my heart twisted. He was hurt, and I couldn't fix it. I couldn't shield him from my mother's accusations. I couldn't erase the lies she had told him. I just hoped he wouldn't believe them. *I shouldn't be tied down here? I shouldn't marry the first boy I date?* How could anyone possibly be blind to our connection? How could they not see that this was fate? I was never more sure of anything than the fact that we belonged together. It wasn't enough that she was ripping us apart, but to ridicule our relationship? How could she?

I watched Nigel walk away. "I love you!" I called out.

He stopped, turned around and faced me. "I love you, too."

He was so sincere that it caught me off guard. He turned back and walked into the darkness. I stood there, frozen for a while. How would I survive without being near him? To never have him walk me home again? To never say goodbye on the porch again, waiting until the last minute to part? I couldn't do it. I felt sick. The cold wind blew against my face, chilling the tears forming in my eyes.

I went in the house, scowling. My dad started.

"Young lady, you have a curfew! Where the hell were you? You just stormed out and didn't say where you'd be! You need to be home to help pack!"

"Help pack? That's all you care about? I'm not going to help pack! You are responsible for us leaving, you pack your own shit!" I ran toward my room. I didn't get far before my father retaliated.

"Now, wait a minute! You don't talk to me like that-"

"Let her go," my mother said, ending the short feud. I continued to my room, went in, and slammed the door as loudly as I could. Then, I pushed my dresser in front of the door so they couldn't get in. I didn't want to see them or talk to them.

I turned off the light and turned on the radio. I crawled into bed and tried to forget this day ever happened.

The next morning, I hadn't set my alarm, but I woke up early. I had an hour before I had to be at school. I tried to decide between going back to sleep or getting up. *I could sleep; what would be the point of good attendance now?* And I doubted my parents would force me to go, as they had better things to do. *Although . . . I could get up. Maybe I could go to school one last day and say goodbye to my friends.* But the only friend I really cared about was Angie and she had graduated last year with Nigel. *Or, I could claim I was going to school but play hooky and spend the day with Nigel instead.* Bingo.

I tried to be quiet as I got up and moved my dresser back into place. I got cleaned up in the bathroom and went back to my room unnoticed. I got dressed and ready, and then went down to the kitchen, but even though I had skipped dinner the night before, I had no appetite.

I ran into my mother. "You're up. I wasn't going to wake you. You could go back to sleep if you want. I don't think you need to go to school this week."

"Well, I want to," I answered defiantly.

"Oh, fine then. Go," she mocked. "You're going to do what you want anyway, right?"

"I'll be home late," I sneered and headed for the door.

"Don't forget your backpack. You know, since you're going to school and all." Her tone was sarcastic. She must have seen through my pretense.

I grabbed the backpack anyway on my way out. Just in case she was looking, I took my usual way to the bus stop, but changed my course at the last minute. I sneaked down a back street and made my way to Nigel's house.

I knew he had an early class this morning and that if I was quick enough, I could catch him first. I arrived in front of his house just as he was coming out.

"Hi."

"Hi. What are you doing here?"

"Ditching school. Do you want to, too?"

He hesitated and looked behind him to see if his parents were watching. They weren't. "Yeah, let's go."

We started walking, and as we walked, we talked and whined.

"I can't believe this! What am I going to do?" I kicked a pebble in my path out of frustration.

"I don't know . . . but you can move back as soon as you graduate."

"As soon as I graduate? That's not for six months! And I won't even be eighteen then! My parents aren't going to let me move across the world!"

He was quiet for a minute, thinking about what I had said.

"Well . . . then I'll just have to move to you."

"What?"

"I'm eighteen. I can do what I want. I want to be with you. I can come with you."

"Come with me? You're kidding. Like your parents are going to go for that."

"Oh well, I'm an adult."

I scoffed. "Be serious." He was quiet again. He started slowing down, and then I slowed to a stop. "Wait. Are you serious?"

"I think so." He put his hands in his pockets and stared down at the ground.

"I've been thinking a lot about it. You can't stay here, but that doesn't mean I can't go to you."

"I-, I don't think you can- "

He pulled his left hand out of his pocket and took mine. Then he pulled his right hand out of his pocket. He had a ring. My heart stopped. He didn't say anything as he slipped the ring onto my finger. He kept his grip on it, not placing it on all the way.

"I love you. Imagining us being apart is unbearable. I don't want you to be away from me for one second, but I know, whether I move or you move, we will be separated for at least a while. I want you to know, I am always with you and I will always love you and I want you to be mine forever."

I was barely breathing. My head was spinning. I couldn't believe this.

"I bought this a while ago. I was waiting for the right time to give it to you," he explained. "I know it's too soon to talk about marriage and all that. Then our parents would really go mad! But, I am promising that I will stay faithful to you and I want a deeper commitment to you. Will you accept my promise ring?"

He waited, braced. I looked into his eyes, slightly wet around the edges. "Yes," I simply said. He smiled widely and pushed the ring down all the way on my finger. He held my hands and gazed at me happily.

"I love you," he told me, though he didn't need to.

"I love you, Nigel. I always will," I told him, embracing him tightly.

We stood in the middle of the street holding each other like we were the only two in the world.

We spent the day playing hooky, enjoying each other, and looking at each other with new appreciation and closeness. I kept admiring my ring- I loved it. It was a fairly plain piece of jewelry, but it was more meaningful than any huge diamond ever could be. I cherished it. I felt so lucky to have it and to have him.

When it was starting to get dark, he walked me home. I didn't expect my parents to be there, but they were. I said goodbye to Nigel on the porch.

"Ring me later?" he asked.

"You bet. Bye, honey. I love you."

"I love you." He walked away backwards so he could maintain eye contact as long as possible before turning around and vanishing. I sighed and went in the door.

"Well, what did you do today?" my mother asked in a bitter tone as soon as I walked in.

"Um, why?"

"Because, I went to your school to get your transcripts and I thought I would get you out early and take you to lunch to apologize. But you weren't there."

" . . . I decided that it would be useless to go to school today since I'm done there. Does it matter?"

"Well, you need to ask permission, young lady. You are a child. You are seventeen years old; you're not an adult."

"You said I didn't have to go today! And you were going to take me out anyway. Why are you mad?"

"Because you think you can do whatever you want lately!"

"No, I know I can't do whatever I want because if I could, I would stay here and live on my own!"

"Oh, because your father and I treat you so badly, huh?"

"No, you don't. You don't even notice me enough to treat me bad."

"I'm sorry we have to work! Do you think mortgages come cheap?"

"Forget I said anything. I'm going to my room!" I stomped past her.

"Wait, this isn't over!" She grabbed my hand. She saw the ring and was silenced for a second. "What is that?"

"A ring."

"Don't be a smartass! Who gave that to you? Nigel? What the hell is it supposed to mean?"

"It's just a promise ring."

"Promise for what? You think you are going to marry him? Are you pregnant?"

"What? No! Why would you even say that?"

"Oh, I don't know. Because you have him alone in the house every afternoon for the past year."

I was silent this time. How did she know? I was careful to hide my tracks.

"Yeah, didn't think I knew, did you? Well, I asked Gertrude to look in on you when we moved here. She watches you to make sure you get off to school and get home okay everyday. She told me when Nigel started walking you home and she told me when he started coming in the house with you. And she told me when he started staying all day, until right before your father and I get home."

I blushed and looked at the ground in shame.

"I didn't want to believe you were up to anything bad, just friends. Maybe some innocent hand-holding or a little kissing. Then, I saw your sheets. I saw that telltale bloody stain that day when you were left alone all day because you had *homework*. Gertrude told me Nigel came over early that day and stayed all day long. I can guess what you did. I really didn't want to believe that my little girl was being a slut."

The word slapped my face. I felt angry and hurt, tears surfaced in my eyes. My mother had never mentioned the stained sheet, and I had forgotten all about Gertrude watching us. I was angry, but I was guilty.

"So, you've been sneaking around having sex with him for a year and now he's giving you a ring? Well, I am glad we are moving. You two should not be together. You are too young for this. You think you're so in love, but you have no idea. It's fun to play house, but let me tell you, you have no clue what you're getting yourself into. That ring, it's worthless. Once we're an ocean away, he's going to move on and you will, too." With those last words, she walked away.

I was stunned and pained. I trudged up the stairs to my room. When I opened my door I was surprised to see that my parents had left packing boxes for me. It was depressing. I really hated all the aggravation associated with moving. I hated boxes and packing them and unpacking them and living out of them. I hated getting situated just in time to have to do it all over again. But I never dreaded moving more than I did this time; to have to leave someone I cared so much for, it was agony. I flopped down onto my bed and cried. All I wanted was Nigel to hold me and pick me up and take me away from all this misery.

And now, after the things my mother had said, I was fairly sure he was not welcome in the house and that our being together was not a high priority for my parents. I wept harder.

I cried myself to sleep. When I woke up and looked at the clock, I saw it was three a.m., I had forgotten to call Nigel. I remembered the last time I didn't call him when he expected me to. I felt guilty, but there was no way could I call him now.

I tried to force myself back to sleep and after an hour or so later, I was successful, though it was only for a couple of hours. My parents were up before seven o'clock, noisily packing and moving things around. I was wide awake, but I didn't want to give them the satisfaction of knowing they had achieved their obvious goal of punishing me by waking me. I stayed in bed and stared at the ceiling, thinking and plotting.

Maybe it wouldn't be so bad, moving home. We hadn't flown to America in over a year- I could see my family again, I did miss them. And, I would be eighteen in nine months, I could move back to Cambridge then. And Nigel could visit me in Detroit. He was right: he was an adult and could do as he pleased.

I was still resentful toward my parents, but I was beginning to let optimism take over. I started packing my things. When I was ready for a break, I went to the kitchen for breakfast. There were boxes everywhere and half of the kitchen was already packed. My mother was on a step stool, reaching for some bowls on the top shelf. As she pulled them down, a casserole dish teetered and fell off the shelf. I dove and caught it before it could hit the ground. My mother gasped and when she saw I had it, she sighed loudly.

"Oh, thank God! That was your grandmother's."

"I didn't know that," I responded quietly, inspecting the familiar dish.

She stepped down. "Well, I guess if we didn't move you away from your family all the time, you might know them better."

I was confused. Why was she talking like that when she should be biting my head off?

"I've been thinking . . . I couldn't sleep last night, that's why I'm up so early today. Look, this is the life we had handed to us. It's not the life I would have chosen for my child, but we have to make do. You and your dad are the only constant in my life, all we really have is each other. I don't like that we have to move all the time, but soon we won't have to anymore. Things will settle down and we can have a normal life. I don't want a strained relationship with you. I don't want to fight anymore. I think we both said some stupid things, but let's just forget about that. We are starting a new life, so let's have a clean slate, okay?"

I thought about it for a minute. She was right. I didn't like it, but all I had was my parents now and we needed each other's support; or, at least, we needed to be cool with each other. "Okay . . . I'm sorry, mom."

"I'm sorry, too." She hugged me. It felt a little weird; she didn't hug me much. I guess she was trying to change that.

"Let me just eat something, then I'll help you pack," I offered.

"No, no, go spend time with Nigel. You only have three more days with him. Your father and I can do this."

"Well, he has class until noon. I can help until then at least."

"Alright, deal."

Things started to change with my folks a bit. I think I was growing up and was able to be more mature and understanding. We tried to be respectful to each other, even if we didn't agree.

I did spend as much time with Nigel as I could over the next few days. We stopped crying and focusing on the negatives and instead talked about our future and anything positive we could grasp.

But the day before I left, I was finding it hard to be upbeat.

We were lying in bed, facing each other. "How am I going to go months without seeing this face?" I asked.

"I know! I can stow away in your suitcase!" he suggested.

"Great idea!" I laughed. Then, I thought about it a bit. "Actually, that would be nice if I snuck you in. I could keep you hidden away in my closet all the time and we could have dirty, forbidden sex whenever we wanted." I licked my lips, getting aroused.

"Ooh, yeah. That's a good plan," he lustily agreed.

"Good, it's settled. You'll come with me."

"Yeah, I'll come with you," he growled and pulled me close. He kissed me as his hands wandered. I was eager to keep him close to me, knowing this was the last time we would be alone together for a long time. That thought made me desire him and his touch more than usual. It was important to me to be united like only lovers could. It was clear he felt the same way. In seconds and without words we ripped each other's clothes off and he had me pinned beneath him, making love to me with more passion and intensity than he had ever before. It wasn't like the other times when we imagined we had forever to experiment and enjoy each other. I didn't want to think of it as our last time, but I knew there was a chance that this was it. I clung to his bare back with my desperate hands. My legs were tightly wrapped around him. He was in me as deep as allowable and he barely stopped kissing me the whole time. I kept my eyes open, studying him, trying to engrave this moment in my brain. I wanted to freeze time, to always have him with me; to always be able to see his amazing brown eyes and his darling, sweet smile; to feel his big hands hold mine; to taste his angel's mouth with his incredible kiss; to hear his moans of pleasure . . . to hear him say, *I love you.*

His motions were becoming a little uneven and he was gasping and grunting uncontrollably. One of his hands, twisted in my hair, held me tight as he looked into my eyes. I softly gazed into his. "My girl. My little girl," he whispered before coming in for another kiss and then climaxing.

On moving day, we had a huge truck come to take our stuff to be shipped to America. We also had a lot of things we were taking on the plane with us. My dad had already turned his company car in, so they called a taxi to pick us up. Nigel was also there with a car. He offered to help us cart our things to the airport.

Between the two cars, all of our stuff was crammed in with barely enough room for the passengers. My parents went in the cab; I went with Nigel. I had Autumn in a kitty carrier on my lap. I tried to comfort her, but she was crying and upset.

"You're going to be alright, baby," I cooed. "We'll be separated for the trip, but when we get home, you'll never leave my sight again."

I doubt it was due to me, but she stopped her caterwauling for a while. Now, it was time to comfort Nigel. I looked at him and he looked back at me briefly, keeping his eyes on the road.

"This is bollocks," he muttered.

"I know. I wish at least I was moving somewhere warmer than here, but Michigan winters are terrible. I have nothing to look forward to. I hate that."

"You'll just have to look forward to your Easter holiday. We can see each other then."

"That's in April! It's only January!" I whined.

"Well, that's all I have," he responded.

I sighed and stared out the windshield.

We were at the airport too quickly. I was shaky. Nigel helped us load our things onto a cart and take them to the proper dropoff point. He stayed with us in the boarding area until we had to get on the plane. We sat together and held hands in silence. A flight attendant approached me to take Autumn away. She was crying, which made me feel like crying. I tried to hold it together. My parents got up, ready to board.

"Just take your time saying goodbye, but don't miss the flight," my dad instructed, trying to give us privacy.

We stood up and faced each other. I could barely speak and I knew once I started, I wouldn't be able to help myself from crying. I breathed heavily, trying to gain control.

"Wow, this is hard," he mustered.

"Yeah," I croaked, staring at my shoes to avoid his face.

"I have something I want to give you that I didn't want your parents to see."

"Oh, yeah? What?"

He pulled something out that he had hidden in his coat. He handed me one of his shirts. It was a red and black striped sweatshirt that he wore a lot. "Something to remember me by."

Instinctively I brought it to my face and sniffed it. It smelled like him. "Thank you, this is perfect. A piece of you to cuddle and keep with me at night."

He looked at me, nodding, thinking for a second; then he pulled me close for a long, goodbye kiss. I'm sure the other passengers around us were staring, but I didn't notice. Only Nigel and I existed at that moment. His arms were around me so tight, as if he could just hold on hard enough, he could keep me with him.

"Last call for passengers on flight 357 to Detroit," an announcement interrupted us.

Our lips reluctantly parted. The kiss turned into a hug. "I'll miss you. I love you so much," he said fiercely.

"I love you, too. I'll miss you every second."

"Phone me as soon as you can."

"I will, I promise." I was crying now.

"Miss? Can I have your ticket?" a flight attendant asked me.

"Oh, yeah. Here it is." I handed it off and looked back at Nigel.

"Okay, you're all set. Time to get on the plane."

"Alright," I answered her. "Bye, honey. I love you!" I called to him, choking up again.

"I love you!" he called back, getting as close to the gate as he could to see me walk away. As I walked down the dark corridor, I looked over my shoulder and saw him, his eyes closed, obviously crushed.

It was the most painful sight I ever witnessed.

I was a zombie on the plane. I stared at nothing as my eyes leaked at a violently heavy rate. The hot tears splashed my lap. I let them fall, not even caring enough to wipe them away. My parents looked at me in wordless amazement, shocked to see this display of emotion, shocked that I could be so affected by leaving some boy. My mother, who was seated next to me, put her arm around me and kept it there for almost an hour. She said nothing and neither did I. My heart was broken.

I spent the rest of the flight in a half conscious stupor. My eyes dried, but they were sore and swollen; my head throbbed and my stomach churned. When the pilot announced that we were approaching Detroit, I felt ill. It was really happening, I was really here, and I fucking hated it.

I was true to my word: I called Nigel as soon as our plane landed. I had no idea what time it was in Cambridge, but I ran to the nearest payphone at the Detroit airport, eager to get a hold of him.

It only rang twice. "Hello?" he enthusiastically answered, like he was hoping it was me. I immediately felt better when I heard his voice.

"Hi, Nigel. I made it."

"Oh, thank God! How was the trip?"

"Well, Autumn is all shook up from being stowed away with the cargo for ten hours, but we're all in one piece." *Barely.*

"Oh, good. I miss you."

"Oh, honey, I miss you, too. I miss you so much, already." My dad approached, rolling his eyes and tapping his watch. I resented having to say goodbye again, but I had no choice. "I have to go. I'll call you as soon as we're settled. I love you. Bye."

We hung up and then my family was off again. My dad's company had sent a van for us to load our stuff in. While we were at the baggage claim area, picking out all of our belongings, one of my dad's former (and now current) co-workers came to pick us up.

"Rick, you son of a gun! How did you ever survive in Limeyville?"

Limeyville? What an ass!

My dad heartily laughed. "Bob, it was a struggle, but we survived."

I stared at my dad. *A struggle?* It was the best thing that ever happened to me. I sneered at them as they made bad jokes about England and its people.

And they did that all the way home. My mother and I sat in the backseat. She smiled as she gazed at the familiar sights. I felt sick; this was no longer home to me.

Our new house was big, the biggest of all. I looked around, astonished, wondering how much my dad got paid to move around the country and abroad. Handsomely, it appeared. Our house was one of many white, two story colonials on large lots. There was a huge front porch and it was beautifully landscaped. Normally I would have found it to be quite lovely, but I hated it instantly. It did not feel like home to me and I doubted that would ever change.

Bob walked in with us. "Well, Rick, I hope you like this place because Reynolds isn't going to move you again. That was it. You're here for good now."

"There's no business in England left to do?" I asked hopefully.

Bob gave me a funny look, and then asked my dad, "She wants to go back?"

"Yeah, she made a boyfriend there," my dad explained in an almost mocking tone.

"You did? You mean you actually kissed one of those nasty British mouths? Oh, God! I hope you got your shots!" He and my dad laughed hysterically.

My blood boiled. My fingers curled into tight fists until my nails dug into my hands.

"Oh, stop it you two," my mom intervened, disciplining the men. "Michelle, go pick out your new room."

I stomped away, heading upstairs. "Not the master bedroom!" my dad yelled to me.

"Ugh," I said to myself, climbing the stairs. I tried to make a mental calculation of days left until I could move out, already.

Chapter 6

"...you will always have me, no matter what."

O ver the next few days, we settled in and unpacked. I called Nigel every day to let him know what I was up to and to see what he was up to. I missed him and I hated not being a part of his life- at least, in person.

As the weeks went by, Nigel and I still kept up with calls and correspondence. He told me about the guys he got to know in art school. They also were aspiring musicians and tried to put together a group. I so wished I could have seen them. Nigel was very excited about it.

"We finally settled on a name for the band."

"What is it?"

"We're calling ourselves Descent."

"I like it, it's original, and it sounds really cool."

"Yeah, doesn't it? We went through about a million names, but we all like this one. It kind of fits us, like we are the product of all the rock and punk predecessors that we admire; but also, like we're descending on the masses, unleashing ourselves on the unsuspecting youth who has no idea we are about to change the face of music as we know it." He sounded proud, like he had really thought this out.

"Wow, honey. So things are really taking off?"

"Yeah, we still have a long way to go but we've got some songs. Well, we started a few songs, they're not quite finished yet, but close."

"Well, describe them to me."

" . . . I can't really describe them. I mean, there are elements of this and that. I started playing bass now so there's a lot of funky bass fused in there. And there are new things, new sounds we're generating. It's very cool."

"It sounds cool. I really wish I could hear you."

"I'll record us for you."

"No, I should be there. I should be your number one fan."

"Well, honey, you will be here, one day. Soon."

I hated that. Soon was too far away. He was moving on. At least, it felt like he was moving on. He was having incredible experiences, he was starting a new life. And I wasn't there.

"You're right. I will be there soon. As soon as I graduate, I'm moving back so we can be together."

"Really? Your parents are gonna go for that?"

"Um, well, I haven't really asked their permission, but that's my plan."

"Well, I'm glad you are planning to come back to me as soon as possible, but I don't know if your parents will allow that."

"I can go away to college like anyone else, right? They wouldn't stand in the way of my education. I'll go to art school with you. It'll be fine."

He was silent, thinking it over. I was silent, too. I only said it would be fine to give him hope. I doubted my parents would be that cool, but we would cross that bridge when we got to it.

Occasionally my parents would ask me about how school was going and if I'd made any new friends. That was code, and I was able to crack it. They really wanted to know if I had met a new boy who would make me forget about Nigel. They obviously didn't know that was impossible. Even though I always had my ring on and we talked very often, they still didn't believe our love was strong enough to last the time and distance barrier.

It was a good thing they were wrong, because on the few occasions during the semester that we were supposed to see each other, something always fell through at the last minute. He was supposed to visit me in February, but a huge ice storm came through and shut down the airport. I was supposed to go to him in April, but my grandmother got ill and we had to go see her. It left us heartbroken, though I think it made my parents quite happy. They were hoping I could just get over him. So silly.

My last semester of high school was a royal waste of time, though I did manage to learn to drive and obtain my license. I had signed up for the easiest classes I could, knowing I would have a hard time paying attention when the center of my universe was thousands of miles away. I had two art classes, which of course I could ace. I wanted to keep a high GPA, but I did have one tough college prep class, advanced placement literature. I had to be adept in my former classes to get in. That was easy, as I was good at writing and interpreting. I chose this class because it sounded interesting. I ended up working harder than I'd ever had to before. The homework and constant essays consumed my free time. I always had a novel to read and report on. The teacher was strict, so I had to learn to be a better writer.

By the end of the semester, I was relieved the class was over and that I wouldn't have to worry about all the writing assignments anymore. However, I realized that it had honed my writing skills and I had a new and more accurate approach to writing than I had before.

When I graduated in late May of 1979, my parents asked me what my plans were for after graduation. I told them my idea, that I wanted to go to art school just like Nigel had. Actually, I wanted to go to his art school. They didn't like that idea.

"Why don't you go to the local university and take some general courses?" my dad suggested.

"No. Why bother taking math and science and all that. I hate math. I'm not going to ever need to know more math than I learned in fifth grade," I pouted.

"Well, what are you going to do in *art school?*" he mocked.

"I don't know for sure. Write, I think. Maybe draw or something."

"Draw or something? How are you going to pay bills with a degree in drawing or something?"

"I can pay the bills with writing."

"That's debatable. Why don't you get a real degree for a real career? You could be a doctor or a lawyer."

I made a face.

"Okay, you could be a secretary or a nanny."

"Thanks for all your confidence in me, dad."

"Well, if you want a real job, you need a real education. If you aren't serious about school, I'm not going to waste thousands of dollars on you for you to have to take a job as a secretary or a nanny or a waitress or something to pay the bills when you realize an art degree won't get you anywhere."

My mom finally broke in. "Hold on, Rick. Let's just calm down. Maybe we can compromise. Michelle, you want to go to art school in England?"

"Yes."

"And we want you to get a good education here."

"Right," my dad chirped.

"Well, what if you agreed to go to college in America- " I whined.

" . . . but, it can be art school."

"No!" my dad grunted.

"Yes. For a semester, at least. This will be the deal. If you want to go to art school in England, you're on your own. That's your choice. Your dad and I will pay for school if you stay in America and you prove that you are working toward a useful degree."

My father looked suspicious. I thought it over, sneering. They knew I didn't have the money to pay for school on my own. They also didn't want me to move away to be with Nigel. My mother acted like she was giving me a choice, but, really, I didn't have one.

"What do you think?" she asked.

"I don't think- " my dad started.

"Shh! Michelle, what do you say?"

" . . . I say, fine. I'll stay here for one semester. But I want to go back to England as soon as I can."

"Okay, let's just take it one step at a time," my mother placated me.

I called Nigel later that day when my parents were out.

"How was graduation?" he asked enthusiastically.

"Oh, fine. I'm glad it's over."

"Well, what's next? Did you talk to your parents about moving back here?"

"Yes. They don't share my vision."

"Oh, I could have guessed that. So, what are you going to do?"

"Well . . . we agreed that I could go to art school-"

"Yeah?"

"Yeah. If I stay in Michigan. They'll pay for school if I go locally. If I move to Cambridge, I'm on my own. And they'll be all disappointed in me."

"So what? You gotta do what you gotta do. I thought you wanted to move back."

"I do! Of course I do! I told them that. All I want to do is be with you. But, this is their idea of a compromise. I don't know . . . Where would I live if I moved back? I don't have enough money to get a place."

"Whoa, whoa. That sounds like your dad talking."

"He did say something along those lines . . . "

"Don't listen to that! We'll get a place together! I'll take care of you."

"You don't have a job!"

"I'll get one! Just promise you won't commit to anything there. I can't not have you around anymore, it's gutting me."

"Me, too. Okay, I'll try to postpone registering for college. But, I can't promise you that I can move back right now. I have to think about things."

"Seriously? I thought this was all settled. When you were graduated you were moving back to England, that was the plan."

"That's still my plan! I just may have to hold off for a little while. I'm not eighteen yet. I can't emancipate myself from my parents. Until I can stand on my own two feet, I kinda have to work with them."

"I get it. But, look, I'm going to get a job and save up some money and then we can get our own place and we can stand on our own two feet together."

"Okay, that sounds really good. I'll call you later as soon as I figure something out."

☙

I decided I would get a job, too. Looking through the want ads in the paper, I found an art supply store that was looking for help. It sounded good, plus it would get me out of the house, and it would bolster my bank account. Really, the only thing I was seeking was a way to be with Nigel as fast as I could. I had a one track mind.

Not long after I found the ad, I was interviewed and hired. It was a small shop and I had been there many times. It was a good atmosphere and it suited me well. I wouldn't be making much money, but every little bit helped. I told Steve, my manager, that I would be willing to work any and every shift. He seemed pleased at what appeared to be my hard work ethic, but in reality, I just wanted as much money as quickly as possible so I could move back to England.

Nigel was still hoping to make money as a musician with his band. Every once in a while he would call me with news that he had a show or a gig or something. They never paid much and he was getting discouraged.

"Am I doing the right thing here?" he asked over the phone.

"Honey, you're doing the only thing you can do."

"Well, I'm not doing a good job providing for us."

"Musicians struggle until they make it big. Everyone does."

"I need to do something more drastic. I need to step it up." He was quiet for a minute, thinking. "I know what I want, I just have to find a way to make it happen."

"You will. You are the most determined person I've ever met."

"Besides you."

"Right, that's why we're so perfect together."

"Right."

"You'll find a way to get the band out there. Soon, you'll be buying a mansion with all your royalties!"

"Thanks for believing in me. I was beginning to think I should give up."

"Hey! Don't ever let me hear you say that again. I have faith in you because you don't just give up. It would be way easier to dump me and have a girlfriend in town. But you aren't doing that. You're hanging in there for something you want even though it's tough and people think you're wrong. Who cares? You have to follow your heart. You have to be a success, because that's who you are."

He sighed. "Okay. I just have to focus. I'm going to be everything you think I am. You're going to be proud of me."

"Too late. Oh, honey, I have to go. I'm working today."

"Alright. I'll call you tomorrow."

"Okay, I love you. Bye."

"I love you. Bye."

ՇՅ

We had planned on seeing each other for his birthday in late June that summer. It would take almost all the money I had earned from work, but that's what it was for.

My parents weren't thrilled with the notion.

"I don't like you going all the way to England by yourself," my mother complained.

"Why doesn't he come here?" my father asked.

"I want to go there. I want to see his band play."

"*His band?*" My dad sniffed with contempt.

"Yes, his band. And he can't exactly bring them all here in his duffel bag," I defended.

"Where will you stay?" my mother questioned with acidity. She obviously thought I planned on sleeping in Nigel's bed.

"I don't know. With the Blakes, I guess."

"No," she quickly snapped.

"I could stay at a hotel."

"No!" my dad interjected. "Not in a hotel alone."

"Or with Nigel," my mother finished. "I'd rather him come here and stay in our guest room."

"Are you sure, mom? You might not be able to babysit us every second."

"Hey, it's not like I don't know what you two want to do. I was a teenager, too, you know."

"But, you aren't going to stop me from seeing him, are you?"

My folks exchanged looks, telepathically determining my fate. After a long pause, my mother sighed. "No," she reluctantly answered. "But, you have to promise to be really careful."

I knew she meant safety and birth control. "Okay," I agreed. "I'll be safe."

Before my trip, my mother took me to see the doctor. She wanted me on oral contraceptives before I saw Nigel, just in case. I felt weird about that, but she kept telling me stories about so and so and a friend of a friend who got knocked up too young and it ruined her life even though she thought she was in love and that her boyfriend would never leave her. "Boys can't handle those things," she'd say. I gathered she didn't think my relationship could withstand a pregnancy. She didn't have much faith in us and assumed we already would have broken up due to the distance. Either way, she didn't want to be a grandmother, but she couldn't stop me from having sex with the man I loved. So we both settled on The Pill.

I called Nigel to finalize the date of our visit before I bought the plane ticket.

"Hi, honey. How are you?"

"Great! You'll never believe what happened!"

"What?"

"Well, I was trying to think of how we could get the band really going, you know? And then I thought, what if we played a regular gig somewhere? So, I went around, looking for a place and I found the perfect spot. This really crackin' club that totally fits our vibe, you know? So, I go in and talk to the owner and, get this: he's so impressed with me and the sound of our band, he agreed to let us play there regularly *and* he's going to manage us!"

"Wow! That sounds great."

"Yeah! We're finally going to get paid and we'll have a real audience and he's going to get us more gigs!"

"Cool! I'm so happy for you."

"Oh, me, too. So, now we have a place to rehearse and write music. It's exactly what we needed. We even get jobs at the club, during the day, you know, so we don't ever have to be distracted. Our lives can revolve around music all the time to keep the creative juices flowing. It all worked out so bloody well!"

"Good, Nigel. I'm really glad."

"Oh, God, I feel so good. I mean, I'll be busy as hell and I probably won't have time for anything else, but, I guess that's what happens when you put your heart and soul into something. You gotta give it your all."

"Yeah," I agreed quietly.

"As a matter of fact, we are going down to the club pretty soon."

"We?"

"Yeah. Me and the guys from the band."

"Right," I replied.

"You know, I haven't asked about you. How is everything going with you?"

"Um, oh, fine, I guess."

"Oh. Good." He could tell I was keeping something.

I decided to divulge. "Yeah-"

"Oh, hey, the guys are here. I gotta go. I'll ring you soon. I love you."

He hung up. I sighed and slowly hung up as well. My heart ached. All I could think about was seeing him since we moved back. Now, when it was so close I could taste it, I was going to have to wait again. I should have mentioned that we needed to iron out the details of my trip, but his mind was miles away. I knew he wasn't too busy to spend time with me, but I decided he was wrapped up in something very important and didn't need any distractions. I wouldn't want to burden him with requiring attention. I decided to send him his birthday gift instead, which was two biographies on musicians he liked. It would be fine. I would just see him some other time. I didn't like it, but I could wait.

But it never seemed like a good time. Whenever I called him, he always had a million things going on. They were all good things and I really was excited for him. But I missed him. I hadn't planned on going so long without seeing his face. We talked a lot and sent letters, but all the correspondence in the world would not give me his smile. I couldn't look into his eyes through the phone.

And then, we started talking on the phone less and writing to each other even more infrequently. He was always busy with his new life. He even started going by his middle name, John, to fit his new persona. I felt like we were growing apart and knew if things continued this way, I would lose my boyfriend.

School was starting soon and I was running out of time. I decided to bring it up during one of our calls.

"Hey, so, I start school in a couple of weeks."

"Wow, is it that time already?"

"Yeah, it is. Summer is almost over."

"Where does all the time go?"

"I don't know. I can't say it's really flying by for me, though. Every day without you feels like an eternity."

"Oh, baby, I hope you don't think I don't miss you. I know I've been busy and all I've been doing is talking about my band, but it breaks my heart that I can't see you."

"Well, I've been saving money for the plane ticket. I could come for a visit."

"Oh, great. When were you thinking?"

"Um, how about next week?"

"Ooh, no, I can't. That is going to be super busy."

"What about the following week?"

"Um . . . Can I get back to you?"

"Sure." I couldn't hide my disappointment.

"I'm sorry. I'm so sorry. I just have to give this my all so my career can take off. Then I can provide for you and your dad won't be able to say anything about me not being good enough for his daughter."

"He never said that."

"Maybe not in so many words, but that is definitely what he thinks. I'll prove him wrong."

"I don't care about what my dad thinks, I care about being with you."

"And I want to be with you, too! Permanently. If I can make a lot of money soon, I can buy us a place to live and we can be together without worrying about how we're going to make it. I don't want you to ever think you made a mistake by choosing to be with me."

"I could never feel that way!"

"I know you love me. But, I want us to have more than love. We need stability. I'm working on that. But unfortunately, that means we won't be able to see each other for a while yet."

I groaned. "Nigel, I don't know if I can wait any longer."

"Just a little while. Okay?"

"I don't have a choice, do I?"

"I can quit the band right now and move to America and get a nine to five job."

"No! I wouldn't ask you to do that."

"I'd do it for you, though. Just say the word and I will. You mean more to me than anything. More than my band."

"No. I can wait. I don't want you to choose. I want you to have everything you want. And you will always have me, no matter what. I'll wait as long as it takes."

"Oh, you're amazing. I love you so much. How many girls would put up with this?"

I wondered about that. "I would think any girl would jump at the opportunity if it was for you."

"Well, I'll just have to take your word for it, cuz there's no way I'd ever even *think* about another girl."

He sounded sincere. I believed him. I felt the same way. "I love you, honey."

"I love you, too, babe."

Chapter 7

"...I want to be with Nigel, and that hasn't changed."

I registered for school in mid August of 1979. I hesitated to sign up because I was still hoping I would end up back in Cambridge, where I belonged. Yet, when I enrolled, I became a bit excited about the classes the college offered. I took intro to journalism, intro to creative writing, art appreciation 101, and basics of sketching. I hadn't decided what to major in yet, so I covered my bases. My dad grumbled about my choices and still tried to talk me into a more formal education, but we had a deal and he had to stick to it.

I thought of Nigel constantly. Everything I saw and heard triggered a memory or a new idea or a daydream. It pained me that we couldn't be together, but in reality, I was as busy as he was. Once school started, I was busy during the day. In the afternoons and weekends, I either had a shift at the art supply store or homework to do.

I was still trying to save up as much money as possible, dreaming about the sweet day when I would be financially independent and could live with my love.

When my birthday came around, I was really looking forward to it. I would be eighteen and an adult. My parents gave me an unexpected gift. Airplane vouchers. It was an invitation to see Nigel whenever I wanted. I couldn't believe it.

"Wow, thank you so much!" I cried out, gleefully.

"Well, you have been working so hard, I didn't want you to have to dump out half of your savings to fly to England," my father explained.

"I'm just surprised. You don't want me going over there. Alone, at least."

"You're an adult now. And it's not a big deal. I'm sure Nigel will take good care of you and make sure you're safe."

"Yes, he will. Thank you." I couldn't believe they trusted us.

"Just, promise to wait to use the ticket until you have a break from school," my mother pleaded.

"Okay. I guess I can wait another eight weeks." Saying those words felt bitter on my tongue, but I had lasted eight months; eight weeks would be nothing.

Nigel called me later that evening.

"Happy Birthday, baby."

"Thank you."

"Did you get my gift?"

"Yes, I did," I said, referring to the stack of records he had sent to me. Albums of hot British bands that were not easy to find in the states. "Thank you very much. You're so sweet."

"So, you liked it?"

"Of course, honey! You always get me the best presents."

"Thanks. So, what else did you get?"

"Plane tickets."

"Plane tickets? To England?"

"Yes."

"Really? For when?"

"Whenever I want. But, I think I'll use them in December."

"December? You can't come any earlier than that?"

"No, I missed that boat."

"Sorry. Oh, well. Two more months."

"I know. I'm counting the days."

"I can't wait."

"Me either."

ဗ

The time dragged on as I waited until the day Nigel and I could reunite. I tried to throw myself into my studies. Being busy didn't help. Nothing could distract me enough to make the time pass quicker.

I settled for planning ahead. I wanted everything to go well when we met up. I started packing a month early. I made reservations at a local hotel in Cambridge for that week. I went shopping for new clothes that he'd never seen before. I knew all this over preparation was silly. He wouldn't care about what I was wearing or where I was staying. All that would matter was that we were finally together.

However, when I arrived in England in early December, I wanted everything to go perfectly. I told Nigel not to pick me up and that I would meet him at the club, since he had a show that night. I took a cab to my hotel and spent hours getting ready.

I had gone shopping at the trendiest boutiques in the metro Detroit area. I hoped to be one step ahead of the London crowd. I settled on skintight black satin pants and a tight black and white striped cotton tank top. I put on a pair of red pumps, tied a red scarf around my neck, and added several thick gold bangle bracelets. I teased up my hair and applied lots of makeup, I looked very glam. But of course, all I cared about was impressing Nigel.

I took a taxi downtown to see them play at their club, The Fox Trot. Outside the doors, I couldn't believe the backup. The line was huge and full of characters. There were women dressed like men and men dressed like women. There were extraordinarily beautiful boys and girls dressed to the height of fashion. I felt extremely plain, despite my careful attire.

I waited in line with the eclectic crowd. I watched as the bouncer let in the unique and gorgeous and rejected the plainer types. I grew more and more nervous as I approached the front of the line. By the time it was my turn to be let in or turned away, I was mostly convinced that I wouldn't fit in. The bouncer gave me the once over and although he didn't look displeased, I wanted to explain myself and my right to be there before he could exclude me. "I'm a friend of the band," I declared, trying to sound confident.

"Oh yeah?" he asked sarcastically. "What's your name?"

"Michelle Casey. I'm here for Nigel Blake."

"Nigel? You must go way back with him. Anyway, your name is on the list; go ahead in. Just, maybe don't go looking for him yet."

"Huh? Why?" I demanded, confused. But the bouncer was already with the next person in line. His comment irked me. I was hoping

Nigel would be waiting for me at the door. I guess I was wrong. Apparently he and his band were a big deal and I was just another girl, even though I knew him when he was Nigel.

Once inside the club, I was awed. Nigel was right, this place was amazing, cutting edge. It was packed with young, beautiful people that all seemed to be glowing faintly purple under the lights. The noise in the club was almost palpable; loud, pulsing music combined with an incoherent buzz of multiple conversations. Everyone seemed to be having a good time. This was obviously the place to be.

The deejay played danceable stuff, but a real mix: disco, punk, new wave. Some I recognized from the American airwaves, some were the new sounds from London. To me they seemed daring, so much more innovative and bold than what I was used to. I respected that; I immediately liked this place. The lights, the music, the people, it was like nothing I had seen before.

I made my way through the hordes of dancing young people and over to the bar. A barmaid approached and took my drink order. As she went about preparing it, I smiled to myself. I wasn't old enough to drink in America, but here, no one even asked my age.

When the waitress returned, I took the opportunity to ask about the band, or more importantly, Nigel. "Excuse me, when does the band come on?" I asked loudly over the music.

"Midnight."

"Where are they right now?"

She gave me a look. "They're busy," she said rudely.

Again, I must have looked like a groupie. "Well, I came to see Nigel."

She didn't look the least bit surprised. "They all do," she smirked.

What? *This* was news. "I'm his girlfriend from America," I said flatly.

Her demeanor changed. "Oh . . . I see . . . He talks about you all the time."

I raised my eyebrows. "Does he? Well, where is he? Can I see him?"

"Oh, no, I'm afraid not. They'll be going on in twenty minutes and they are still getting ready. There will be time after the show, though. That's usually when the guys take their girls and- " she trailed off.

"And what?"

"Um, talk and dance and have some drinks. You know."

"Yeah, I can imagine."

She tried to recover and make small talk. "So, where in America are you from? What's it like over there?"

"Different," I said coolly. She took the hint and went back to her work.

America *was* different from England; but whatever country you're in, men are the same. And no man can resist popularity, fame, and adulation, especially one who never had it before. *So girls were throwing themselves at him? These girls?* I gazed around. All the women either looked like models or artists. Either way, they would be interesting to him; maybe more than me. And I had been gone. He had surely been lonely. I trusted him and believed he was a good boy, but with all this temptation, how optimistic could I be? I stared into my drink, playing with the little straw.

Then, a gentleman approached me. "Now, you look far too depressed to be in here. Let's get her another drink, shall we?" he insisted to the barmaid. "On the house," he said to me, smiling. Who was this guy, I wondered. He was handsome, but I hoped he wasn't hitting on me. He must have some connections here. Maybe this was the club owner Nigel told me about. "So you're John's American girl," he stated with a charming smile.

Yes, he must be the infamous owner/manager. I attempted to smile back at him. "That's me."

"Michelle, right?"

"Yes," I answered, suddenly in a better mood. I was grateful he knew my name. Nigel *did* talk about me.

"I'm Patrick Fox. This is my club. What do you think of it?"

"It's very, very . . . unique. I've never seen anything like it."

"Perfect. There is nothing like it, especially around here."

My next drink arrived. He picked it up and handed it to me. "Here, why don't you follow me?" He led me into the back, behind the bar, avoiding the crowd. We went through the kitchen and storage areas. We wandered through the winding hallway as he informed me of the growing success of the band, filling me in on trivial information. I got the feeling he was trying to distract me.

I wondered where we were going. The further we walked, the louder the crowd was getting. We emerged on a balcony to the left of the stage.

"This is the VIP box," he joked. "I'd be honored if you watched the show from here tonight. Best seat in the house."

"Really? Thank you."

"No problem. Let me know if you need anything. I'll stop by from time to time to check on you. Now, I have to go back to being the manager," he winked, then disappeared back into the maze.

I looked down onto the crowd; the place was packed. I couldn't believe my little boyfriend had created such a successful enterprise. Moments later, the lights lowered and they were announced. There was a lot of fog, then a strange electronic sound cut through. Multicolored lights dissipated the darkness and five men came into view. Applause ensued. The song kick-started, the guys dove into their performances. All of them were very handsome and very well dressed. Actually, they were *fashionable*. Shaggy, yet styled hair, unusual but avant-garde clothes and makeup- they were definitely wearing makeup. I had never seen it on Nigel before. He looked good, very good. He wasn't wearing his glasses. He wore tight black pants and a puffy, ruffled blouse. His hair was different- it was dyed a reddish color and it hung longer over his eyes. I barely recognized him; he looked like one of the musicians on one of his many record album covers. He confidently danced a bit behind the bass guitar he skillfully played. The lights flattered him. He looked amazing on that stage. I stared at him wide eyed and enjoyed the view. Looking down at the crowd, I noticed that I wasn't the only one. Most of the people were dancing and minding their own business, but some were clinging to the stage, gazing adoringly at the band. My jealousy rekindled. I tried to pay attention only to the music, which was quite good. The show was impressive, especially for such young guys.

When they finished their set, they escaped into the back. The lights became a bit brighter and the deejay began playing dance music again. I stood up and peered over the edge of the balcony, hoping to see Nigel somewhere. I looked all over and couldn't find him. I was bent over the railing, determined to be the first girl Nigel saw after the show. I then felt a hand on my ass. I turned around angrily, expecting to find Patrick, but it was Nigel.

"Oh my God! Nigel!" I cried, clutching my heart.

"Nigel? It's been a long time since anyone has called me that here."

He was smiling. He'd obviously hurried from the stage right up to me. He was sweaty and still had the makeup on. I couldn't have cared less, I threw my arms around him. He squeezed me tightly. I had forgotten how much I missed his arms around me. I couldn't let go. "Pat told me you were up here," he said to me during our embrace. "You look amazing!"

I finally let him go. "I'm so glad to see you. I've missed you so bad." I looked him over. "God, you look so . . . different."

He laughed. "Yeah, this is my alter ego."

"John, huh?"

"Yeah, John. That's what everyone calls me."

"Not everyone," I reminded. "You'll always be Nigel to me."

"Okay," he agreed. "So, do you want me to show you around? I can introduce you to the guys!"

"Do they know who I am?" I questioned him, afraid that I might have gotten lost with Nigel's identity.

"Of course, they know who you are! Although, they don't believe you exist, they think I've got an imaginary girlfriend in *America*. Everyone else has a girlfriend *here*."

I was glad he said that last part. "Everyone else," meaning everyone but him. He hadn't replaced me. I smiled, and felt so relieved. He offered his hand, I took it and he led me away.

Backstage, the guys were all burning off steam, drinking and loudly laughing and joking around. "Hey guys, calm down for a minute. There's a lady present," Nigel announced. He pulled me by his side and proudly smiled down at me. "Everyone, this is Michelle, my very real girlfriend. Michelle, this is everyone."

"Hi guys. It's nice to meet you all," I said politely.

"Ah, the American girlfriend. I was sure he made you up. I mean, what woman would be seen with this bloke?" the guitarist teased.

I was surprised to hear that. Judging by the reaction of the girls in the crowd earlier, he surely couldn't have a hard time getting female attention. I must have had a confused look on my face, Nigel noticed.

"Don't mind him, he's just jealous. That's Randy. And that's Mick, Sammy, and Rodney," he pointed out the members.

"Don't listen to that guy," Sammy, the singer, said pointing at Randy. "John talks about you all the time. He's always goin' on about how pretty you are and how great you are and how much he misses you. Don't you, John?"

I looked at him. "Is that true, *John?*" He looked embarrassed. I squeezed his hand and smiled at him.

Patrick appeared. "Well, what did you think of the show?" he asked me.

"I was blown away! The sound is so fresh, so different. And I like how you have that tough guitar element, that's unique. It's really catchy."

"Not like the new American music?" he inquired. The guys all were waiting on my commentary.

"No, not at all. It's mostly rock dominated there. Kind of stagnant, I think."

They all seemed pleased to hear that. We chatted for a while. It was after two in the morning when everyone started to leave.

Nigel got up and I did the same. We all said our goodbyes and went our separate ways. Nigel hung by my side. "Where are you staying?" he asked.

"In town, not far from here," I answered. "What about you? Do you have to go home?"

"Well, no, I mean, my parents know I have crazy nights and they don't really expect me to be home at any particular time."

"So . . . do you want to stay with me tonight?"

"Yes, I would," he smiled.

I smiled back. I really had missed him and wanted to be with him, but after seeing him tonight, I couldn't help but feel some distance between us. It was like he was a different person living a life I didn't know much about.

We walked to my hotel, keeping the conversation steady, but light. Mostly we talked about the show and the band and the club and things like that. When we got in my room, there was awkward silence. Neither of us knew what to say or do with each other. Part of me wanted to ask him a million personal questions. I wanted to know how he felt about me now. Part of me wanted to get naked with him right away. I didn't know what to do, and he seemed as uncomfortable and unsure as I was.

I sat on the edge of the bed, staring at him. Here, away from the club, under fluorescent lights, he looked so out of place, like in a Halloween costume on November first. I tried to look past that, to the boy I met in literature class two years ago.

"Are you tired?" he asked me with concern. "This must have been a long day for you."

"I am, but I don't want to sleep. I'm too revved up. I can't believe this. I'm here with you again. And now you're a star!"

He rolled his eyes. "I'm not a star. I just play bass in a band. I also wash glasses and clean up at the club, it's not all glamorous."

"It looks glamorous. I mean, look at you. *Totally* glam. It's hard to recognize you."

"Don't say that. It's still me, same old Nigel."

"Is it? Are you still Nigel in there?"

"Of course I am. I just think we need to get reacquainted. It's been too long."

"I agree. And I want to know the details of your new life and career. Tell me everything."

"Alright, you too. But first, let me just wash all this makeup off."

I opened my mouth to say something as he got up and headed for the bathroom, but thought better of it. I was glad he was taking off his face paint, but it was odd that he was the one who needed to wash off his makeup instead of me.

While he was in the bathroom, I changed out of my clothes and into the pajamas I wore almost every night- his old striped shirt. It was quite faded and ragged now, but I loved it. It reminded me of him, and it made me feel like I was still sleeping with him, even if he wasn't with me.

He came out of the bathroom, toweling water off of his face. He had taken his shirt off to wash up. All of the makeup was gone, and I could recognize him again.

His hair was partially wet. Water continued to drip down his neck and chest. When I looked up from my suitcase I was frozen, paralyzed with lust. Simultaneously, he caught me, wearing nothing but his old shirt, oversized on me. His arm fell limp at his side and he dropped the towel. I stood up straight, eyes still fixed on him. He took a step forward toward me and then instantly we rushed into each other, madly kissing and embracing.

I was extremely turned on; I knew he was, too. He threw me down on the bed and pawed me, kissed me, grinded on me. I clutched him, anxious to have him close to my body again. He savagely kissed, licked, and nibbled on me as I squirmed to get his pants down. I struggled, desperate to unveil him. He quit sucking my neck and shifted to rip his pants off while I took off my shirt.

Wordlessly, he repositioned himself on top of me and entered. We both grumbled, mine a surprised gasp, his a comfortable moan.

"God, I forgot how good you feel," he groaned lowly in my ear.

I was too overcome to reply, but I felt the same way. I had also forgotten how good it felt to be with him and how lonely I was without him.

Also, the way our bodies fit together and worked together was magic. I had missed that. I was trying to concentrate enough to immortalize every moment in my head, but my current state of bliss had me practically on another planet. I felt the smile push my cheeks up, my eyes gently closed. Pleasure lapped over me like warm waves on the shore.

"Oh fuck," he broke my trance.

"What?"

"I almost came. I don't have a condom or anything. "

"It's okay. I'm on The Pill."

"You are? Why?"

" . . . Um, I thought I might want to have sex with my boyfriend."

He looked confused for a minute, like he was afraid I was having sex with someone else. After all, I had only started taking birth control after being away from him for months. He looked as if he figured out that I had done it for him and resumed.

I was glad I was on contraceptives. It was easier, more convenient and no hassle. I was sure he appreciated it, too, because he seemed to enjoy himself on a new level.

We were back on that familiar plane of ecstasy. The pleasure increased, higher and higher. I could feel him swell inside me and he surely felt me tighten around him. My toes curled. He stopped panting and seemed to stop breathing altogether.

With an astonished moan, he thrust deeply. Then he finished with a few final thrusts before collapsing down onto me, face buried in my hair.

He was sweaty and warm. I sighed with satisfaction and put my arms around him. He lied there, heaving, eventually catching his breath, but too depleted to move. His weight on me decreased my ability to catch my own breath, but I didn't care. I preferred him to be as close as possible.

He lifted his head and looked into my eyes. He smiled. He didn't say anything, and he didn't have to. I read his expression and reciprocated with one of equal warmth and meaning. We continued the gaze for a long moment. His eyes traveled around my face, as if soaking it in. He brought his lips to mine. We kissed, holding each other, trying to achieve the same level of closeness and contentment. I was happier and more fulfilled than I'd been in far too long.

We lied in bed, staring at the ceiling, enjoying the moment. His arm was around me, my head rested on his chest. I listened to his heart beating. He played with my hair.

"I've missed you so much," I confessed.

"I've missed you, too."

"I miss this, I miss being next to you. Holding you, hearing your voice."

"And the sex isn't bad either."

"No, it's not. It's great. I'm really happy right now. I just don't want it to end."

"I wish it didn't have to either. . . . Hey! Move back home! That was your plan anyway, right? We can get a place together!"

"Live together?"

"Yeah! Why not?" He sat up, all excited. "We could support each other! We can live out our dreams! I'll have my band and you can be a famous writer. . . . This is perfect! Don't you think? You said it yourself, the scene around here is so cutting edge, so much more is happening."

I slowly sat up, wide awake now. "Yeah, but . . . "

"But what?" He picked up my hand and held it. "I want to be with you. It's too hard having you across the world. How long do I have to wait to have you in my life again?"

If he had any idea how much power he had over me, I'm sure he would have asked me to do more than just move in with him. And I would have done *anything* he asked. If it was a choice between living with my parents in a lush neighborhood in America and living with Nigel in a cardboard box in a third world country, the choice was obvious.

Still, I was unsure if we could survive on our own. Also, I was less positive that our relationship was as strong as it was before I moved away.

"Are you sure you want to do this? Maybe we should sleep on it."

"I'll feel the same way when I wake up."

"So, this isn't just the sex talking?"

"No, it's not. Well, maybe a little bit, but can you blame me?" he kidded. " No, my heart wants you here. And my hands want you here," he said, squeezing mine. "And my lips want you here." He kissed me. "And my eyes and ears, so I can wake up to your beautiful face every day and hear you say, "I love you."

His eyes were soft and dewy. He meant that. I understood from his tone that he meant more than just that. I felt like he was attempting to commit on a deeper level, to try to explain how much he loved and needed me.

"Nigel, I- . . . I- . . . I think I need to think about it for a while."

His eyes changed from adoring to disappointed. It broke my heart. It wasn't that I wasn't sure I loved him, it was just that moving in together was a big step that we hadn't really discussed before and now that it was on the table, I was scared.

I tried to console him. "I love you. Come here." I lied back down and pulled him close to me. I hiked up the blankets around us and combed his hair out of his face with my fingers. He closed his eyes as I continued to stroke his hair. It wasn't long before his breathing turned shallow and quieter as he drifted to sleep. I reached over and turned off the lamp.

As my eyes adjusted, the dim light coming from the shrouded window and the glowing alarm clock were all that illuminated the room. I could see his face, though. And despite the fact I was in an unknown hotel room, thousands of miles away from my house, I felt like I was home.

I woke up later in the morning, not knowing where I was at first. For a moment, I was frightened, and then I heard Nigel murmur in his sleep as he snuggled closer to me. My heart melted.

I looked at the sleeping angel beside me and I felt better than I had in months. I had gotten used to the loneliness and longing. Familiar pain. With him, I always felt whole, like I was where I belonged. I was home, no matter where we were. Those feelings rushed back with a euphoric tidal wave. It felt good. Familiar joy.

I felt a chill, and then remembered I was naked. Then I remembered what had happened earlier that morning. It was good. Not just physically, but to be spiritually reunited was what I longed for.

It felt like old times- just me and him. Together, the way it was meant to be. I was crazy to think his fledgling musical career would put an obstacle between us. He was still the same; I was the same. The real obstacle was distance. *I* had put the obstacle there. *I* had to fix it.

I liked being in America, where things were familiar. But home truly was where Nigel was. I had to be with him, I couldn't leave him again. I surely couldn't ask him to move to me. He had started something amazing here. He was realizing his dream. My biggest dream was to be with him.

It was settled. I had to move back to Cambridge.

I looked over at him to check if he was still asleep. He was. I wanted to wake him for two reasons. One, to discuss my decision with him. Two, to look into his beautiful eyes, to interact with him, to prove this wasn't just a lovely dream.

He looked so peaceful, so perfect. I studied his face. I wanted to capture this picture in my memory.

"Stop staring at me," he mumbled, never opening his eyes.

I laughed. "I'm sorry. If you weren't so cute, I wouldn't."

"Well, I can't help that," he groaned out with a stretch.

"I know you can't," I teased. "Did you sleep well?"

"Yeah, I did. Better than I have in a long time. I think it's the way you smell. It comforts me."

I needed to hear that.

"What time is it?" he asked.

"Almost noon."

"Aww . . . I have band practice soon."

"Really? You do?"

"Yeah, we have another show tonight. And I have to go home first. Check in with my parents, change my clothes, you know."

"Oh, right." I was disappointed. I wanted to talk about our future. I didn't want to drop a bomb and then say goodbye. "When can I see you again?"

"You'll come to the show, right?"

"If you want me to, I'll be there."

"Of course I do! But I think tonight, after the set, I'll just take off so we can be alone to talk."

"That sounds good. It's a date."

He went home and I knew I had to call my parents and explain that my week long vacation was going to turn into a permanent residency. I had a very hard time making the call. I stalled, trying to kill as much time as I could. Finally, I mustered up some courage and dialed. My dad answered.

"Hello?"

"Hi, Dad. I'm in Cambridge."

"Oh, good. You got there safe?"

"Yeah . . . I'm here safe." I dreaded giving my news.

"Okay. When is your flight back?"

"Well, that's what I wanted to talk about . . . I want to move back here."

He was silent. Angry, I'm sure. "You want to live there?"

"Yes. You know I never wanted to move away."

"Is this only about Nigel? Can't you find a boyfriend in America?" He was getting louder and irate.

"No, I can't. I mean, I can but I won't. I need to be with Nigel."

"So, you're choosing him over your own family?"

"No, I'm not choosing! I'm not leaving you! I just want to be with him."

"You're going to drop out of school and live- where? Who is going to support you? Nigel? Did he start making six figures since we left?"

"I haven't decided yet where I'll live. I'll get a job."

"A job? Any job you're going to get is not going to pay your rent and all those expenses you don't even know about *and* your tuition."

"Well, then, I guess I won't be going to school!"

" . . . What? You're going to throw your life away on some boy who is probably not even going to last six months with you in the real world?"

"Well, I think I'd rather take my chances with him than come home to you! I'm so sick of you and mom criticizing every decision I make- "

"Then stop making stupid decisions!"

"You never support me! You're never proud of me! Only when you're disappointed in me do you pay any attention to me! No wonder I'd rather be with someone who values me and my company."

"Trust me, I know what he values and he knows he can get it every night, now."

I felt like I had been slapped in the face. That was a low blow. I hung up. I sat stunned on the hotel bed for at least ten minutes, replaying the conversation in my head, especially the last part. How could a father say that to his little girl?

I remembered other fights we'd had. There weren't many, but usually they got pretty nasty. And no one ever apologized, all was swept under the rug . . . at least until the next big fight.

I imagined what was going on at my house right now. My father telling my mother what had happened; her taking his side, no doubt. If he'd told her the last thing he'd said, I'm sure she would disapprove, but silently agree. They never understood my relationship with Nigel. But why did they have to speak badly about him? He was nothing but respectful. Did they resent him for taking my virginity? Did they dislike him because he wasn't the typical, boring American they would've preferred? Or were they jealous that our love was deeper and stronger than their love was and that moving me away from him didn't destroy that?

I had no idea what the reason was. Even though I was infuriated with my parents, I was also greatly saddened that things turned out this way. I felt like a failure for disappointing them, but I had no choice. Still, I wished things could have worked out amicably. I wished my parents were happy for me for once. I wished I didn't have to choose between pleasing them and pleasing myself.

I was depressed. I took a shower to try to wash away my funk. It didn't work. When I got out, I intended on dressing up again to go to the club, but instead I put on casual clothes and sat around, unable to focus or care about anything.

I thought about my living arrangements. Where *was* I going to live? Could we afford it on our own? What if things didn't work out? Could

I go home again? Would I be welcome? Was this all a mistake? Would I ever talk to my parents again?

Questions spun around my head. My emotions raged, everything from anger to disgust to bitterness and sadness. I lied in my bed, crying on and off. Although I hadn't eaten since the day before, I felt sick when I thought about food.

I lost track of time completely. Between the fight and the jet lag and the excitement, I was wiped out and fell asleep. Without meaning to, I slept for almost twelve hours. I was awoken by a knock on the door.

"Michelle, are you in there?"

It was Nigel. I sat up quickly, but was dazed. My blurry eyes read the glowing alarm clock numbers. "One a.m.?" I mumbled with disbelief. I hurried to the door, tripping on the way. I opened it and saw Nigel looking frantic.

"Where the hell were you?" he demanded.

The tone of his voice was like salt in my wounds. I was not ready for more retaliation. He evaluated my face: my puffy eyes, my red nose, a frown I couldn't get rid of.

"What happened? Are you alright?" He changed in demeanor, suddenly worried and upset.

"I'm sorry. I should've been at your show." I backed away from the door, making room for him to come in, and then shut the door behind him.

"I don't care about that, I thought something happened to you when you weren't there. I was scared to death when no one saw you or heard from you. I ran down here right after I knew you hadn't shown up."

I nodded, looking down, feeling the tears start to well up. "I got in a fight with my dad," I said quietly with a wavering voice.

"You did? What about?" He took my hand and led me to the bed to sit. He sat closely beside me and put his arm around me.

My lips trembled. "I told them I wasn't coming home, that I wanted to stay here with you."

He sat up straight. "You're staying?"

I nodded. He smiled brightly, like a child on Christmas morning.

"You're STAYING?" he repeated.

I couldn't help but grin in spite of myself over his enthusiasm. It distracted me from my depression. He jumped up and pulled me up. He threw his arms around me and squeezed me tightly.

"Oh my God, I'm so happy! My girl is back! Oh, I love you so much." He kissed me hard, taking my breath away. "This is great news! No need to be sad!"

"Well, my parents are going to be really mad. My dad pretty much told me I was a dumb slut."

"What? Did he really? Fuck that! Fuck your dad! Listen, we're starting a new life, me and you, and it's going to be great. All we need is each other! Let's promise, nothing is going to tear us apart again. Not parents, not distance, nothing." His eyes were intense, he stared into mine, waiting for a response.

"Okay," I answered quietly.

"Okay?" he questioned my response.

"Okay," I agreed, louder and more assured.

"Okay?" he probed.

"Okay!" I shouted, laughing. I believed him. He made me believe him. Everything was going to be alright, and it was going to be good, because we were together.

I stayed in that hotel for a week. It took that long to find an apartment that was in the right area at the right price. I was lucky, too, because I didn't even have a job. Nigel knew a guy who knew a guy who owned the building. I had all my money wired to Cambridge to pay the first month's rent and the deposit. However, all my things were in America, so I would need to go back.

Nigel offered to go back with me, but one round trip plane ticket was expensive enough, though I really wanted the support. I fretted about the meeting with my parents from the time we had the fight over the phone until the moment I stepped on the porch. I had taken a cab from the airport, not wanting to ask them for the favor of picking me up.

I knocked twice before finding my key and opening the door. No one was home. That was a relief. My mother had decorated for Christmas while I was gone. I felt a twinge of sentimentality and desire to be home for the holidays. I pushed it aside. I almost felt like I wasn't a part of the family anymore. I convinced myself that Nigel was my family and my future.

I went to my room and started going through my things, making piles of what I wanted to take with me most. Some things I hadn't even unpacked, though I had lived there almost a year. I was so engrossed in my sorting that I didn't notice the sound of my mother coming home. She entered my room quietly.

"You're home," she stated. "I thought there was a burglar in the house."

"Yeah, I'm sorry I didn't give you any warning. I just didn't want to call and upset you more," I admitted quietly, still organizing my things.

"Well, you and I didn't get the chance to talk about this. I think we should," she said gently, sitting down on my bed.

"Okay. But I don't know what there is to talk about. I told you from the very beginning that I want to be with Nigel, and that hasn't changed."

"I understand. Do you have to move right away, though?"

"Yes! I already had to spend the past year without him and that was hard enough. I don't want to say goodbye to him ever again."

"Alright, alright," she said calmly. "Just don't be mad at your dad. He was far too hard on you, but he was upset. He doesn't want you to move and neither do I. I know you love Nigel, I guess more than I thought you did, but you are our only daughter, our only child. We don't like the idea of you living on another continent. You're only eighteen. You're still our little girl and we want to take care of you."

"Well, if Dad had phrased it like that instead of instantly lashing out and calling me a whore, maybe I would have considered staying here. But I promised Nigel I was moving back, and my last conversation with Dad really made me want to. Nigel will take care of me. He loves me."

"I know, I know. But, he's what, nineteen? Is he going to be able to support you? Does he even have a job?"

"Yes, he does. And I'll just have to get one, too. We'll be fine. We'll be just like every other couple starting out."

She relaxed a bit, realizing I was right. But the worry never left her face. She took a deep breath in and slowly exhaled. Then she changed the subject. "How long are you staying here?"

"I didn't know if I should even spend the night. I mean, the way things were left when I talked to Dad last- "

"Of course you're staying here! Dad feels terrible about the way things were left. He'll be glad to see you."

"Okay, I'll stay. But I'm only here until tomorrow."

"Okay." She got up and was about to walk out the door, but turned around. "I just want you to know that if things don't work the way you had planned- "

I scowled at her for insinuating that.

" -or if you and Nigel ever want to live in America instead, you always have a home here. Don't forget that. You are always welcome. And we will always love you." She walked out.

I felt tears burn the corners of my eyes. I had really mixed feelings toward my parents. I could never tell how they felt about me and I wasn't totally sure about how I felt about them. I had no concept of family and what that was supposed to mean. It felt odd to hear things like that.

I continued packing and sorting. I heard the front door open and slam shut as my dad came home. I heard low murmurs, my mother likely explaining that I was home and that my dad should be nice to me. I heard him converse with her, but I couldn't make out the words. I was getting nervous. I was not looking forward to the discussion we were about to have.

Footsteps creaked on the stairs, giving me warning. I busied myself. My dad knocked on the open door. "Can I come in?"

"Sure, it's your house," I retorted.

"It's your house, too."

"Is it?"

"Yes, of course. It will always be your home."

"No plans of moving again, then?" I mocked.

"No, we're here for good. Why don't you stay, too?"

I bristled. He was being nice to coerce me into staying in America with them. "No. I promised Nigel."

"So, he means more to you than your own parents?"

"*He's* always shown me love and support. And not because I'm *easy*."

"Okay, I'm sorry I said those things on the phone. I didn't mean that. I know he loves you and you obviously love him. Does he love you enough to move here? Would he be willing to give up everything that you'll be giving up to be with him?"

"He would have moved here a year ago if he had the money!"

"I'll *give* you money. Tell him you both can live here now."

"No, Dad. I want to live there. And I want to do it on my own. We'll be fine, but this is something we need to do ourselves."

My father looked disappointed. I didn't like that I hurt him, even though he had hurt me so much recently. "I understand," he finally said.

"Good. I'm glad." I went back to my packing.

"Maybe, if I'd made more time for you when you were growing up, it wouldn't be so easy to leave your daddy."

A lump appeared in my throat. I tried to swallow it and hold in my tears. "May*be*," I quietly responded

He nodded. " . . . Okay, then. Go be with Nigel. I'm glad you have someone who cares about you as much as he does," he said softly with remorse as he walked out of the room.

When he was gone, I could no longer hold in my tears, but I kept packing up. I was eager to get out of the house. It was too emotionally draining.

୯ଓ

The next day, my parents drove me, Autumn, and all the things I could cram into their car to the airport. There were hugs and goodbyes and promises to keep in touch and commitments made to come home if things didn't work out. It was a sad departure, but there was a chasm between us. I needed to start fresh and stop living under their thumb. I was ready to start being an adult, but I was glad I wouldn't have to take the leap alone. I thanked my lucky stars again for Nigel.

He was there to pick me up at the airport with a smile so wide and warm I fell in love with him all over again. I ran to him. He held me tight and said, "C'mon, let's go home."

Chapter 8

"It's more like a social thing."

Nigel, Autumn, and I moved into our tiny apartment. We were thrilled . . . and broke. Christmas was around the corner. I sent home gifts to my parents and they sent me money as my present, which was greatly needed. Nigel and I had a ten dollar (or, rather, ten *pound*) limit on the gifts we exchanged that year. He bought me a tenner's worth of used records that he knew I would like. I bought him a few interesting looking guitar picks and spent the remainder on the best chocolate I could afford to make him cookies. Despite the low monetary value, I think we put more time and effort into those gifts than any other we had ever exchanged. Of course, we already had the best present of all- each other.

We spent our Christmas day with his parents and our Christmas night in bed.

When the holidays were over, it was time to get serious about supporting ourselves. It was 1980, a new year, a new decade, and a new life that was bright and promising. Nigel quit college, which I wasn't happy about, but he was convinced he was better off concentrating on his music instead of art studies. I didn't even have the opportunity to go to school; even if I wanted to, we couldn't afford it. He made a little bit of money at the club, and whatever was left over after buying equipment and clothes and supplies went into the house fund.

I got a job in a boutique downtown. It was great. They had the trendiest clothes, vintage and unusual modern stuff. With any money I had leftover, I pieced together an awesome wardrobe. Nigel would come in and visit me during the day. Sometimes he'd bring in one of the guys from the band, usually Mick (the fashionable keyboardist) and they would buy something to use in their elaborate costumes. I was impressed with their audacity to wear makeup and women's clothes. It was taboo and very sexy to me.

We gradually furnished our apartment with hand me downs, thrift store specials and other bits and pieces we were able to afford. The first thing we bought was a bed. Of course, that was the most important thing, and the most used thing in the place. We had a lot of fun shopping and choosing how to represent ourselves to the guests who would visit our home, carefully selecting artwork to display and other odds and ends. But none of that really mattered; all we really cared about was that we had our own little place where we could be together and share our love.

We were happy, truly happy. We didn't have much money, but we both had so much hope and so many dreams that we were sure would come true. It was hard not to, he was already in a great band. I was constantly inspired to write and paint. And, we had each other- the ultimate dream come true.

And yet, occasionally, Nigel would enter a dark period where he was moody and quiet. I loved his smile so much, but all I would get was a frown. He didn't want affection, he didn't want to talk; he would just shut down and pick fights.

One night, after a show, we were sitting around with the guys. All of them, their girlfriends, some bouncers, and people who worked at the club were sitting around a few tables together. There was booze flowing. The bar was open to us and there were pints and bottles and glasses everywhere. Everyone was drinking, some more, some less. Everyone was having a good time- telling stories, listening to stories, joking around, a bit of making out was involved . . . Randy, in particular, could get the attention of the crowd with a great tale about his lively past. I remember Sammy trying hardest to win over the random transient females. Rodney was pretty focused on his steady girlfriend.

Mick, gregarious as usual, drink in hand, was chatting someone up. Nigel was the only one I couldn't figure out.

Usually he was the life of the party. Laughing, smiling, and joking around, everyone's favorite guy. But something was different about him lately. He didn't act the same. He was paying me less attention, and I could handle that, but there was something else about him. He was never focused and he would disappear throughout the night. I missed him. I felt like we already spent too much time apart and sometimes, after the show was the only opportunity we had to see each other.

He would stay at the club, socializing and partying with the group of guys. I would have to go home and get some sleep before work the next morning. Sometimes I could talk him into coming home with me, but often he resented the fact that I had a day job and those responsibilities when his line of work caused him to be a night owl. He perceived me as being a wet blanket, I think. But in actuality, I was trying to provide a foundation for us in case his band didn't do as well as he expected. This was a source of tension for us and caused many fights. I wanted him home with me and all he wanted to do was party.

Many mornings at work, I would complain to my coworkers. I tried to explain his behavior and they would listen and sympathize. Of course, when women talk, it's usually hearsay and man bashing, and this was no different.

"He sounds like he's on drugs," my coworker, Victoria said.

"Shut up, don't say that to her!" another coworker, Sarah said.

"No, really," continued Victoria. "This sounds quite a bit like something that happened to my cousin. Her boyfriend was in a band and all these dodgy guys were always hanging around him. She noticed he was acting different and getting testy and he was usually such a sweetie. Anyway, before long, she caught him shooting up heroin."

"Heroin? Come on now. Nigel isn't like that," Sarah defended.

"Okay, I'm sure he's not on heroin, but it kinda sounds the same, doesn't it?"

I didn't answer. She was right, the stories did sound similar.

"We're in a band and we don't do heroin," Sarah pointed out.

"You guys started a band?" I asked, intrigued.

"Yeah, just a few weeks ago," Victoria answered.

"So, not long enough to get into heroin, huh?" I joked. Victoria snickered.

Sarah intervened. "Hey, don't worry about it. It's probably just a phase. He's got a lot of things going on right now, he probably doesn't know how to deal with it. Why don't you talk to him about it?"

"Yeah, I guess I should," I said quietly. But I didn't want to. Just like that guy in Victoria's story, Nigel, who was usually a sweetie was also testy lately. I wondered how he would react to my inquisition.

After thinking about it all day, I decided how to go about discussing the matter with Nigel. He didn't have a show that night, just rehearsal in the afternoon, and would be home shortly after me. I hurried back to our apartment after work and began making dinner.

"Hi," he greeted as he came in the door.

"Hi, honey. How was your day?"

"Ugh, we were trying to write some new songs and it's so hard to get everyone to agree on the right sound, you know? It's like, I feel like I know what direction to go in, but then, we all have to agree and it's so irritating." He sank down on the sofa with a groan.

"Are you hungry?" I asked from the kitchen.

"No, not really."

"I made dinner."

"Oh, okay then. I'll eat." He reluctantly picked himself up and moseyed to the table as I set it. He sat in his usual seat, leaned back and sighed.

"You don't have to eat if you don't want to." It was my turn to be irritated.

"No, no, it's fine."

I turned my back to retrieve some silverware and made a face I didn't want him to see. I finished setting the table in silence. I didn't like talking to him when he was in this type of mood; he was too easily set off. But I knew I had to broach the subject of his recent behavior.

I picked up his plate and filled it halfway with food, knowing he didn't want to eat at all. He didn't look up. He looked like a tired, mopey child. I didn't like it. I set his plate in front of him and watched him slowly pick up his fork and play around with his food as I made up my plate. I was beginning to lose my appetite, too.

But, I decided to break the ice. "It's been a long time since we had dinner together at home."

"Yeah, I guess it has been."

"I miss this, when it's quiet, just me and you."

He smiled at me. "Me, too." Then he looked back at his plate as he stabbed at his dinner. "We should appreciate these moments, I doubt it will be like this when the band takes off."

I frowned. "What do you mean?"

He looked puzzled and aggravated. "What do I mean? Don't you realize I'll be going on tour? I mean, think about it, I'll be gone for months at a time. I won't be home for *dinner*." He said the last word with disdain, like he didn't think things like that were important.

I was quiet, taken aback. Not only was he telling me he was planning on leaving for 'months at a time', but he was also talking to me like I was too stupid to realize that that was the plan. He was also quiet, still stabbing at the food on his plate while apparently contemplating.

He started again. "You know, why didn't you think I would be going on tour when the band takes off? Do you not think we'll be successful?" His tone was half hurt, half accusing. "Because I thought you were the one person who believed in me fully, even more than I believe in myself."

"Nigel, you know I believe in you. I think the band you started is amazing. It's not that I don't think you'll be successful, I guess I just didn't see that as an option. I didn't think our future would consist of you always being on the road, touring every country, gone for months at a time."

"Well, this is my job. That's what happens when you're good at your job. That's the goal."

"Well, we've never talked about this before."

"So, let's talk about it now."

" . . . Okay."

"You don't like the idea of me going off, is that it?"

"How could I like the idea of you going off?"

"I'm doing this for us, for our future."

"What kind of future are we going to have if you are never home?"

"Hey, we didn't stop loving each other when you lived in America for a year!"

"I had no choice! I didn't want to leave you. It was the hardest thing I ever had to do!"

"I don't want to leave you either, but if you care about me as much as you say you do, it shouldn't be a problem."

"You don't think I love you enough, is that what you're saying?"

"Well, you aren't happy for me, you don't want me to further my career. You know how much this means to me. It's all I want!"

"*All* you want?"

"Don't. Don't read into that. This is my calling, this is what I'm supposed to do with my life."

"Not start a family with me? Being a rock star is the only thing you care about?"

"I'm not ready to start a family. Are you? We're too young to start this shit. Isn't it better that I go do this now before we're tied down?"

"News flash, buddy. You are tied down! You aren't some free bird, you are mine! And this is important. If all you care about is being a big shot, you might not have a girl to come home to!"

"What the fuck are you saying? You want to break up with me? Is this how it's going to go down?"

"No, I don't want to break up. I want my Nigel back!"

"*News flash, buddy.* Nigel is gone! Stop calling me that, I'm John!"

"John, huh? Well, John, why don't you go back to your drugs and leave me the fuck alone."

His eyes blazed with anger. He stood up and powerfully threw his dish to the side. It crashed and splintered, splattering food all over the floor. He gave me a foul sneer and headed to the door.

I wanted to get one last crack in before he was gone. "Hey John, if you ever see Nigel again, tell him to come home, *he's* the one I love."

He slammed the door so hard I thought it would split in half.

I sat with my head in my hands for a long time. I was too upset to care about the food stains setting into the carpet. I couldn't believe we had a fight like that. I couldn't believe my plan of having a nice dinner with meaningful conversation ended up this way. Usually I was so patient with him and so good at controlling my anger. But this time, I had enough. I was tired of his attitude and couldn't keep myself from showing it. Yet I really hated that he was gone and was so pissed off at me.

I wondered where he was. Where could he go? To a friend's house? Did he have some groupie waiting for me to mess up so she could swoop in? All I could fathom was him in another girl's bed, him complaining about me, her comforting him, saying *she* would never act that way.

As my jealousy fueled ridiculous daydreams, Autumn had come out of hiding after our argument and was helping herself to the food on the floor. I shooed her away from the shattered dish fragments. I leaned against the wall, sighed and closed my eyes. I needed to pull myself together. I was making myself crazy. I needed a distraction. I cleaned up the mess before the cat got into it again. Then I put away what was left of our meal. Then, I did the dishes and put those away. I went around, tidying up the rest of the apartment to vent my frustrations. I wore myself out. I decided to wash up and get ready for bed. I didn't know if Nigel was going to come home that night or not. I just wanted to forget about it and go to sleep.

I took a shower and then while drying off, walked into the bedroom to put on my pajamas. I picked up my nightshirt, his old shirt I always wore. I dropped my towel.

"Stop." I heard a voice from behind me.

I jumped and screamed at the same time.

Nigel laughed. "Don't put that on."

All I wanted to do was cover up, I was naked and uncomfortable. "Why?"

"You cleaned up. You picked up all the mess *I* made, and now you're putting on *my* old shirt?"

I looked at him strangely. "Yeah . . . "

"I'm just surprised. I thought I was going to come home to boxes and suitcases. Or worse, an empty flat and a 'Dear John' letter."

"No. I would at least write a 'Dear Nigel' letter," I quietly joked.

He laughed. He put his arms around me. "I'm sorry."

"*I'm* sorry. I can't believe I said those things."

"No, *I* said terrible things. I wish I hadn't."

"Please don't think I don't want your dreams to come true," I begged.

"I don't! I don't think that. I shouldn't have reacted that way. I don't know what came over me."

I was wondering that myself, but I just wanted to put it behind us. "Well, we can't go back, so let's just forgive each other."

"Agreed . . . So, what are you willing to do to make it up to me?"

I giggled. "Oh, I don't know. I can think of a few things."

"Hmm, like what?"

We started kissing and soon he was also naked. We crashed down onto the unmade bed and wrestled around. We made love for a short, but intense period. When it was over, we lied close to each other, wordless and satisfied. I lightly stroked the soft hairs on his arm. I was totally contented, but Nigel seemed preoccupied.

He finally spoke. "Michelle, I want to talk about something."

I could tell this had to do with our fight earlier and I was reluctant to bring that up while I was on cloud nine. "Okay."

"You said . . . You said I was on drugs."

I swallowed hard. "Okay," I hesitantly repeated.

"Why did you say that?"

" . . . Um, I don't know."

"Yes, you do."

"I guess, sometimes it seems like . . . something is different about you and . . . I don't know, I thought maybe you were taking drugs." He was quiet. I elaborated. "I'm sure I'm wrong. But there *is* something going on with you lately."

"No, you're not wrong." Now, it was my turn to be quiet. I stared at him, disbelieving my own accusations when he admitted them. "Some of the guys at the club, they have . . . connections. We just were sitting around drinking one day and they pulled out some stuff and offered it up. I mean, we were partying, you know? So, we tried a little. And then, it just kind of became a thing we did sometimes."

"Sometimes? When?"

"Usually after the shows. Sometimes before."

It suddenly clicked as to why the staff at the club had been trying to keep me away from Nigel that first night before the show. As I remembered, he misread my silence as anger.

"I'm not addicted to anything," he defended. " It's more like a social thing."

"It's not heroin is it?"

"What? God, no! Mostly pot. It's really fine. Everyone does it, it's no big deal."

I still didn't like the idea. And I really didn't like that he had an alter ego when he was using. I was away from Nigel enough, I didn't want to not be with him when we were in the same room

"Okay, if you say so. Just, don't do it around me, alright? I don't want to see you like that. I prefer you like this."

"Okay, deal." He cuddled closer to me and kissed my head.

We drifted to sleep in each other's arms. It felt good to have my Nigel back.

When I went into work the next day, there were flyers in the front window. When I went inside, there was a stack of flyers by the cash register.

"What's this?" I asked Sarah, pointing to the pile of pink papers.

"They're advertisements for our show next week!"

"Oh, you're kidding? That's great! I can't believe you got a gig already, that's huge!"

"I know. I'm so excited! So, will you come?"

"Of course, I'll be there. I don't know who will close that night, but I'll go."

"Well, the show is at one a.m."

"Oh, well then, I guess closing won't be an issue."

"Hey, do you think the guys would go?" She was referring to Nigel's band.

"Um, yeah probably. I'll give them a flyer."

"Give them a bunch! Have them pass 'em out! I want this show to be huge and if the crowd sees Descent there, they will think we're big stuff."

She was right. Nigel's band was creating a bit of a stir. They were known as trendy, cool, and cutting edge, at least around our town.

That night, I was hanging out at the club with the band and their usual group of followers. I tried not to watch Nigel like a hawk, but I could tell he felt my judging eyes on him. He made a point of acting upbeat, fun, and sober. I did my best not to be suspicious.

"Hey guys, want to go to a show next week?" I asked enthusiastically.

"What show?" Nigel asked me.

"Who's playin'?" Randy asked.

"An all girl punk group. You know Sarah from the store? She started a band. They'll be at the Moonshine Pub."

"Oh, yeah? That might be interesting," Mick quipped.

"All girls? Okay, yeah," Sammy volunteered.

"Alright, let's give 'em a shot," Randy agreed.

"Great! They'll be thrilled," I beamed.

ଔ

The next day, when I told Sarah they would be there she screamed and hugged me. "This is going to be bloody marvelous! Everything has been going right! I hope it continues. I really don't want to work here forever. I'd love to be a professional musician. I guess I should learn how to play better . . . "

"Yeah, it's hard to practice when you're stuck here, folding shirts all the time," I joked.

"That's true. Man, if we had a better lead singer, we would have more gigs. Then, I could get paid to rock instead of ring up clothes." She looked solemn. Their current lead singer was Sarah's rough roommate, Suzy.

"Oh well, at least you get a discount on your band's apparel."

She brightened. "You're right. This was a good stepping stone. Next step, sold out arenas!"

All week, Victoria and Sarah were buzzing about their upcoming show. I was very excited to see it, too. I had heard enough about it.

I offered to help the girls with their makeup and costumes before the show. Sarah and I had put together the wardrobe at the boutique and when the girls were dressed, I was impressed. Their mission was to appear incredibly cool without seeming to care, and we nailed it. Sarah, Victoria, and Suzy were decked out in red leather and purple lace, stiletto heals, and combat boots, juxtaposing punk and sex. And, of course, their faces were painted over with thick black eyeliner, hot pink cheeks, dark red lips, and multicolored eyelids. They looked amazing, like they were already stars.

The four of us were crammed into this makeshift dressing room in the back of the pub. We didn't care that it was crowded, everyone was half drunk anyway. It was a lot of fun to be involved in their band. I could understand why Nigel liked this so much. Although I wasn't part of the fold, I felt like I was one of them.

"So, are you our groupie or what?" the lead singer, Suzy asked me.

"Well, since this is your first real show, I don't think so," I kidded her.

"No, I think she's an honorary member of the band!" Sarah announced and put an arm around me. "I mean, she's been helpin' us with our look, workin' our shifts so we can practice, *and* she got Descent to come here!"

I was proud. I felt needed and appreciated for the first time in a while.

"Yeah, but they might think you guys suck and throw their beer bottles at you. And Rodney has a wicked arm from all that drumming," I joked. Sarah pushed me, playfully.

"Ey! Speakin' of that, go out and see if Nigel's got the guys here yet," Suzy demanded in her thick accent.

I snuck out and peeked around the wall to check out the crowd. I first saw Mick with his platinum hair, and then was able to spot Rodney, Sammy, and Randy. Where was Nigel? I visually searched the vicinity and saw him by the bar. His back was to me. He was talking to someone. A girl. Who? I couldn't see . . . he was blocking my view. All I could make out was wavy blonde hair and a red dress.

"Well?" Suzy had crept up behind me. "Are they here?"

"Yeah," I said, turning away from the crowd and back behind the wall.

"Good. We'll be goin' on in ten minutes." She stumbled back to the "dressing room."

I was so nervous for them. I did feel like a member of the group even though I didn't play in the band. I sure had a lot of butterflies in my stomach. But, was it for them, or because I was worried about that girl Nigel was talking to? She could have been a waitress for all I knew. Or an old neighbor. Or someone from school. Or a sex crazed groupie who spotted him. I slowly walked back to the girls while fretting over the possibilities.

"Hey, where are you going to be during the show? Just in case we need anything?" Sarah asked.

"Um, I don't know. Where should I be?"

"You know, you should probably be out in the crowd so you can see how we look and sound. Just keep an eye on us. If we need you, I'll give you a signal."

"Like this one?" I held up my middle finger, playing around.

"Actually, yeah. We have to fit the persona, right? Punk rock bitches. But in England, we stick up two fingers, like this." She made the inappropriate gesture.

I laughed. "Okay, I'll keep my eye out for that."

"Thanks. Well, here goes nothin'."

"Good luck. You'll kick ass."

"I know," she said with a tone that conveyed no confidence at all.

I left them to get on stage and made my way through the crowd to stand alongside the guys. Again, I was able to find Mick first in the sea of people.

"Hey! Thanks for coming!" I shouted over the roar of the crowd.

"Oh, yeah, I'm really curious to hear them!"

"The girls are so excited you are here!" As I said that, I thought of the girl I had seen with Nigel. I looked around for him. Mick saw me. He entangled himself in the masses, trying to get to Nigel to tell him I was looking for him. I watched as he poked Nigel's shoulder. He looked up with annoyance. I couldn't hear, but I read Mick's lips say, "Michelle is looking for you."

Nigel looked up and over to where I was. I watched with questioning eyes as he spotted me, looking just a bit guilty. He turned back to the girl and said something quickly before hurrying to my side.

"Hi, baby. How is everything going?" He kissed my cheek.

"Um, good. They're about to go on any minute."

"Cool." The lights dimmed. He turned to the stage and put his arm around me. I took a breath, ready to ask him some questions when I was interrupted.

The announcer came on the stage to introduce the band.

"Ladies and Gentlemen, please give it up for Dirty Sweet!"

Nigel took his arm off of me to applaud and hoot. I halfheartedly did the same, still preoccupied with my worries.

The girls came out, Victoria taking her place behind her drum kit,

Sarah on the left behind her guitar, and Suzy front and center behind the microphone with her bass. They played great. They sounded good, they looked good, and their songs were good. They had the place roaring. I checked around me to see how everyone else was enjoying it. The guys were all bobbing their heads and/or dancing around. The rest of the crowd was doing the same.

As I scanned the audience, I found the girl in the red dress. She stood fairly close by, on the opposite side of Nigel as me. She looked like she was trying to get closer. I didn't want to stare, but I frequently looked her way. Yes, she was getting closer. I could see her more clearly now. I did not recognize her. She was pretty. Quite pretty. I caught her looking at Nigel, not noticing me. I looked over at him, he was fixated on the band.

I was unsure if this girl had intentions for him that he didn't know about or if he had been flirting too before he knew I was around. I looked back again for the blonde, she was gone. I realized I was supposed to be paying attention to my friends on stage. What kind of honorary member was I?

The set lasted about forty minutes and when it was over, the crowd was cheering like mad. The girls all reveled in it, bowing and waving. Sarah flipped off the crowd, which only resulted in more applause. At first, I laughed, but then I realized that was my cue. "I have to go! I'll be back!" I yelled to Nigel over the noise.

Heading back to the dressing room, I caught up with the girls. "That was unbelievable! The crowd really liked it."

"Yeah? You think so?" Sarah asked.

"Oh, definitely! I checked!" I confirmed with a smile.

"Well, let's go out there and talk to our adoring audience!" Victoria suggested.

All of us made our way back to the dance floor. The lights were a bit brighter now, making it easier to see. I found Nigel and made a beeline for him.

"Hi, honey!" I greeted him loudly in case that blonde vulture was standing by. I began visually searching around for her.

Nigel gave me a strange look. "Hi. What are you looking for?"

"Me? Oh, nothing in particular. Just checking the crowd. Lots of people here tonight. That's a good sign."

"Yeah, that was a great show. I think it was a success," he said to the band.

"Thanks. Thanks for coming," Sarah applauded.

Mick appeared. "It was very interesting. Your songs have a different edge. You had everyone dancing, that's for sure."

"Wow! Our first real show and I already feel like we made it!" Victoria beamed.

"So, anyone else here tonight worth mentioning?" I interrupted, really only asking Nigel. He had a confused look on his perfect face. I tried to compose myself. "You know, any other bands or local celebrities or . . . anything."

Randy chimed in. "Yeah, if you count this guy who, no joke, looked exactly like Cher." He exploded into laughter. Nigel joined in, too, nodding in agreement.

He apparently either didn't catch my drift or was avoiding the question. I was curious as to who that blonde was, but maybe she really was no one, or at least, no one to him.

But I couldn't get it out of my mind.

That night, home in bed, Nigel was reading a book. I was just sitting up, staring at the wall. Every once in a while, he would look over at me and ask, "Are you okay?" I would nod my head and mumble, "Yeah, fine," until he was convinced and went back to his book. After a few times, he put his book down with a sigh and turned over toward me.

"What's going on? Why do you look like a zombie?"

"Huh? I'm not doing anything."

"I know. You're just staring at the wall. What's up with you tonight?"

"I just- I just have a lot on my mind."

"From the show? Did anything exciting happen that I don't know about?"

"You tell me." It slipped out before I could edit myself. I cringed.

"What does that mean? Why have you been acting so strange lately?" He was irked and defensive. I hadn't meant to upset him, I just wanted an answer.

"Who was that blonde girl you were talking to at the bar?" I blatantly threw the question out there. Couldn't tiptoe around it now.

He looked puzzled. I couldn't tell if he genuinely didn't know what

I was talking about or if he was trying to decide how to answer. "I don't know. Some girl. I never met her before tonight."

"So she was hitting on you?"

"I don't know. She was asking me stuff. She didn't give me her telephone number or anything!"

"Well, what did she say?"

"She recognized me. She asked about the band. All we talked about was music and shit." He was starting to take an annoyed tone with me. But I wasn't going to let this go without getting to the bottom of it.

"She recognized you? She's a groupie?"

"Groupie? We don't have groupies! We have some people who come to our shows because they like our music."

"Or they like the view," I muttered quietly and spitefully.

"What? You don't think girls would like our music, just our looks?"

"I didn't say that, I just meant . . . I see the way some girls stare when you're on stage."

"Well, that's bound to happen, isn't it? We want to draw a crowd! We want to look good onstage! But, we are there to play, not to pick up chicks!"

"I just- I don't know if you know how good looking you are. I don't know if you ever did, but especially now. Everyone else can see it but you! That girl could have been a model. And she wanted you! She would be a more fitting mate than me!"

"Okay, so you're insecure and you don't trust me! That's nice. Do I have to wear a chastity belt when we go on tour?"

"What? When are you touring?"

"I don't know! Whenever!" He stared at me, waiting for my rebuttal. I didn't respond. I just looked at him sadly. He calmed down a little bit. "You're gonna have to trust me," he warned.

I sighed. I trusted him. I trusted that he loved me. I didn't trust the women that would follow him. They wouldn't care that he was in a committed relationship. They wouldn't care if he was married! And he was right, I was insecure. At one time, he and I were kind of loners: dateless, inexperienced, and chaste, but then we found each other and it all was right. Now, he was turning into a rock star and I was afraid I was going to lose him.

"Do you trust me?" he demanded.

I knew what I should say. "I do," I answered hesitantly.

"That was convincing," he muttered.

"I'm sorry, Nigel. You didn't do anything wrong here. You're right. I have to get over this. I'll never get any sleep for the rest of my life if I don't."

He looked like he accepted. "Okay. Well, I think for now, we both should get some sleep, alright?" I nodded and he smiled and turned off his lamp. "Goodnight. Love you."

"Love you," I quietly returned in the dark as he situated himself in the bed, facing away from me. No sex? Normally he couldn't keep his hands off me at night. Again, I was jealous and insecure.

And it was hard not to be. As the weeks went by, Nigel's band was really picking up steam. They were being interviewed by the music press. Their manager was finding larger and larger gigs for them. Their fan base was growing. And then, in early 1981, they were offered a recording contract.

Chapter 9

"...please don't let me stand in your way."

Nigel came home one day and told me all about getting signed.

"Michelle, I have some incredible news! We had two record companies fighting for us. For *us*! So, we had to choose and I think we picked the right one. They are giving us a retainer already! Can you believe this? It's really bloody happening! I can't believe this! Can you believe this? I'm going to call my mom." He bounced away to the phone in the kitchen.

He hadn't given me an opportunity to respond. I tried to conceal my disappointment as he told his mother the news. I couldn't help but immediately feel sad about this. I wanted him to have everything he wanted, but I knew it was going to put a terrible strain on our relationship. I couldn't bear to think about him being gone all the time for touring and recording. I didn't want to think about a growing female fan base throwing themselves at him regularly while I was miles and miles away from him. He was on the fast track to Excitementville and I couldn't compete with that. Not nearly.

He came back in the room, dancing around with glee. "So, where do you think we should buy our first house?" he asked optimistically. "The country or the city? Or both? Should we also have a place in America? Hell, maybe one in France, too!"

I couldn't help but smile. "Honey, anywhere you want is fine with me. As long as you're there, I will love it."

He chuckled and kissed me. "Come on, let's go celebrate." He led me to the bedroom.

Every time we had sex, it was different. Not necessarily better or worse, just different. I never knew what was coming and that was part of the fun.

Nigel was captive to one of his ever-changing moods, but I couldn't tell which one. As he slowly and methodically undressed himself, my mind was far off, wondering if this was the last time we would have a moment like this, untainted by his fame. I was having a hard time focusing on the moment.

When he was nearly naked, he began with me, taking off one item of clothing at a time until I was completely undressed. He didn't seem overly hungry for gratification, more contemplative. We stood there; he looked at me, almost studying me or trying to see into me. His eyes were sharp and focused, but I couldn't read his mind. Although I hadn't been quite in the mood, Nigel quickly changed that with his intensity. He was taking his time, conjuring heightening desire between us with slow caresses in safe zones before advancing toward the most sensitive parts. His big hands held my face, he kissed me in a manner that left me wanting more. As my lips struggled to continue his seductive kiss, he pulled away, casually enjoying the distress this caused me. His fingertips, so lightly gliding down my jaw line and down my neck had my whole body quivering. I closed my eyes, breathing deeply but quietly, anxious and eager. He wrapped his arms around my naked body and sank his lips onto my neck. My heart jumped and momentarily my head flopped to the other side as he erased all traces of my strength. I was totally under his control. And he knew it.

His once sweet kisses became voracious, his formerly docile touch became forceful as he scooped my now limp body into his strong arms and heaved me onto the bed. He remained dominant, tasting my flesh, moving from my neck down to my chest as he groped and suckled. My restless legs were slowly dancing around on the bed as my desire for him grew unbearable. He liked that. He knew what he was doing to me. I noticed a devilish smile crossing his lips through my barely open eyes. His manly hands went to work, one, grabbing hold of my buttock, the other, readying himself to plunge into me. It happened quickly, and I was appreciative because I couldn't wait another second.

I moaned involuntarily, turning my head away from him, falling into an out of body happy place.

"Hey." He broke my trance. "Look at me."

I opened my eyes, but was too dazed to respond. He pulled my chin toward him. "Look at me," he again commanded, more forcefully. I had no choice now.

His eyes locked on mine. They blazed with intensity. I was hypnotized. I knew it excited him to control me this way and I was excited, too, as I'm sure he could tell.

I barely blinked, still staring into his brown eyes, as my peripheral vision captured the quiver of his lips, the ruddiness of his cheeks, the sweat forming on his forehead. He breathed heavily through flaring nostrils, his blessed tongue darting out to lick his shapely lips periodically. He unintentionally closed his eyes for a moment, gasping and grunting. I continued to stare, wide eyed at my master. I was completely under his spell. Exactly where I wanted to be.

He squeezed my body to his, thrusting feverishly as he climaxed with high pitched moans.

He continued to gradually decrease his pace to slower and more shallow thrusts until he was satisfied. He looked into my eyes and smiled.

"I love you," he sighed, kissing me again and again in gratitude.

"I love *you*," I returned, feeling like I was the grateful one.

With a groan, he released himself from me and anchored his body to my side. I could feel the wetness of our love dribble across my leg and I didn't care. I kept one arm around him, cradling his body to me, I stretched the other arm over to stroke his hair away from his face. His amazing face. That face had more power over me than anything I could imagine. It was able to transform me into a submissive sex toy, a protective maternal figure, and a doting schoolgirl all at once. Minutes ago, it was a sex face, completely confident. Now it was the face of a little boy, my sweet little boy.

I kissed him again. I loved him so much I thought I was going to burst. I squeezed him tighter, fearing this incredible love we shared was doomed.

Nigel wasn't home much over the next few weeks. Because it was his band, he felt personally responsible to be there with the manager during all of their business deals. Then there was the recording, which took longer than expected as problems came up and pieces had to be rewritten and such. He tried to explain it all to me but it was almost another language and I could not exactly follow. But I listened and I cared and I supported his ambitions.

And I missed him. Studio time was available only at night and I worked during the day. He would get home shortly before I had to wake up, reeking of cigarettes and geared up to tell me about how everything went.

I really hated getting up early, but so much was my love for him, I would sacrifice my precious sleep for the chance to spend some time with my dearest and hear about his day. He would come into the bedroom and wake me with a kiss. Then he would have to wait until my initial grumpiness was over before turning on the lamp and starting a conversation.

Then usually we would take a shower together, sometimes doing more than washing each other's backs.

This went on for a few months. I was getting used to this crazy life when the first single from the album was released. We were driving around one day when we heard it on the radio for the first time.

"Holy shit!" he exclaimed incredulously. "Turn it up!"

I couldn't believe it either. "You're on the radio! You're on the fucking radio!" I screamed.

He laughed, amazed. "Oh, my God. This is it. We've made it!" He smiled, shaking his head as the song played on. He pulled into our parking space as we reached our apartment building, and we sat there listening until the song was over. The deejay announced, "And that was Descent, a brand new group all the way from Cambridge. Hot off the presses, that one is. These boys are starting to cause a big stir. You can still catch them playing at the Fox Trot on Friday nights. Might want to jump on the bandwagon before they get too big for their britches. And now, on to an old favorite . . . " Nigel turned the volume down low.

"Did you hear that? We were talked about on the radio! Can you imagine how many people are going to see us now after that publicity?" He wasn't looking at me as he asked that question and he wasn't really anticipating a response.

" . . . That's really, really great." I finally sputtered softly, trying to hide my concern. I could feel the grip of fame tightening around my boyfriend. I was afraid it was stronger than I was.

"I gotta go call Mick." He bolted out of the car. I followed him, trying to catch up.

ଓ

When Friday night's show came, Nigel was right, it was even more crowded than usual, with curious kids clamoring to see this hot new band with the intriguing infectious single. I was there, of course. I was in the VIP box with the other girlfriends. I had also brought Sarah with me for support. I had confided in her my phobias of Nigel morphing into a self indulgent rock star with a bad attitude and no time for a nagging old lady at home. She tried to comfort me.

"There's as many boys in the audience as there are girls. These kids just want to see a show! What did you think was going to happen?"

"I don't know. I guess I had visions of screaming girls or something."

"Screaming girls? For this kind of music? I don't think so." She had a point. Their sound was edgy new wave, not exactly sexy. "Besides, everyone thinks they're gay," she said nonchalantly.

"What?" I shrieked. "What do you mean?"

"Michelle, look at them! They're totally camp! Five pretty boys in makeup and frilly shirts. Look at the crowd, look at who they're attracting. Sure, there are some pretty girls, but they aren't the only ones. Look at these people!"

It was true, they had an eclectic audience, studded with transvestites and crazy characters. It seemed that I could only see the beautiful women who appeared to circle like sharks. Nigel had called me insecure before and, damn it, he knew me too well.

"Okay, so should I be worried about women hitting on him or men hitting on him?"

"You shouldn't worry about either. Nigel loves you and he will be faithful to you," Sarah said sternly.

But I couldn't believe it. I felt so unworthy of him now. He wasn't the "plain" boy I fell in love with anymore and he never would be again. What could he possibly see in me when compared to these stunning women?

And still, I caught him looking up at the balcony, flashing me his paralyzing smile from time to time. I should have known how deep his love for me ran. But I just couldn't believe it.

It only got worse. At home I was either standoffish or overly possessive. I stared at him a lot, trying to capture his face in my memory, sure that this good thing wasn't going to last. And that killed me. I was sulky and depressed and I took it out on him. He didn't understand my mood and I didn't want to explain. He tried to reach out, but after getting burned too many times, he gave up and spent more and more time away from me, choosing to hang out at the club instead.

When he came home late, my eyes searched his body for any signs of infidelity- long hairs on his clothes, lipstick on his collar. I tried to smell him to see if I could detect women's perfume on him. Inconspicuous as I tried to appear, he saw through me.

"What are you doing?" he asked coldly, irritated.

"Nothing."

"Fucking stop this! I know what you're doing! You think I'm cheating!"

"Why would I have a reason to think that?"

"No! Don't try to trick me. I have given you no reasons. They're all in your head. Get over it!"

I tried. I wanted to trust him. He was right, he did nothing wrong. It was all me and a lifetime of rejection that made me this way.

All I wanted was to be close to him and all I ended up doing was push him away. It hurt me so much, and I could tell it hurt him, too.

That's when he started doing more drugs, trying to escape his wounds, his pressures that he faced not only with his career, but at home also.

Bitter as things became between us, I was still the first one Nigel wanted to tell his good news to. Coming home from a band meeting one day, he was floating on a cloud. "Sweetheart, you will never guess what happened today."

I was instantly happy to see him so thrilled with whatever was going on and was genuinely glad for his mood. "What, honey?"

"We just got signed up for our first tour! Two weeks, ten shows across Europe!" He was beyond excited.

I knew this was coming and I had tried to make my peace with it. I was as calm on the exterior as I could be, trying to be supportive. "Wow. That's really wonderful! I'm proud of you. Congratulations." I gave him a kiss and a tight hug.

"You're not upset?" he asked in our embrace.

"Um, no. This is a great opportunity for you. This is your dream. It's fabulous news."

He pulled away from my hug. "You know you can't lie for shit."

" . . . I know. But, no, I am really happy for you. I mean it."

He gave me an unconvinced look, knowing how many fights this tour issue had caused us.

"I'll prove it. I'm going to throw a huge party for you and the guys. It will be like a congratulations/going away party. Yeah. We'll invite everyone. It's going to be the party of the year! I'm going to make everything perfect and you'll see that all I care about is you and your happiness."

By this time, he believed me and was beaming.

"Baby, you don't have to do that. Just knowing that you can accept this and trust me is enough."

"No, no, no. I *want* to throw this party. As an *"I'm sorry"* and a *"good luck"*. I've been terrible and I know that. I'm really sorry. You don't deserve that. So, let's put that all behind us and look ahead to the bright future."

ଔ

I had two weeks to plan the party before the guys took off. We decided to have it the day before they left. I had invited everyone I could think of and asked the band to invite anyone they wanted as well. I knew our apartment couldn't hold as many as we'd like, but I didn't care. The neighbors would be mad at the noise and traffic, but again, I didn't care. I wanted everyone to have a good time.

When the party began, my place was loaded with booze, beer, and food. Records were playing, the lights were dimmed, and already there were more people than I imagined buzzing around.

And that continued. A constant mill of people going in and out. Music, laughter, loud voices, and singing filled the room. The smell of perfume and cigarettes was thick in the air. It appeared that before long, the bathroom was the designated area for blow jobs and drug taking. No one had any qualms about smoking pot in the open, so I could only assume what was happening in the bathroom was more risqué. I tried to ignore that, and it was fairly easy because as the hostess, I was constantly busy with replenishing food and drinks, as well as socializing and keeping watch on the crowd. And my eagle eye didn't fail as it moved in on Nigel hovering around the bathroom door.

It was hard to keep watch on him with so many people obstructing my view, but I managed to bob and weave around until I saw him go in with an unfamiliar fellow. My stomach turned upside down. I knew what was happening and I didn't like it. What would happen when he was on tour? What kind of trouble would he get in? He'd have no restrictions. And he wanted to live the rock and roll life. Try as I did to be cool about all this, it was wearing on me.

I stood like an enraged mental patient, staring at the door without blinking for minutes before Sarah approached me.

"What is up with you? You look bloody insane."

"Nigel's in the bathroom," I said monotonously.

It was a simple statement that usually would have implied nothing irregular, but she understood at once, which only fueled my fear that he was up to no good. "Uh oh. Do you want me to go break it up?"

"No. He's a big boy. If that's what he wants to do, let him do it."

"You're not okay with that."

"No, I'm not. But I'm not going to try to control him either. He'll just rebel. He doesn't like boundaries."

She gave me a look that I only saw out of the corner of my eye. I was still fixed on the bathroom door. We both flinched as it opened. He came out with the stranger right behind him, laughing and wiping his nose on his shirt sleeve. My heart deflated. Sarah patted my shoulder as my worst fears were confirmed. My head drooped and I closed my eyes.

Seconds later, Nigel was at my other side. "What's wrong? Do you not feel good?"

"Yeah, Michelle. How do you feel?" Sarah asked sarcastically.

I looked up in time to see Nigel give her a questioning but irritated expression. "Hey," he said, putting an arm around me to steer me away from Sarah to talk more privately. "I have an idea. Why don't you and I go in the bedroom and take a little break from the party?"

"Huh? What are you talking about?"

"Come on, don't you think it would be hot to have sex with all these people right outside the door? Kind of dangerous, you know? Thinking about that really turns me on." He took my hand in his and rubbed it over the hard bulge in his pants.

I pulled my hand away, embarrassed. "We have a house full of guests! And, if you haven't noticed, our bedroom has been occupied all night by everyone else in the place who wants to do it!"

"Yeah, I have noticed. And *I'm* the only one not getting laid and it's *my* fucking bed!" He stormed off into the crowd.

I sighed, frustrated. Sarah returned to my side. "What was all that about?"

"I don't know. I hate when he gets this way. I can't stand being around him."

"Well, if it gets too bad, you can always stay at my place."

"Thanks. I hope it doesn't come to that though. Wouldn't it be terrible to have to leave my own party? Especially since this is supposed to be my farewell send off to the boys," I sulked.

"Come on, let's have a drink," Sarah commanded. I followed.

I tried to appreciate the evening. I was starting to have a good time, visiting everyone and laughing and forgetting my woes. Every once in a while, I would look up to find Nigel and he was either joking around with someone or glaring at me. It was pissing me off.

I was about to go up to him and tell him so, when Victoria grabbed me by the elbow and stammered. "You gotta hear this story, Michelle. Go on Suzy, tell her. Tell her!" she laughed and babbled in a drunken stupor.

"Alright, 'ere it is . . . " Suzy began with an equally drunken slurring. She commenced reciting what I'm sure was a fascinating tale about something or other, but my mind was far off. She didn't even notice I was looking at Nigel, not her, as she spoke. I had him in my sights. As soon as Suzy was done with her endless story, I would go talk to him.

But, as I watched him, that blonde bombshell from a while back approached him. *Who invited her? Well, half of Cambridge was here, why wouldn't the beautiful skanks come, too?* It seemed to happen in slow motion, she came up to him and tapped him on the shoulder. He turned around and smiled when he saw her. Smiling like, not just a polite smile, but a smile like he'd been waiting for her all night. I watched her pull a small white bag out of her bra, just enough to flash it to him. He looked at it, then at her with big eyes. She nodded toward the bathroom and he followed in like a puppy. My face burned but my blood felt cold in my veins. I felt like I had been socked in the stomach. And then, I was.

"Hey! Hell of a story, ain't it?" Victoria elbowed me too roughly in the gut.

She had no idea I had tuned out the whole thing. I struggled to speak.

"She's speechless!" Suzy shouted. "Fuckin' right. I can't believe it myself."

I left the two of them cackling about whatever it was and stood up, just wanting to get away. I stumbled toward the hallway, hoping Nigel would exit the bathroom before I could get to the door. No such luck. I pushed my way through the mob and left the apartment. I didn't know what the plan was from there, but it didn't matter because my legs gave out and before I knew it, I was sinking to the floor. I sat against the wall, cradling my knees to my chest, head down, trying to hold in the tears. Moments later, the door opened. "Fuck," I whispered to myself, not wanting to be seen.

It was Sarah. "Hey, what's going on?"

"Nigel is in the bathroom with some bimbo," I mumbled.

"What? Some bimbo?"

"Yeah, this girl who is always hanging around, trying to get him to talk to her. No, let me rephrase that. He seems to *enjoy* her company. And, right now, they're either doing coke, doing each other, or both!"

"No. No, he wouldn't cheat on you."

"He probably doesn't even know *what* he's doing!"

"Get in there and talk to him. Beat down the damn door if you have to! It's *your* loo and that's *your* man. Don't let some tart hit on him in *your own* home!" She held out her hand and helped me up. She was right.

We walked back in and saw Nigel looking innocent with the girl nowhere to be seen. Sarah, who had been right behind me, silently faded into the background. I came up to Nigel and tapped him on his shoulder. He turned around with a dazzling smile, only to lose it when he saw that it was me. He looked guilty. He tried to recover. "Oh, there you are. I've been looking for you."

"Really?"

"Yeah, really." He put his arms around my waist and held me close to him. He was in a completely different mood than last I saw him. He had been angry and agitated but now he was back to happy and horny. "I missed you."

"Oh, you've been lonely?"

"So lonely," he agreed, not sensing my sarcasm.

"No one to keep you company?" I continued.

He finally caught on. "What are you getting at?"

"You aren't even trying to be secretive!" I blew up, too loudly. People started to stare.

He took my elbow forcefully and yanked me off to an empty corner of the room. "What do you think you're doing, making a big spectacle like that?"

"Am I the one at fault here?"

"And what is it that you think *I've* done?"

"Nigel, who is that girl?"

"What girl?"

"Stop playing dumb! You know what I'm talking about! Who the fuck is she? Why is she here? Why are you going off with her behind closed doors?" I was screeching now. The crowd could've heard me three blocks away.

"Will you calm the fuck down?" he demanded in a hushed and bitter tone. "Nothing has happened between us."

"That sounds like you're anticipating that something *will* happen between you. Just waiting for an opportunity? Should I go? Give you two some alone time?"

He shook his head. "You're being paranoid. And jealous. And possessive. And it's not becoming. *And*, it's annoying as shit," he told me matter of factly. "You know, you're making it very easy to leave. And why would I want to come home to this? All you're going to do is interrogate me when I get back because you won't be there to watch my every move while I'm on tour. You can't even trust me in my own fucking home!"

"Okay, spin it so it's my fault. I'm the bad guy, fine. Just tell me right now if I *should* trust you or not. What were you doing in the bathroom with that girl?"

I watched the look on his face turn from sour and indignant to scared and guilty. He was speechless, searching for an excuse to be there that sounded good.

"Okay," I began after letting time pass as he stared at the ground. "Since I'm making it so easy to leave and you can't think of a reason to come back, I guess we don't have a future, do we?"

He raised his head with an apologetic look in his eyes. "Wait, no, I didn't mean that- "

"I'm gonna go. I don't really want to stay and watch you break my heart right under my nose. When you get back from your tour, I'll be gone." I said it all so quickly that I barely had time to make the decision before I told him about it. I just wanted to run away. I wanted to hurt him, and I wanted to ruin his party.

"Don't. Don't go." He put his hands on my arms to hold me.

"Why not? You don't even want me. I think you want to be single so you can enjoy all the female attention. Well, please don't let me stand in your way. Have your fun, Nigel. Get your dick sucked by every pretty girl you see. Get drunk, get high, have a ball," I said bitterly. He let his hands slide off of me as I watched the look on his face go from concerned to utterly betrayed and hurt.

A part of me couldn't bear to see him in pain, but I couldn't take it back now. And I didn't want to. "Enjoy your party," I said sarcastically.

He opened his mouth to say something to stop me, but no words came. I walked away, finding Sarah on my way out. "I need to go," I simply said, but she understood. She grabbed her purse as I got mine and we left with Victoria and Suzy hot on our heels.

Luckily Sarah hadn't been drinking much that night and was sober as we left. She got behind the wheel, I got in the passenger's seat, and Suzy and Victoria tumbled into the backseat. It wasn't long that we were on the road before I totally fell apart. I was wailing so loud that Sarah was distracted from the road. She fought the urge to console me physically, and instead hurried home. Victoria, who sat behind me, put her arms around me.

"Now, now. Don't you worry. Everything is gonna be alright."

"How?" I managed to yell between sobs. "My life was shit before I met him. And it was shit while I was away from him. And now it's going to be shit again because even if we stay together, he won't ever have time for me!" I bawled so loudly, it hurt my own ears.

Sarah's eyes bulged, amazed at my reaction. "We're almost to my carpark. You can ring him from my flat if you want to. Tell him it was all just a cock up."

"Fuck that!" Suzy interjected. "If my boyfriend ever pulled what Nigel's doin', I'd cut off his fucking bollocks."

I cried harder. When we pulled up to Sarah's apartment building, the girls had to help me in and up the stairs, which was tough considering two out of three were plastered.

I plopped onto Sarah's couch once we were in. Moments later, Sarah was there with a blanket and a box of tissues. She sat beside me. "Is there anything I can do for you?" she asked quietly.

"I don't know. I don't know if there's anything I can do or he can do to make this better." I stared down at my left hand, at the promise ring he gave me a year and a half before. I wondered what it meant now. "God, this sucks so bad. I need him, Sarah. I need him. He's my soul mate. He's my everything. I can't function without him."

"You know he feels the same way! He's probably cryin' on Sam's shoulder right now sayin' the same thing."

I stopped my whimpering for a second. "You really think so?"

"Yeah. Don't you think so, Vic?"

"For sure," Victoria answered vehemently. "Right, Sue?"

Suzy was elbows deep in a cardboard box, searching for something. "I don't know. Men are wankers, mostly."

"You don't feel that way! If you did you wouldn't be running off with Colin," Victoria scolded.

"Running off?" I questioned.

"Yeah, Colin wants me to move in with him in his new London flat. I can't wait to get out of this stinky suburban shithole."

"What? When are you going?" I pondered.

"Tomorrow. Same as Nigel."

I began to wail again as I realized he was soon to be out of the country. Sarah and Victoria shot evil stares at Suzy.

"What? She asked!" Suzy defended herself.

"She's right. He *is* going to be gone tomorrow. Is this how I should be spending my last night with him? I need to see if we can talk things out. I mean, maybe we won't be together when he gets back, but we could at least have one more night together. I should go see if I can fix things."

"Are you sure? Do you want to phone him first?" Sarah asked.

"No, no I want to just go back and talk to him in person," I insisted.

"Okay, I'll take you back," Sarah offered.

"No, I'll take a cab."

"Are you sure?"

"Yeah, it's fine. You have done enough for me today. Thank you so much. I'll call you tomorrow and tell you how it went."

"Alright. But, if things go badly, you can always come back here," Sarah comforted me.

"Yeah, and after tonight, there will be an empty room!" Suzy added.

"Great," I responded unenthusiastically. I didn't like the idea of having to move out of my home. Although I appreciated having a back-up plan, I hoped I wouldn't need it. I didn't want to leave Nigel for real; I shouldn't have left him at all. It didn't feel right. "Thanks for everything you guys. Goodbye Suzy, and good luck." I walked out the door and onto the street, eventually hailed a cab and headed home.

When I arrived, I paid the driver and searched for my keys in my bottomless purse as I made my way up to my door. Victorious, I unlocked it and went in. I was so preoccupied with finding my keys, I hadn't noticed the noise was much lower now. I had only been gone for a little more than an hour but there were not many people left, and those still hanging around seemed either wasted or were making out on the furniture. I looked around for Nigel, fearing he was one of the ones making out under some random floozy.

I sighed with relief, finding this was not the case. The bathroom was empty, he wasn't in there either. Whew! I wasn't sure he was even home as I continued down the hallway to my room, afraid I was going to walk in on some orgy.

I didn't. It was just two people. But they were having sex. The woman I recognized first-that damn slutty blonde. She was on top of some guy. She gasped when I opened the door and turned around to look at me. Then, so did her partner. Now I was able to see who it was.

"Nigel?" I barely squeaked out, stunned and hurt.

"Michelle! Oh my God! Oh fuck!" he cried.

The blonde dismounted and grabbed her dress. I barely noticed as she threw it on and raced out the door. My wobbly legs threatened to give out under me. Nigel was there in a moment, having put on his pants in a hurry. He supported me before I fell, panic all over his face. I couldn't speak.

"Oh, God. Oh, Michelle I am so sorry. Oh my God, I am so fucking sorry. Oh my God, I can't believe I did this. What the fuck was I thinking? I'm so sorry, baby. I'm so sorry." He kept repeating apologies, trying to get a hold of himself. He held me and I was too dazed to realize what was happening. "Michelle? Michelle? Say something. Please, say something baby."

That sparked something in me. "Baby?" I whispered. *"Baby?"*

He sighed and looked like he regretted begging me to talk.

I pushed him off of me. "Is this how you treat your *baby?* Were you calling her baby, too?"

"No! No! She means nothing to me! I swear! I never would have done that if-" he stopped himself.

"If what? If you weren't high? Or if you thought I was coming home? Or, if I had fucked you earlier like you wanted? Is that it?"

"No, that's not it. I only wanted to have sex with you. But you left and- "

"And what?" I cut him off. "If you get horny on the road, I won't be there, so you're just going to fuck any random girl who's available?"

"You walked out on me. I thought you were gone for good."

"Gone for good? You didn't even try to talk to me! You didn't come after me! You were just going to let me go? End it just like that? I was right when I said you wanted to be single, wasn't I?"

"No! I love you!"

I laughed for a while like he had just told a very funny joke. Then I snapped. "What the fuck is wrong with you?"

He looked down, ashamed. Like a dog being scolded.

"I gave up everything for you! I left my family and school and my *country* to be with you! And now you are leaving me for your big shot band, but before you can do that you have to betray me and show me how fucking *stupid* I am for wasting my life with a selfish dickhead who doesn't give a shit about me! Damn it! I can't believe this!"

I was still seething with anger, my blood practically boiling. He was sitting on the edge of the bed with his hands holding his head. I felt a twinge of sympathy. I was so full of rage and hurt, but I loved Nigel so deeply that his pain was my pain. He was crying. "I'm so sorry. I can't believe I did this to you. I will never forgive myself."

I didn't know what to do. My knees were weak and I sat next to him on the bed. He immediately threw his arms around me and wept on my shoulder. I didn't have it in me to comfort him and forgive him this time. But I knew it was the cocaine that had made him act the way he did. It turned him into someone else, someone I didn't like. *My* Nigel would never do that to me. As I watched him crying, it was getting harder to stay angry. He was the little boy I loved, sensitive and emotional. Easily hurt, fragile and fallible.

But he was also the man I trusted who betrayed me. I sat like stone as he sniveled on me, obviously wanting me to give him some warmth. I couldn't.

"You don't love me anymore," he accused between sobs.

His words ripped my heart in half. "Nigel, if I didn't love you I wouldn't be heartbroken now."

"You still love me?" He perked up, hopefully.

I was silent, not knowing how to answer. It didn't matter; he was reborn.

"Marry me!" he said with a smile. "Marry me. I'll be good. Just like old times. Remember? We were so in love. We can be like that again- but real family. Let's get married!" He blurted all this out quickly and excitedly.

I felt my mouth fall open, but that's all I could feel. I was beyond shocked.

He kept smiling, misconstruing my silence for overwhelming joy. In reality, I found it totally inappropriate. We were both on an emotional roller-coaster and now was not the time to make life altering decisions.

"Well, what do you say?" he eagerly demanded.

"I- I- I don't know."

"You don't know?" He was offended. "You don't want to marry me? I thought you loved me?" His enthusiasm changed to depression.

"I need to think about this."

Depression turned to anger. "Are you kidding me? I thought you loved me! I thought you didn't want anything in the world more than me! And here I am, offering myself and the rest of my life to you and you don't know if you want it? You're fucking kidding me, right?" He was enraged.

I couldn't understand his myriad of emotions. "Nigel, calm down."

"No! Don't fucking tell me to calm down!" He stood up and paced angrily around.

I was frightened. "What's wrong with you?"

"Wrong with me? Wrong with *me*? What's wrong with *you*?" He picked up a framed picture of us, smiling and very much in love. He looked at it for a moment. Suddenly solemn, he continued. "I don't even recognize these people anymore. How long has it been since we were happy?"

"It wasn't that long ago," I answered quietly, not knowing if he wanted a response or not.

"You think we can go back?"

I took a deep breath. "Things . . . things are different now."

"Because I fucked everything up? Is that what you mean?"

"That's not what I said."

"Good. Because I'm not the only one who ruined this. You have been pushing me away and accusing me of cheating and *you* were the one who walked out on *me* at our own party, so don't think I'm the only one to blame, here."

"*I* didn't cheat on *you*! *I'm* not some crazy drug addict throwing tantrums!"

"I'm not throwing a tantrum! You want to see me throw a tantrum?" His eyes were wild and wide. With all his strength he heaved the picture in his hand at the wall. Then, he violently swept everything off of the dresser. I shrank back from the tirade. He picked up a hand mirror, looked into it briefly, and with a cry of rage, chucked it at the wall. The glass shattered and the mirror ricocheted back and hit me in the arm. He turned around quickly, with fear and concern on his face. "Oh my God, are you alright? I'm so sorry. What have I done?"

"I'm fine." The site burned, but I didn't feel pain. I was in shock; I was trembling. I had never seen a violent side of Nigel before. It was clear that certain substances had altered his behavior.

Nigel sat on the bed beside me. I flinched as his hands took my arm, inspecting the newly forming welt. He tenderly checked the wound. "I can't believe I acted like that. I don't know what came over me," he said softly, his voice cracking. Then, he was crying again. "I'm a monster. No wonder you don't want to marry me."

Again, there it was. He was crying and all I wanted to do was hold him and tell him everything was going to be alright. I wanted to tell him I could never stop loving him and he truly was the only thing that mattered in my life. But I didn't say any of that. My heart wanted him but my brain told me to go. I was torn. I looked over at him and he looked up to meet my gaze. His eyes were red and teary, his face was pale, his dry lips quivering, droplets slowly streaking down his cheeks and chin. My heart was winning the battle. I put my arms around him and cradled his head to my chest. He cried harder and I began crying, too, as loud and hard as he was.

We didn't talk, we just sat there, soaking each other, whimpering and sniffling. It had been a long night. All the fighting and crying had taken too much out of us. I felt too weak to sit up anymore. I leaned us back on the bed, forgetting the infidelity, only aware of holding on to Nigel like I could make all our pain disappear if I didn't let go. It was too easy to ignore his mistakes. I was mad, but I had told him before that nothing he did could ever make me stop loving him, and I meant it. He betrayed me, he broke his vows that he made when he gave me my promise ring, but no matter how upset with him I was, I couldn't turn off my love for him. He needed me more than ever to stand by his side and help him with his growing drug and alcohol problem. I could forgive him even though it would be hard. I would be there for him, always.

He clung to me, gently whimpering, on the verge of falling asleep. I stroked his hair, dozing off myself.

Chapter 10

"We'll work it out!"

I had no idea what time it was when we fell asleep. When I opened my eyes, it was bright outside. I was cold. I looked over, and Nigel wasn't there. I sat up, wondering why I was sleeping sideways on the bed, on top of the blankets. Then I remembered everything as the slow wave of wisdom washed over me with increasing pain and panic. I looked over the other way and saw the rumpled sheets and cringed, thinking about what had happened there last night. I felt incredibly sick and I had to get up.

I stumbled out of bed, groggy and disoriented. I made my way down the hall and was relieved that none of the party guests were passed out in my living room. Good, no one was there. But, neither was Nigel. I looked at the clock; it was almost noon.

"Fuck," I whispered to myself. "He's gone." The band had to be on a bus by ten a.m. that morning. I didn't say goodbye. I didn't have the chance to say anything. And that was really bad timing because there was so much to say, so much to resolve.

I sighed and sank onto a kitchen chair. Just then, I noticed a folded note with my name on it on the table. I picked it up, Nigel had written it:

> Michelle,
>
> You were right to deny my proposal. You were right to leave me. I do not deserve you and you do not deserve

to endure all the strain my dreams are causing us. You are right, how can I promise I won't sleep around with random girls when I am on the road if I am always drinking or partying? What kind of life will you have, always wondering if I am staying true? This is probably the start of many tours to come. I can't ask you to waste your life on me. I love you too much to let that happen to you. I'm sorry, but it's over.

With shaking hands, I dropped the letter. I sat stunned for I don't know how long before it really hit me. Then, a loud wail emanated from the bottom of my soul and tears poured out of me. I shook so hard I thought I would fall apart. And I wouldn't have cared if I did. I wanted to die. My life was over.

My mind was dotted with memories of our first encounter, our first touch, our first kiss, the first "I love you,", the first time we had sex, the first fight, the look on his face when I left for America, the look on his face when I came back, the look on his face last night . . . a montage of our happiest and lowest moments, and all in between. Remembering him took me out of the current moment of utter despair and back to a time when I first felt true happiness. To leave that place and be thrust in the lonely present was unbearable. "I don't want to live! I don't want to live!" I shrieked as I cried, hoping God was listening and would strike me down.

No such luck.

I folded my arms on the table in front of me and rested my head on them, weeping uncontrollably, though quieter now, until I had no tears left. I sat there for hours. My spirit left my body, my mind shut down in self defense. I could hear Autumn crying for food, but I couldn't even pick my head up, let alone tend to her.

The phone rang, the shrill noise cutting through my bubble of misery. The sound made my throbbing head hurt and I just wanted to silence it. I didn't want to talk to anyone and I thought I was unable to get up to answer it anyway. I was only able to muster up enough strength when it occurred to me that it could be Nigel on the other end. As quickly as I could, I staggered to the phone and tried to speak clearly.

"Hello?"

"Hey, what's going on?" Sarah asked from the other end.

The tears came back. "He's gone! He left me!"

"What? You mean he went on tour, right? Don't worry, he'll be back in a fortnight."

"No, he's never coming back! He broke up with me! I came home and found him in bed with that blonde slut and- "

"Hang on. I'll be right over!" She hung up and so did I. I just stood by the phone and leaned against the wall, crying pitifully. Then, after summoning all my strength, I made my way to the door and unlocked it for Sarah. The phone rang again. I stumbled back to it and answered, thinking it was Sarah again.

"Hello?"

"Hello, Michelle? This is Patrick Fox. Look, we're at a truck stop in France right now. I need you to talk to John. He's a fucking mess. You've got to talk to him, no one else can get through to him."

"What? He's a mess?"

"Yeah, hang on, he's right here."

I listened as I heard the receiver being passed and a reluctance to pick it up. I thought I heard Randy saying, "just talk to her, man" in the background.

"Hi," Nigel eventually said.

I choked up. "Hi," I answered, voice cracking.

"Oh, God, I'm so sorry baby," he cried, sobbing.

"How could you do this? How could you do this to me?" I could barely say.

"I don't know, I don't know. I love you so much. I wish I was home so I could hold you."

"I wish you were home, too. I can't do this without you. I can't- " I was crying too hard to speak. "Nigel, Nigel, don't leave me."

"I don't want to! Don't you know I don't want to?"

"Then come home! We'll work it out!"

"Honey, we can't work this out. I can't keep coming home just to leave you again all the time. What kind of life is that for you?"

"I won't have any life if you aren't in it! Please, Nigel! Please don't leave me!"

"Michelle, I . . . I want you to move on." He tried to sound steady and strong.

"No! I-"

"Yes! Don't waste your life on me." His strong voice wavered with the pain those words caused him. "I'm sorry. I'm so sorry. I love you." It sounded final.

"Nigel, wait!"

"I'm sorry." He hung up.

I didn't breathe. I held still, keeping the receiver next to my ear as if he would suddenly come back on the line. Sarah put her hands on me. I jumped.

"I'm sorry, I came in while you were on the phone. The door was open, so I thought . . . " she trailed off. "Nigel called?"

"Kind of. From a payphone in France. I can't even get a hold of him if I wanted to," I muttered with my tired, teary voice.

"Come sit down." She guided me to my couch. "I'll make you some tea."

"I don't want anything. I don't want anything but Nigel." I started crying hard again. She sat beside me and held me until I was mostly done.

"Can you tell me what happened?" she inquired.

"I can try . . . It doesn't even seem real. It's like, it doesn't make sense! I mean, we had some problems lately, but, I just can't believe it's over. It's not right. It's not supposed to be this way. Nigel and I belong together."

"I believe that, too."

"You do?" I was cheered up a bit.

"Yeah, of course I do! Anyone could see that. That's why this doesn't make sense to me either. It doesn't seem like something Nigel would do, cheat on you and break it off with you."

"I know! He's so different now from who he was when I left for America. I don't know what changed him. The band, maybe? A little fame going to his head?"

"Or the drugs?" Sarah suggested.

I shamefully looked at her concerned face as she pointed out what I tried to ignore most of the time.

"It was a party. Everyone was doing it." I quietly defended.

"No, not everyone. I wasn't, you weren't. A lot of people weren't."

"He was just having a good time before going on this trip, enjoying his friends and relaxing before the tour."

"Wouldn't he enjoy his friends, not to mention his *girl*friend, more if he actually knew what was going on?"

"See, that's it Sarah. He didn't even *know* what was going on. He didn't mean to cheat on me, I'm sure. He was so out of it. I'll bet he just took more than usual because he was upset that I left him. And I *did* leave him! He didn't know I was coming back, maybe ever. He is so sensitive, I should have known better than to do that to him."

"Why are you blaming yourself for his infidelity? Why do you keep making excuses for his behavior?"

I sighed and finally said, "Because I understand him, Sarah."

She looked at me curiously.

"I know he has a drug problem. I know he's using more than we realize. I know that's why he's different now, and I know that's why he needs me more than ever."

Sarah listened, absorbing my words, neither judging nor agreeing.

Eventually she said, "So then, are you just going to wait for him to come home and try to talk things out?"

"Would that make me pathetic?"

"No, of course not! But, maybe a break is just what you need."

I frowned. "Ugh, the thought of him not being mine is so brutal. It's literally physically painful." I explained.

"I know. Well, did he give you any indication that he would be back? Did he sound like he knew he had made a mistake?"

The tears rose to my eyes again. "No. No, he sounded sure, actually."

"Oh," Sarah looked down, sad for me. Seconds later she seemed brighter. "Maybe you should move in with me," she suggested.

"What? Leave my home? Our home?"

"Yes. This place is just too full of painful memories. You don't want to be reminded of him constantly, do you?"

"Sarah, since the day I met him, I have not been able to stop thinking about him. Every day, every hour, he is always on my mind. And that's the only thing that keeps me smiling."

"Well, will you still be smiling when you think about him now?"

"I don't know." His face flashed in my head and I began weeping again.

"Just think about it. I have an empty room now. It might be fun. And, you'll have someone there to talk to. It doesn't have to be permanent, you could always move back if things work out with Nigel."

She made sense. I wouldn't even be able to sleep in my own bed now, after the incident. And I was tired, and I didn't want to be alone. Sarah's offer was sounding more tempting.

I considered it, but the apartment was my home. It was where I began a new life with my soul mate. It was where we learned to be adults. It was where we had meals and spent long nights talking and laughing. It was where we fought and where we had incredible sex. It was where Nigel proposed to me. I looked down at my ring finger and at the promise ring I'd been wearing for years. I remembered what he said to me when he gave it to me, that he would always be faithful and would always be committed to me.

I looked around again. This place was also where he lied to me, cheated on me, and broke up with me. I felt cold and sick remembering that. I slowly put the fingers on my right hand around the ring on my left. I took a deep breath and pulled it off.

ം

I took Sarah up on her offer. She helped me pack a few things and drove me to her home. I spent the first night on her couch and I was so exhausted that I fell asleep immediately. Over the next week, I moved in the rest of my things. I took only what was mine from my apartment, including my cat. I left everything else behind, including my ring.

Sarah was great. She pulled her weight and mine at home and at work as I struggled to cope with my new, depressing life. I was starting to realize that things might really be over with Nigel and I tried to prepare myself for that. Of course, I was still hopeful and tried to be optimistic. It was hard, but, day by day, things got a bit easier, though I was still grieving in a major way.

Two weeks later, Sarah and I were in the boutique, setting up a display when Nigel walked in.

"Michelle! Where have you been? I've been phoning the flat with no answer."

"I moved out," I stammered, totally shocked to see him.

"I saw that. I just got back today and I went home and you weren't there. And your stuff was gone."

"Yeah." It was hard to talk to him. Hard to see him.

"You left the ring," he stated quietly.

"I don't really need it anymore, do I?" I was also quiet, but bitter.

He looked hurt. I couldn't tell if it was because he broke his promise to me or because I returned the meaningful token. He was silent for a while as he tried to compose himself. "You can keep it, though. It's yours. I bought it for you."

"I know. I remember when you gave it to me. What you said . . . " I started getting choked up thinking about his sincere words and bleary eyes that day. I shook my head, trying to clear it. "I don't need the reminder. That's why I had to move out."

"I understand. I guess I just thought that . . . "

"What?" I asked eagerly, hoping he had changed his mind about our breakup.

"Well, I figured I would be the one moving out and you would keep the flat."

"Oh," I said, unable to hide my disappointment.

"Suzy moved to London and I thought Michelle shouldn't be living on her own," Sarah interrupted. She had been eavesdropping. "We've been doing great, haven't we?"

I was still too floored to function properly. I didn't speak. Sarah left us alone.

"So, you're okay?" Nigel asked, unconvinced and afraid I was over him already.

"I wouldn't say that," I answered quietly.

"Michelle, I'm really so sorry. I've been really worried about you. I wanted to come back home so badly, but I couldn't."

"No, I know. I know where your priorities lie," I jibed.

He was taken aback. He sighed. "Yeah, I deserve that."

"So, your tour went well?" I asked, half hoping it was unsuccessful and he would quit the band and come back to me.

"Yeah, actually it did. I mean, I was miserable and all I could think about was you." I perked up. "But, the shows were great and we made some money." I was deflated again. "And now, we are going to be doing six shows next week all over England."

"Oh," I responded unenthusiastically.

He looked sad. "See, I told you. I'd be the shittiest boyfriend in the world if you stayed with me. I'd never be around. And I have to put my career first right now. I don't want to put you second."

"So instead, you are going to be totally selfless and cut me loose, huh?"

"Hey, you know how much this is hurting me, too."

"You say that, and I would believe you, but here's the difference between us. *You* are the most important thing to me. Nothing could ever top you. But for you, fame is more important than me. So, don't say you're hurting as much as me, because that's shit."

"I wouldn't want you to give up your dreams for me."

"You are my only dream! You're the only thing I've ever wanted!"

"Well, I'm sorry I want more than a happy home! Go ahead and hate me forever because I'm trying to do the right thing!"

That angered me. Two weeks of suppressed fury shot out of my mouth like ammunition. "Wait a minute! You think you're doing the right thing? Do you realize what you're giving up? We had everything! But that's not enough, is it? You can't even promise to stay faithful to me and that's beyond pathetic. You aren't even trying! Instead of attempting to stay sober enough while you're gone to keep your dick in your pants, you are planning on getting plastered to the point where you won't even know who you're fucking! And that's your reason for leaving? You'd rather be promiscuous and stoned than sober and monogamous?"

"If I can't even do that when I'm in our home, how can I promise to do that when I'm gone?" he argued.

At first, I thought that was a pitiful excuse. Then I realized, Nigel was addicted. He didn't see it as choosing the drugs over me, he didn't think there was a choice. He had been doing this for a long time and was depending on them more and more. He needed them. He needed them more than me. I was silent. The truth felt like a very heavy blow that knocked the wind out of me. He watched me try to cope with his response, anxious for a rebuttal. "Well?"

"Nigel, I think you have a problem."

"What do you mean?" He was offended.

"If you can't plan on staying sober, if you think you can't be a rock star without getting smashed, I think . . . I think . . . " I couldn't say the word '*addiction*'.

"What?" He wasn't quite following. He didn't seem to think there was anything wrong with his partying. "It's all part of the life, it's what everyone does. It's no big deal."

"Look at what you're giving up! I think it's a very big deal!"

"Michelle, you have no idea how guilty I feel about what I did to you before I left. It was all I could think about. I will never forgive myself. It was a mistake that I don't plan on repeating, but even if I stay sober all the time I will be hurting you on a daily basis and I can't live with that. I'll never be there for you. I can't be who you need now."

It hurt so bad to hear him reiterate his reasons for breaking up with me. I slumped over. I almost fell. He quickly put his arms around me and held me, resting his chin on my head. "I love you so much. I have to stop hurting you."

"Then don't leave," I whispered, choking on tears.

"I have given this a lot of thought. I think it's the only choice." He took a deep breath in. "This is killing me. God, this is killing me." He pulled away and held me at arm's length. "I love you. I will always love you." He let me go and walked out the door.

I fell to pieces again. Luckily there were no customers in the store.

Sarah reappeared, her face white. She had been spying and saw the whole thing. "Go in the back, I'll handle things up here."

 timesCG

A month went by and I had neither seen nor heard from Nigel. Hope that he would come back to me was diminishing. Every once in a while, I would hear his band on the radio and it only reminded me of his success and how he had chosen it over me. I would often wonder where he was, what he was doing, who he was with. As for me, I usually spent my free time moping around the apartment. I still slept with that old stuffed lion he gave me every night, often using it as a handkerchief to dry my tears. I was definitely not over him.

I tried to get on with my life, though. I tried to involve my brain with thoughts other than him. Sarah and Victoria definitely helped. Instead of trying to set me up with new guys, they planned girls only afternoons and weekends. They were still working on their own band, which for some reason didn't remind me of Nigel and his band. Maybe because it was all girls instead of all boys, I don't know. They were only a two piece now since Suzy was gone. We were sitting around the apartment talking about that one night.

"Where in the hell are we supposed to get a new singer?" Victoria whined.

"No fucking clue," Sarah retorted.

"Where have you looked?" I asked.

"Um, pubs, other bands, friends of friends, even some customers from the local scene," Victoria answered.

"And no one is any good?" I couldn't believe it.

"Well, maybe they look right, but they can't sing. Or, they sound decent but they're too old or something. We need someone who looks like they go with us."

"And someone who can write good lyrics," Sarah added.

"You need a songwriter?" I inquired.

"Well, yeah. That's usually the singer's domain," Sarah responded.

"I can give you some songs," I offered. The girls looked at me like I held the goose with the golden eggs. "What?" I was surprised. "I've been writing songs and poems and stuff for years."

"Where are they?" Victoria jumped on it.

"In my room."

"Go get 'em!"

I hurried to collect my journals and notebooks full of lyrics and verses. I handed them off. The girls flipped through them, ignoring some and rereading others.

"There are a lot of sappy ones in here," Victoria complained.

"Yeah. Most of them are about how much I love- er, *loved* Nigel."

"Some of these have potential," Sarah commented.

"You think so? Cool."

"Do you sing?" Victoria asked bluntly.

"Um, I can sing. I don't do it much, though. And not in front of people."

"Could you?" Sarah pressed.

"Well . . . I guess so. If you guys are really desperate for a singer."

"We are!" Victoria said quickly.

"We haven't been able to do any shows since Suzy left. And that's fine, because we needed an image overhaul. So, maybe this is it! What do you say? Are you in?" Sarah and Victoria looked at me with wide, hopeful eyes.

"Oh . . . Okay," I replied.

They jumped up and screamed and hugged me.

☙

My twentieth birthday was approaching and I was not really looking forward to it. In America, twenty one was important; in England, it was insignificant. Being twenty back home would've meant only one more year until I could legally drink. Being twenty in England just meant your youth was vanishing. I was not ready to start growing old alone. Nigel had celebrated my last four birthdays with me; this next one was a ticking clock of doom. The girls made it fun, as much fun as it could be. We went out drinking and dancing. I drank until I forgot that Nigel hadn't sent a card or called to wish me a happy birthday. It really was over.

But my musical career was just beginning. I was glad to have more distractions from Nigel. However, I used the opportunity to write about him and our failed relationship in angst riddled songs that fit the band's tough but cool facade. Our image was angry, rough sex kittens. Girls you didn't want to piss off, but you wanted to fuck. When we practiced, I found that it wasn't hard to sing in front of people when I was fueled up the way I was with passion and loathing. It was cathartic.

The only problem was that I didn't play any instruments.

"I can teach you enough to get you by," Sarah offered. "You can play bass."

I gave her a vicious scowl and she retreated.

"Sorry, forget I said that. You can just sing. I'll find someone else who can play a little bass."

And that's what we did. We found a fourth member of the new and improved Dirty Sweet, a cute but quiet young girl that frequented our boutique. Her name was Lila and she was good enough to join the band. We were synchronized and we thought we sounded pretty decent. Before long, Victoria had booked us a show. It was a small gig, and we were only asked to play three songs to open for an up and coming local band, but we were thrilled anyway. I was scared, but with my best friends around me, I had enough courage to belt out our raspy tunes.

From there, we played other small venues and word of mouth was starting to spread. With every show, we were getting better and because of that, we were able to book larger and longer shows. We were far from famous, though, far from making it big with our music. Our biggest break was when Victoria scored us a gig in a midsize club on a weekday night. Our set list was four new songs and three covers. I was nervous but excited, ready to unleash myself on the world, but afraid they wouldn't like me.

We were as well rehearsed as possible. On the night of the show, we were actually confident that this could be the start of something big. We spent hours getting ready, practicing and dressing up in our trademark punk prostitute chic clothing.

When we walked on stage, it was very dark, and I was glad. It took some of the pressure off. Victoria took her place behind the drum kit, Sarah on the left of me with her electric guitar, Lila on the right with her bass, and I stood behind the microphone stand.

I had to introduce us. "Hi everyone, we're Dirty Sweet and we're about to knock your socks off. Let's go!"

Victoria banged her drum sticks together. We all counted out loud. "One, two, one, two, three, four." Then, boom, the girls kicked off into our first number. I followed, trying to match their furious enthusiasm.

By the end of the first song, the crowd was responding better than I had anticipated. That gave me a confidence boost for the next song. This continued. Our sixth song was slower, almost a ballad. The lights dimmed further. When the song was over, the audience exploded and the lights brightened a bit. I was so relieved and happy. I couldn't help but smile out to the audience, forgetting my supposed pissed off demeanor. As I returned the love to the crowd, I saw a familiar face. Nigel was there. He was clapping slowly, staring back at me. I was fixed on him, dumbfounded. It was almost a minute before I could snap out of it.

"Hey!" Sarah screeched in a loud whisper. "Introduce the next song!"

"Oh yeah," I muttered. I tried to ignore Nigel's presence. "Okay everyone, we've got one more song for you tonight and it's a fast one, so get up and let's do this!"

Sarah cranked on her guitar and Victoria started pounding away on the drums. I found Nigel again in the crowd as I waited for my part to come. This time, I noticed who he was with. The band was there with their usual crowd, but there was someone new with them. A pretty brunette stood beside to Nigel, very close. Her arm was linked in his. She didn't notice I was staring at her with confusion and resentment.

I couldn't think about it anymore, it was time to sing. And the song couldn't have been more fitting- an angry number about a bad breakup. I tore it up, fueling it with rage and emotion like never before. Mostly, I kept my eyes closed, but occasionally I would open them to see Nigel looking guilty, a bit scared, and uncomfortable. Shortly after, the song was over, the girls fizzling it out into a grand finale.

"Thank you! Good night!" I shouted as we stood and bowed before exiting the stage.

"That was fucking great!" Victoria cheered as we walked off.

"Damn straight!" Sarah agreed.

"Yeah," was all I could muster. I was almost a zombie after seeing Nigel with another girl already.

"What's with you?" Victoria demanded. "That went perfectly!"

I didn't answer. I had zeroed in on Nigel, pulling the arm of his latest trick out of the club in a hurry. They rushed past us toward the door. There was no need to explain to Victoria why I wasn't as high on life as they were. The girls looked at me like I needed comforting again.

"Come on, let's get a drink," Sarah suggested.

They led me to the bar and just as we gave our order to the bartender, a man's voice from behind us said, "It's on me."

I turned around, about ready to smack any man who dared talk to me right now when I saw it was Sammy. My fury softened to appreciation.

"Would you girls fancy joining us? Free drinks. To congratulate you for your show."

"Can't say no to that!" Sarah answered for all of us. We took our drinks and followed Sammy to an out of the way table in the back of the club. He held out a chair for me and after I sat, he sat next to me.

"We didn't know you joined the band."

"Yeah, just a couple of months ago," I answered.

"That was a great show, ladies!" Randy cheered.

"Wasn't it?" Sarah agreed. They all laughed and talked about gigs and performing and venues and such. The guys talked about their latest shows and budding success when they were prodded, though they seemed to be in a hurry to change the subject for my sake. It was starting to feel uncomfortable.

"Hey, guys, don't feel like you have to walk on eggshells for me," I said.

In unison they all began saying "No, No. Not at all" and the like to placate me. But their faces said it all. It was like "Sorry our friend dumped you for us."

"So, what's next for your band?" Mick asked.

"Um, I don't know. We haven't really thought about it yet," Victoria said.

"No plans to travel and tour the world?" Randy probed. "It's a blast! There is nothing like it!"

Then, total silence. The room grew tense. My face fell.

He tried to recover. "Oh, shit! I didn't mean- Listen, John's a fucking idiot for letting you go. No tour beats a great girl."

"Don't worry about it. I think I'll go now, though." I felt like I had been punched in the stomach.

Sarah and Victoria stood up. "No, sit. You guys stay. I'll catch a cab home. Goodnight everyone." I turned to go.

Sammy stood up. "Wait. I'll drive you home." I nodded. He escorted me out of the club and into the parking lot toward his little red car. He opened the car door for me and shut it behind me. He then got in on the other side and slid behind the wheel in silence. He drove, seemingly debating with himself over something. I stared out the window, letting him think,

"John's really torn up, you know," he finally blurted.

"Oh yeah?"

"Yeah, he is."

"So, that girl he was with tonight, she was his psychiatrist?"

He fumbled for the right words. "He's trying to get over you."

"Why? He could have me back in a second! He doesn't need to be *torn up*. He made his decision. He deserves to hurt over it. God knows I am."

We were pulling into the parking lot of my building. Sammy parked and turned to me. "Just, don't think you didn't mean the world to him. Since I met him, all he ever talked about was you. And during that European tour, God, all he did was blubber over your breakup. He didn't eat, he drank way too much, he took more pills and shit than any of us, but he didn't even *look* at any girls. He was just trying to escape his pain, and I think that's why he brought that girl with him tonight. None of us knew you would be there. If we did, we wouldn't have gone, because he's not over you."

I believed him. "I'm not over him either. I can't take seeing him with other girls. I don't think I'd ever be okay with that. I think I need to leave England. It's his turf, not mine."

"But what about your band? You just started."

"You know, I don't care about that stuff. I don't want fame and everything that goes with it. That won't make me happy…" I didn't finish my thought, I didn't need to. It was obvious that only Nigel would complete my life. "But I wish you well. Good luck with everything. Thanks for the ride. Goodbye, Sammy." I opened my car door and was poised to get out.

"Don't give up on your dreams. You never know what will happen in the future. If you are meant to be with John, you will be," Sammy prophesized.

I nodded. "Right." I got out and shut the door.

I made up my mind by the time Sarah and Victoria got home that I was going to move back to America. They were not happy.

"What? You can't leave!" Victoria screamed.

"I have to. I can't be running into Nigel every time I turn around."

"You aren't! Come on, don't go!" Sarah insisted.

"I think I need to. I need to go home and try to have a normal life."

"What about the band? We're on the verge of something big, here. I know it!" Victoria whined.

"You don't need me for that. Have Lila sing. I know she can, I've heard her. She's probably better than me!"

"But she's not you! We don't just want you to stay for the band; we want you around. We'll miss you." Sarah confessed.

"I'll miss you, too. You guys are wonderful and I have really appreciated having you as friends and as my support, especially lately."

They looked somber, like they realized I truly meant business. I had made up my mind and I was sure about it.

"When do you think you're going back?" Victoria asked.

"Next month, I guess. Long enough to get everything in order."

"We can't talk you out of this?" Sarah pleaded.

"No. Sorry."

"Damn that Nigel!" Victoria cursed.

"Michelle, you don't always have to run away when things get tough," Sarah insisted.

"What are you talking about? I'm not running away," I was baffled.

"You are too! That's what you always do when you get upset. You just run."

"Sarah, ease up," Victoria intervened.

"Stay out of this, Vic. She needs to hear the truth."

"Well, I don't know what you're talking about," I said defiantly.

"Of course you don't! You can figure everyone else in the world out, but not yourself. You don't even know you're doing it, but you always run when things go bad. I'm telling you this as your friend, as someone who has gotten very close to you over the past couple of years. As someone who doesn't want to see you go." Her eyes were tearing up, her face morose. My irritation at her accusations faded into equal sorrow because I was not just saying goodbye to the life I had built, but to my best friend, too.

"I'm sorry. I don't want to leave you. I love you. It has meant so much to me to have a friend I can count on, especially with . . . well, you know. But, I just can't stay here anymore. I just can't. It's too hard. I need to get away from all these reminders. I have to start over. But, maybe I'll see you again. Maybe one day, you'll move to America," I suggested with a laugh. Victoria joined in halfheartedly.

Sarah just looked heartbroken. "You know, you always have a place to stay if you change your mind."

"Thanks, I really appreciate that. You guys are the best." I hugged them both.

But I didn't change my mind. I was sure I needed to get out of England. Everything reminded me of Nigel. Places we'd been, the local accents, posters of his band advertising upcoming concerts. It was too much. I called my parents to tell them I was done with Nigel and was moving back to Michigan. My mother seemed pleased, a bit smug, but pleased. They never wanted me to move away and they never wanted me to pursue my relationship with Nigel. Their wishes were coming true, as mine were blowing up in smoke.

Chapter 11

"...some purpose and direction."

It was the fall of 1981when I got back to America. To me, that was significant. Fall meant death. Just like the flowers and grass and leaves, my life too was over. I was feeling incredibly low. Several months ago, I had everything I had ever wanted. Now, I was starting from scratch. And worse yet, I was moving back in with my parents.

They met me at the airport, at the claiming area where I was picking up Autumn. I could read their faces and their thoughts. On the surface they seemed happy to have me back home with them, but I could sense the I-told-you-so attitude underneath.

"Welcome home!" My mother extended her arms when I met her at the gate. I fell into a halfhearted hug.

My father copied the move as my mom passed me down to him. "Hi, Dad," I greeted with zero enthusiasm.

"Good to have you back, kid," he said, but I doubted he meant it. I knew he was still pissed off at me for causing a rift, for disobeying his orders to follow my dreams, for moving across the ocean to shack up with a musician . . . What I'm sure he meant was it was good to have me back where they could control me and keep me away from my Kryptonite.

We drove home, practically in silence. Occasionally my mother would try to ask me a question, to which I would respond as monosyllabically as possible. She tried to fill me in on the goings on at home and with the family, but I couldn't feign interest. I tried to keep my focus on Autumn.

When we got to our big, white house, my soul sank lower. This was it. It felt like jail to me. Instantly I regretted not finding my own apartment, or shack, or cardboard box to live in. I thought of Nigel, probably living it up right now while I was regressing back to my thirteen year old self. I cursed him in my head. He ruined all my plans. Why did he have to be the way he was? Why couldn't I be enough for him like he was for me?

I let Autumn out of her carrier and watched her with cautious mother eyes as she sniffed around and re-familiarized herself with her new home. Before long, she was out of sight and I decided to go to my room and settle in.

As I was unpacking what I had brought, I heard a tap on the open door. My parents were standing there, poised for lecture. An uneasy feeling swept through me. "We need to talk," my father insisted.

"Okay," I mumbled.

My mother started. "We just want to lay down some ground rules. Things have changed since you lived here last and we think we should make some things clear."

"Like what?"

"Well . . . " My mom hesitated.

"Curfew," my father interjected loudly.

"Curfew?" I couldn't believe my ears.

"Yeah. I don't know what the hell you were up to in Cambridge, but that's not gonna fly here. We don't need to be up all night waiting for you to come home, and we don't need you waking us up at three a.m. either."

My mom nodded. "And no boys in the house. We don't want any repeats of that. No boys sneaking in."

I couldn't believe I was hearing this. What did they think of me? Obviously I was some sex crazed, night prowling slut who needed to be put on lockdown. Couldn't they tell I was a brokenhearted shell of myself?

"And you have to do what your mother and I tell you to do. This is our house and if you want to live here, you can, but you have to obey us."

That one I understood loud and clear. They were bitter that I hadn't done what they commanded me to do and they were punishing me for that now.

"That being said, we want you to go back to school," my dad continued. "And none of that art school shit, you're getting a real diploma that you can use."

"We thought you could go to the community college. They have a lot of courses to choose from. I took a booklet from their office." She handed me a paperback manual filled with career opportunities.

I stared down at it, unable and unwilling to meet their gaze or say anything to them.

"Well, we'll leave you alone now," my mother said and guided my dad out of the room, shutting the door behind them.

I sank down onto the bed, feeling paralyzed with impending doom. It all just seemed to be getting worse. First I lose the love of my life, then I lose the home I had made for myself; then I'm forced to move back to live with my parents where I'm treated like a child/prisoner, and now, coerced into college!

That was too much. If I had to follow their rules while I lived under their roof, fine. But to ruin my whole future by making me choose a job I'll surely hate? That was too much!

Worse yet, I wanted to call Nigel and cry to him. He was the one I wanted to turn to and still the first one I thought of. I realized now I had no one. I was alone. Outnumbered in my own home. Treated like a guilty convict.

I sighed. This was a lot to take at once. Tears started to build in my eyes. Then I heard a scratch at the door. Autumn had found me. I got up to let her in. She pranced into the room, continuing her quest to smell everything in the house. I shut the door and sat and watched her study everything, happy for the distraction. When she was finished, she leapt on the bed next to me, purring and snuggling. Looking at her darling face changed my perspective. She got comfortable and was sleeping in no time. Poor thing, she was surely exhausted after the trip. So was I. I managed to lie down without disturbing her too much and stroked her little head until I too fell asleep.

I woke up when I heard Autumn scratching at the door to get out. I looked at the alarm clock. It was after three in the morning. I got up to let her out, then laid back down, hoping to fall back asleep. I couldn't. It was too early to start my day, but my mind was racing with woes. I turned on my bedside lamp. I noticed the college manual on the night-stand. I picked it up, hoping it would bore me into slumber. All the choices sounded entirely unappealing. It was depressing. I scanned the pages as I fell asleep again.

When I woke up later, it was to the sound of the back door slamming shut. My parents had left for work. I was relieved to have privacy, relieved to have a break from their lectures and clucking tongues. I trotted down the stairs to the kitchen. I found a note on the table on top of the newspaper:

Find a job or decide on a major
before I get home

It was my father's handwriting. I looked down at the newspaper, the want ads were right on top.

"Unreal," I complained out loud, shaking my head. I contemplated finding an apartment and moving out instead of following their demands. I picked up the want ads, looking for apartments to rent when a request for the art supply store that I had worked at before caught my eye. They were looking for a manager. I was intrigued. I thought it might be the perfect answer. I could work there, get money while getting my parents off of my back and be able to afford my own place in no time! I hurried to the phone and dialed, the number still in my memory.

My old manager, Steve, answered the phone.

"Hi, Steve, this is Michelle Casey."

"Michelle? You're in town?"

"Yeah, I moved back. Listen, I saw your ad in the paper- "

"You want the job?"

"Well, yeah. I have experience there, obviously. And while I lived in England I worked my way up to co-manager of a store."

"Okay, sounds good. Why don't you come in today? Say, one o'clock?"

"Sure, yeah, absolutely! Thank you!"

I was excited. My scheme might just work out. I had hope for the first time in a long time. A bright spot in what I was sure would be a dreary day.

When I went in for the interview, I was pleasantly surprised to see familiar faces around the store. They all looked shocked to see me back, but happy as well. It was nice to be greeted by smiles instead of rules.

Steve met me and led me to the manager's office. "So, you want to be the manager?"

"Yes, I think I'd be good at that. I kind of know what to expect."

"I guess you would. I'll be honest with you. I need to fill this position ASAP and all the other candidates, well, leave something to be desired."

I nodded, my hopes rising.

"Give me a name and number to check on your last job, and if you get a good recommendation, you got the job."

My eyebrows lifted in surprise. "Really? Wow, awesome."

He slid a pad of paper and a pen at me to write down the information. I wrote the phone number to the boutique and Sarah's name, sure she would give me a sterling review.

"So, Steve," I asked as I scribbled, "Why are you in such a rush to find a new manager?"

"I'm going back to school," he stated proudly. "I'm ready for bigger and better things."

"What are you going for?" I asked, truly interested.

"Accounting! I had no idea what I wanted to get my degree in, but accountants make a ton of money. My brother-in-law is one. He's got a huge place and a brand new car, *and* he gets all these company perks. So, he tells me I should try it. And I think, why not? I mean, this job involves math and numbers and money, and I can swing that. So, I took a few classes in night school and it turns out, I'm really good at it. Now, I've decided to go full time and finish my degree so I can start making the big bucks."

His face was shining with optimism. I was glad he had found something that suited him and made him happy. I was also glad for the title he was leaving to me. I was more than happy to take his leftovers.

"That sounds great! Good luck!"

"Thanks. It feels right."

I nodded again.

"Well, hey, I'm gonna have to call on your reference check. So, I'll call you later to let you know how it went."

"Okay, very good. Do you still have my number?"

"No, I don't think so. Give it to me again."

I jotted it down and made my way out of the store, waving goodbye to the employees I spotted as I exited. I walked home quickly in the brisk November air, making a mental note to myself that the first thing I saved up for would have to be a car, not an apartment.

By the time I got home, my outlook had changed. I was feeling confident that things could turn around for the better. The walk had cleared my head. I was on my way up to my room to check out the college course manual to see if I could find some night course to get excited about like Steve had when the phone rang.

"Hello?"

"Hi, Michelle? It's Steve. I called your reference and it checks out. You got the job."

"I do? Oh good!"

"Yeah. How soon can you start?"

"Oh, um, right away, I think."

"Okay. Can you be here tomorrow at nine?"

"Yeah, yeah I can."

"Great! Thanks. I'll see you tomorrow then."

"Okay, see you tomorrow!" I hung up, jubilant, forgetting all about my college plans.

When my parents got home, I was proud to tell them my news. They were happy to hear it.

"So, you don't think you want to go to college, then?" my mother asked.

"I don't know if I'll need to. But I can always go back later if I decide that's what I want," I answered, recalling Steve and his ambitions.

"Well, like I said, if you want to go to school, we'll help pay for it," my dad reminded me, not seeming too disappointed that I was rejecting school, thus saving him thousands of dollars.

"Thank you. I'll let you know."

And after that, they dropped it. No more lectures. They were happy I had a job that could support me.

And so was I. It got me out of the house. It distracted me from thinking about Nigel all the time. It gave me some purpose and direction.

ॐ

Steve showed me the ropes for the first two weeks, and then he quit altogether to pursue his education. I was comfortable. I knew what to expect and I loved being in that little art shop.

He was right about the math, though. There was more math involved than I anticipated. Luckily for me, it was all within my scope. Most of it was money matters and inventory and such. Before long, I was very good at calculating all the figures I dealt with. Steve was right, it was kind of fun.

Within a few months, I was able to afford a car- a used car, but a good car. It drained my bank account and I had to start over again, saving up as much as I could so I could afford to move out. Things were going better at home, but I didn't want to live under my parents' roof any longer than I had to.

Although I saved up as much money as possible, I wanted more, and I wanted it now. If I stayed a manager of an art supply store, I would have enough to live on. I could support myself and pay my bills, but I wouldn't be able to live as comfortably as I wanted to.

I would think about Nigel, making millions as a famous musician, living lavishly, sitting in a hot tub, wearing gold chains, drinking champagne with beautiful bikini clad models straddling him as his butler offers caviar to him on a silver platter.

Then, I thought of me in a dark, dingy apartment, bundled up in an old coat and mittens, sharing a can of cat food with Autumn by candle light- our only source of light and heat.

I knew those were ridiculous thoughts, but I understood why Steve felt the need to persevere, to try to make more of himself, to achieve a better life. I wanted that, too. And I didn't want Nigel to have the world while I had nothing. By this time, he and his band were growing more and more famous. They had regular airplay on the hottest radio stations and were frequently on television in live appearances and interviews. I hated the thought that he was out of my league, that he was leaving me in the dust as he was growing into a superstar. I couldn't allow that. Maybe I didn't want to be a famous musician or anything, but I wasn't going to be a pauper either. If he ever saw me again, he would see a success!

It was silly to base my goals around that fantasy (like he would ever just drop by to see me!), but it fueled me anyway. I looked in that college manual and found those night accounting classes that Steve had taken and decided I would do that, too.

My parents were happy with the notion. "Accounting. That's good and stable," my dad beamed.

"So you think you'll be able to handle working all day, then going to school at night?" my mother asked.

"Yeah, it's not like I have a life or anything. Besides, I still want to save up money, so I want to keep working. I can handle it all," I said resolutely. And I meant it. I was stubborn. If there was something I wanted, I wouldn't take no for an answer.

And that's what I did. In the fall of 1982, I enrolled in college. I worked from nine to six in the store Monday through Friday and went to class from seven to ten four nights a week, then from eight till noon on Saturday. I barely had time to do anything, but it didn't matter. Like I told my mother, I had no life. None of my old friends were around anymore. I was chummy with the employees at work and although I went out for a drink with them for my twenty-first birthday, there were very few times when we hung out outside of work. I didn't really mind. My life wasn't full of fun, but it *was* full. And I couldn't be lonely when I was so busy. I had no time to think about it.

So, I definitely was not looking for a new boyfriend.

But a boy in my business class wanted to change that.

He sat next to me and little by little got to know me. First he would ask me little things like, "What did the teacher just say?" or "Do you know if it's supposed to rain today?" Then, it was on to borrowing pencils and notes, making small talk and getting basic personal information.

I didn't think anything of it at first. I didn't mind this stranger chit chatting with me. He was alright. Funny, nice, friendly. That was it. I could see it coming though, and a few weeks into our semester, it happened. He asked me if I had a boyfriend one Thursday as class was letting out.

At first, I didn't know how to answer. I didn't have a boyfriend, but for some reason, I didn't consider myself available. I guess a big part of me felt attached to Nigel, like our breakup was only temporary until he came to his senses. I felt like he was still my future. But, in reality, I was single.

"No, I don't," I finally replied.

"Oh. I'm kind of surprised. Glad, but surprised." He smiled.

"Surprised?"

"Yeah. Pretty girl like you . . . how could you stay single for long?"

I scoffed at the compliment. I didn't believe it, my self esteem was very low. I tried not to seem rude, though. "Well, it hasn't been long," I admitted quietly, looking down. After the words came out of my mouth, I realized it had been a year already. It still felt like yesterday. The pain was fresh. It was slowly diminishing, but it was always there.

"Oh, I see. Breakups are tough. You're probably not ready to date anyone else yet, but . . . " he seemed to be working up the nerve to finish his thought. "If you ever want to talk or get a drink or something, here's my phone number. My name's Will, by the way. Will Benson."

I took the piece of paper. "I'm Michelle Casey. Maybe I'll take you up on that one day."

"Cool. Well, have a nice weekend," he said, grinning, and walked away.

I looked at the paper with his name and number on it. It felt wrong. I felt dirty just having it in my hand. I crumpled it up and jammed it in my purse.

Driving home that night, I kept thinking about Nigel, Will, and myself. Why did it feel so wrong to consider dating someone else? I knew Nigel was. I knew he was more than just dating other people. Why did I feel guilty?

Maybe it didn't feel like guilt. It felt more like infidelity because I envisioned myself invisibly bound to Nigel for so long. Did it just feel weird because I wasn't over Nigel yet? Or was it something else?

I pondered that all night and all the next day at work. It was Friday and I was glad to not have to see Will until the following Tuesday. I wasn't ready to tell him yea or nay.

By the afternoon, all the worry caught up to me and I felt exhausted (or was it the forty hour work week plus school and homework?). I sneaked into the break-room to relax for a moment. Sinking down into a chair at the little table, I groaned and closed my eyes. About a minute later, I opened them and saw Nigel.

He was on the cover of a magazine someone had left on the table. I lunged for it and scanned it quickly. The headline read:

"Descent's hottest playboy, John Blake, dating three models at once!"

And there was his picture, sure enough, up to his elbows in three gorgeous women. He wore a huge smile, open and laughing. I had seen that smile so many times before, but it didn't seem recognizable that *my* Nigel was *this* John. *Playboy?*

I shook my head, trying to clear it. *How could he be having so much fun while I was still grieving over our breakup? Wasn't he devastated, too? Apparently not!* And I was worried about having a drink with a guy? Just a regular guy, not three incredible male models at once. My heart was racing and I felt my face redden with pain and anger. My fingers- still gripping the magazine I stared at helplessly- felt like they were going to burn through it.

One of the employees came in, Tonya, a young girl, maybe fifteen or so. She saw me staring at the cover.

"Oh, do you like him, too?"

I gave her a crazed, confused look. She misinterpreted it.

"I know! He's so hot! I can't believe how lucky those girls are. I mean, to be so close to John Blake. . . . How could you stand it?" She was giddy.

She was also clueless. No one here knew about my relationship with "John," or anything about my life in England for that matter. It wasn't worth telling. No one would believe me, and I didn't want the questions and attention that would go along with it if they did.

"He's not that great," I said coldly, getting up and slamming the magazine down on the table.

"Yeah, okay," she teased. "I saw how you were looking at him. Like you *love* him. Don't deny it."

I sighed and stormed out of the room and into my tiny office. Shutting the door behind me, I felt unstoppable tears fill my eyes.

"Damn you, damn you, damn you," I whispered, cursing Nigel as fat teardrops poured down my face.

I tried to calm down. "Stop crying, you idiot! Pull yourself together!" I whispered to myself. I reached into my purse for a tissue and pulled out the wadded up phone number I'd stuffed away yesterday.

I was about to throw it into the trashcan, angered that it wouldn't be useful in drying my face and wanting only that. Before my fingers released it, I changed my mind. I kept it in my hand while I successfully hunted for a tissue.

Blotting my eyes, I unraveled the crumpled memo, looking at it with a new perspective. Someone wanted to buy *me* a drink? Someone thought *I* was special enough to take out? Someone thought *I* was good looking? It was the reassurance I needed, and a drink sounded like the perfect medicine.

I picked up my phone and dialed Will's number, nervously playing with the cord while it rang. He answered and sounded excited that I had called. We made a date for that evening.

We met at a bar near school. He was there waiting when I arrived. He saw me and waved me over to the booth he was in. He stood up when I approached.

"You look nice," he said as I sat down.

"Thank you," I responded, surprised that my simple efforts tonight would impress anyone. I had to remember, this was a regular guy, not a rock star.

"So, what will you have?" Will asked. "I'll go up and get it for you."

"Um, how about a Cosmo?"

"You got it!" He was gone in a flash.

Huh, I thought to myself. He was treating me like I was a celebrity or something. I had gotten used to Nigel's self important attitude and self absorbedness. Will was back in a hurry, almost like he was afraid I would leave if I had the chance.

"Thank you."

"No problem."

"Um . . ." I hesitated, trying to make small talk. "Do you live around here?"

"Not too far. You?"

"Not too far either. Which is nice, because I had to work before I could get home to get ready tonight." I hoped he understood my explanation for the simple jeans and a sweater ensemble I had thrown on. I didn't look grungy, but not glammed up the way I used to when I went out with my previous boyfriend.

"Oh yeah? What do you do?"

We waded into a back and forth conversation about ourselves. We talked about school, work, and family- the basic intro to dating.

After three drinks, I realized it was getting late. The time had gone by quickly. I was enjoying my time with this simple boy. It was easy to talk to him. I didn't feel naive and unworthy around him. I felt . . . above him. Like he was putting me on a pedestal. And why? Was I that great? Nigel apparently didn't seem to think so.

"I have to go. I have class in the morning," I explained.

"Oh, okay. Well, let me walk you out."

"Let me pay for my drinks." I reached into my purse.

"No, no! On me. Please."

"Are you sure?"

"Yes! I asked *you* out for a drink. I didn't realize you would drink half the booze in Michigan, but that's my responsibility."

I laughed, being far from drunk. He was funny. He threw down some money on the table and escorted me to my car.

"Thank you for a lovely night," I said, standing by my car, the cold autumn air sobering me up quickly.

"Yeah, I had a good time. Maybe we can do it again."

"Sure, that sounds good."

"Okay, um, I'll talk to you in class, then."

"Okay. Goodnight."

He stumbled awkwardly, not knowing whether or not to kiss me. He decided on a quick peck on the cheek. "Goodnight."

He walked away fast, seemingly embarrassed. I smiled as I got into my car. I remembered when Nigel was awkward around me physically. It seemed like an eternity ago.

I felt good on the short drive home. Maybe the alcohol relaxed me. More likely, it was because Will had validated me. For the first time in a long time, I felt desirable and worthy.

I decided to keep seeing him. He was delighted. He thought I was a princess even though I did nothing *I* perceived to be impressive. I was just myself. He looked at me differently than Nigel ever looked at me. Of course, Nigel always looked at me adoringly because he loved me almost from day one. But Will looked at me like Tonya looked at that picture of Nigel/John on the cover of the magazine. It felt good.

And I liked him, too. He was decent looking, though I wasn't particularly attracted to his features. Nigel had kind of spoiled me for other men, but I liked Will more for who he was on the inside. A big part of me wondered if my involvement with him was a rebound effort or if I truly wanted him around.

Whatever the reason, we spent more and more time together. I found out that he was an orphan and was raised by an adopted father who had died two years prior. It was sad, but he didn't let it get him down; he was very accepting of all the tragedy he underwent in his young life. It also explained his gregarious personality, always trying to charm those around him into liking and accepting him into their hearts.

It worked on me.

Eventually I invited him to my parents' house one night for dinner. They liked him immediately. After some basic small talk over the meal, we congregated in the living room for cake, and eventually, heavier conversation.

"Well, young man, what are your goals for the future?" my father asked in an embarrassing, intrusive paternal act.

"Um, I go to school full time, I'm working on my master's degree in Marketing. I should be graduating this spring. I also work part time for a marketing firm as an intern and I'm hoping to secure a position there when I graduate," Will summed up effectively.

My dad looked pleasantly surprised and exchanged a look conveying that to my mother, who also had questions.

"So, do you live with your parents, Will?"

"No, my parents died when I was very young." I winced, instantly regretting not mentioning this to my parents before. Will was composed and he continued. "I was raised by a great man, but he also passed away a couple of years ago to cancer." The room was thick and tense. I could feel my mother's embarrassment. He tried to lighten it up. "But, he left me his house and a substantial amount of money to tide me over." Will kept taking deep breaths, trying to control his emotions. "He was always very generous with me, he was an orphan himself. But, he didn't want to spoil me, even though he did," Will added with a light laugh. "He wanted to teach me how to become a self sufficient man. And I hope I'm making him proud."

"I'm sure you are, dear," my mother said with big sad eyes, looking ready to cry.

Just then, like a perfect mind reader, Autumn came into the room, mewing and strutting around. Great distraction. Will was attentive.

"Hi kitty. Come here, kitty kitty."

"That's Autumn," I explained.

"Aw. Hi Autumn." He scratched her head when she came near his outstretched hand. "I've never had a pet. Must be nice. The old man was allergic to everything."

Again, my mom looked ready to cry, saddened at his lack of animals while growing up. My dad noticed and tried to keep the conversation light.

"Yeah, we got that cat for Michelle for her sixteenth birthday when we lived in England."

"You lived in England?" Will asked, looking at me.

"She didn't tell you?" my dad asked. "She didn't tell you about her musician boyfriend and all that stuff that happened over there?"

"No. I guess she was embarrassed she dated some poor musician. Probably couldn't get a real job, huh?" he half joked with my dad.

My father busted with laughter. I didn't think it was funny for several reasons. One, I hated that my father still undermined my relationship with Nigel. Two, it wasn't my father's place to tell Will about my past. Three, Will said "musician" like it was a dirty word. Four, why was Will trying to butter up my dad instead of siding with me? It was the first thing he had ever done to upset me, and to me, it was a big thing. It seemed that Will's attitude was more like my parents than my own. I tried not to jump to conclusions. I didn't even have time to think it over before my mother joined in.

"Why didn't you tell Will about any of that? And why didn't you tell us he was an orphan? That would've saved us an awkward conversation. Why are you always so secretive?"

I had three pairs of eyes on me now, waiting for an answer to too many questions. I hated confrontations.

"I'm sorry, I should have warned you about Will's parents. And I didn't want to tell him everything about my past right away. I was going to wait for the right time. I wasn't trying to be secretive."

I felt like a child who had just been reprimanded in public. Embarrassed, ashamed, all eyes on me. Autumn continued to try to demand attention, but things were too uncomfortable for her to distract us.

Will broke the tension. "It's getting late. I should go home now."

He stood up, and we all followed his lead.

"Well, it was very nice to meet you, Will," my mother crooned.

"You, too. Thank you so much for dinner. It was great."

"Our pleasure having you, son," my father shook his hand.

"Thank you. Good night," he said, looking at my parents. Then he turned to me. "Michelle, do you want to walk me to my car? I'm not sure if I trust this neighborhood," he joked, rationalizing the need for me to accompany him.

We all laughed at the fake slam against our posh street. He started toward the door, pausing to turn and wave goodbye to my parents as I followed him out.

"I'm sorry if that got weird in there," I apologized.

"No, I'm fine. Are you fine?"

"Yeah, fine. Are you fine?"

"Yeah, fine."

"Fine," I nodded.

He looked at me, questioningly. " . . . So, we're fine then?" he teased.

I laughed. "Yeah, I think my parents like you."

"Yeah, I'm a crowd pleaser."

I laughed again. "Well, thanks for enduring that . . . I should go in. My parents will think we're bad mouthing them if I'm out here too long."

"Okay. Um . . . I guess I'll see you in class, then."

"Yeah, see you in class. Goodnight." I gave him a little peck on the lips.

He smiled happily. "Goodnight." He got into his car and I watched as he drove off, waving.

When I went back in the house, my parents were still in the living room. I was sure they had also been discussing the dinner. I waited for the onslaught.

"He's a nice boy," my mother commented.

"Yes, he's nice," I replied.

"A lot more suitable for you than the last one," my father judged.

I was silent, offended. "Yeah . . . I wish you didn't have to bring Nigel up during dessert."

"I just assumed you had told him. I mean, you were barely able to talk about anything else for the past five years."

"That's not true- "

"Oh, stop it you two. That's all in the past. William is the future," my mother interrupted.

"Wait, mom, Will and I have only been dating a few weeks. Let's not get carried away, here."

"Well, he's just the type of guy you should be with. Your father is right. You and Nigel? No, he wasn't right for you. You didn't belong together. You and Will look like you belong together."

What was she talking about? I had never felt any connection so strong in my life than the one I had immediately with Nigel. Did they think he was too fast for me? Or too foreign? What was their beef with him? My mother seemed to be reading my mind.

"Now, your first love will always be special to you, but don't make it out to be more than that, especially with Nigel. I mean, who knew he would end up a rock star? I saw him on the cover of a magazine with *three* models today! Obviously, you two don't fit together."

My dad snorted.

My face burned. What was she saying? That my once nerdy first love was now way too hot for the likes of me? That's why they thought things didn't work out? Was that what she was saying? I was pissed.

"Okay, conversation over. I'm going to my room."

"Of course you are," my dad mumbled, though I was able to hear it. I also heard my mother ask, "What did I say,?" slightly confused.

I stomped up to my room, slammed the door shut, and locked it behind me. I flopped on my bed, angry. I couldn't understand my parents and they obviously didn't understand me. I liked Will, but nowhere near as much as I had liked Nigel. He didn't stir up those kind of feelings. I doubted he ever could.

And apparently, my own mother and father thought I wasn't good enough for Nigel anymore! Wasn't cool enough, wasn't pretty enough, or did they just hate him and want to convince me to move on toward a more realistic mate?

I couldn't follow their thought processes and I really didn't care. They didn't know me, even though we lived together all my life (save those two years I lived with Nigel). They never understood our love. And they certainly didn't know what was best for me!

I wasn't going to break up with Will to spite them, but I wasn't going to rush out and marry him either, like I'm sure they would have loved. I was determined to take it slowly and weigh my feelings as things progressed, untainted by my parents' approval or disapproval.

Chapter 12

"...I mourned the loss."

When the holidays came, my parents wanted Will to come over. I felt it was a little too soon for all that, but since he had no family of his own, we all made the exception. I still wanted to take things slow, so we decided no gifts and no giving in to the holiday hysteria that pushed fledgling couples into getting more serious than necessary. It was easier for me to stay detached, since I wasn't over Nigel, but Will was more anxious to secure our relationship. I understood why, but I couldn't force my heart to feel more for him. I almost felt numb.

1983 began and the days went on unremarkably. I tried to live as normal a life as I could. I tried to forget my past life that was full of music, sex, drugs, dreams, excitement, stardom, sex, fighting, love, happiness, depression, sex, fun, fads, and sex.

My new life was a ripple in a pond compared to the hurricane of emotion in England. After a while, it seemed like the old me had died eons ago. I had become a different person who had extricated herself from those stormy waters and now was rowing down a calm stream.

On a never ending cloudy day.

Because, although it was safe and easy, my sunshine was gone. And some days, the clouds would rain on me.

Like when I would be in a store, minding my own business, and I would see Nigel on the cover of a tabloid:

"Pin-Up Rock Star Can't Keep His Nose Clean"
"John Blake Spotted with Hollywood Starlet"
"Egomaniacs of Descent Destroy Hotel"

It was hard to feel stable when things like that rocked my world every week or so. I felt bad for Nigel to be criticized by the press, but I felt worse for myself. I ached at the thought of him with those flawless women. Even though he had been a careless jerk before we broke up, I still loved him and still wished I could be with him. I would have given up everything in my serene life in a heartbeat to be with him again, even if it meant being thrown back onto a sinking ship during a typhoon.

Mostly, I knew the tabloids and magazines were touting pure garbage, but one day, a more trusted publication caught my eye:

"The Real Story Behind Descent"

I picked it up and scanned it. Maybe it was more trash and lies, but maybe it was legit. I bought it and hurried home to read it.

When I finally had the chance, I found the article contained actual interviews with direct quotations from the band members. The journalist asked questions about women, drugs, their albums, music videos, and tours. However, it seemed the article was swayed to portray them as self serving jerks who cared neither about the fans nor their own music, choosing only to be as rich and famous as they could be to score women and free cocaine.

It was false, I could tell. I knew these guys and I could see that their quotes were taken out of context and edited intentionally. Still, I was curious to read on, anxious to see if there was any morsels of truth amongst the array of venomous trite.

Nigel was under the magnifying glass more than any of the other members, and I (along with millions worldwide) was privy to the dirty insider information. My stomach churned as I read about the heaps of pretty girls anxious to get close to him and the stories about the goddess-like actresses, singers, models, etc., who succeeded. I saw too many pictures of him with too many ladies.

And if that weren't enough, the allegations of drug use were irrefutable.

I was mad and worried and heartbroken.

I was also disappointed as the quotes from "John" were arrogant and snide. They didn't sound like something my darling would say. But occasionally he would use a word or phrase or something familiar and then I knew no one had put those words in his mouth- it was Nigel, sure enough.

He was different now. Not my Nigel anymore. Even if I were to see him again, I would barely recognize him, physically or emotionally. And we would probably never connect the same again. He was alien to me and I'm sure I was too dull and plain for him.

The last thread of hope I had for our love surviving was mercilessly slashed and I mourned the loss.

All I could do was concentrate on putting a new life together. I didn't escape into art anymore, as I was unable to summon up any inspiration. Instead I focused on my job, my school, and my new relationship. The more time I spent with Will, the more I was starting to like him. He really was just what I needed at the time. I had been lonely and down, he was always around when I wanted him and he gave my confidence quite a boost. I stopped thinking about Nigel so much. And, although I did have to fess up about my time spent living in England, I left out a lot of details. I carefully avoided mentioning that my musician boyfriend turned out to be John Blake. I also left out how intense our bond was and how much I cared for him. Will was quick to change the subject and didn't ask many questions.

As our relationship progressed, things started to become more and more physical. I tried to keep things as restrained as I could for as long as I could because I wasn't ready to give myself to someone the way I had given myself to Nigel yet. But it got harder to say no to Will and to deny myself and it was getting easier to succumb as more time passed since the break-up. Also, the knowledge that Nigel was no saint helped ease my reservations. Eventually, we began exploring each other, moving from first base to second base and then on to third base. I still wanted to wait until we went all the way. He was patient with my request.

He was making it very easy for me to love him. But I wasn't sure I was able to have those kinds of feelings for someone other than Nigel. I had different feelings, though. I loved Will, but not in the same way or for the same reasons. It was incomparable.

As time went on, I thought about Nigel less. That was good. The open wound in my heart was always stinging, but eventually it started to scab over.

However, certain things did trigger memories of him, usually pleasant ones. Often they made me smile. Occasionally they made me cry. I was jealous of his girlfriends. I was still aroused when I saw his face on the cover of a magazine.

I was getting over Nigel, but I would be forever under him to a degree. He could always lure me back in if I let him. It stunned me how much power he still had over me. I still cared about him and it still hurt me that we weren't together. It seemed like a cruel joke that I had the love of my life in my arms, promising to always be mine, only to have him ripped away. That wasn't how it was supposed to be. We were supposed to be together. Even though I knew it wasn't possible, I still considered him my soul mate, my future.

One Friday at work, I was closing up and counting the money in Tonya's register.

"So, did you see that John Blake is doing an interview on Channel 7 tonight at eight?" she asked.

"What? He is?" I hadn't heard, but was intrigued.

"Yeah. I thought you would be interested, since you have a huge crush on him and all," she mocked.

"Tonya, I don't have a huge crush on him," I corrected, shaking my head.

"Please! Deny it if you want to, but I know where you're going to be tonight at eight." She had a huge satisfied smile on her face. I tried to assert some authority.

"Go straighten up aisle four," I reprimanded.

Her smile vanished but she did what she was told. With no witnesses, I allowed myself to react to Tonya's news. Normally I was strong and tried to ignore my feelings for Nigel, but I was desperate to see that interview. I had plans with Will, but given the choice between the two, I preferred to spend the evening alone in my room with Nigel on the TV than in the company of my actual boyfriend.

As soon as I could, I went into my office for privacy and shut the door. I called Will and made an excuse about not feeling well and told him I wanted to go home and rest in bed. He sounded disappointed, but I didn't waver. There was nothing in the world that would keep me from seeing Nigel, even if it was just on TV.

When I got home, I rushed to my room, ensuring everything was all set for my night of lust. It was a bit ridiculous, but this was the closest thing I had to being with him again. I turned off the lights and sat inches away from the screen.

When the interview began, it was bizarre to see his face on television, but it was nice to hear him talk. He seemed so much like my Nigel, it warmed my heart. He was his old self, but something was different. There was a sadness about him that was unfamiliar. He had a tendency to get depressed, but it was more than that. It was like he was terribly down but trying to cover it up with occasional smiles, laughs, and jokes. I could see right through him. It hurt to witness his evident pain. I badly wanted to reach into the television and hold him. It was clear he had a nagging gloom, just like I did. *Is he not over me?* I wondered.

And then, with perfect timing, the interviewer asked if he had a girlfriend.

My heart stopped beating.

"No, I don't," he simply answered. My spirit soared.

"Why not? You surely can't have a hard time finding women. We see you with models and celebrities all the time."

"Yeah, but, it's nothing serious . . . I guess I'm still carrying a torch for someone," he confessed sadly, eyes cast down.

"The one that got away?"

He nodded.

"What happened there?"

He was thrown off. He obviously didn't anticipate this coming up and having to explain it to the whole world. "Um . . . well, I guess . . . it was that the music got in the way, you know? It's like you have your home life and your jet-set career and the two just don't mix. It puts a strain on things," he summarized, trying to seem professional and detached.

"So, you're just keeping things casual for now? Just having fun?"

"Well, yeah, I'm having fun. This is amazing. I can't believe how lucky I am to be where I am. I'm being interviewed on TV for millions to see!" He laughed, trying to bounce back and appear upbeat and playful.

I didn't buy it. The segment ended and I leaned away from the screen, finally able to breathe and think again.

I couldn't believe what I had just heard and seen. He announced to the world that he wasn't over me! He confessed that he wasn't into any of those dumb models he was seen with! He was still brokenhearted over our breakup! He felt the same way as I did!

As happy as this news made me, I was still upset. I hated seeing him so sad. I wondered if he was in a funk during the interview or if he was always this way. Or worse. Who was comforting him? Who was listening to him? Who cared for him?

I doubted any of those trophy girlfriends did. They were probably using him. These revelations dug at my heart. Nigel needed love. I'd bet he didn't know he could still call on me for it.

Or maybe he did! Maybe he was trying to get a hold of me, maybe he was sick of being apart! Maybe he realized he had made a terrible mistake and thought we could pick up where things left off!

Of course, it wouldn't be that simple. There would be a lot to sort out. Hurt feelings to mend, apologies to be made, deciding what kind of future we would have. . . . We would have to get reacquainted all over again.

And then, there was Will.

It was clear that Will was not my top priority, like he should have been, but I couldn't help that. My heart was in the driver's seat and it would always steer me back to Nigel. I knew that if Nigel were to ask me to come back to him right now, I would say yes without hesitation.

I was a terrible girlfriend.

It occurred to me that maybe I should break up with Will instead of leading him on. But, then I thought there was no harm in continuing to see him for the time being. We were taking things slowly and as long as that stayed the same, no harm done.

That night, the next day, the next week, the next month, every time the phone rang, I tried to be the one to answer it. I assumed Nigel would be calling, considering he was still "carrying a torch" for me. I hunted through the mail every day, hoping to find a letter or something from him. I started buying all the teen magazines or any publication with him in it, searching for another interview in which he mentioned me or his longing for me. I spent my free time hugging my stuffed lion and gazing at all the centerfolds of him I had been acquiring, dreaming about our reunion.

But it was all in vain. Nigel never called, wrote, or stopped by. He never reiterated his feelings for the one that got away in any other interview. My heart broke again. I was bitter. Even when I heard the news from Tonya that Descent was going to be playing in Detroit, I decided not to go. I had seen footage of their concerts, it was a sickening mass of screaming girls. I wasn't about to be one of them. Besides, he would never see me in the crowd. I didn't want to get my hopes up by going to the show that he would spot me, pull me out of the audience, and take me onstage for a big hug and kiss. And I knew that's how I would envision it, and that it wouldn't happen, and I would fall apart all over again. It was time to stop my foolish dreams. It was time to get over him.

Spring was coming and Will was due to graduate. The firm he worked for offered him a full-time executive position with an impressive starting salary. He was elated. I was proud of him. He had worked very hard and had overcome so much to get where he was.

My parents had gotten quite attached to him, more than I had, it seemed. My mother decided to have a post graduation party for him at the house. He was invited to bring over as many people as he wanted and he okayed the fact that my mom wanted my whole family to be there, too.

When the day finally came, the small soirée we had envisioned had become a swarm of people, food, and festivities. It was a good time and a definite cause for celebration. The house was packed, inside and out. It was overwhelming to Will. I caught him sitting alone on the stairwell, hidden from sight. I climbed up and sat next to him.

"What are you doing?" I asked him.

"Oh, just taking a break from the chaos," he answered quietly.

"Yeah, lots of people here. Is it too much for you?"

"Um, no, I mean, I'm glad everyone came today. It's just that . . . I'm not used to being surrounded like this. I'm not used to family and get-togethers and all that. It's a lot to handle all at once."

"I'm sorry. Maybe I should have planned a quiet dinner out instead."

"No, it's fine. It's nice that you and your family went to so much trouble. I like that. It's nice borrowing your family." He managed a wrinkled smile.

I returned one. I took for granted the fact that I had a family who was around. Even if we didn't get along well all the time, I still had them. And now I had all my extended family nearby also. He didn't have any blood relatives or even non-blood relatives anymore. I pitied my little orphan and mentally kicked myself for not appreciating what I had.

"Well, consider yourself one of us," I responded, standing up, offering a hand to him. It was a friendly gesture and he was my friend. I didn't really see him as more than that. I loved him, but not in a passionate way. It was a comfortable companionship and it felt like it was enough for me.

He took my hand and stood up also. He inhaled with a grin and seemed strong and ready to face the party again.

We went back out and wandered around, eating, drinking, and socializing. We had a lot of fun. He seemed to be enjoying himself more than usual. I was glad I could give him this party, remembering another party I had tried to throw for a boyfriend that hadn't gone quite so well.

My dad stood up on a folding chair and clinked a fork on his beer bottle.

"Everyone, let me have your attention, please. I would like to make a toast. To the man of the hour! A fine gentleman who my daughter is very lucky to have, considering her taste in men isn't always . . . realistic." I scoffed, insulted that he would bring up me in his speech and allude to Nigel in front of Will. "Let's hope he can put up with her!" The crowd laughed, but not as hard as my dad who I suspected wasn't joking at all. "Anyway, this lad has struggled and he has triumphed.

Here's to Will, may you always be successful in everything you do! Cheers!"

"Cheers!" Everyone exclaimed in unison, clinking their drinks together. As they were busy tapping glasses and bottles, Will also stood on a chair.

"I'd like to say something, too." The audience was totally attentive. "I want to thank Michelle and Paula and Rick for throwing me this party. I also want to thank this wonderful family for welcoming me. Thank you all for coming. So, friends, family, I would like you all to know how special Michelle is to me. She has given me a home in this world. She has made my lonely existence lively and loving." He turned his gaze to me. "Michelle, I am so thrilled you have let me into your family, now I was wondering if I could do the same for you. Will you marry me?"

Simultaneously the group gasped and awed and held their breath. I felt all the blood drain away from my vital organs and into my cheeks. I was beyond shocked. Everyone stared at me, including Will. Of all the times I imagined being proposed to, it was never the way it actually happened. I fantasized about the perfect setting, the perfect words, and, of course, the perfect fiancé- who I had thought would be Nigel. But even when *he* proposed to me, it was far from perfect. I wasn't bursting with delight then, and I wasn't now either. The only difference was that I declined Nigel's proposal and I felt *in*clined to accept Will's. Everyone waited. I didn't know what to say, but he looked so happy and confident enough for both of us. "I don't know, let me think about it" was what I wanted to say, but what I actually said was . . .

"Yes."

The group roared and Will smiled proudly at me, his face lit up like a jack-o-lantern. He stepped down and made a beeline for me. He wrapped his arms around me, squeezed me, and picked me up, twirling me around, kissing me. This only got the crowd cheering more. He put me down, kissed me on the cheek and smiled at everyone. I tried to hide my worry. What had I done?

Hugs, handshakes, and congratulations ensued. Everyone was so happy for us. I couldn't believe the difference between the reception of Will and I versus Nigel and I. Considering Nigel and I were soul mates, I hoped my loved ones could see that he was the one I was meant to be with, that he was the one who made me unbearably happy. That was not the case. Will was safe, though, safe and comfortable. *Realistic*, as my dad put it. To my family, I guess that meant more than true love.

But I knew better. I knew I would never love Will like I loved Nigel, but I figured that ship had sailed. My time with Nigel was glorious and life altering, but it was history. Will was the present, and it looked like he was the future.

It felt good to see so many smiling faces happy for me. I was getting wrapped up in the enthusiasm in spite of myself. The idea of getting married, the idea of being Will's wife, became more appealing to me. It felt like a logical move.

We celebrated our engagement with making love for the first time. It had been a long while since I had sex, which made the first time a bit awkward. I couldn't tell if the problem was me or him, all I did know was that it wasn't as fluid and natural as it was with Nigel. It was different. But, sex wasn't the most important thing.

∛

We decided to wait until I graduated before beginning to plan the wedding. But Will was eager to start house hunting. He put his inherited house up for sale and with that plus his savings and the large paychecks he started earning, he was able to afford a very nice house in a nice neighborhood.

He scheduled showings with his real estate agent for when I had free time because he wanted the house selection to be a joint decision, even though it was going to be purchased with his money. House hunting was fun and made me all the more excited to move on with my life with him. I was beyond ready to move out of my parents' house. Maybe that wasn't a good reason for moving in with him, but it felt right at the time.

After several months of looking, we settled on a house. It was newer construction and was in move-in condition. It was even bigger and nicer than my parents' house. I was looking forward to living there.

 C8

I began my next year of college. I was taking more classes this semester, as many as I could cram in. I had been in school full time for the past year and I was more than full time in this fall semester, eager to graduate. I cut back my hours at work to make time for school and the new house. Will insisted that I quit my job because he could take care of me financially, but I wasn't comfortable with that. I wanted to pay my own way. And so, I agreed to move in with Will before we got married only if I could help with the bills.

As winter descended, I was busy with finals, holidays, work, and moving in to our house. Time was a commodity. Unfortunately, this meant Will had to do a lot of the furniture shopping and decorating himself. My mom was all too happy to go with him and he was delighted to have a mother in his life for the first time. Often I would stop by the house with a box of my stuff or a bag of groceries to find that little by little, my home was being furnished without my influence.

It couldn't be helped, I knew that, but I remembered how much fun it was for Nigel and I to collaborate on decorating with the small touches that made our home *our* home. One day, off on my winter break from school, I suggested Will and I go shopping together. He hated the furniture, artwork, and designs that I was drawn to. He preferred more old-fashioned types of furnishings. We couldn't agree on anything.

"I never have this much trouble when I'm shopping with your mom," he would comment.

It wasn't just that, either. After Autumn and I were moved in, I realized how much television he liked to watch. The focal point of the living room was not art pieces or interesting furniture, it was the TV. It was always on. This bothered me because I was not a big fan. I preferred having music on and conversation in the living room. He attempted to give me my way by buying a very large television and putting it in the basement. He commenced turning the basement into a den with big recliners, a fully stocked bar, a pool table, and other things that men were attracted to. He did a nice job, it was neat and orderly, but it was not something I would have planned to have in my house. I didn't object; a small part of me understood that this really was Will's house and not mine.

☙

The new school semester began, and I had to crack down and spend all of my free time working on this or that. Will was patient and supportive with my demanding schedule, but he expected me to fulfill the "womanly" duties of the house as well as uphold my work and school responsibilities. He worked long hours and would be exhausted when he got home. He wanted dinner to be ready and the house to be clean; laundry done, pressed, and folded; and a special treat waiting for him at bedtime. When I couldn't do all that he wanted, he was adamant about me quitting my "silly little job" because it was taking time away from more important things. True, my job wasn't very important, but it mattered to me. I didn't want to be a housewife, my only purpose being a slave to the house and husband. I needed my own life, I needed to be myself. He didn't understand that about me.

I was coming to find he didn't understand much about me.

One day, being a good little girl, I was making dinner and finishing up some chores. With the stereo on, I was able to breeze through my work, singing happily as I went. Will came into the kitchen. "When is dinner ready?"

"Soon," I replied.

He walked into the living room, annoyed at the music. "What is this shit?"

"Siouxsie and the Banshees," I answered like it was common knowledge. They were one of my favorite bands and I played them often.

"It sucks," he commented. "I don't get this music. I don't understand all this garbage you like."

"It's garbage because you don't get it?"

"No, it's garbage because it's not real music. All that artsy crap. Who are you trying to impress?"

I didn't know if he was asking me or the "artsy crap" world in general. Either way, I was fuming. He was such a simple person with a simple mind. One of the most basic things about me was my creativity. I had to express that part of me. Nigel understood that and he was the same way. I had to surround myself with stimulation and stimulating people. To him, that was a waste of time. Why be inspired when you can just watch TV?

"So, when is dinner ready?" he asked again.

"Um, it's ready now. Just grab a plate and serve yourself. I have to get to my class."

"Your night class doesn't start until seven," he argued.

"Yeah, but I have to do some research in the library first. I gotta go," I lied as I gathered my things and rushed out the door. He gave me a disbelieving look.

I drove slowly to the campus, trying to kill time. I blared my music in rebellion, trying to drown out the nagging voice in my head that told me I was fooling myself by thinking Will was the man I should marry. I just turned the volume up higher and tried to focus on The Doors tape I was listening to.

Fate seemed to be in the car with Jim Morrison and I.

The next song played and though I had heard it many times, I never really listened to it:

"Think that you know what to do
Impossible, yes, but it's true
I think that you know what to do, yeah
Sure that you know what to do
You're lost, little girl
You're lost, little girl
You're lost, tell me who are you?"

It felt like the song was written exclusively for my ears.

I wondered if I was making a mistake by being with someone who didn't understand me and was so different from me. I had thought we worked well together even though we didn't have much in common. But now that we were living together, the differences between us felt overwhelming. I felt suffocated, unable to be my real self. Trapped into conformity by the pressures of responsibility and doing what was expected of me. My sense of self was fading. I no longer had the time or inspiration to write or draw. I dressed conservatively to look professional. I settled for a safe partner instead of one who I could relate to.

All I had to immerse myself in now was my music. And apparently, I couldn't even have that.

If he didn't even know me, how could he be in love with me? Was it just the idea of me he loved? Was it the shell of myself that he was attracted to? If he couldn't see the inside of me, where all the important stuff is, what was it about me that he thought was so great?

I dawdled in the library, ensconced in my worries. I couldn't pay attention in class, and even by the time I made it home, I couldn't shake my feelings.

Will noticed.

"Hey, I'm sorry about earlier," he said while lying in bed as I was getting ready to go to sleep in our room. "I think I offended you and I didn't mean to. I mean, that's your world, and maybe I don't get it, but I shouldn't dump on things you like. So, I'm sorry."

I smiled and sat on the bed by him. "Thank you. I appreciate that." I felt a little bit better, but I was wiser now. "I guess we should get to know each other more before we get married."

"What are you saying? Are you having second thoughts?"

"I just mean there are some things that we obviously don't see eye to eye on and we shouldn't be strangers when we walk down the aisle, should we?"

"No, we shouldn't. But, just because we don't feel the same way about everything doesn't mean I don't love you."

"I know. I love you, too."

He looked pleased. "Good. Now get in bed."

CB

From then on, we tried to be patient and understanding with each other. I tried to get into what he was into and vice versa. Usually this meant settling on something we could both agree on whether it was what movie to see, where to go on vacation, or how to spend our Saturday nights. We became very good at compromise, and found many ways we could both be happy.

And, actually, I *was* happy. Content. My life was different than I had envisioned, but it was satisfying. I was overloaded with classes and homework, but I managed to make everything work. Being busy all the time, I rarely had an opportunity to reflect on my choices and decide if I was still where I wanted to be. My eyes were on the prize; I wanted to graduate as quickly as I could and be done with school once and for all. Yet, whenever there was free time, Will and I tried to do something fun. We settled into our own little lifestyle and it was satisfactory.

In May of 1985, I finished school and with his help, found an accounting firm with a great reputation that hired me. I hated leaving my little art store, but I had to graduate into a real career. I did enjoy the nights and weekends off, and, of course, the better paychecks.

Will was ecstatic. I had so much more time for him now; although, I wasn't in a rush to start the wedding plans. It didn't feel like fun to me, it felt like work, and after all the constant stress of school responsibilities, I just wanted a break. I explained this to Will and he understood. I wasn't sure I did, though. The idea of planning a wedding had always seemed fun and joyous to me before. What had changed?

Sometimes Will would casually ask me if I was excited about getting married to him and I would have to think about it first. It obviously bothered him that I wasn't very enthusiastic about it, but I couldn't lie. I was content enough with the present, I didn't know how I felt about the future. I couldn't even imagine myself walking down the aisle with him. I guess I still felt numb to love and the happy ever after I wasn't expecting to have with someone other than Nigel.

Even the idea of taking his name felt odd. Michelle Lynn Benson. I didn't really like the sound of it. I chalked it up to not being used to it yet. My initials would be MLB. MLB, just like they would have been if I had married Nigel. I liked *that*.

I just wanted to have fun with Will and avoid messy emotional stuff and drama. It worked for us. We had lots of expendable cash and did a lot and went on lots of little trips. Yet, most nights, we stayed home, eating dinner and having cocktails in our little bar. It was the life of a settled down married couple and we weren't even there yet.

But it was comfortable. I had everything I needed . . . pretty much.

Then one day in August, I got an unexpected visitor.

Chapter 13

"Sometimes things have to get messy."

I had just gotten home from work and was about to change my clothes when I heard a knock on the door. I went to answer it and nearly fainted.

"Nigel?"

"Hi, Michelle." He looked shy on my front porch; nervous, but even more handsome than I remembered. He was dressed well, his carefully coiffed hair highlighted, but he didn't have any makeup on. He wasn't wearing all the rock star get-up I was used to seeing him in on television or magazine spreads. He had filled out a little bit, more like a man than last I saw him. My heart was racing and I couldn't think straight. I held onto the door frame for support.

"What- . . . What are you doing here?" I was too stunned to articulate properly.

"I was in town. I looked you up. I didn't know if you'd be home or not."

"Yeah, I just got here."

"I'm glad. Can we talk?" he asked hopefully.

I gestured for him to come in the house and he looked relieved. "I didn't know if you'd agree to talk to me."

"You obviously went to some trouble-"

He threw his arms around me, cutting me off mid-sentence.

"God, I have missed you." He squeezed me so tightly that I wouldn't have been able to breathe even if my lungs continued to function, which they didn't at the time. I was too shocked over it all to care about a silly thing like breathing. I was also too shocked to hug him back, and I didn't know if I would have wanted to anyway.

It didn't seem to bother him. After a moment, he released me. His hands slid down my arms and grasped my hands, holding them. Then a devastated look crossed his face. He noticed my ring.

I looked down at it, too, almost wishing it weren't there. He didn't speak.

"I'm engaged," I answered simply but quietly, just a little ashamed that I had moved on.

His face fell. "So it's true. You're getting married."

"How did you- "

"I phoned your mom a few weeks back. I thought you still lived with her. I really wanted to get in touch with you again, but she told me that you had moved out a while ago . . . with your fiancé."

I felt guilty, even though I didn't need to.

He tried to pull himself together. "Well, what did I expect? That you'd wait for me forever?"

I couldn't look at him as I defended myself. "If I had any reason to think you'd come back, maybe I wouldn't have gotten involved with anyone else. It's been years since I've seen you. You never even called or wrote or anything. I just assumed that it was over for us."

"Yeah, right, I know." He nodded, looking down, taking full responsibility. "I mean, I wanted you to move on. That's why I never tried to interfere in your life after we broke up. It would be too hard for me to see you or talk to you from time to time and then have to say goodbye all over again. I couldn't do it. And I didn't want you to wait around, wasting your life on me. I knew I would be gone all the time and I couldn't stand the thought of you being alone and lonely all the time."

I suppose that was unselfish of him, but the words still sounded as bitter as they had four years ago when I heard them the first time. And I didn't want to hear it again today.

"Seems like you moved on, too, from what I've seen and heard."

"No. It's all for distraction," he responded.

"Right. Surrounding yourself with models- "

"Alright, yeah, it comes with the territory. But, I mean it, it's all for distraction."

I stared at him with wide eyes. I couldn't believe this. What was he saying? None of it seemed real. For so long I had wanted him to come back to me, but instead I was left behind as he climbed to the top of the world. As time passed, that longing turned to bitterness and rage; and by this point, indifference. But now, seeing him again, it was as if no time had passed. We were different people, but there was no change in the love that burned within me from the day I met him. But I was still incredibly angry with him. I couldn't tell if my love or my hate was stronger.

He looked around for the first time, and then really looked at me for the first time.

I felt like I was under a magnifying glass and I felt uncomfortable. "What?"

"I'm sorry. This is just - this is not how I was expecting to find you."

"What were you expecting?"

"I don't know, I guess." He looked at me like he was saddened. I wondered what it was that disappointed him. He broke the tense silence. "This is a nice house."

"Thanks," I returned halfheartedly.

"So, what do you do for a living? The last time I saw you, you definitely weren't wearing *business attire*. Are you like an editor or something?"

I felt like I was being mocked a little bit. "I'm an accountant now," I tried to sound proud.

"An accountant?" he asked in total disbelief.

"Yes, an accountant. What's wrong with that? We can't all be rock stars. The rest of us have to pay the bills somehow," I defended.

"I'm sorry, I didn't mean to offend you. I'm just surprised," he retracted.

I loosened up a bit.

"I can *see* you found a way to pay the bills," he said, looking around.

I felt like a bad host suddenly. I was so surprised with my guest that I forgot all about manners. "Do you want me to show you the house?"

"Alright," he agreed unenthusiastically. He wordlessly followed me around. Something was bothering him that he just wouldn't say. I had a million questions for him, too, but neither of us wanted to bring up anything unpleasant, knowing it would cause a huge fight.

We went through the living room, dining room, kitchen, and the game room/family room in the basement. I showed him the second floor, the guest room, the office, and the master bedroom.

"And that's it," I concluded as I led him back down to the kitchen. "Do you want something to drink?"

"Um, sure."

I gestured for him to sit on one of the stools at the counter. "Is wine okay?"

"Yeah, whatever you want is fine." He was still uneasy. I could tell he was holding his tongue. I waited for the blow, as I prepared our drinks.

He searched for something to say. "Your house is very . . . neat."

"Oh, thanks. I like to keep it that way."

"Huh." He sounded unconvinced. "You know, I never would have imagined you here. It's not exactly your style," he observed.

"How's that? It's simple and uncluttered. That's how I like things. Orderly, no unnecessary drama," I explained, slightly irritated at his judgment.

"I'm sorry, don't take offense. It's a nice house," he repeated. "It's big."

I poured two glasses and handed one to him. "I'm sure it's very mundane to you. I mean, it can't compare to what you're used to."

He was sipping as I spoke. He lifted his eyebrows at my assumption. "I'm a nomadic musician. I don't have the luxury of a normal life in a normal neighborhood. This is nice. Anyone would be happy here."

I shrugged in agreement and corked the wine bottle and put it in the refrigerator.

"Well, anyone would be happy here, but not you," he remarked.

"Excuse me?" I asked, slightly offended.

"Am I wrong or have you turned into someone completely different from the girl I knew? This-" he gestured around, "-this is not you. All of it! The house, the clothes, the job. It's not you!"

"Nigel, what did you come here for? I haven't seen you in years and now you show up out of nowhere, come into my home and tell me my life's a sham? What is this?"

He stood up and approached me. He calmly said, "I'm sorry. I didn't want to insult you; I wanted to catch up with you. It's just . . . it's just so odd to see you as a *completely* different person than you were the last time I saw you."

"The last time you saw me was four years ago! And I'm not completely different. So what if I have a real job and a steady home life? That's what regular people do."

"Yeah, but we," he pointed to him and me "aren't regular."

"Well, I am. I had to grow up. Sometimes that means giving up your dreams."

"That's not true. You didn't have to give up everything."

"What was I supposed to do, Nigel? Everything changed when we broke up. I kept hoping you would come back for me, but you didn't, so I had to move on. I couldn't just sit around, waiting around for you, wasting my life- "

"No, not waiting around for me. Creating your own destiny! You are throwing away your talents! I wanted to be a musician, so I did. You wanted to write, or paint, or sing- so you go off and become an accountant? *An accountant?* You don't even like math!"

"Okay, I get it!"

"No, you don't. The house, it's so . . . perfect. Too perfect. You had no idea I was coming over today but look around- it looks like you've been cleaning for days! Everything is in its place. So neat, so controlled."

I scowled at him for using that word. He ignored that and continued.

"So, you can't control your life, so you'll control the house, and I'm willing to bet, the boyfriend."

"That's enough. I think you should go." I walked into the living room to lead him out. He followed.

"Why? Is your fiancé going to be home soon?"

"I just have a lot of things to do before tomorrow," I lied.

"Really? And what time do you start work in the morning?"

"Seven."

"Seven? You hate getting up early!

"Nigel- "

"Look, I didn't come here to do this, and I'm sorry. But I can't not tell you that you are obviously living a lie. It's all wrong. And why? You don't have to settle for this."

"Settle?" I asked in disbelief. "You left me because you wanted me to move on. And now that I have finally put my life back together, you tell me I'm settling?" I couldn't believe this. I had more questions. "Why did you come here today? To accuse me of changing? To catch me being a boring professional type?"

"No! I'm in town and I looked you up. I wanted to see you again."

"And now you have." I was bitter that he hadn't bothered to "see me" in years nor had he bothered to call me to tell me he was stopping by today. "Why? Why now? Why didn't you ever try before?"

He came up to me with a calmer demeanor. "I'm so sorry. I've wanted to. So many times I've wanted to. I thought you must hate me. I thought you would slam the door in my face."

"Oh, come on Nigel, what a spineless thing to say! You were afraid to confront me because you know how badly you messed up and you thought I would call you on it," I accused. I believed I was right. He didn't oppose me. He seemed calm and ready to accept my verbal bullets without flinching.

He inhaled deeply, collecting his thoughts. "I am sorry things turned out the way they did for us, but we can't change that now. But you can change your future if you want to."

I stood there frozen, his words barely registering.

"Maybe I should go. I didn't come here to try to take you away from your fiancé or your house or your life. I just wanted to see what you were up to and if you were okay. And I see that . . . that you're not. But, hey, maybe I'm wrong. Maybe this is who you are meant to be and I'm just being a prat. I guess we aren't who we were when we were kids, eh?"

I kept staring at the wall, avoiding his face.

"I wish I hadn't upset you. This was not how I planned on things going. I don't know when your fiancé gets home, but I guess I should be gone before he does." He searched his pockets and pulled out a card and a pen. "I'm going to be in town for a few days . . . " He scribbled a number on the card and handed it to me. "I'm staying at the Monarch Hotel, room 1451. Come by or call, if you want."

I took the card from him and lifelessly looked at it, keeping my eyes on it and away from him.

"Look, I'm sorry. Don't be mad. I care about you too much to keep quiet, but if that's what you want, I will. I'll leave now." He kissed my cheek. "I hope to hear from you soon. Call anytime, please. I think there's a lot left to say."

He walked out, gently shutting the door behind him. After it clicked into place, I walked over to the window and peeked out the curtain at him getting into his car and driving away. I couldn't tell if it was anger or longing, but I felt sick as I watched my unbreakably attractive ex drive away from my house.

"Damn him," I said out loud, exasperated that he still had such an influence over me. I stomped into the kitchen and downed my wine, then the rest of his. Then I poured myself a full glass and walked into the living room. As I sipped, I looked around. I had a nice house, practically a dream house.

Just not *my* dream house.

"Fuck," I whispered to myself. "He's right."

It seemed I had never noticed it before. I felt like I was a stranger taking a tour in my own home. Who decorated this place? Where were the mementos of my past, my style? This house wasn't me. I walked up the stairs, scoffing at the cheap, soul-less paintings on the wall. I ended up in the bathroom at the end of the stairs. "Decorative soaps? Why?" I asked myself in disbelief.

I looked into the full length mirror. "What am I wearing? Why do I look like this?" Suddenly I couldn't stand the sight of myself, looking like an old lady, hair pinned back, boring professional ensemble. I frantically tore off my business suit and took down my hair. I looked at myself again, wearing only underwear. It had been a long time since I saw myself undressed in a mirror. I was shocked. I was fat. "What is this?" I panicked, noticing bulges, flab, lumps.

"Where did this come from?" And as soon as the words came out of my mouth, I realized the habits I'd been forming. Drinking too much to "unwind". Eating instead of having sex for pleasure. Driving everywhere, never walking. Big dinners always followed by dessert; then, being too full and/or drunk to move until I fall asleep…early. "Uh oh."

Immediately I felt ashamed. My first thought was, *"How did I let this happen?"* Thought two was, *"How could I let Nigel see me this way?"*

I had apparently been in a daze, not noticing who I was becoming. It was not the person I wanted to be. Then I realized why I felt like Will didn't understand me. He was seeing the character I was playing. The responsible achiever. No wonder he didn't know I was a passionate artist. It wasn't his fault that he didn't know me well, it was mine. I was confusing him. I didn't tell him about my past, I didn't share my true desires with him. I was deceiving him and being untrue to myself. I fell deep into a puddle of guilt, not knowing how long it consumed me before a slamming door broke my spell.

"I'm home!" Will loudly announced.

"Quickly, I dashed into my room and grabbed the clothes at the top of a pile of clean laundry. I threw them on before I could be seen that way. Sweatpants and a baggy T-shirt, it was my usual attire. The attire of the out of shape and hopeless. I groaned, infuriated with myself and stomped downstairs.

"Hi honey," Will greeted me and kissed my cheek. "What's for dinner?"

"Dinner?" Making dinner was my responsibility and it was usually ready before he got home.

"Yes, dinner. You know, that stuff we eat at the end of the day. Usually comes on a plate. You remember, right?" He joked and then headed into the kitchen.

With all the drama, I hadn't even thought about dinner. My mind was on a million other things. I wondered if I should confess that my ex had just been over for a visit. I followed him toward the kitchen, waiting for the right moment to come clean. I hesitated. When Will saw that I had no food prepared, he turned around and frowned.

"Well, you don't look like you're dressed to go out. So, leftovers, then?"

He had no tone of dissatisfaction or annoyance. I appreciated that. I grinned and nodded as he knelt in front of the open refrigerator, searching for food. He pulled out several containers, face buried in the fridge.

"Lasagna, macaroni and cheese, pizza. Ooh, there's cake, and . . . stuff to make nachos. Yeah, I'm having nachos. Want some?"

I was horrified. Frozen. I loved to cook. I prided myself on making everything from scratch. And this is what I made? A myriad of artery-clogging, love-handle-causing comfort food. The same question kept popping into my head, *"What happened?"* I stared at the piles of unhealthy food on the floor. Autumn came out to inspect the dishes on the floor, checking to see if she could get to the contents.

"What's wrong?" he asked, arms full of food.

" . . . I'm not hungry," was all I could think to say.

"Oh, that's why you didn't cook?" He was clueless that Nigel had been here. "That's okay. I gotta eat. I'm starving, and Danny never has any food."

"Danny?"

"Yeah, I'm going to Danny's for poker tonight. Remember?"

"Oh, I guess I forgot." I was disappointed. I really wanted to talk to Will. I wanted to tell him everything that was on my mind for once. There was so much I needed to say.

"Is something wrong?" he asked while assembling his dinner, tossing a piece of cheese on the floor for the cat.

"Um . . . no," I lied. I figured I would just tell him later.

"Alright. I gotta eat quick, then I'm gone."

"When will you be back?"

"Probably around midnight." He was busy with his dinner.

I went in the living room. I caught my reflection in a mirror on the wall. I leaned in to see better. My face looked so puffy. Why hadn't I noticed it before? I stepped back, surveying the rest of my bloated body. I sighed. "I can fix this," I said quietly to myself.

"Did you say something?" Will asked from the kitchen, mouth full.

"No," I responded. "I mean, yes." I walked into the kitchen. "I'm going for a walk."

"A walk? Why?"

"It's a nice day. I want to get some air."

"*Okay.*" He looked skeptical, and I couldn't blame him. I never walked or exercised or did much at all besides work and eat. He got up, wiping his mouth and putting his plate in the sink. "I'll be gone when you get back but I'll leave the back door unlocked." I nodded.

He kissed my cheek. "Have fun."

"You, too. Say 'hi' to the guys for me."

"I will!" he said loudly, making his way upstairs.

I went outside. It was a nice day. I started walking, thoughts pacing between my depression and Nigel. He reminded me of who I once was and who I was now: so far from the person I wanted to be. The walk helped me put things into perspective. If I wanted my old body back, I would take it. If I wanted my old life back, I would take it. And if I wanted Nigel back, I would take that, too! Wait! Nigel back? Is that what I wanted?

I was walking quicker now, sorting things out in my mind just as quickly. I thought Nigel and I had no future. Maybe he thought we did. Maybe that's why he came by. Is that why he said there was a lot left to say? Did he want me back? Did I want him back?

I started running. Didn't I love Will? Of course I did. He was a good man. He gave me everything he could. With him I had stability and security, something Nigel couldn't provide. Not anymore, at least. And nothing could change that, right?

I realized I didn't know Nigel anymore. What if he'd become a great man? Like the boy I loved, only more mature and responsible. What if I was meant to marry him and not Will? It made sense. Maybe that was why we could never really get over each other. But, if Nigel was so perfect, did I deserve him? How could I compete with the gorgeous Hollywood types that were always throwing themselves at him. Look at me!

No, no, my depressing physique was only temporary. I would take care of myself and my appearance and I would change my dull life-style. I felt empowered. Without knowing, I had been running so long, I didn't know where I was anymore. I slowed to a stop and looked around. I was surprised that I wasn't tired. It wasn't dark yet. It was a wonderful summer day. The air was warm, the flowers were blooming, and things were changing. Everything was changing.

I found my bearings and ran back home. When I got in, I was panting and sweaty, but I felt alive and energized. I felt better than I had in ages, like I was able to control my life.

I stretched as I walked around the kitchen to cool down. I poured myself a glass of water. As I drank it, I walked into the living room. Something white on the floor caught my eye. It was the card with Nigel's number on it. I must have dropped it. I picked it up and looked at it, contemplating.

I showered and went to my room to change. I tried on several pairs of jeans, nothing fit. I groaned. I went into my closet, searching for an alternative. Buried deep between formal wear was Nigel's old shirt. I had hidden it from Will. I pulled it out and sighed. "Nigel," I whispered to myself.

I drifted away down memory lane, remembering our tender moments involving that silly shirt. Seeing him wear it, the effect it had when he saw me wear it, the day he gave it to me . . . It still had the power to stir up deep emotions.

Finally, I came back to the real world and tried to get dressed. I stashed away the shirt again, reluctantly, and found a dress that I had always liked. I tried it on, and it still fit! Looking in the mirror, I discovered it didn't look bad. It hid all my problem areas while accentuating my bust. I was happy. I don't know what I was dressing up for, a confidence boost I suppose. I began giving myself a makeover-hair, nails, the works. When I was done, I felt really good about myself. All I had to do was try. By this time, I was hungry and I went downstairs to prepare a light, balanced dinner.

Afterward, I started to feel a little lonely. I was all dressed up with nowhere to go, no one to see. I called Danny's house to talk to Will. Danny's wife answered the phone and gave it to him.

"Hi, dear. What's up?" he asked.

"Oh, nothing. Just feeling lonely."

"Well, it's almost eight o'clock. You'll be going to bed soon."

I cringed. Was I really that lame?

"Why don't you call a girlfriend? I'd love to talk but I'm on fire tonight."

I felt a little betrayed. "Oh, well, I don't want to keep you. Have fun."

"Okay, I'll see you later tonight. Don't wait up, I think I'll be late. Okay, goodbye."

"Bye." I hung up. I tried to call a few friends, but no one was home.

Everyone had lives, it seemed. There was only one person I knew who might be free. I went downstairs to get Nigel's phone number. Nervously, I dialed and was connected to his room.

"Hello?" he answered, hope in his voice.

"Hi, Nigel."

"Michelle. I didn't think you would call me."

"Well, I thought I might take you up on your offer. Are you busy?"

"No, not at all. Bored, actually."

"Can I come see you?"

"Yeah, yeah. I'll be waiting."

"Fine, I'll be right there." I hung up. What was I doing?

ങ

I drove far too quickly to his hotel, clutching the business card with his room number on it. *"Why am I in such a hurry?"* I wondered. I should have felt guilty, I mean, what was I doing going to my old flame's hotel room? I was engaged, after all! But, something was compelling me to go; I didn't question it and I didn't hesitate.

I checked myself in the vanity mirror of my car before practically running in. I entered the mirrored main door of the hotel; it was the nicest, most expensive hotel in the area. My heels clacked on the shiny marble floor as I sped to the elevator. I was glad no one else was in there because I was visibly shaking with anticipation.

The elevator dinged and opened. I stepped onto his floor. My heart raced as I found his door. I tried to compose myself before knocking, but he opened the door before I could.

"Hi!" he said enthusiastically.

"Hi," I answered breathlessly. "Look, I'm sorry about earlier, I- "

"No, no, *I'm* sorry. I shouldn't have-"

"No, you were right-"

He didn't even hear it, he was too busy apologizing, standing in the doorway. "I had no place talking to you like that-"

"I'm glad you did."

He froze. "You are?"

I nodded. "It hurt to hear it, but you were right. And, it took a lot of courage to say all that. At first I thought, 'what does he know?'. But you were able to see all my problems so clearly because you know me so well. . . . "

"I guess I thought you had changed. I figured you weren't that girl anymore and the new you didn't want me in your life."

"I'm still the same girl you knew, Nigel," I explained, trying to assure him.

His mouth relaxed into a soft smile. "Please, come in." I entered the room and he shut the door behind me. "You look great. This is how I remember you."

I felt a little embarrassed as I walked in. I must have looked like such a geek earlier. And here he was, a rock star. I was beginning to regret coming.

"Do you want a drink?" he offered, heading toward the little bar in his upscale hotel suite.

"Um, no, I shouldn't." I followed him in, looking around.

"I'm glad you came." He must have sensed my apprehension.

"Really?" I breathed, relieved that he wasn't mad or disappointed in me.

"Yeah, I mean, there's so much I wanted to say. And the way we left things earlier today . . . "

"Forgotten," I interrupted. " . . . Well . . . not *forgotten* . . . The person you met today is not who I am. You know who I am. I just-, *I* don't know me anymore." I sank down on his couch. He sat beside me, looking concerned. He didn't say anything, he just quietly waited, ready to listen.

"After we broke up, it was a really low time for me. I was really confused. I mean, I kind of had my whole life planned and then, boom, it was over. I had to start from scratch and I had to make compromises."

He slumped, ashamed. "Michelle, I'm really sorry about leaving you."

I held my hand up. "Nigel, don't. Don't apologize. I'm over it. I understand why you did what you did."

"You do?"

"Yeah. That doesn't mean it didn't hurt and, God, it still hurts so bad, even now. But I know why you did it."

"I'm so glad to hear you say that. I still think about that day all the time. I haven't forgiven myself for breaking up with you."

"You did what you thought was best."

"But I was wrong."

I wasn't expecting that. "What do you mean?"

"I thought I needed to force us both to move on with our lives, separate from each other, because we wouldn't have survived all the chaos of the music business. But that was totally daft. It's true that we would have had to spend a lot of time apart, but, to still have you in my life, that would have been so much more rewarding than what I have now." He was remorseful, like he committed a terrible crime that he couldn't undo. "I hated seeing you the way I found you today. Defeated. It wasn't supposed to be that way. It wouldn't have been that way if I hadn't . . . "

"Nigel, please stop blaming yourself." I put my hand on his shoulder.

"I can't. I not only fucked up my life, but I fucked yours up, too."

"Hey, you weren't the only one who made mistakes. I had a hand in our breakup, too. As for my *fucked up life*, I'm a big girl, I made my own decisions. If I'm living the wrong life, I can fix things. Didn't you just tell me that earlier today?"

"So, you don't think it's too late to fix things?"

"I guess it's never too late. Wait- " I realized he might have been referring to our relationship. I wanted him to clarify. "What do you mean?"

"Michelle, I didn't have a reason to be in town, well, other than to see you. I can't stop thinking about you and us and . . . I want you back. I need you. I don't give a shit about all those dumb models. They don't mean anything to me. They can't replace you. Nothing can. Not a day goes by that I don't think of you. Don't you think of me?"

I didn't want to confess, but I couldn't lie for shit, as he once told me. "Constantly," I replied reluctantly.

A relieved smile brightened his face. "Really? You're not over me?"

"I tried to convince myself I was, but you don't get over a love like ours," I confided. It was the truth.

"No, you don't. That's because it's a once in a lifetime thing. True love. Do you feel like that's what you have with the man you're about to marry?"

I was silent. I hadn't really thought of it that way. "It's different. It's comfortable, it's realistic, it's safe . . . "

"So, the answer is no."

"I feel like we fit together. Like you and I used to."

"We still do."

"Do you really think so? I mean, when we met, we were in the same league. But now, you live in a totally different world from me, a world I know nothing about. Look around. Look at what you're used to."

"You don't live in a hovel, Michelle. And we have the same upbringing. We're still the same; at least, I know I am. I feel the same as I did when I was that seventeen year old nerd you met. Remember me back then? I thought you were the best thing I'd ever seen and I still feel that way now. Looking at you, it takes me right back to that time. I was so happy then. *We* were so happy then. Please don't think you aren't good enough for me now. The truth is, I'd be lucky to have you."

"You always were," I teased.

"See, that's the girl I remember. I've missed you."

I looked into his smiling eyes, my heart bulging. "I've missed you, too, Nigel."

He took my hand and squeezed it. "You don't have to miss me anymore. You don't ever have to spend another day without me in your life."

It sounded incredibly tempting. "So, you want me to leave my fiancé for you?"

"Only if you want to. If you think he is better for you than me, I guess you should stay with him. But I can't imagine he loves you more than I do. We have shared so much together. I know everything about you and I *love* everything about you. Does he?"

Again, I was silent, and that gave him his answer. Deep in my heart, I knew Will and I didn't click and even if I came clean and stopped hiding myself from him, we could never be as well suited for each other as Nigel and I. But, something was stopping me from falling headlong into Nigel's arms now. His words were pretty, but I had reservations.

"Nigel, I need to ask you something. Where is all this coming from? Why now?"

He looked down again. "I've been going through a lot lately. There's just been so many things happening, bad things. It made me realize I need someone who would be there for me. Someone stable who I can count on and lean on and talk to and hold at night and share things with. I mean, my life is like a roller coaster, too many ups and downs. There's just too much pressure, too much is riding on me, and I have no one to turn to. And I know, I *know* I'm drinking too much. It's unbelievable how much I drink now."

"Is that it? Only drinking?" I alluded to his drug use.

He sighed. "No, that's not it," he admitted. "But, it's like, what everyone does. You know, you go to a party and it's everywhere. It gets crazy and it's out of hand, but it dulls the pain. It helps you forget. And it helps you continue the party."

"Is that the kind of life you want?"

"No, it's not. I need security. I need someone who cares about me to stand beside me and save me from myself. I'm sick of being alone. I don't want to be single anymore."

I didn't like the sound of that. "So are you here because you want me, or because you think I'm a sure thing?"

"I don't think you're a sure thing! I came back here not knowing if you would even speak to me, and I was betting that you wouldn't. But I had to take the chance and I'm so glad I did. I couldn't give up. Even when your mom told me you were engaged. And that *killed* me! I hadn't been so depressed since we broke up. And I thought, '*Well, you really cocked things up*', and I tried to accept that. But I couldn't. I'll be damned if I don't try to get you back. I never should have let you go in the first place. I love you. I love you so much."

"You love me? Or you need me?"

"Both! It's both! I need you *because* I love you. No one else could ever be what you are to me. You're my soul mate and I'm yours."

I knew he was sincere. I believed him. It felt so good to hear him say these things. It made me realize how wrong my life had been without him in it. He was luring me in.

He stroked my hair. "Do you have any idea how mad I was about you when we met? I thought I was going to be alone forever, but then, this beautiful American girl came out of nowhere and wanted to sit by me on the bus. Not only that, for some reason, she thought I was great, she thought I was beautiful. She loved me, right from the start, and, God, I loved her. It was like she could see right into my soul, you know? It was amazing."

My eyes filled with tears that began to overflow and stream down my cheeks as he brought back those tender memories. He delicately wiped them away with his fingertips. He continued.

"And not only that, this girl, she made me a man. She did things to me I could only dream of. She was so hot…" he whispered in my ear, his warm, moist breath made my flesh tingle. "…and so tight…" he nuzzled his face into my neck. "…and so wet." He put his hand on the inside of my thigh and slowly moved it up, under my dress. "I still think about those nights we had together," he growled.

I was completely under his spell. It was like old times, dangerous, forbidden, alluring. He kissed me and I forgot everything else in the world. We fell back on the couch, our kisses rapidly turning into something more.

It was like we were teenagers again. I wanted him so badly. It felt so right to be back with my first lover; like we were made to be together, spiritually and physically. It made me realize that it never felt this good with Will. *Will!* His face popped into my head. I pushed Nigel away.

"I can't do this! I'm engaged."

"To the wrong man!"

"Maybe so, but I can't cheat on him. I could never do that."

"Michelle, I need you. It has been so long since I've been with you," he pleaded, desperate to continue what we had started.

But I was adamant. I couldn't cheat, not even for Nigel. Then, a thought occurred to me. "Yeah, it has been a long time. Do you remember the last night we spent together? It was right after *you* cheated on me." I stood up.

He was taken off guard as I made a one eighty. He also stood up, trying to calm me down. "You're right. I'm sorry. I wish I could take that back."

"Me, too! I've wished that for four years. But we can't."

"No, we can't. All we can do is move on. I'm so sorry I got high and slept with that girl. It was the dumbest thing I ever did. I hate that I did that to you. Do you think we can move past that?"

I wasn't sure, remembering that night was still so painful. And I could envision it so clearly, like it was happening all over again. I wondered about all the other women he had been with since we broke up. The realizations felt overwhelming.

"I don't know if this is right."

"What? I thought we had everything worked out."

"No, we don't. You just cruised into town out of the blue and tell me that you shouldn't have left me four years ago and now you want to pretend like it never happened because you think you'd be better off with me, even though I'm attached."

"Michelle, I love you! And you love me. We belong together! You know I'm right!"

"No I don't. I'm really confused. This has been a really confusing day!"

"Okay, let's talk it out."

"What is there to talk about? What's going to happen tomorrow, or in a few weeks when you have to go back to your life? Where do I fit into that?"

"You'll be by my side where you always belonged. Come with me!"

"You want me to leave everything behind and come with you?" I was flabbergasted. "Nigel, why wouldn't you let me come with you before?"

"You said you understood! You said you forgave me!"

"I have forgiven you!" I shouted. "So, why am I still so hurt?"

He didn't speak. He just stared at me, waiting for me to continue.

"Because I still love you *so* much! I look at you now, and it's like no time has passed. But it has. It's been years since I've seen you, but it's like it was just yesterday that you cheated on me." He slumped on the couch, guilty and sad. Angry tears surfaced as I unleashed four years of fury onto him. "How could you do that to me? I was so devoted to you. I was so fucking crazy about you, there was nothing I wouldn't have done for you! But, we have a fight and without even trying to work things out, you jump into bed with the nearest slut. Our bed? It was such a happy place. When you were sick, I nursed you in that bed. You used to come home to me in the early morning and wake me with a kiss in that bed. And all those amazing nights we shared in that bed. And the nights we just lied there talking or holding each other . . . And you could fuck some sleazy wench in that bed?"

Nigel was silent, his head was down, his fists against his temples. He was beating himself up. I suppose the pain was still as fresh for him as it was for me.

I didn't want to cause him more misery, but I had to go on. "I could forgive all that. Even that night, I was so mad and hurt but I didn't stop loving you. I didn't stop wanting you. Even though it destroyed me, even though you betrayed me, I forgave you. But when *I* begged, you wouldn't take *me* back?"

"I couldn't forgive myself!"

"So you punished *me?* You should have just killed me because my life was over! But the worst part was that after everything, I *still* wanted you back. I didn't care how much you hurt me, I would have given anything to have you again. I waited and waited, always hoping, but no. And now, now that I have started to put my life back together, here you are, ripping open my wounds, asking me to come with you?"

He bolted up. "Yes! Yes I am! You can't be more mad at me than I am with myself! You can't have suffered as much as I have! All you lost was me. I lost *you!* You were my whole world."

"*You* were everything to *me!* Like oxygen. Like water."

"I know exactly what you mean. But, Michelle, we don't have to hurt anymore. Don't you want to go back to being complete? I do! Say you'll come with me."

It was so easy to give in to him. The pain in his voice, the stress in his eyes. I had always wanted to keep him safe and protect him above all else. Even if it meant I would be the one to suffer.

I had a feeling that's what would have happened.

I hushed my heart and let my head take over.

"I don't know if I even know who you are anymore. I don't know anything about your new life. So much has happened over the past few years. Can I really believe things will just go back to the way they were? Can I believe you won't devastate me again?"

"Of course you can. I've changed."

"Maybe that's the problem. You used to be my soul mate, but you changed." I was making up my mind on the spot that this wasn't going to work. "It was Nigel I fell in love with, not John."

"No, wait! I'm still Nigel! Let me prove I'm still the man you fell in love with. Don't just convince yourself that I'm not. Why can't you see I'm sorry and I'd never abuse your trust again? Why can't you see how much I care about you? Don't you believe me? Why are you so ready to throw away our future? Is this because you think it's better to stay in your boring comfortable world instead of taking a chance to be happy?"

His accusation stung me, but I didn't contest it. I was bewildered, but the more we talked, the more confused I became. "I need to go."

"Stop running away from me! You can't keep pretending like you're done with me. I can see you still love me! But that scares you! You're just refusing to run away with me because that's the logical thing to do. That's why you are where you are right now, stuck in your buttoned-down predictable life. That's why you tried to just forget me. It's simpler that way, isn't it? *Uncluttered? No unnecessary drama?* It can't always be that damn tidy! Sometimes things have to get messy."

I didn't know what to say. I hated confrontations. And what was worse, he knew me too well. I didn't want to hear it, but he was right.

"Stay. Please stay," he pleaded. His eyes were desperate. I knew he could easily coerce me into doing whatever he wanted if I looked into those eyes for too long.

"No, I can't look at you. I can't think straight when I look at you." I grabbed my purse and headed to the door.

"Don't you think that's significant? You're still in love with me." I looked at him for a moment, almost reconsidering, then went back to the door. He tried to block me. "Alright, I promise I won't try to kiss you or anything again. But, please stay. Let's talk. Don't just walk away from this. Please."

He was begging. His face looked tortured. I had such trouble not giving in to him when he was in pain. But, I found the strength. I tapped into my anger.

"I said something like that to you a few years ago. Remember? I begged you not to go. I *begged* you to talk it out with me. But you thought you knew what was best. And now, I think I do, too." I opened the door.

"Damn it, you're stubborn!" he shouted as I walked out, slamming the door behind me.

I walked a few steps and froze. *I could turn around right now,* I thought. *I should turn around right now.* I felt the same way that he did. I was only complete when I was with him. But I didn't want to go back to him and make the same mistake twice. I slowly walked to the elevator, weighing my options. I heard a door open and I turned around. He was there, standing in his doorway, watching to see if I would go back.

Chapter 14

"...feeling quite confused."

He looked so sad, crushed. I felt similarly. We stared at each other for a moment. He started walking toward me. I started walking toward him, a bit faster. He looked so glad that I was coming back, I thought he was going to cry. He quickened his gait, I started running. We collided into each other's arms, instantly locked in a passionate kiss.

When we were finally able to break our lip-lock for a moment, he said "This is where you belong. I love you, Michelle."

"I love you, Nigel. I love you. I love you," I repeated over and over.

"Huh?"

It was Will. I had been dreaming, and I guess talking in my sleep.

"What did you say, honey?" he asked, voice groggy.

"Sorry, go back to sleep," I whispered.

He grumbled and turned his back to me. Seconds later, he was snoring away. I sighed. I was having a good dream. It was better than reality had been.

In reality, I had run away from Nigel, not to him. I got on the elevator, I didn't go back. As the doors were closing, I caught his reflection in a mirror in the hallway across from his room. He looked devastated that I had left like that; he put his head down and backed into his room and slowly shut the door.

Remembering that, I felt like someone had stabbed me in the heart with a dirty, dull knife. I couldn't believe I hurt him that way. Why didn't I turn around like I did in the dream? Why didn't I tell him that he was all I ever wanted and I would take him back in a second?

I knew why. I was angry. During the whole drive home last night, I was cursing him out. All the bad memories I had tried to repress and forget were stirred up and back to the forefront of my mind. When he cheated, when he broke up with me, how he chose stardom over me. . . . What kind of love is that? Then after that, I'm so torn up over our breakup that I have to leave the country while he's already dating other women. And he is on TV, on the radio, on magazine covers, on top of the world! And then, he has the audacity to barge into my life and tell me he's missed me for years but never bothered to call or write or see me!

Also, he has the nerve to tell me I'm living a lie. That I've changed and have made wrong decisions, that my whole life is messed up. And why? Why did he have to say all those painful things? Why couldn't he just leave me alone?

Because he loved me. He loved me. He flew around the world to tell me that.

When I had arrived home the night before, I went straight to bed. Will wasn't home and wouldn't be for hours yet. I was glad, because I couldn't face him. I felt guilty for being with Nigel and for almost leaving him. I was torn and had no idea what side to choose. My head ached with tortured emotion. My mind was spinning. In one day, my whole world was flipped over. Nigel had me questioning everything, the most important question being, '*Do I want him back, too?*'

I was pretty sure I knew the answer. I cried myself to sleep. I was literally wailing, reliving all my memories. I cried thinking about how much it would hurt to break up with Will. I cried out of guilt over my infidelity. I cried because I was agonizing over *Nigel's* infidelity. I cried because I didn't trust him enough when he said he loved me and would never hurt me again. I cried thinking about what I had just given up, the chance to have what I had been missing for the past four years. I cried because I was mad and I cried because I still loved him. Maybe I would always love him, but did that mean we were good for each other? We were once, but now? I was incredibly confused.

The next day, I slept in. I didn't set my alarm intentionally. I didn't care about going to work or anything else. I just needed a break from consciousness. I didn't know when I fell asleep, but I did sleep hard, as I didn't wake up when Will got into bed, which must have been after midnight.

When he woke up in the morning to his own alarm clock, he was surprised to see me in bed and tried to rouse me.

"Get up! Your alarm didn't go off. It's eight o'clock!"

"I'm not going to work today," I decided on the spot.

"What? Are you sick? Oh, you must be really sick because you never call in," he remarked. He looked at me and saw the red eyes, nose, and haggard appearance. "You look terrible."

I thought it would be easier to play along than to explain. "Yes, I'm very sick. I need to stay home today."

Just then, the phone rang. Will answered it. "Honey, it's work. Should I tell them you're too sick to come to the phone?"

"Yes, please. Tell them I'm sorry I didn't call sooner but I can't come in today." I tried to sound as feeble as possible. I overheard Will reiterating my statement into the phone. When he hung up, he came to my side.

"They said they hope you feel better. Can I do anything for you?"

"No, I just need to rest."

"Okay, I'll try to get ready for work quietly so you can sleep. Call me today if you need anything." He kissed my head.

"Alright, thank you," I softly said. He smiled at me and left the room, shutting the door behind him. When he left, I snuggled in the bed. It felt really good to be in bed past six a.m. on a weekday. Nigel was right, I hated getting up early. I grimaced, realizing that he was right. I had been so mad at him for his base analysis of me after not seeing me for years. But all the things he said, though I didn't want to hear them, they were true. It must have taken a lot of courage to say those things. And he had to say them because he cared too much about me to see me wasting my life. And I *was* wasting my life, because a life without him really wasn't much of a life. At least it was no life I wanted, not the life intended for me.

Last night, I was so confused, but today, everything was clear. It would be scary to completely change my life and go back to Nigel, but

I was willing to do it. I had to do it! I just hoped he would understand why I needed to think it over for a while.

I heard the door slam shut; Will had left for work. I jumped out of bed, not sure of what to do, but knowing I had to do something.

My first thought was to call Nigel's room. I looked at the clock, 8:45. No, Nigel was probably still asleep. Or maybe he couldn't fall asleep last night either. Or maybe he was already gone! He didn't say how long he would be in town, especially after being shot down. I bolted down the stairs to find my purse that had his card in it.

I dialed the phone so frantically that I misdialed three times before successfully reaching the front desk. "Yes, hello, can I please be connected to room 1451?" I asked quickly.

"1451? I'm sorry, ma'am, but the gentleman in 1451 checked out almost an hour ago," the clerk reported.

"What? An hour ago?" I was speechless and deeply disappointed.

"Yes, ma'am. Is there anything else I can do for you?"

"Um . . . yeah, he didn't leave a number where he could be reached or a message for someone who may be looking for him, did he?"

"No, he requested privacy," the clerk said curtly. I understood. Nigel was probably used to girls finding out his location and trying to get into his room. The clerk must have assumed that I was one of them.

"Okay, thank you," I softly replied, defeated. I hung up. I stood there for a while, not knowing exactly what to do. Three minutes ago, I had every intention of trying to make up with Nigel and start a new life, the life he thought I deserved. Now I had lost that chance. I had no idea where he went, how to reach him, or if he even wanted to bother with me now after I had rejected him and his advice. I was depressing myself as I realized all this. I moped up the stairs and collapsed into bed. I knew I wouldn't be able to sleep, but I wanted to evade my depression, so I tried.

I spent almost all day in bed, only getting up occasionally to go get some comforting junk food to sustain me. Yesterday I cared, for a moment, about getting my body back. Today I didn't care about anything; not my job, not my health, and maybe not even my fiancé. I had been ready to just walk out on him for Nigel; what did that say about my love for him? I felt ashamed. Will trusted me and I trusted him. He would never walk out on me. He thought I was the best thing that ever happened to him and he told me often. But I never told him back, I guess because I didn't feel the same. That wasn't right. Maybe I didn't deserve him and his unfailing love. Sure, he had his imperfections, but he was good to me.

Yes, he was good to me, but was that enough? Was he good for me?

Suddenly I was questioning our whole relationship, from start to present. Looking back, I wondered what drew me to him. Was it the security and stability? Nigel was a wild ride and I was kind of sick of it by the end, but I knew why I was with him. We had a real connection that I never had with anyone else. Not with Will. I went through half a box of cookies while I compared the two. They took turns coming out on top in my head. I was feeling quite confused when I heard the back door slam shut, interrupting my thoughts.

"I'm home!" Will called out. Moments later he was thudding up the stairs on his way to the bedroom. "I got off early to take care of you." He had a grocery bag in his hand. "I brought you some stuff. Ice cream, in case your throat hurts. Cold medicine, drowsy and non-drowsy. Soup, ginger ale, tissues, crackers, and I bought a few magazines you like. Did I miss anything?"

I was amazed and touched. "No, you got everything I could possibly want or need. Thank you so much, that was so sweet of you." I sat up and gave him a hug. That was one point for Will. Nigel, zero.

"Did I do good?"

"Yes, Will, you did." I tried not to sound irritated, but it always bothered me that he needed constant patting on the back for everything he did right, even for small things. I was very grateful at his hospitality, but Nigel would do nice things for me out of his own goodness, not to look like a hero. That was one point for Nigel. Now the men were tied.

"So, how do you feel?" Will asked.

"Well, actually, I'm not sick at all. I just needed the day off to get a grip on myself."

"Why didn't you just tell me that? I was worried all day about you."

There he went, making everything about him. He didn't care that I was having a mental breakdown, he only cared that I put a damper on his day by making him worry about me. How dare I? That would be another point for Nigel, he wasn't a selfish man. "I'm sorry to worry you but I've just been really depressed and I couldn't bear to go in to work today. Do you understand?"

"Yes, I understand. Listen, I'm here if you need to talk or anything. Maybe I should take you out tomorrow to cheer you up. Would you like that?"

"Yeah, that would be really fun. I feel better already." And I meant it. See, unlike Nigel, who was so involved in being a rock star, Will's world revolved around me and that was worth a few points. Nigel was lagging behind.

"So, what's been bothering you anyway?"

"Um . . . I don't know where to start. I guess lately, I've just-"

"You know, I've been pretty depressed lately, too. I think a fun weekend is exactly what we need. Hell, it's Friday, let's start now. Get dressed, let's go out to dinner! I'll go make a reservation." He jumped up and ran downstairs.

I felt totally ignored. Obviously I was having a big issue if I couldn't even get out of bed. He couldn't even pay attention to me for more than one sentence without bringing it back to himself. He never listened to me, and mostly I brushed that off, but this time I was in crisis and I couldn't count on him to hear me out. It really bothered me. We had discussed that in the past. I was a good listener, more of a listener than a talker. He was a talker, and he always had to be the subject. And if he wasn't, he would bring it around to him if he could, the way he just did. I had been blaming myself for not being more open with Will, for not bearing my soul to him, but on second thought, I had my reasons. Whenever I tried to talk to Will about anything, his eyes would glaze over or he would interrupt me. I didn't talk because I felt like I wasn't being heard.

I frowned. I was more mixed up than ever.

I got up and got dressed anyway because I was sick of being in the house. I put on pants with an elastic waistband and a blouse that would conceal belly bulge. I had eaten too much today and I didn't care.

At the restaurant, we had drinks, appetizers, dinner, dessert, and more drinks. I wasn't hungry at all, but I forced the food in, I suppose

I was trying to satisfy the void Will left me with. I tried to push the negativity and brutal truth out of my thoughts and concentrate on delightful, pleasant food. It worked.

We made it home safely later that night. I was still tipsy. I staggered upstairs, Will at my heels. He started kissing my neck, trying to initiate sex. I wasn't really in the mood.

"Come on, we haven't done it in . . . forever," he whined. He was right, I couldn't remember the last time.

"Alright." I gave in. He started tearing off my clothes and pushed me down on the bed. In my drunken daze, my mind wandered as my body was being humped. I thought back to the time when Nigel and I were making love for the first few times and how great and special that was. I could remember the pleasure so well. I pictured the look on his face, the lines of his young body, and his luscious mouth. I recalled the waves of excitement I felt. I sensed a smile creep onto my face. Though my head was far away, my body was receptive. Will thought he was in rare form, but I was enjoying the sex so much more tonight than usual because I was thinking about having sex with Nigel.

Not too long later, we were both done and laying on our backs in bed, panting and smiling. "I rocked your world, didn't I?" Will half joked.

"Oh yeah," I half teased back. I wasn't going to let him take full responsibility for my delight.

"I'm beat. Goodnight." He kissed me, then rolled over to fall asleep.

"Goodnight," I whispered back and closed my eyes, remembering how Nigel would hold me and kiss me after making love.

I didn't want to end my Nigel trance. I found it funny that when I was with him, I wanted to capture every moment and savor them. With Will, I was wishing he were someone else because who he truly was didn't satisfy me. Staying with Will would be the smart choice, but was it the right choice?

I thought again about their score cards. I was trying to decide if they were even. It was close.

The next morning, I got up and went in the bathroom. I leaned on the counter to get a close look in the mirror. "You know what you have to do, don't you?" I asked myself. My heart sank as I thought about breaking up with Will. "Coward," I sneered.

I couldn't do it. I wasn't happy and I didn't want to spend the rest of my life with Will, but I couldn't bring myself to hurt him. I couldn't crush his dreams. He wanted a life with me; marriage, kids, gray hair, all that.

To me, it sounded like a prison sentence.

I heard him snoring in the bedroom. I smiled.

I guess a big part of me still loved Will deeply even though I knew our relationship was doomed.

But at the same time, I was falling out of love with him and I couldn't deny that. Whenever he wanted to make wedding plans or talk details, I would come up with an excuse not to or change the subject. In my head, I was planning my future and it didn't involve him.

ဢ

Four months passed and I still hadn't ended things with Will. At first, I waited for Nigel to call me, thinking that the time would be right to leave Will when Nigel came back into my life. He never called. After a few weeks, I tried to get in touch with him. I couldn't. I then realized that I didn't need Nigel to take me away because I already knew that I needed to move on. The only problem was that I lacked the courage to do it.

I kept putting it off for one reason or another. I told myself that I didn't want to be hasty, I wanted to be sure. We had plans to go away for my birthday, so I didn't want to do it then. And the holidays were right after, also not a good time. I held my tongue and waited for the right moment.

The New Year came and as 1986 began, I had a very important resolution to make. It was time to be more proactive about my life. I stopped eating so much and so unhealthy. I stopped drinking and exercised more. I tried to rediscover myself and figure out what I wanted from life. I knew the first step would be to break up with Will, but I couldn't bring myself to do it.

I began to spend more and more time locked up in my bedroom, just to get away from him. I also encouraged him to take business trips when they were offered. "Take the over time," I would say. "We can use the money to pay for the honeymoon."

One Sunday afternoon, while he was on a ten day trip to New Mexico, I was bored and started cleaning out my closet. I came across a box that had some teenage mementos in it.

"Aww," I said out loud to myself as I dug into it. I was surprised to find letters from Nigel. They were from our first Christmas together, the ones he wrote me while I was away from him. I sighed and read every one of them, instantly ensconced in the young love we had begun in 1977.

"Wow," I said softly, reminded of how strong that love was, right from the start.

When I had read all the letters, I searched the box for more treasures. I found the self-addressed envelopes he had given me to write him back. There were two left that I hadn't used. I held them in my hand, staring off into space as my mind wandered.

I wonder what Nigel is up to now. I wonder where he is. Does he still have the notes I gave him? Probably not, he has been moving around for years. Maybe he has a box of stuff from his childhood at his parents' house. The letters may be in there. His parents' house . . . his parents' house! I have their address! I could write to them! They would know how to get in touch with their son! They can tell me and I can talk to him and we can get back together and rekindle our love!

My heart raced as I thought about seeing Nigel again, or at least talking to him. His parents surely would be willing to help me get in touch with him. They always liked me.

Wait! Am I nuts? What am I doing? If I think I'm going after Nigel, shouldn't I break up with Will first? I'm going to sneak behind Will's back to write a note to the Blakes to try to reconnect with their son? That's conniving! Who would do that? Damn it, if you want to get Nigel back, have the balls to break up with Will.

"Okay, that's it. I'm breaking up with him. Maybe Nigel won't even want me back, but I have to try," I said to myself.

I sat down and wrote a letter to his parents.

Dear Mr. and Mrs. Blake,

Hello, how are you? I hope life has been treating you well. It has been a long time since I saw you last, and that is a shame. I always hoped someday we would be family. You know I cared deeply for your son, and I still do.

I miss him greatly and would like to contact him, but I don't have a way to do that. I was hoping you would be able to pass along a phone number or address or something. If nothing else, please tell him I'd like to speak with him the next time you see him. I appreciate it so much. Take care.

All my love, Michelle Casey.

With a sigh, I folded up my letter and put it in a new envelope. I carefully addressed it and over-stamped it, wanting no delay in it reaching Cambridge safely and quickly. I put it in the out-going mail before the pick-up time.

To my surprise, I got a response six days later, on the following Saturday. I was glad the letter arrived before Will came home. I ripped it open and scanned it.

Dearest Michelle,

Joe and I were pleased to hear from you. It has been a long time, hasn't it?
I wish things would have gone differently for you and Nigel as well, but life has a funny way of working out.

I think it is time you and he have a talk. Here is his phone number and address. Good luck and God bless!

Love, Joe and Jan Blake.

My heart thumped in my chest. From the sounds of the letter, Nigel's parents wanted us to be together! And he was living in California now! I felt that I was close to reconnecting with him and felt excited for the first time in far too long. I didn't want to waste any time, I wanted to talk to Nigel right away. I ran to the phone and dialed. After several rings, a woman answered. She sounded irritated. "Hello?"

"Uh, hi. Is Nig– is John there?" I asked, totally thrown off.

"Hang on," she said and I heard her in the background calling for him. Who was this person? A housekeeper? A friend? Something else?

He picked up the phone. "Hello?"

"Nigel?"

"Michelle? . . . Hi."

"You recognize my voice."

"Not many people call me Nigel. Especially American women."

"Oh. Well, how are you?"

"Um, good. Frantic at the moment, but good."

"Frantic? What's going on?" I wondered.

He was silent for a moment. "I'm– I'm getting married next week," he admitted. I was silently stunned. There was a pause. "Michelle?"

"Married?" I whispered.

"I'm sorry. Look, can we talk in person?"

I tried to collect myself. "What's there to say?"

" . . . I'm having a baby. My girlfriend is pregnant and we think it's best to get married as soon as possible," he blurted out.

My heart stopped. My visions of the future evaporated.

"I didn't know how to tell you. But it doesn't matter, does it? I mean, you're getting married, too, so I guess we're even," he pointed out. The knife in my heart twisted. I remained quiet. "I'm sorry. This isn't a good way to tell you, but there is no good way . . . I needed to move on, too. . . . You wouldn't come back to me. What was I supposed to do?"

I still couldn't speak. It was agitating him.

"Say something! Please."

"C– Congratulations," I quietly stuttered and hung up. My hand lingered on the receiver; it felt heavy and numb. All of me felt numb. I couldn't believe it. Nigel had prodded me to take hold of my life, to fix what was broken. Until a minute before, I thought I had a chance to do that. The mistake that I wanted to fix most was when I decided not to take him up on the offer to get back together when he asked me to six months ago. If I had, I would be his girlfriend. Maybe *I* would be having his baby. Then he would be marrying *me*.

That's the way it was supposed to be! The tears were unstoppable. I felt grief and loss like I'd never known. More than when we first broke up. It felt so final. He was having a child, with another woman!

I picked up the letter from his parents and read it again. Suddenly, I was interpreting it totally differently: " . . . *wish things had gone differently . . . life has a funny way of working out . . . you two should talk.*"

They knew what was going on! They were going to be grandparents! Things were working out, for everyone but me!

I cried so hard, mourning our ill-fated love and the baby *we'd* never have. I cried thinking about that other woman taking his name, holding his hand, being in the position meant for me. I cried at my own stupidity for wasting my opportunity and for thinking that Nigel would just come back to me now. What did I expect? He saw me moving on; he had every right to move on, too.

I sat there, soaked in tears, wiping my nose on my shirt sleeve. It was a while before I was able to stand up. When I finally could, I was confused. Where did I think I was going? Nothing mattered, I couldn't see the point of going anywhere or doing anything.

And with that, I headed for the kitchen. I dove into my stash of junk food. I washed down bites of fatty, salty, and or sugary poisons with a rum and Coke that was equal portions of each. I didn't care. I ate and drank voraciously until it caught up with me, which, due to my emotional paralysis, wasn't for almost an hour.

Suddenly very sick from the crying, over eating, and heavy drinking, I went upstairs and vomited out everything I'd ingested for the past two days. I was crying and puking so hard, it took all the energy I could muster to pick myself up off the floor and get to the sink. I splashed my face with water and rinsed my mouth. Toweling off, I looked up and saw myself in the mirror. Red, puffy eyes with dark gray circles beneath them. Pale lips, flushed cheeks, disheveled hair. Even though my head was spinning, I could still focus on my own self hatred. I didn't want to be alive. For a moment I thought about taking all the pain pills I had in the medicine cabinet at once. I settled for the next best thing to killing myself and went to bed.

It didn't take long to fall asleep and once I did, I was out for fourteen hours.

I woke up to Autumn licking my face. I was startled and unamused, and I had a bitch of a headache. I stumbled to the bathroom to take something. Upon opening the medicine cabinet to look for the aspirin, I saw my prescription bottles and remembered what had happened the night before, from the bad news from Nigel to the suicidal thoughts before bed.

"Ugh," I groaned out loud before throwing two tablets down my throat and putting my head beneath the faucet to gulp down some water. I wearily and slowly made my way downstairs to the kitchen. I saw the huge mess I had made the day before: food wrappers, empty bags and boxes, an empty bottle of Captain Morgan's. So much excess. I felt sick again just remembering what I'd done.

I was in no position to clean up, so I wobbled over to the living room and sank into a chair and let my head spin. When it was all calm, I realized something—I was going to have to pick up the pieces sometime. I couldn't be a fall-down drunk or a six hundred pound woman and expect to be happy.

I started talking to myself, like I so often do when I'm depressed.

"So, you thought Nigel would make you happy? But it's too late for that. You fucked that one up nicely. So, what will make you happy? Another man? No, no, I think I need some time alone to figure things out. Yes, I need to figure things out. I don't know who I am anymore. I have strayed quite a bit, haven't I? Well, since I am not happy with this person I've become, I guess I need to be someone else, don't I? I used to be so cool. I loved that me. The me that was unique and unafraid. The me that followed her heart and did what felt right instead of taking the safe route. Can I still be her? Wait! I am still her! Well, what would she do right now?"

I thought about it for a moment. "I think I need to make a big change. I don't like my life. I don't like anything about it. I don't like my job, I don't like this house, I don't think I should be with my partner. I need to get away from all these things and start fresh. I need a career that satisfies me, that I can be happy with. I want to live somewhere warm and sunny, in a cool house that I can express myself in. I want to surround myself with positive people who understand me and love me for who I am."

I sighed, feeling very optimistic. It was all possible. I was going to take charge of my life. I was ready. "Nothing is going to stop me from being happy. Nigel or no Nigel."

My head started to clear, whether it was the aspirin kicking in or the personal revelation, I don't know.

I got up and went upstairs to take a shower. When the fog in the bathroom had dissipated, I saw myself. I didn't look as horrible as I had the past few times I studied my reflection. Something was different.

"Huh," I said to myself, pleasantly surprised.

I wrapped up in a towel and went into my bedroom to change. I opened the closet, searching for clothes. I hadn't put everything away after cleaning out my closet a week ago. I tried to shove the mess out of my way to get to an outfit. As I did, I noticed a photo album on the floor and was compelled to look in it. When I opened it, a picture fell out. It was my friend Sarah. She was in Florida. I remembered when she sent this picture to me, it was about six months ago. The letter that came with it was stuffed in the album. I brought it out and read it.

> Dear Michelle,
>
> I hope you are doing well. I think about you often, especially now. I have moved to America! Remember how I always talked about how much I hated the dreadful weather in England? Well, I finally did something about it. I love Florida. There is so much to do and see and everyone adores my charming accent!
>
> I don't know why it took me so long to change my life and be happy. I should have done it a long time ago. I hope you are as blissful as I am. If ever you are in the area, please come see me- it's so beautiful here.
>
> All my love, Sarah

There was a phone number and address. I smiled, thinking about Sarah. She was always such a good friend. I really needed a good friend. I suddenly missed her badly, and so I called her right away.

"Hello?" she answered.

"Hi, Sarah? It's Michelle . . . Casey."

"Hey, how are you?" she asked excitedly.

"Oh, um, okay. How are you?"

"Fabulous, darling. I love it here. My life has just been amazing since I moved to Florida."

"Really? I'm glad you like America so much."

"Well, I know you thought England was so great. Probably because of Nigel, eh? I guess, the grass is always greener. . . . "

"Yeah, my grass has been looking pretty dead lately."

"Why? What's going on?"

" I am just really confused. So much has happened recently that has made me rethink every decision I've ever made. I think I really screwed up my life."

"Stop right there. You sound just like me before I moved. What you need is a fresh start. You have to say goodbye to all the negative things and people in your life and begin again. I was miserable and my surroundings were making me more miserable. Then, I decided to do something about it. I quit my job, broke up with my loser boyfriend, and moved to a warm, sunny climate. I changed my entire perspective and for the first time in a long time, I am truly happy."

"I don't remember what it feels like to be truly happy."

"Oh, no. You need help. You need drastic measures. Why don't you come stay with me? Oh, you'd love it here! And I can help you get your life back." She was so enthusiastic, it was contagious.

I thought about the mental list I had made. Warm weather would do me good. Michigan wasn't very appealing to me and I just wanted to leave everything behind. "You want me to run away?" I teased her.

She laughed. "Alright, I see how sometimes running away is the healthiest thing to do. So, yes, do the natural thing for you and run away from your problems."

"Okay!" I agreed. What did I have to lose?

"Really? Oh, this will be so fun! You should come straight away before you can change your mind."

"Well, I have to- . . . talk to a few people first." I didn't want to mention I was going to break up with my fiancé.

"Hey! Don't let anyone guilt you into staying where you don't want to be, doing what you don't want to do because it pleases them. Only you matter! Be selfish, this is your life."

"You're right. I'll be there within a few days. You're sure I'm not imposing? I'd have to bring Autumn with me."

"No! I'd love the company. It will be like old times!"

"Great! I'll call you when I get everything straightened out. Bye!"

I hung up. I couldn't believe what I was doing. I didn't do impetuous things like this. Not anymore, at least. *That's your problem, Michelle! And look where it's gotten you.*

The first thing I did was call work. It was a Sunday and no one would be there, but I decided to leave a message on the answering machine while I had the courage. "Hello, this is Michelle Casey and I'm sorry to say that I am no longer able to work for you. There has been an emergency, and I will need to take my vacation time right away. I will be moving out of state. So sorry. I'll be in tomorrow morning to collect my things." I hung up. A huge smile creased my face. "Whoa," I whispered to myself, feeling like a two ton weight was lifted from my shoulders. It felt so good I couldn't stop smiling.

The slam of the back door changed that.

"I'm home!" Will called out.

My heart jumped. *Oh, no. Am I ready for this? Yes, yes you are. You can do it! Take charge of your life!*

I went down the stairs and saw him in the living room.

"Was there a small tornado in the kitchen while I was gone? I didn't hear anything about it on the news," he joked.

"I'm sorry. I'll clean it up." I wished I hadn't made such a mess. It made me feel like a worse human being than I already did.

"It's fine. I'm just glad to be home."

I cringed, feeling overwhelmed with guilt. "How was your trip?" I asked.

"Alright. I missed you. Did you miss me?"

I was scared and shaky. This was it. "Um, honestly . . . No."

His expression soured. "Oh, that's nice." He got mad. "What's going on lately? I've been gone working all these extra hours to pay for our wedding and, frankly, it doesn't even seem like you want to marry me."

I took a deep breath. " . . . I don't."

He was stunned. "What?"

"I don't want to marry you." I was quiet, letting him absorb that.

"Where did all this come from?"

"I'm not happy. I don't want this life or this house or any of it."

He was reeling. It took him a moment to collect himself. "Fine, you want to move? We can move. But I thought you wanted this house."

"I think I did at one point. But, I was just lying to myself. I couldn't have what I really wanted, so I just settled for what was within reach."

"Like me? You settled for me?" He was getting very angry.

"No, I don't mean that you aren't a great guy. But I don't think you are the right guy for me. You should be with someone who appreciates you."

"You're damn right! I can't believe this shit! All I do is kiss your ass and this is how you repay me?"

"Well, I don't think you kiss my ass, but either way, who asked you to? That's not what I want! I want someone who I can relate to, someone I can talk to."

"So, talk. I'm listening."

"Now! Now you're listening! It's too late. I've made up my mind, and I'm sure this is the right thing to do. Stringing you along isn't fair to you and I'm just wasting my time and yours. We should just end it now."

"I can't believe this. I can't believe you are doing this to me."

"I know it doesn't seem like it but I think I'm doing you a favor. You should be with someone who loves you unconditionally, someone who really appreciates you. I'm sorry, but that's not me."

He sank into a chair. He started crying. My heart was torn up. A part of me wanted to say, "Just kidding!" and hold him. But I knew there was no going back, and there shouldn't be. It took a long time to get where I was today and I needed to be strong and go through with it. I tried not to cry, but I couldn't help it.

With my strongest voice I said, "I'm moving. I quit my job and I'm moving in with a friend. I'll be out by tomorrow. You can keep the house." I took off my ring and set it on the end table beside him.

I trudged upstairs, sniffling, leaving him sobbing downstairs.

He spent that night in the basement, most likely drinking. I spent the evening packing and stuffing everything I could into my car. I only took my things, nothing that was ours. Every once in a while, he would come up and ask me if I was sure or if there was anything we could do to fix things. I had to convince him that I wasn't going to stay, no matter what. It was so hard to have to continue to crush his hopes. He would mope away, coming back later to yell at me and say that I was making a huge mistake and that it was wrong of me to leave him. It was a terrible night.

When he was leaving for work the next morning, he wanted to see me again. I was busy, trying to get everything done as quickly as I could, eager to get out of the house.

"Are you absolutely sure about this? Don't you think you should give it more time?" he asked sadly.

I kept packing as I answered him. "I am sure. I've known for a long time that it wasn't going to work. I was just hoping that I was wrong. But I knew then and I know now that I have to do this. It's better that I go now before we waste more time."

I didn't want to look up. I didn't want to see his face.

"Yeah, you've already wasted over three years with me. I don't want to be in your way anymore." He started walking away.

I had to stop him. "Will, I'm sorry. I'm so sorry. I don't want to hurt you, but it's not right to stay with you just to keep from upsetting you. And I don't think I've wasted the past three years with you. I just now figured out who I am. And I don't think it's who you think I am. I hope you find someone who fits you better."

"Fine, whatever. I hope your new life makes you really happy," he returned sarcastically.

"I know you don't mean that, but I do hope you will be happy."

"Right. Well, have a nice life," he sneered and walked away.

"Goodbye, Will," I said quietly.

෬

Breaking up with Will was incredibly hard to do. It killed me that I was hurting him, and the break-up hurt me, too. I still loved him; even though it was not enough, I loved him. It was tougher than I thought it would be to say goodbye to him and leave my home. It wasn't what I wanted, but it was familiar and comfortable. There were good memories. I cried as I packed up and loaded my car.

I put Autumn in her carrier; she was the last thing to go in the car. I stopped by my bank to close my account and withdrew all my money. I also had one more stop before I made it to the highway. I went to my office to officially quit. I briefly contrived an excuse for my boss and gave him my new address to forward my paychecks to. I collected my few personal items and was on my way.

As I made the long drive down south, I had too much time to think. I was torn, half elated and half depressed that I was leaving it all behind. Starting fresh sounded good, but it was also starting from scratch. It felt as overwhelming as it did liberating.

Autumn and I spent that night in a motel in Kentucky. I missed my bed and the comforts of home. I told myself that although it was unpleasant, it was only temporary. It was a step I had to take to propel myself into a better life. I had no idea what that life was going to be like or what I was going to do with myself, but it was an adventure that I was looking forward to.

Chapter 15

"...I felt like things were finally starting to go right."

My life had changed so much in the past six months. But now, on my way to Florida with everything I could pack into my car and a purse full of cash, I felt like things were finally starting to go right.

By the time I got to Sarah's house, it was near sundown. I pulled up in her driveway and honked. She ran out on the porch, screaming, heading right for me. I got out and she threw her arms around me.

"Oh, it's so good to see you! I'm so glad you're here! Come on in, we'll unpack later."

I looked around as the sun was setting behind Sarah's little yellow house. It was so unlike the atmosphere I had come from. Here it was warm and inviting. The grass was green, the flowers were alive and flourishing; there was no snow and no cloudy skies. The humid air was tinged with smells of the nearby ocean. I took a deep breath in and appreciated it all.

I picked up Autumn's carrier and followed Sarah into the house. She gave me the grand tour. She showed me my room: it was small and had tacky old-fashioned purple and white wallpaper on the walls. It was perfect. I loved her house, from the wacky turquoise paint on the walls to the hodgepodge furniture. It was cozy and unique, and it seemed like the perfect place to rebuild my life. For the first time, I felt sure that I had made the right move.

I was instantly hopeful that this was the type of environment I needed to lick my wounds and start fresh. I could feel the shackles of my old burdens slowly disappear and the life blood of the real me tingle in my veins again.

As we sat at the table, she poured us some wine and said, "Okay, so what's the story?"

"Huh?"

"Why did you move here? What are you escaping from?"

I was silent. I didn't know where to start. She had no clue that I had just made quite a drastic change.

"I talk to you for the first time in almost five years just two days ago and you pack up all your shit and race down to move in with me? What's up? Anxious to get the band back together?"

I sighed and launched into the whole explanation, starting from when I first moved back to America to the current day.

"When I moved home, you know it was because of Nigel. I wanted to get away from him and all those reminders of him. But even so many thousands of miles away, he was always there, like he was haunting me. Not just in my head, but on all those fucking magazine covers and all over the radio *and* TV! I just couldn't escape him. It took a really long time to get over him. . . .

"So, I start working to distract myself, and my parents talk me into going to school for a real job, and I meet this new guy and it all, like, happened so fast. All these seemingly little harmless decisions suddenly shape my life into something I never intended, and don't want! But I follow that road because I'm, like, too numb by this point.

"Then guess who shows up at my door after I'm fucking engaged? Nigel. Yeah. So, he comes crawling back, says he made a mistake and needs me and loves me so much and wants me to leave my life and join him. And I'm so confused, I have no idea what to think. But, I decide to talk to him. Then, he goes into the whole thing, we're soul mates, we're meant to be, all that shit. And he's almost got me back, and it feels good. But then I start thinking, hey, this guy left me when I had done everything I could to keep us together. He didn't come back to me when I begged him! And he fucking cheated on me and now he's out bangin' sluts all the time and getting shit-faced and he needs me to save him from himself 'cause he's a fucking mess without me. And I'm like, no! Fuck that! You had your chance! Yeah, I loved you and I probably will always love you but, come on, you want me to leave a man who is loyal for a man who will always put me second to his career? No! No way!

"So, I go home and I realize the man I'm going home to is not the love of my life, not the one I want to marry; and, not only that, my whole life is one big mess. Suddenly I see, Nigel was right. And even though he cheated and left me and ignored me for four years, I want him back more than anything! Crazy, right?

"I realize that Nigel was the only thing I ever really cared about and that my life was totally bleak without him in it. He was dumb and made mistakes and, yeah, they were big fucking mistakes, but, they weren't enough, nothing could be enough to make me stop wanting him, or stop loving him. He was right. We *are* soul mates.

"So, I call him up the next morning to tell him I changed my mind, but he'd left by then and I couldn't get a hold of him. And I couldn't get a hold of him until, like, six months later; and when I do, he fucking tells me he's getting married because he knocked up his girlfriend! Can you believe that? So, I figure, my life is over and I might as well settle for that. But, I couldn't take it anymore, Nigel or no Nigel, I had to start over. So, I quit my job, pack my shit, break up with my fiancé . . . and, here I am."

She listened patiently, nodding and interjecting "yeah" and "oh" where applicable. It felt good to be heard and it felt good to sort it out.

"Wow. I had no idea your life was so dramatic after you left England. That's some pretty exciting stuff."

"Yeah, I can do without exciting and dramatic for a while."

She drummed her fingers on her wine glass, trying to think of something to say to lighten the mood. "Well, shit, if you wanted a boring life, you shouldn't have moved here! It's a nonstop party. On any given day you can see old man Winkler walkin' his poodle down the street wearin' nothin' but a Speedo. And there's this perverted hippie who lives behind me who grows his own pot in his backyard and tries to get me to come over to smoke in the nude."

I laughed. "Is it wrong for me to think this is an improvement over my old life?"

She shook her head. "I'm glad you came here. I can't believe it took you so long to do this!" Sarah smiled. "Being unhappy for so long, and feeling guilty about changing that? Tsk, tsk."

I smiled back. She always made me feel better.

"I haven't told my parents yet."

"Oh, no?"

"Nope, not a thing. They won't approve."

"Well, I can see why you're putting that off. I think you've had enough negativity for a while. At least, wait until tomorrow."

I was more than fine with that. I was drained. The crying, the packing, and the driving had taken a lot out of me. Sarah could see that on my face.

"Hey, you, just look absolutely knackered. Why don't you get some sleep? You have the rest of your life to sort everything out."

The rest of my life. A new life. *My* life. It felt good.

ভ

Over the next week, I got settled in. I hadn't brought much with me, only what I couldn't part with. It was cleansing to start fresh. I felt like I was in a much healthier place. It was good for my soul.

It was also good to have a girlfriend around to confide in. I had forgotten how much I missed having Sarah in my life. We got along so well, it was like no time had passed since we moved from each other. She was still the same quirky, ballsy chick she always was. She was upbeat and in charge, exactly the kind of role model I needed.

I no longer felt like I needed food to fill a void in my life. I felt more complete than I had in a long time. Sarah and I went on crazy eating and drinking binges every once in a while, but for the most part, we ate quite healthy. We wanted to have fun and indulge, but we also wanted to look hot. I followed her lead of balancing decadence with abstinence. It was easier than I thought it could be. I enjoyed all the wonderful fresh produce from fruit and vegetable stands on every corner. The food was crisp and tastier than what I was used to up north. Also, we walked almost every night, which to me was unusual to do in the winter. It was gorgeous in Florida and I appreciated it thoroughly. I looked forward to getting out on the sidewalks near sundown and seeing palm trees, orange skies, and bright, blooming flowers.

Over time, I lost my excess weight. I felt like my old self again, in many ways.

Sarah worked out of her house, making jewelry and selling it to local vendors, so she was usually home. I envied her career. It was like what I wanted for myself. Being paid to be creative on my own terms would be a dream come true.

I needed to take direction in my life. I needed to figure out what I wanted and how to go about getting it. I was having a hard time focusing, perhaps because I was still weighted down with guilt and fear. I knew I had to confront my parents and tell them what was going on for my own peace of mind. When I got up the nerve, I called my mother.

"Hi mom, it's me."

"Well, hi. I haven't heard from you in a while. What's up?"

"Well, a lot actually. I broke up with Will and quit my job and moved to Florida."

She was totally quiet for a long time.

"Mom?"

"Are you kidding? Tell me you're kidding."

"No. It's the truth. I just needed to- "

"Young lady, you can't just walk away from everything! You need to go back and beg Will for forgiveness, and your boss! How could you just- "

"I'm not doing that! I don't want Will or my crappy job. I hate it! I'm not going to live a life I hate because you think it's the right life for me! I know what's best for me- "

"If you knew what was best, you never would've done this! This is a big mistake! You obviously didn't think it through."

"No, I did think it through. I thought about it for a long time. This finally feels right, I'm finally happy. I did the right thing."

She didn't even acknowledge that. "How are you going to support yourself? Who is going to support you? You're going to find some redneck who lives on welfare and be miserable. Will loves you. He was the safe bet. I don't know what the hell you're thinking!"

"Mom, I'm an adult. I get to make my own choices. You can't force your opinions on me. I have to make my own decisions."

"Fine. Make mistakes. Screw up your life. Just don't come crying to us when you're alone and broke and sorry."

"No problem." I hung up.

I turned around and saw Sarah leaning against the wall. She had been eavesdropping. "Good for you," she cheered.

"Ugh, I hate fighting with my parents, but they don't understand, you know?"

"I know. My parents are the same way. You have no idea how much they yelled at me when I said I was moving here. No matter how old you are, they still want to control you. And no matter how much they fuck up their own life, they always think they know best and you're just a daft child."

"Exactly," I pouted.

"So, what are you going to do now?"

"I'm not moving back!"

"No, no, I know you aren't. I mean, what are you going to do with your life? What's the next step?"

I shrugged and sighed. "I don't know. I guess I have to figure out a way to pay the bills."

"Damn straight! That call to your mom probably cost me seven bloody dollars!" Sarah joked.

I laughed. "I just don't know what to do."

"You have to do something you like. No- something you *love*. Something you have a flair for. Something that makes you want to get up in the morning."

"That's how you are with your job, isn't it?"

"Oh, yeah! I love my job! I could never have a boring desk job, it's not my style. And, obviously, it's not yours either. So, what is your dream job?"

I thought it over for a moment. "I'd like to do something artistic, too. Like . . . paint or write or something. That's what I intended to do when I graduated high school."

"Oh, yeah. You were always a great writer. You could write for a living. You could be a millionaire if you play your cards right."

"Yeah, but I don't know where to start. I mean, what do I write? Songs? Books? Screenplays? Greeting cards?"

"All of the above! Any of the above!"

I laughed. "Well, you need inspiration to write. I don't have anything to inspire me."

"What? Hello? You have just gotten into a fight with your mother, you broke up with your fiancé, you moved across the US with two days notice. Hell, that's a country song right there!"

I laughed. "Okay, you have a point."

"It will come to you, I'm sure. Just remember, you can have whatever you want once you decide what that is. You just have to take it."

CB

I kept thinking of how to go about becoming a writer again. It was tough. In my youth, I couldn't keep my pen still. Now, I was sitting at a desk with a blank piece of paper mocking me. The pen was apparently in a coma.

"Argh!" I got up and walked around. Sarah was right, I had enough drama recently to write a soap opera, and yet I couldn't transfer my feelings and experiences into something worth reading.

Have I lost it? Is this a skill unlike riding a bike? Maybe I'm not able to be the creative type I once was. Damn. What the hell will I do now?

I paced the halls. Sarah was in her workshop/spare room making jewelry, looking up every so often as I passed by. After four or five trips, she spoke up.

"If you're going to wear out my carpet, you better plan on replacing it."

I popped in to the room and slumped in a nearby chair. "I have writer's block," I whined.

"Yeah, sometimes I can't find inspiration to create, either."

"What do you do?"

"I look for it. Sometimes it's a fashion magazine or looking at a painting or listening to a song. Lots of things inspire me. What inspires you?"

I thought about it. "Nothing inspires me like love."

"Great, focus on that. Now, go away. I can't concentrate with your negative vibes wrecking my flow."

I snickered, but I did what I was told. I went into my room and flopped on my bed. I closed my eyes and tried to conjure up some poetic feelings.

It didn't go so well. I could summon up bits and pieces of songs, but none that I could get excited about. And my plan was, like Sarah suggested, to write some country music songs. I was always a big believer in things happening for a reason. So I knew there was a reason I had moved here and I assumed it would be for that- to write country songs. After all, we were in the south. But my story of love gone wrong and mama not understanding her little girl ain't a little girl no more wasn't exactly Grammy worthy.

Days went by and still nothing. My trash can was overflowing with crumpled up paper. I almost gave up, but instead I decided to take a break from writing and concentrate on something else for a while until I was inspired. Sarah needed help with her business and I was able to sort out her finances properly. I didn't mind using my accounting skills to help her. She almost made it fun. It felt good to be useful.

We were together all the time. We lived together, worked together, shopped together, but we rarely fought. I think we both appreciated having the other to talk to and lean on.

She was incredibly supportive and never tried to push me to do more with my life as the weeks went by and I still hadn't found a means of supporting myself. But I didn't want just any old job, I wanted to find my *calling*. I needed to prove to myself and any naysayers that I had done the right thing.

I still wanted to write, but nothing good was coming from the recent pain and upheaval I'd been through. I almost didn't want to write about that. It was ugly to me and I didn't want to dwell on it.

For days, Nigel had been on the brain. I didn't know why, but he kept popping into my thoughts. I would remember our good times and smile. I would remember our rough patches and feel sick. I replayed the stories in my head, my own voice narrating them, like I was describing some incredible tale of love and misery between two teenagers who became broken adults.

I was stuck on that. The incredible tale. I was able to put it all in order, I was able to describe it, it was interesting, why not tell it? I played with the suggestion, thinking at first it was a dumb idea and it would go away. It didn't.

"I took his virginity. I took his virginity." I could not get the phrase out of my head. I wrote it down and whoosh, a flood of inspiration bled from my pen. I scribbled away, barely taking breaks to think, the transgressions rushing to the front of my mind. I couldn't stop, and I didn't want to stop. The story was good, and it was mine. I would write it, but maybe I would just keep it to myself. Maybe I would share it with my children on my death bed so that they would know their mother was once hot and cool enough to score a rock star.

As the paragraphs flowed, I thought to myself, '*Hey, this is kind of juicy*'. And it was all true. I just told it in vivid detail; not making up the events, just describing them in picture-like phrases. I spent hours without stopping- writing, writing, writing. Whenever I had a spare second, I picked up my notebook and began from where I left off. It felt so good to create again, to take ideas and turn them into art. To express myself for the first time in a long time felt like therapy. I couldn't stop if I wanted to, which I didn't. The book became an obsession; it became my full-time job.

I decided it was too good to keep to myself. I shopped around for a publisher. When I found one, they agreed that it was interesting enough to captivate a large audience. They jumped on it, and I was very excited.

By the end of 1986, my book was complete. I couldn't believe I was a published author. It was my dream come true. A dream (like so many of my other dreams) that I thought was unattainable. But I did it, and I was proud of myself.

ॐ

Within a few months, the book started taking off. I began making money from something I actually enjoyed doing. It was an amazing feeling. I felt validated, like I had made the right decisions and they were paying off. I finally knew what I was supposed to do with my life; I had found my calling. Only one thing was missing from my nearly perfect life.

I had almost everything I had ever wanted, except love. My true love. Life was incomplete without that. I had been so busy healing from my heartaches and rebuilding my new life that I was numb to that emptiness Nigel had left me with.

I couldn't hide anything from Sarah if I wanted to, but it was clear I was lonely and unsure what to do with my life.

"Alright, so what's next?" Sarah asked me. "What are you going to do with yourself now that the book is done?"

"I don't know."

"Maybe it's time you get a new boyfriend."

"Maybe. I'd like a man in my life, but I haven't met anyone who interests me."

"You're too picky."

"No I'm not. I just know what I want."

"And what's that?"

"Um," I thought. "Well, he'd have to be romantic, and charming, and artistic, and creative... It would be nice if he played an instrument. He's not afraid to be silly . . . he has to make me laugh and he *has* to be good in bed," I laughed. "He has to be handsome and sweet and caring and sensitive . . . "

"Is that all?" Sarah teased.

"Okay, maybe I'm being too specific."

"No, that's not what your problem is."

"So what is my problem then?"

"You're still in love with Nigel. You just described your perfect man and it's Nigel."

"Oh, please. I'm on the rebound from Will, not Nigel!"

"No, you're over Will! But you never got over Nigel! How can you even deny it? You just wrote a novel about him, for God's sake!"

I was stunned.

She continued. "Even the way your story ends, it's like you're still waiting for him to come back into your life. How can you move on and be happy with someone else when you aren't even over the one that got away five years ago?"

I blankly stared at the wall as I pondered her accusations. It only took seconds before I realized she was right. Of course she was right, it all made sense. The reason I left England, the reason I never really gave my heart to Will, and why I eventually left him. The reason I changed my life, the reason I wrote the book. The reason I get out of bed every morning! For Nigel! He had been the drive of all of my major decisions since the day I met him and still was to this day. Over him? Not at all. I just didn't see it until someone pointed it out.

That was me, though. Always so oblivious when it came to my own issues.

Now that the truth was out, I had to make a choice. Either move on or devise a way to get him back.

"So," Sarah pressed. "You never answered my question. What are you going to do now?"

"I have no clue."

"Alright, say you're rewriting the ending to your story and it can go anyway you want it to go. What would you do?"

I shrugged. "Maybe my happy ending is supposed to be with someone else."

"You don't believe that."

"Well, how long can I wait for Nigel? You said it yourself, we broke up over five years ago. And now he's married, for fuck's sake!"

"Michelle, how do you want your story to end?"

"But, I- "

"Hey! *How do you want your story to end?* Whether it's pure fiction or stark reality, anything is possible. You're in control. So tell me, how do you want your story to end?"

I didn't say anything. I felt too foolish to confess what I truly wanted. She saw right through me.

"Fine. Don't say it. But if you never admit to it, you'll never get what you really want." She crossed her arms and left the room, leaving her wisdom like a heavy veil over me. I sat and considered the situation. It was true, I was scared to admit to wanting something that seemed too unlikely, even for fiction. After fretting about it for a while, I collected myself enough to get up and go to my room. I flung myself on to my bed and let my mind wander.

Now I had always been a dreamer and always hated rules and conformity, but to even *think* about me with Nigel again felt wrong. He was off limits. He was married, *and* he had a baby. And even if I took that out of the equation, so much had happened between us, I didn't know if it could ever be the way it was before. Was I just building some perfect relationship in my head? Would the reality be a disappointment if I ever got it?

But on the other hand, to think of myself with anyone else felt more wrong. I meant what I said to Sarah earlier, about my perfect man. Nigel was everything I ever wanted in a mate. And he was so much more. He was amazing in ways I never knew I craved until I saw them in him, and thus became addicted to those little idiosyncrasies. I didn't just appreciate him, I needed him.

Stewing over all the many thoughts and questions swimming in my mind didn't lead to any answers. I needed to write it all down. I reached under my bed where I kept my old journal, the journal Nigel had given me almost ten years ago, and poised my pen to jot down some brilliant solution.

Nothing. No words came through me, but it wasn't writer's block. I was forcing myself to edit my feelings and thoughts before I could get them out.

"Stop it. Don't over think, just write," I commanded in a whisper.

Still nothing. There was too much emotion in me to have nothing to say.

Then I remembered what Sarah had said: I was in control. I'd never get what I wanted if I couldn't even say it. What did I want? What was my ideal ending?

I hesitated. "Okay, head, take a break. Heart, it's your turn."

Again, I put my pen to the paper, not knowing what, if anything, would come of this. It was something I wasn't expecting.

A letter to Nigel.

> *Dear Nigel,*
>
> *I want to ask you something. Can you think of anything more pathetic than a dumb girl carrying a torch for a man who left her five years ago? I can. A girl who can't get over that man despite the fact that he is now married. He has moved on, yet she is still as*

helpless for him as she was when she first fell in love with him.

Would it surprise you to hear that I am that pathetic girl? Maybe it wouldn't, because you had to know that I was an absolute fool for you since the day we met. Maybe it would, because you gave me the opportunity to be in your life again and I turned it down.

It seems that I am not only pathetic, but I am stupid and careless. Stupid because I gave away all I ever wanted; Careless because I didn't see how much you needed me. You were trapped in a burning house, calling out for help, and I callously let you suffer. You needed me and I rejected you. At your lowest point, you reached out to me but I was too bitter to give you what you yearned for most, a trusted, loving friend by your side.

I am absolutely tormented now. In a way, I'm glad you were single when the band took off so I wasn't in the way of your freedom or your fun. But, I wasn't there when you needed support. I didn't hold your hand. I didn't cradle you at night when you slept in strange rooms alone. I wasn't there to calm you down and save you from yourself. I wasn't there when you were sick to make you feel taken care of. I wasn't there to support you, to comfort you, to protect you. I wasn't there to make you see that no matter how bad you mess up, you would always be the most loved and cherished man on the planet.

Nigel, my dear, we have both made so many mistakes. There are many obstacles in *our way. It would seem to anyone that we have no chance. But, anyone else's opinion doesn't matter. No one else can feel what we felt for each other, no one else could explain our connection. No one else can tell me you don't belong with me, and I know you do. You always did and you always will. You are my everything. And I love you more than I could ever describe.*

Yours forever,
Michelle

When I finished it, I tossed the notebook onto the floor. It was something I would never let anyone else ever read, especially Nigel. It was such a pathetic sounding letter, but that's how I felt at the time. Desperate, lonely, willing to do anything to get him back.

Sarah tapped on my door. "Hey, I was wondering, do you think Nigel has read the book?"

"What? I don't know. I never thought about that."

"You never thought about that?" she asked, incredulously.

I realized what I had done. "Oh, no! I'm so embarrassed."

"Why? The book is a success. It's a great story, and besides, it's not like you portrayed him in a bad light. You didn't lie about anything. "

"Yeah, but I didn't hide anything either. I put every thought and feeling I had about him into that book."

"So, what? He knows you fancied him."

"Ugh, I just practically published my diary. There's things in there I didn't want him to know about!"

"You're so damn secretive. Good God. If anything, he'd appreciate your honesty, I'm sure."

"Okay, maybe, but what about his wife?"

She closed her mouth and thought about that. I groaned and flopped face down into a pile of pillows.

Chapter 16

"If you want me to stay, I will."

One morning in the spring of 1987, I was driving to the bank, listening to the radio. At the commercial break, the deejay announced that Descent was coming to town next month and that tickets were going on sale at ten o'clock. It was nine a.m. My heart pumped furiously. I didn't know why but I felt compelled to go to the show.

My sweaty hands barely made the turn into the bank parking lot. I sat for a moment, frozen in my seat. *Am I really going to the show? Should I? For what reason? I couldn't get backstage to see Nigel, anyway. Could I?*

I slowly got out of my car and walked into the bank, mentally fighting with myself the whole way. *Am I actually going to do this? Is this pathetic? No, what's the problem? Worst-case scenario, we don't see each other but I get to see a concert. That's fine. Maybe, I don't even want to see him. Yeah, right! I have to see him! I have to do this!*

By the time I made it to the teller's window, I had decided.

"What can I do for you today, ma'am?" she asked.

"I'd like to make a withdrawal," I stated.

After taking out what I hoped would be enough money for the best tickets available, I hurried to the ticket broker. I had forty minutes until the tickets went on sale. There was already a line, I began to worry that I wouldn't get the vouchers I wanted.

When my turn arrived at the window, I asked the attendant, "Is there any way I can get backstage passes for the Descent concert? Money is no object."

He laughed. "I'm sorry dear, can't help you. I do have front row tickets, though."

"I'll take that! Two, please."

I handed over a small fortune to the grinning cashier. In return, I was awarded two glorious tickets that couldn't have been worth more if they were made of solid gold.

"Thank you, so much!" I sang.

"You're very welcome. Have fun at the concert."

I could not wait to tell Sarah. When I got home, I was walking on air. I unlocked the front door and entered the living room; she was on the couch, lazing around. She looked away from the TV and saw me, beaming.

"What's with you?" she asked lightly.

"Descent is coming to town. I just bought two front row tickets!"

She sat up. "What? You're going to see Descent?"

"No. *We* are going to see Descent!"

She was on her feet. "What? Aghhh! You got us front row tickets to Descent?"

"Yeah! Aghhh!" She grabbed me and we hugged and jumped simultaneously.

We were screaming with glee, then Sarah's face soured. "Wait a minute! Why are you going to see them now? You haven't been to one of their shows since you left Cambridge. Is this about Nigel?"

I drooped to the couch. "Well . . . I guess. . . . Mostly, I mean . . . I don't know."

She snickered. "Yes, you do."

"Alright! It *is* about Nigel."

"Of course it is. I know how much he still means to you. He's the one that got away."

"No, he didn't get away. I let him go," I sighed. "And I kick myself every day for doing that." I slumped down, my head falling into my hands. "Ugh, I was so damn stupid! My whole life has been one huge mess since we broke up. Everything would have been okay if I had taken him back when he asked me to. Why couldn't I see that?" I felt tears rising. "I just want him back, Sarah. What am I going to do?"

She sat next to me and put her arm around me. "Well, I think this is a good start," she began, pointing at the tickets. "You can try to get his attention at the concert. If he sees you, and let's make sure he does, he'll probably ask you to come backstage and talk. Then, maybe, I don't know, you can see if he's still happily married. If so, you can at least get some stuff off of your chest to get some closure."

I took a deep breath. "You're right. That's all I can do. I'll just try to be at the right place at the right time and the rest is up to fate."

∞

I spent the next two months mentally preparing for the concert. I tried to envision things going well, things going bad, nothing happening at all, and everything in between. My stomach was constantly knotted. I was always thinking about it. I worried, I giggled, I had every emotion in existence.

When the day finally came, I was a nervous wreck. Sarah just laughed at me in all my tumult.

"You'd think it was judgment day," she mocked.

"In a way, it is," I replied.

"Well, I hope something happens between you two because I don't know how much bloody more of this I can stand."

I wanted to get to the show as early as possible. I made Sarah drive because I was too shaky. She tried to calm me down on the way there.

"You're going to have to be cool. Otherwise, he's going to take one look at you and wonder why he ever dated such a barmy bird."

"I know, I know. What if he sees me and he hates me now? What if he read the book and is totally pissed off that I used him and his story?"

"I don't know, but either way, you're going to have to face him. I think it's good that you're doing it now, the waiting is making you crazy."

I was in a daze. I barely remember getting to the arena, finding our seats, waiting for the show to start, or hearing the opening act. The haze only lifted when the lights lowered and they were announced.

My heart stopped. My blood was cold in my veins. I didn't breathe. The music started and colored lights shined down on the band. Next to me, Sarah was cheering and clapping, along with the rest of the crowd. I was a statue.

The music boomed in my ears, but I barely heard it. It was surreal. This experience was so different from when I saw them play last at the Fox Trot. Their sound was obviously more polished since they began in 1980. They were all grown up, no longer the foppish teenaged boys they once were, they were men, handsome, tailored men who had conquered not only the music charts, but the whole world. I was amongst thousands of screaming fans, but they all seemed to disappear as I looked onto the stage.

Sarah shook me. "Hey, Nigel is right in front of us! Great seats, huh?"

I didn't respond. I was in shock. She was right, Nigel was directly in front of me. He was no more than five feet away. I stared at him, unbelieving. I hadn't seen him perform since he was twenty one. It was so hard to associate this rock god with the sweet, shy seventeen year old boy I met in high school.

He played his part so well. He was a seasoned veteran of the stage. He worked the crowd, he was on his mark, he was the target of too many whistles (for my taste, at least). I became aware of my surroundings, aware of the multitude of fanatics around me. I was just one of them.

I suddenly felt so stupid being here. What was I trying to accomplish? His gaze was out over the crowd but not on anyone in particular, certainly not on me. I, on the other hand, couldn't take my eyes off of him. Even though this persona wasn't the one I fell in love with, I could still see beyond to the sensitive darling that used to love spending the evening curled up in my arms, just talking.

A few numbers into the set, Sammy paused to speak to the audience about the next song to be played. Nigel fiddled with his guitar a bit and casually looked around. Toward the front row. Toward me. He saw me. I saw a look of confusion, then recognition on his face. He stared, frozen. I lifted my hand in a halfhearted wave. The song began and he started playing along with it, trying to get his concentration back. I sighed, wondering what he was thinking.

Sarah poked me. "He saw you!"

"I know."

"What do you think that means?" She had to yell.

I shrugged. "I wish I knew."

I couldn't pay attention to the music any longer. I was preoccupied with wondering what Nigel was thinking about. He didn't look at me again.

After a few more songs, the show seemed to be over. The band waved goodbye and walked off the stage. The crowd roared and chanted, "Encore! Encore!"

During the chaos, a security guard came up to me and said, "Are you Michelle Casey?"

"Yes!" I yelled over the noise.

"Your presence is requested back stage after the show." He handed me a pass.

"I'm with her!" Sarah announced loudly. The guard gave her a look, but issued her a pass anyway.

Within seconds, the band reappeared and kicked into their encore performance. The rest of the crowd went wild, but I just wanted the concert to be over so I could talk to Nigel. I was thrilled he wanted to talk to me, but at the same time I was worried that he wasn't going to say what I wanted to hear.

After three extended songs, the show was actually over. The lights came up and the crowd started filing out. Sarah was almost more excited than me to go back stage. "Come on, let's go!" She pulled my hand.

"I'm scared!" I whined, though I let her pull me.

"Let's get this over with! Besides, I want to see the guys again!"

We were escorted back stage by another security guard. He led us down a long corridor.

"Geez, you'd think the Queen was here," Sarah observed as we passed all the bouncers.

Our escort knocked on a white door and we heard a "come in" from behind it. The guard let us in and stayed outside. My heart was thumping so loud, it must have been audible. I saw Sammy first.

"Hey, I remember you!" he teased and approached me for a big hug.

"Hi Sammy, how are you?" I held him with shaking hands.

"Fabulous, of course." He looked over at Sarah. "Hey, now, you brought this riffraff? God, they'll let anyone in here, won't they?"

"Ha, ha," Sarah laughed and embraced her old friend.

The other guys trickled in. Nigel was the last to come through. He was holding a towel and wiping sweat off of his face. My tachycardia slowed to a stop. Everyone else seemed to be watching us with baited breath as we stared at each other, twenty feet apart.

"Hi," he finally said.

"Hi." I couldn't think of anything to say, my brain was empty. Sarah was behind me, she gave me a gentle shake to revive me. "You remember Sarah, right?"

"Of course, my God! What are you doing in America?"

"This is where we all end up, isn't it?" she joked.

"Yeah, I guess." He turned to me. "Florida? I thought you still lived in Michigan."

"Sarah talked me in to moving here," I said quietly.

He nodded, waiting for an explanation. "Do you want to talk?" he asked when I didn't appear to intend to go on.

"Yes," I replied. I looked back at Sarah.

"Don't mind me, I can take care of myself," she said, putting an arm around Mick. He smiled and as I walked toward the back of the huge room with Nigel, I could hear jokes and laughter erupt.

Nigel led us to a quiet place with a few chairs, the dressing area, I presumed.

"I'm sorry if my being here bothers you," I confessed immediately.

"It doesn't bother me. I'm just curious."

"About what? About what I want? Or why I'm here? Or about the book?"

"All of the above."

"You know about the book?"

He nodded. I blushed. "I'm sorry. I should have asked your permission first-"

"It's fine. I actually tried to get in contact with you when I heard about it. I called your house, or what I *thought* was still your house. Your ex answered and said you moved out over a year ago."

It was my turn to nod.

"Then I found your mom's phone number and called her and she said she had no idea where you were or how to reach you."

"We aren't really speaking."

"Okay, so, what's going on? You have never come to one of my shows before, at least, not to my knowledge."

"No, I haven't," I shamefully admitted.

"You know, I always had a weird fantasy of running into you when we played in Detroit."

"You did?"

"Yeah, well, I *hoped* that you would come to see me." He looked disappointed.

"I had a lot of those fantasies, too- that I would be somewhere and run into you or something. Or you would show up on my doorstep one day."

"I did that. You didn't seem too thrilled to see me."

"I'm sorry, it was just so incredibly confusing. It was the last thing I expected and it didn't go the way I would've imagined."

"Me either. I imagined you would either say 'fuck you' or fuck me on the spot. But, you were never very predictable, were you?" I chuckled. "I was hoping that you wanted me back, too, though."

"I did."

He looked surprised. I tried to explain my actions.

"I know I fought with you and I pushed you away and I ran because I was scared and really mixed up. And I was angry and I just wanted to yell. But, after a while, I cooled down and thought about it and I realized, you were right, damn it. You were right about everything. I tried to call you the next morning but you were already gone."

"I left early. I didn't want to hang around. I thought you were done with me."

"Yeah, you never think I'll come right back after I leave you, do you?" I snidely teased. He laughed uncomfortably. I changed tactics. "I guess you didn't waste time moving on, huh?"

"Well, I needed to get over it."

"I see. How is your baby anyway?"

"She's good. She's getting big."

She? He had a baby *girl?* It was hard to hear that. I always wanted a girl, and ever since I met him I wanted *his* child.

I bit my lower lip, trying to hold it together. "That's nice...I hope your little family is ...is- making you happy." I stumbled for the right words.

Now was his turn to be uncomfortable. I watched him struggle to be positive. "Yeah . . . It's hard work, but, yeah . . . "

"You're happy?"

"I'm happy," he responded, not at all convincing, but I didn't question him.

"Good." I paused, hesitating to say what was in my mind. Then I thought better of it, knowing I might not have another chance. "You know, it's hard for me to not be *the one*. The mother of your child, your wife, taking your last name... But all I really care about is your happiness, even if I'm not the one who's lucky enough to be by your side."

" . . . She didn't take my last name," he quietly confessed.

"What? Why not?"

"She already had her own identity."

I was flabbergasted. I couldn't imagine an identity more important than that of being his wife. "Oh, I see. Well, no offense to her, but I would be so honored to take your name. To have a little Blake family. That's the dream. At least, that was *my* dream."

He was sadly looking down at the floor. I could tell the conversation was bothering him. I think I hit a sore spot and I didn't want to upset him.

"I should go." I stood up.

"Um, you don't have to rush off. I get so tired of only having those daft blokes to talk to, you know?"

"If you want me to stay, I will." I sat back down. "I'd do whatever you want me to." I didn't know why I was so brazen. I should have had more tact when dealing with a married man. I think I embarrassed him a little bit. "Did you want to talk about something in particular, or did you just want to shoot the breeze?"

"I kind of figured you had something in mind. That's why you're here, right? You didn't come just to see the show. What is it?"

There was no use in faking the truth. He knew me too well for that. "I guess I missed you."

"You guess you missed me?"

"Okay, I miss you. I really miss you. I think about you all the time and I have been since I saw you last. I made a terrible mistake. *I should have said yes* when you asked me to come with you. And now it's too late. You're married. And, what's worse, you're happily married."

He snickered, but didn't say anything.

"I know I have no right to say this, but I get sick when I think of her saying all those things I used to say to you, doing all those things we used to do. Kissing you, making love with you. Looking into your eyes, holding you at night, hearing all your stories and your worries and your dreams."

He didn't say anything.

I assumed he was irritated with me. I tried to defend myself. "I'm sorry. I know I have no right to be jealous, I guess. But, the thought of you coming home to her, and her telling you how much she missed you and loves you, ugh, I can't stand it. I loved taking care of you and holding your hand. Laughing with you, crying with you, it was the best time of my life. I just hate to think that you have that kind of connection with someone else."

He was still quiet and it was making me nervous. I was sure he was mad at me for disrespecting his marriage. When I checked his face to see how he was receiving the news, I saw him looking away, at nothing in particular, but unable to meet my gaze. He wasn't mad at all. He looked depressed.

"Hey, I'm sorry. I know I shouldn't be talking like this. It's not my place."

"It's fine. I dropped in on *your* life and was brutally honest with *you*. I didn't edit my feelings for your sake."

"No, you didn't. And I'm glad. It was good to know how you really felt."

He nodded. I couldn't tell if it was because he felt the same way.

Suddenly I understood why he had been so quiet. "Um, as someone who thinks she still knows you well, can I tell you something?"

He looked up in anticipation.

"You don't seem incredibly happy." He looked back down. "You haven't said much but you also haven't agreed with anything I've said about her taking my place."

"What did you say when I accused you of not being happy with your ex? You said 'it's different'. That's how it is with me and my wife. It's not like it was with you and me, *it's different.*"

"Okay, well, with me, *different* meant not as good. Is that the same for you?"

He thought about it briefly. "I don't know. It's different," he muttered.

That answered my question. I continued, too curious to leave it alone. "But, you have a good thing going, right? You have what you need?"

"Michelle, why are you doing this?"

"Why can't you answer me? Can't you tell me you're alright?" I stared at him, searching his face for an answer. I didn't find one. Another thought occurred to me. "Nigel, you stopped with the drugs and alcohol right? You don't need them anymore, right?"

He looked guilty. "I'm trying . . . "

I was confused and concerned. "But, isn't it easier now to get straight with a loving wife by your side?" Again, my question went unanswered. "Isn't she supporting you and helping you through this?" Silence. "Is she making it worse?" I asked in exasperation. He gave me a sneer. I didn't care. "Well, I'm waiting to hear you defend her. Just tell me she loves you more than anything and I'll shut up."

He got up in a huff and paced away from me. I followed.

"Nigel, I'm getting the feeling that she doesn't give you what you deserve. I mean, does she think you are the most wonderful man on the planet? Does everything about you make her squeal?"

Still he was speechless.

"That's how *I* feel about you! Don't you think your *wife* should, too? You told me the last time I saw you how much you needed someone beside you to comfort you and take care of you, and it broke my heart. Tell me she does that for you."

He looked pained. I didn't want to hurt him.

"I'm sorry, Nigel. Truly, I didn't come here to break up your marriage. But, can't you give me one reason you want to stay with your wife?"

"Yeah, my daughter. I don't want to tear up her home. I can't. Even if things aren't going so well, I have to try to make it work for her sake."

"I know. She's your number one priority." I felt guilty for even thinking about suggesting he end his marriage when a child was stuck in the middle. Yet, I couldn't stop myself from spilling my soul. "But, you're mine! You don't want to see *her* hurting, I don't want to see *you* hurting. Break-ups are so hard, I know that. And I don't want you to go through that torture, I'd spare you from that if I could. But sometimes, it's healthier to split up than to live in misery. That thought is what gave me the strength to end my dead-end relationship. And, even though it sucked, I'm glad I did it. I wasn't where I was supposed to be and I wasn't with who I'm meant to be with. I feel like I'm meant to be with *you*. That's why I came here tonight, to see if there was even a tiny part of you that feels the same. How could I live with myself knowing I had the slightest chance of making you mine and didn't take it?"

He kept his head low, looking at the ground. I couldn't tell what he was thinking and I was afraid I had hurt him. That was the last thing I wanted.

He finally spoke up, very quietly. "Look, I appreciate how much you care about me. But I can't leave my wife. I'm sorry."

I tried to rebound fast, taking a deep breath. "Don't be sorry. You are doing the noble thing. Self sacrifice, right?" He looked into my eyes, trying to read my emotions. I honestly was fine. I wanted him to be happy and it seemed he was where he wanted to be. That was good enough for me. "Well, I can't say I'm not disappointed, but at least I tried. I guess it's just not meant to be. But, if things change, if you ever find yourself alone and you need someone to take care of you, remember me. Think of me as your Plan B."

He chuckled. "Plan B?"

"Yup."

"You're going to settle for that?"

"It's not settling. Wasting my life on someone else would be settling. I tried that, remember? It didn't work. I can't do better than you. There *is* no better than you, for me, at least. So, yes, I will wait. I'd wait forever if I have to. What else can I do? You said it yourself, what we had was true love, and it only comes once in a lifetime."

He looked at me, eyes questioning, trying to soak in the impact of my words. I could tell he was confused about his feelings. I put my hand on his shoulder.

"Nigel, I think I should go now. I really didn't intend on turning your world upside down tonight. I didn't even know if I'd get a chance to talk to you. But I swore to myself that if I did, I wouldn't waste it. I just wanted to let you know how loved you are. And if you ever need someone to love you through and through, I will, and I always have, and I always will. I don't even have a choice."

He was still silent. I took that as a hint.

"Goodbye." I turned away.

"Wait," he called to me. I turned around. "Don't you want to say goodbye the proper way?" He held his arms open for a hug.

I took a deep breath, thinking about it. "If I hold you again, I won't ever let you go," I spilled.

He let his arms drop, defeated. I knew he couldn't promise to return everything I had offered and didn't want to lead me on. "I understand. But, before you go, I want to say thank you. For loving me and caring about me."

I nodded. "Always." I walked out. He didn't follow.

Chapter 17

"...the puzzle was complete."

I found Sarah chatting in hushed voices with Sammy and Mick. I gathered they were talking about me and Nigel. They didn't hear me approaching.

"Sarah?" I asked. She jumped. "Can we go home now?"

"The guys invited us out for drinks," she told me.

"I don't- I don't think I'm up for that."

"Actually, you do look like you could use a drink," Sammy tried to joke.

"Drinks won't help me," I said solemnly.

Sarah looked torn.

"I can take a cab home if you want. I don't want to ruin your night just because mine was difficult."

"Hey! There's no way I would let you take a cab home! Let's go."

She said the last part funny: *"Let's go."* I didn't think that much of it.

"We have plenty of booze *at the house,*" she said loudly, still sounding funny. "Yeah, I think going back *to the house* is a *very good idea.*" She put her hands on my shoulders from behind me.

"Did you take drugs?" I asked, bewildered.

She just laughed and steered me out of the back room. We maneuvered quickly out of the bustling building, past the gaggles of barely dressed women and girls who were attempting to sneak into that back room. We hurried out of the huge, noisy theater. We emerged into the parking lot, the instant quiet was refreshing. I hadn't had the chance to ask Sarah why she seemed a little off beat, I was still unconvinced that she was sober.

"Hey, do you want me to drive? Because I can." I offered as we headed toward the car.

"What? No! I'm fine." She sounded normal again.

"Are you sure? You seemed totally high in there."

"No, I'm fine. I'm great, actually." We got into the vehicle. "It was great seeing those guys after all those years. I forgot how fun they are."

"Yeah. I'm so sorry I ruined your night."

"Stop! You didn't ruin anything. Trust me, it's alright."

She had assured me. "Thanks. You're a great friend. I love you, Sarah."

She laughed. "I know I'm a great friend. And I love you, too. So, uh, speaking of love . . . How did it go with Nigel?"

We talked the whole way home. I told her every word, every detail, every inflection of his voice, every expression on his face. She listened carefully, asking questions, truly interested. She really was a great friend.

When we got home, all I wanted to do was wash up and go to bed. I headed for the bathroom.

"Are you sure you want to go to bed? Come on, have a drink with me. It's such a nice night. Let's sit on the back porch and have a margarita," she insisted.

"I don't know . . . "

"Come on. One drink. You can have one drink with your best friend, can't you?"

"Well, I suppose since I kept you from a night of binge drinking with those wild boys . . . sure. I'll have a drink."

She clapped with glee. "Smashing! I'll go and get 'em started."

"Okay. While you're doing that, I'm going to change into my pajamas."

"Pajamas? Why? The night is still young. You don't want to change yet. Just wait."

"Sarah, it's almost midnight and I'm tired. What should I wait for? Is there a dress code on the back porch? Is that creepy neighbor out there again?"

"Probably."

"I'll take my chances."

"Well, before you do that, let's have a toast."

"You haven't even made the margaritas yet!"

"I know. Let's just take a shot of tequila."

"Really?" I cringed.

"Yeah, come on. One shot."

I groaned, knowing it was useless to argue with her. "Fine."

She hurried to the kitchen and poured two overflowing shot glasses with the tequila. She carefully handed one to me. "Okay. Let's drink to second chances."

"Second chances? Is that a dig on my failed attempt with Nigel?"

"No, of course not. How about a toast to . . . better things to come!"

"Well, can't get any worse," I said bitterly, raising my glass to hers and clinking it.

"Cheers!" We threw back the foul liquid.

"Whew."

"Yee-hah!" she shouted and began preparing our next drink. "Margaritas will be done in five minutes!" she shouted happily.

"Okay, then. I'm going to go wash up." I started walking away.

"Wait! Can you get the margarita glasses? I think they're in the basement."

"Are you sure? I think they are up in that cabinet."

"No, I packed them away last week thinking we never use them."

"Well, we don't have to use them now. We could just use the regular- "

"Hey! This is a special occasion! Let's make it fun! Now, go get those glasses. I think they are in a box by the Christmas decorations."

I sighed, but I couldn't deny her request. She was going to great lengths to cheer me up. I stomped down the stairs and began my task of searching for the illusive margarita glasses.

After looking through every cardboard box in sight, I was coming up empty. Every time I shouted up the stairs to tell her they were MIA, she turned on the blender and couldn't hear me. Fifteen minutes later, I gave up.

I went back up the stairs and I didn't see Sarah in the kitchen. I found her in the living room, looking out our front window. I didn't ask why.

"I couldn't find those damn glasses anywhere."

She popped up and tried to hurry past me as I headed for the kitchen cabinet. "I'll help you look."

"Forget it, let's just use the regular glasses!" I beat her into the kitchen and reached in the cabinet for a glass when the margarita glasses caught my eye from the top shelf. "What? These were in here the whole time! You didn't pack them away!"

"Oh, shit. I thought I did. I'm so sorry. What an idiot I am! Here, I'll take care of this. Sit down, I'll pour you a drink."

I watched her do so and I noticed the full blender carafe. "Hey, why did you make so much? You said one drink."

"One for you! Can't I have more?"

"Damn lush. Alright, I'm going to change now. I will drink my margarita in my pajamas, if you don't mind."

"Actually I *do* mind," she informed me. I gave her a look. She recovered. "But, go ahead. I'll be waiting for you on the back porch. Take your time."

I did take my time. The gravity of the situation finally weighed on me. I decided to take a shower to try to wash away my bad memories. It didn't work. I slumped against the shower wall, barely able to hold it together. I felt like my broken heart would stop beating.

Eventually, the hot water started running out and I managed to pull myself together enough to get out and dry off. I put on my pajamas that were hanging on the hook on the back of the door. The faded nightshirt I loved to wear, Nigel's old red and black striped sweatshirt, the one that he had given me eight years ago. I sighed when I picked it up, realizing it was time to get over him, but I put it on anyway.

I was about to head out to the kitchen to start my night of booze swilling when I noticed my bedroom door was closed. I heard Autumn mewing and I went to open it.

Opening the door, I tried to comfort her. "I'm sorry baby, did I lock you in-"

I stopped mid-sentence. She was in my room, and so was Nigel. He sat on my bed, wearing casual clothes, an old Rolling Stones t-shirt and black jeans. He wasn't the rock star I had just seen, he was my familiar friend. He was a sight for sore eyes. In one hand, he held my journal, in the other hand, he pet the cat on his lap. My mouth fell open. He looked up at me, and his did the same.

"Nigel, what are you- "

"You're wearing my shirt."

I looked down at myself, a little embarrassed. The shirt was worn and tattered and barely covered my unmentionables.

"You're still wearing my shirt," he repeated incredulously.

I had no words. Did I seem pathetic to him, still clinging to a dream?

He stood up slowly, letting Autumn adjust off of him though he never took his stunned eyes off me. No words spoken, eye contact never breaking, he walked up to me, took me in his strong arms and kissed me deeply.

His mouth on my mouth felt euphoric. I had waited so long and wanted it so bad that it almost didn't feel wrong. After what surely was a least a minute, though time seemed to stop dead, I realized what was happening. It took a tremendous amount of strength to detach myself from his perfect, addictive lips, but I managed.

"Nigel," I tried to catch my breath between sentences. "I can't do this. You're married."

He held me still, but looked slightly ashamed. Then another thought crossed his mind. "You told me if you were in my arms again, you wouldn't let go."

I nodded.

His soft brown eyes became wet. "So don't let go." He held me tighter, his head on my shoulder, squeezing me like I would escape. He was wrong, I could never escape. I never wanted to let him go.

I held him, my poor, sweet little boy. The boy who just needed to be loved. All I ever wanted since I met him was to be that one who could give him more than anyone else could. And I could. It was too easy to love this man, I was specifically made for the task. Everything he went through that made him who he was reciprocated perfectly with every-thing I was, due to my own experiences. We were puzzle pieces. And with him in my arms again, the puzzle was complete.

I felt my shoulder getting wet as sobs racked his tall body. My heart broke into a thousand sharp pieces. I squeezed him and stroked his hair. He cried harder. I just let him have it out, rubbing his back.

Moments later, he attempted to stand upright, no longer leaning down on me.

"I'm sorry. I just . . . ugh," he muttered, wiping his eyes on the back of his hand.

I went over to my nightstand for some tissues. I sat on the bed and patted the space next to me. "Come here, honey," I demanded sweetly.

He did as he was told. I handed him a few tissues. As he dried his eyes, I put my arm around him. "Can you tell me what is going on?"

He cleared his throat and tried to compose himself. "It was what you said earlier. You came and said all those things. You didn't have to. You could have said, 'fuck you,' and that's probably what I deserved. But, no. You come and offer your undying love? After I let you down so many times? After I tell you I need to stay married, you tell me you'll wait for me forever?"

He looked at me, I stared back into his tear-stained face, silent, waiting for him to continue his explanation.

"My wife wants to end things."

I was stunned. I had no idea. My mouth fell open again.

"I didn't want to tell you earlier because I thought her and I were going to try to work through it. I mean, I didn't want to fail at this, you know? I wanted to try my damnedest to keep my family together."

"Then, why are you here?"

"I changed my mind."

"That quickly? Nigel, I didn't mean to confuse you. I don't want you to rush into anything in the heat of the moment. This is all very sudden."

"It is, I know. But, it's also very familiar."

I looked at him, confused.

"We've been here before. The tables were turned, but it was the same," he explained. "Two years ago I came to you with no warning, told you how I felt about you, and asked you to come with me. You were scared and you ran. I understand that now. Maybe you knew you weren't in the right place or with the right person, but you had accepted that and were fine with it. The first instinct would be to stay where things are familiar and comfortable."

"Yeah," I agreed.

"But after thinking about it, you realize what you need to do. It may be a tough move, but it's a move you have to make."

"Yeah."

"How long did it take you to realize you had made a mistake and wanted to be with me?"

"About an hour," I confessed.

"Same here. I couldn't stop thinking about us. And it made me happy," he smiled a smile that I hadn't seen in a long time.

"It did?"

"Yeah," he confirmed.

"Well, if I had gone right back to you instead of sleeping on it that night we could have been together all this time."

"I know. I remembered you saying you tried to call me the next morning but I had gone already. I didn't want anything like that to happen again. I didn't want to take the risk of losing you again. I had to make a choice. I mean, I had to decide right there between you and my wife."

I froze. I didn't like the idea of being responsible for his divorce, but I definitely couldn't be his mistress. "Nigel, are you sure you are making the right decision? This is all so sudden. I mean, I'm so glad you're here and I want you more than anything but your happiness means more to me than my own. If you think you should work on your marriage, then that's what I want you to do. Don't let me stand in the way."

He shook his head, organizing his thoughts. "No, it's not like that. My wife is about ready to walk out the door if I let her. I've been trying to prolong things and putting off divorce, but now I'm wondering why. It can't be fixed. It was never right, something was missing."

"How long have you felt this way?"

He sighed. "It's been a while."

"What makes you think you're ready to end things now?"

He looked me in the eyes. "You."

I stared back into his wounded brown eyes as he continued. "I felt like shit as soon as you left. I didn't know if it was because it was an old wound reopened or because I was disappointed in my marriage, but I realized it was because I had you back in my life for a few minutes and that felt good. Then you left and it was like, like someone locked me in a freezer, you know? All cold and dark. It's not like that around you. You're warm. And you're bright. And I feel so good when I'm with you. Like I'm home and safe. Like I'm taken care of. And loved . . . It has just been a long time since I felt that way. I've really missed that."

I couldn't believe what he was saying. My face burned as so many emotions swirled over me. He continued.

"So, Sammy comes to check up on me and I can barely hold it together. And he says, 'Well, Sarah gave us their address. She wanted to make sure you had it if you needed it. But, she wants us to come by tonight. And we want to go, it'll be fun. Do you want to come?' And at first, I think it would be too hard for both of us. But then I thought, I can't let this go. I have to see Michelle."

My heart was about to burst in my chest. I also realized why Sarah had been acting so strange as we were leaving the dressing room and why she kept trying to stall me from getting ready for bed.

" . . . Then I get over here, and I'm scared shitless. I had no idea what to do or say. Then Sarah points down the hall and says you're down there. I figured you were in your room and this seemed to be it. The one with Autumn sleeping in it."

I laughed, nodding.

"And I didn't mean to invade your privacy, but I saw that journal and I recognized it. The one I gave you for our first Christmas. I picked it up, it was open, and I saw my name written on that page. So I kind of read it. Then I read it again and again and I just couldn't believe how sincere your feelings are for me. No one has cared about me as much as you do. With no agenda. You don't want anything from me but my company. You just want to give your love to me, and God, I need it so badly."

I stared at him softly, my eyes filling with tears.

"And then, you come in here, oblivious, wearing my old shirt. You still wear my old shirt."

"I love it. It's yours."

"See, that's it. That's what I mean. You just can't stop loving me. When I read your book, it was like I was looking into your heart. The things you said in there . . . It's, like, even surprising to me how deeply you care about me. I never got that feeling from my own wife. You embrace my flaws and love me in spite of them. You don't tear me down over them. That's true love. It was a little bit of a kick in the ass for me to see that."

"Really? I didn't think you would find that appropriate. I felt kind of guilty, still loving you so much considering you're married. But I just can't help the way I feel. I tried, but I can't stop loving you," I admitted quietly, voice breaking.

"Good. Please don't. Please don't ever stop loving me." He put his head on my bosom and his arms around my body. "I never stopped loving you. I didn't. I just got so wrapped up in the life, you know? I wanted everything. But I didn't have what I *needed*. You're right. No one was there to take care of me. No one made me feel secure and loved. And I needed that so much. So, I just drank more and did more coke. I just tried to replace it all with women and alcohol and all that. I was so stupid."

"None of that matters anymore. All that bad stuff is behind us now, and we'll work through everything else."

He lifted his head and looked into my eyes and smiled a wrinkled, heartfelt smile. He leaned us down on my bed so I was lying in his arms. He squeezed me. Words couldn't explain how satisfying it was to be held by him again.

"You belong in my arms. You fit just perfectly. We fit together just right."

I agreed. "This feels like we're in high school again."

"Yeah, it does. Like it's the first time. Like it's naughty."

I giggled. He was right. "Well, maybe it is naughty."

"Oh yeah, you always liked that naughty stuff. You get turned on when it's wrong," he growled and stroked my arm, sending tingles through my whole body.

"You remember. But, this time, it *is* wrong, and it's *not* a turn on. I can't get physical with a married man."

He let his grip go limp and stopped stroking me.

I continued. "I really would like nothing more than to make love right now. Then again, and again, and again and forever . . . but, we can't do that. And you're on tour! You have to leave me tomorrow." I realized all this the moment before I spoke the words.

"I know. I can't stay in town for long. Tomorrow didn't cross my mind. Things just happened so fast, I just went with it."

"Okay. So, what next?"

He sighed, thinking it over. "How can I leave you?"

"That is such a recurring theme for us. We have had to say goodbye too many times over the years!"

"But we still end up together. That's what counts. Look, it's going to be a while before we can really be together for good. But, be patient with me. I will be back with you as soon as I can."

I nodded. "I told you before. I'd wait forever if I had to."

He smiled such an amazing smile it nearly took my breath away. "God, I love you. Who else would put up with my shit?"

"Luckily for me, no one," I teased.

"No, luckily for *me*." He squeezed me. We laughed, playing around until a squeak from the floorboard down the hall interrupted us. Nigel sat up and tried to peer out the cracked door.

"Hey!" he reprimanded in his perfect tone that evoked no fear.

"Sorry, I was just curious to see if she had killed you." Sammy approached. I sat up in the bed and covered myself as much as possible, trying to look more demure. Sarah was right behind.

"We just wanted to see . . . um, what you guys were up to." She was transparent.

"I could've told you about it in the morning," I said through clenched teeth.

"But, then we wouldn't hear about it 'cause we won't be here in the morning!" Sammy half joked.

"I will," Nigel added quickly. Three pairs of eyes went to him, including mine. "I'm staying here tonight." He looked at me. "I have to leave in the morning, but I'm not leaving you. As soon as the tour is done, so is my marriage." He looked to Sammy and Sarah now. "We're getting back together," he said proudly, beaming.

My heart melted. Our little crowd cheered. Sarah spoke. "Oh my God, that is so great! Well, we have to celebrate! Come on, let's go. Drinks are waiting!"

They were off before Nigel and I could even exchange a look.

Nigel gave in. "Alright. I guess we can go socialize with them for a while since I get to spend the rest of the night alone with you. No hanky-panky, though, I swear."

"Good. It'll be tough to resist you, but I will try to manage."

He laughed. Then, he got serious. "I mean it, Michelle. As soon as I can I'm ending things with my wife."

"What about your daughter?"

He shrugged sadly. "That's the tough part. I've been putting this off for her sake, but I don't think it would be best for her to live in a home where mommy and daddy are always fighting and yelling."

"Is that how it is?"

"Kind of. I mean, we only got married because we felt like we had to. There's nothing much between us anymore."

"Still, I don't want to break up your marriage."

"You aren't."

"Are you sure?"

"Yeah."

"It wasn't because I wrote the book? Because I didn't mean to cause any harm."

"I know, I know. It wasn't the book. I told you my wife has been wanting to end things for a while now."

"But you weren't ready- "

"No, I wasn't, it's true. But now, I see everything more clearly. You made me see things that I tried to ignore. You showed me my life as it really is, not just the illusion. And it's not what I want."

"Alright. I'm glad you feel that way, but we can just take things slow. I don't want you to rush into anything. I want you to be sure about this before you make all these decisions that are going to radically change your life."

He chuckled. "Always looking out for me, aren't you? Thanks. But I'm sure. And don't feel like you're to blame for ending my marriage, it was already damaged. I have to do this, but I'm doing this for me. I can't waste my life with someone who isn't right for me, especially now that I know what I'd be missing." He took my hand. "You know, you inspired me today."

"I inspired you?"

He laughed. "Hey, it's not the first time! But, the way you took control of your life again. You dug yourself into a hole, but you climbed out. That's what I have to do now. I want to take back my life. I want to get sober."

"That's wonderful! Can I help you?"

He smiled. "Well, your support is very helpful. I appreciate that. But this is something I need to do on my own. It is going to make a big difference having my own personal cheerleader by my side, though."

"I will be by your side, Nigel. I will hold your hand and listen to you and do whatever I can. I'll be there every step of the way."

"Do you really mean that?"

"Of course."

"So, when I leave town, you're going to come with me?"

I didn't answer right away. It only took seconds to realize there was nowhere I'd rather be than by his side, wherever that was, through good and bad.

"I'd love to. I don't ever want to say goodbye again."

"Neither do I." He looked proudly at me, his brown eyes staring deep into mine. It was as if all the ugliness and loneliness and pain and betrayal had vanished. It didn't matter that it had ever existed. We were just the two souls who had met by chance, that had a connection so strong the most powerful things in the world couldn't destroy it. Not money, fame, power, distance, family, anger, jealousy. Nothing.

Sarah yelled from across the house "Are you guys coming or not?"

I looked at Nigel. "Maybe a night of drinking isn't wise, huh?"

"I don't need to drink tonight. I want to see things clearly," he answered, gazing adoringly at my face. I felt a little self conscious with no makeup or anything. I timidly turned away from him. He put his hand on my chin and gently pulled me back.

"Look at me, sweetie. I want to see that face. I've missed this face."

I smiled, finally confident that he wanted *me* and loved *me*. After all, he had chosen me over hundreds of prettier, wilder girls.

He held me tighter. "Remember when we were teenagers and all we wanted was to be able to spend the night together? That would've been a dream come true. And now, look at us. We're living the dream. Maybe it took us a long time to get here, but I don't think anything will tear us apart again."

"I won't let that happen," I vowed.

"Me either," he assured me. "I miss this, lying in bed with you, holding you and just talking. Not that the other things we did in bed weren't fun," he laughed, "but, times like this are very special." He took my hand and wove my fingers with his.

"Yeah, And it's kind of strange now. It feels like no time has passed but so much has happened to talk about."

"Right. And the last few times we spoke, we were always running away from each other. Nothing ever got resolved. We would just fight and run."

"Yeah. I hate that."

"That won't happen tonight."

"Nope," I agreed.

He was silent for a moment. "Can I ask you something?"

"Yes, of course. I have about a million things I want to ask you. But, you first."

"It's about the book. Why did you write it?"

I was unprepared for this question. "Um . . . I just felt like I had to."

"To get my attention?"

"No, not necessarily. Actually, I'm glad you asked me this. I guess I should explain myself. I never meant to upset you or wreck your marriage . . . I just had so many feelings bottled up that wouldn't go away. I had to get them out. And I thought this story was kind of beautiful, and definitely enthralling and dramatic. I wanted to share it."

"Oh," he nodded.

"I'm glad I did it. I needed an outlet and I needed to create again. This book helped me put my life in order. It helped me rediscover myself."

"I see."

"I'm sorry I put you in the middle, though. I'm sorry if it makes you uncomfortable for everyone to know our business."

"Yeah, you didn't hide anything, did you?"

"You know me. Can't lie for shit. Way too fucking honest."

"Yeah, but that's okay. You can't help how you feel. And, in a way, it's kind of nice to read the unadulterated truth."

I smiled. "Indeed."

Look for

Stay With Me

the continuation of *Come With Me*,
due out in 2011